But God

But God

Lula A. Scott

PALMETTO
PUBLISHING
Charleston, SC
www.PalmettoPublishing.com

Copyright © 2024 by Lula A. Scott

All rights reserved

No portion of this book may be reproduced, stored in a retrieval system, or transmitted in any form by any means—electronic, mechanical, photocopy, recording, or other—except for brief quotations in printed reviews, without prior permission of the author.

Paperback ISBN: 979-8-8229-5425-0

Early Praises for *But God*

What an amazing piece of literature!

The book, **But God**, the life of Lula Scott, written by my aunt, shows in true form just how God is able to keep us through whatever trials come up in our lives, from the time that we are born until the time God decides to call us home. **But God** is full of laughs, joy, crying moments, and suspenseful moments that will make you give God praise as you read it.

If you have the pleasure of knowing Lula Scott you will understand how she became the amazing woman she is, and if you don't know her, you will have an in-depth picture into her life and feel as if you have known her all your life. I thank God that he decided to make her my aunt/mother and I pray that this book reaches the masses, so that people who feel life is destroying them and they can't go on will know that GOD is able and willing to see them through to victory in Christ Jesus.
Eric Brigham- nephew/son

Lula and I met about 30 years ago. She was a private caregiver for a hospice patient I was assigned to as the hospice nurse. The care she gave was so tender and loving that Lula stole my heart. And in return, when she finished that case, I stole her. I wanted the best for my patients and there was no one better than Lula. For close to 10 years we worked as a team. She has been an inspiration to me and a treasure in my life. Lula is a woman of deep, undying faith who brought comfort to both families and patients at their lowest point. At my time of need, I entrusted her with the care of my most beloved - my mother. I watched them become like sisters and she grieved the loss of my mother with me. Some call her Aunt Lula. Some call her Mother Scott. I just call

her my Momma. I thank you for the honor of your friendship and trust. I love you dearly!
Nancy Ostoff- daughter

For over 35 years I have been blessed to be able to call Lula Scott my teacher, mentor, supporter, confidant, and friend. Not just to me, but she has been all these things and more to her family, members of our congregation, attorneys, victims, and witnesses in the Philadelphia Criminal Justice System, neighbors, and anyone in need. People like Lula are few and in between. Where do they come from?

This book helps shed light on how God forged this servant leader, orchestrated her experiences, and instilled His wisdom. Lula's story confirms that "all things work together for good to those who love God, to those who are the called according to *His* purpose". I thank God for his perfected work and for placing Lula Scott in our lives.

Thank you, Lula, for sharing the story of your journey.
George D. Mosee, Jr., Esquire
Former First Assistant District Attorney, Philadelphia District Attorney's Office
Assistant Pastor, Mt. Calvary Family Worship Center

I had fainted, Unless I had believed to see the goodness of the Lord in the land of the living. Wait on the Lord: Be of good courage, and he shall strengthen your heart. Wait, I say, on the Lord.
Psalm 27:13-14

DEDICATIONS

This page is dedicated to the ones who knew my story and still held my hand.

Firstly, in memory of my husband, **Dennis Scott,** who loved me in spite of, saw the best and worst in me, walked beside me, held my hand, and always supported me, my hopes, my plans, and my dreams.

In memory of my parents, **Anna Bradley and Troy Bradley,** for their love and care and giving me life and family.

In memory of my baby son, **Eddie,** who left too soon and was always promising to give me five grandchildren. Thank you for the memories.

In memory of my Goddaughter, **Beatrice,** who called me Momma, and did anything to keep me happy. You loved me unconditionally. Thank you.

In memory of **Fannie,** my mom, my sister, and my friend, I will always be grateful to you. You are the greatest woman who God ever created.

To my sister, **Gwen,** we were always together as partners, even in our crimes as children. The things we did, if Momma knew it, we would have really gotten a beaten. But I thank you because we are strong and grown-up now. We love each other and we have really learned how to depend on God's promises. Thank you sister because you are the best.

To **Clyde,** who my daughters call, my little Jesus, I love your smile and I love it when you say, "Mommy, do you need anything?" You never miss a day saying it. Thank you.

To **Marlene**, my precious daughter, you are always on call. "Mom, where are you? I am on my way." No matter what the circumstances are, you have always been there. Thank you.

To **Sharon**, my baby, you ask me, "Mom, why are you crying? What's the matter? Let me wipe your tears away." You always try to take my pain. Thank you.

To **Eric**, who I have watched grow from a baby to a man, one who takes care of and loves Aunt Lula. Thank you for being my baby boy.

To Godbaby, **Dr. Karen Wells**, I could write a book about you. You are the one who said if you were a snowflake, I would save you. I don't know how you would have done it, but thank you.

To **Theresa**, my daughter, with a heart of gold, you were the one, when your dad died, did not leave my side until you knew that I could sleep in that bed again. Thank you for every act of kindness then and now.

To **Nancy**, my daughter, who has been through the storms always with me, always with loving care. I love you and thank you for letting me be your mom.

To **Nita**, my daughter, you always say, "Mother, are you okay?" You have always shown me the utmost concern. Thank you for being who you are to me.

To **Adrian**, the one who God entrusted to me for a few months, you're quiet and you sit and you just look, but you warm the room. Thank you for just being there. Thank you for the talks that we had.

To my best friend, **Kim Wells**, who has been an anchor, you're always there. I never wake up a morning when I don't hear your voice saying, "Good morning. Is there anything I can do for you today?" Thank you.

To my son, **Millard**, not son-in-law, my son, who was instrumental in moving me out of my home and coming to live with you and Sharon. I thank you for loving me. I thank you for letting me make you laugh. I thank you for making me laugh. I really thank you because you are making my last days, some of my best.

To my beloved nieces and nephews, you add delight and joy to my life each and every day. I am so glad that God placed each of you in my life. Thank you for loving me and allowing me the chance to love each of you.

Special thanks to my niece Troynett, nephews, Bobby and Eric, and great-nephews, Michael, Lynn, and Brandon, I cherish each of you and appreciate the love and kindness shown to me to make my dream become a reality. God bless each of you and I love you all so much.

Chapter 1

So where do we begin. Let me first introduce myself. My name is Lula Scott. I decided to write this book so that it may be a help to someone who has issues that they are dealing with, or they were not able to come to grip with their feelings, or they do not know why. I was born in Winston-Salem, North Carolina. The earliest memories I have of myself was when I swallowed a straight pin and I can remember being turned upside down. I was made to vomit until they were able to find the pin that I had swallowed.

I don't remember anything about my mother and father living together. I only know what I've been told. I know that when my mother was 28-years-old, I was born and I was her seventh child. What I have been told is that my mother was abused by my father. My mother took me and my siblings to my grandmother when I was nine-months-old and she left all of us there, me, my sisters, Fannie, Pearl, and Gwen, and my brother, Bunk. My brother, Samuel, had died before I was born and my sister, Annie, was living with family in Philadelphia.

My father later came and took me and my sisters with him. My daddy had me by the arm and Gwen by the hand. My sister, Fannie said, "Can I go?" My daddy said, "If you can keep up, you can go." My poor brother was hollering. He said, "Daddy, don't leave me." But my daddy had to run. He couldn't get my brother because my mother's brother, Uncle George, was running after my father because he had come to get us.

LULA A. SCOTT

Before my father had come, Fannie later told me, there were times when she was working in the cotton field and she would cry out, "Lord, please let somebody come and get me." She said when my daddy came, she was so happy. Fannie ran as fast as she could.

My mother, she loved my brother, Bunk so much, after my father took us, she went and got him from her mother. She didn't have shoes to put on him so she put her nursing shoes on Bunk. When we were older, we laughed about that because he came home on the train with Momma's shoes on his feet. He made it out of there.

The next recollection that I have is when I went to live with my aunt and uncle. While I was born to Anna Bradley and Troy Bradley and I had six siblings, what I really knew of myself was that I was living with my aunt and uncle, Nedith and Sam Mayes. I called my aunt Mommy and I called my uncle, Uncle Sam. They could not understand why she was the Momma and he was the Uncle. My aunt and uncle had one son and they had me for a daughter and I really thought I belonged to them for many years.

When I was five, my aunt enrolled me in school. My teacher's name was Mrs. Farabee. I remembered going to kindergarten. My aunt would dress me up every morning before she went to work. My uncle was driving a Nash car. Black people didn't have many cars during that time, but I remember a T-model Ford and a lady riding down the street, tooting her horn. It was so exciting to see a lady with a car. We didn't have that kind of car, but we had a car and that was a big thing to me because I would ride to the school.

I remember as a kindergartener, I believed I was the apple of Mrs. Farabee's eye because she really loved me. We were doing a play and she gave me the best part. I was Little Miss Muffet and I remember being dressed in a pink and blue homemade uniform, something that they made for me to wear in that play. I said my speech with everything that I had because I was a fast learner. Once they taught me what to say, I could speak, I could mimic them, and I did it flawlessly.

But God

I remember going to Skyland School. It was 1945. The school had been a school for whites only and then they closed it and made it a school for black children. It was a big thing for us to be the first class of black students to go to Skyland School. The news people and everybody came and we were very important.

I also remember that we lived on a street called Cameron Avenue. On Cameron Avenue, there were only doctors and teachers, and lawyers, those type of people. My family were workers in the tobacco factory. A lot of the children at school were still living in places where they had outside bathroom facilities. The water was outside, but where we lived there was an inside bathtub. I had my own room, we had a living room, dining room, and a kitchen. So we were living with the upper class people as you would call it, but I also remember that during those days, being dark-skinned was not too good in the South.

At school, they put all of the light-skinned kids in the front, and the darker skinned children, like me, would have to sit in the back of the class. My aunt would say things to me and tell me that I had to be very smart. Sometimes, I would try to hang with the light-skinned children because I thought they were more important than me. But my aunt would tell me, "You're beautiful."

I had long black hair. They would press my hair and give me Shirley Temple curls. My aunt would put the finest clothes on me that she could afford to buy. Later, I realized that she couldn't really afford to buy me those clothes, but she wanted me to look nice.

When I was in second grade, I remember there was a girl named Jean. She was light-skinned so she sat in the front of the class. I decided that I could out read Jean. I would raise my hand for everything. My teacher, Mrs. Hayes, would say "Bradley, you can read." And boy, I would read Mack and Muffin, Jane, and see Puff run. Run Puff run. I would read loud. I could read well. When I got my report card I got all As. My aunt would always laugh. She would say that I rocked in a little rocking chair and read until I would almost turn it over on the heater. I would be reading and rocking.

Every Saturday night, my aunt would put me in a big tin tub and give me the nicest bath. Every morning before I would go to school, she would wash me up as we call it. She had one son, his name was Lee. He was like a brother to me. Lee also went to Skyland School. As I got a little older, he would walk me to school.

Lee was kind of mischievous. He would hooky school. One day I wanted to stay out of school. I begged so hard and I threatened him that if he did not let me stay out of school, I would tell. So he let me stay home from school. But on this day, my aunt or my uncle, one of them came home early, and Lee and I had to run out the back door. Lee told me to go to the school, stand up on the commode, so if the teacher came in, she couldn't see my feet. I did what he told me to do, but somehow they caught me anyway. They took me back in the class and they told me never to do it again.

Well, Lee and I did it another day, that is, played hooky from school again. That day when we came home, Lee forgot the key so he put me through the window. When I jumped through the window, my aunt was there with a switch. She gave me the best beating I ever had. I laugh about it now. I think Lee knew my aunt was there, so he put me through the window so I could get the switch. But I never cut class again.

We would go to church on Sundays. My uncle was a pastor. We would go to Lexington, North Carolina. Lee could play the piano. He had piano lessons. Lee would play the piano and the people would sing. I was a little girl and I would shout in the floor. My uncle would preach. When we stopped going to Lexington, we came back to our home church. We had to go to church in the morning, we went in the afternoon, and we had to go back for night service. We were in church all day on Sundays.

But God

My aunt would cook on Saturdays. The only time she would cook on Sundays was breakfast when the Bishop would come to eat at our house on Sunday mornings before church. I remember my aunt would get up early on Sunday mornings and cook for him.

I remember when the tobacco factory, where my aunt worked, went on strike. My aunt had to march the picket line and she would take me. I would also walk the picket lines.

Later on, for some reason, we moved off of Cameron Avenue and onto 8th Street. When we moved to 8th Street, I would be outside playing. This lady would come by. She would say, "Hi, baby." I would speak to her and talk to her. One day, a lady told me, "That's your mother." I said, "That's not my mother. My mother is in the house and her name is Aunt Nedith." Somehow, she was Aunt Nedith and Mom, too. I didn't think much about it. I was happy, playing, and having a good time. I later found out that my aunt took me when I was two-years-old and that she was not my mother, but my father's sister.

One day, the lady who I would come past, took me to the store. She told Mr. Lamb, who owned the store, "Whenever she comes into the store and she wants some cookies, you give them to her." I thought that was a big thing that I could go into the store and eat cookies. I didn't tell my aunt. But while she was at work, I would get the cookies and eat them before she came home. Sometimes I would be so sick that when she came home, I would spit-up because I had eaten so many sweets.

Then this man would come to the house. I would say, "Here comes Uncle Troy. He's going to give me a nickel." When he would come, he would give me a nickel and I would eat more sweets. As time went on, people would say that he was my father, but I continued to call him Uncle Troy and he let me call him that. He was Uncle Troy to me.

As time went on, the church we went to, I later found out that my sisters, Fannie, Pearl, and Gwen were members. My brother, Bunk, he did not come much, but my sisters were always there. The more I went to church, the more I became closer to my sister Gwen. We were close in age and we would play after church. I would see them at church, and I would go home and I would be sad because Gwen would be going one way and I would be going another way. When I realized that I had a brother and sisters and I wanted to be with them. I had a longing.

After I went home to my Aunt Nedith and Uncle Sam, I wouldn't see Gwen because my siblings and parents very seldom visited our house. I didn't have too many friends. I only had one friend. Her name was Sandra. We went from first grade to tenth grade together in school. Sandra was my best friend.

I must have been about nine-years-old, and I remember something happened at church and I was crying. My sister Pearl saw me and evidently she went home and told my mother what had transpired. Pearl came and told my Aunt Nedith that my mother said to send me home and if she didn't, she would come and get me. They had a few little exchanges and my aunt asked me did I want to go with my mother. My aunt told me, "Well, that's your mother. Do you want to go?" I said, "Yes, I want to go." My aunt said, "Well, if you really want to go, I'm not going to give you all of your beautiful clothes." I loved the beautiful clothes, but I still wanted to go. I could remember that my aunt changed my Sunday dress and she put my school dress and my school shoes on me and I went to my mother's.

But God

Aunt Nedith & Uncle Sam's home

Lula A. Scott

Skyland Elementary School

But God

ME AT SKYLAND ELEMENTARY SCHOOL

Lula A. Scott

ATKINS SENIOR HIGH SCHOOL

But God

ATKINS SENIOR HIGH SCHOOL

CHAPTER 2

I left my aunt's house with no clothes. The day after I went to live with my mother, there was a woman named Miss Scott, who was a seamstress, and somehow my mother had material at Miss Scott's house. I went to Miss Scott's house, she measured me, and made me clothes. I was very happy.

Then there was a lady named Miss Maxine who did hair. My mother sent me there to have my hair pressed and curled. I went there for a while. So everything went real good.

We lived in a three-room house. I had left that beautiful house with my beautiful bed, where I lived with my aunt and uncle, and I went to my mother's. In that three-room house, there was my mother, her husband, who I called Mr. Nichols, my brother, Bunk, and my sisters, Fannie, Pearl, and Gwen. When you came in the front door, that was the living room. You walked to the next room, that was the bedroom. When you walked to the next room, that was the kitchen. The toilet was outside. The sink was outside. The next door neighbor shared the sink and toilet with us. When you stood up off the toilet, the toilet would flush.

Gwen and I had chores. We had to bring the wood and coal into the house for heat. We had to carry the wood, carry the water, and keep the outside toilet clean, which two families had to use.

We had an icebox. There was no refrigerator. Anything that we needed to keep cold, we had to chip from a block of ice. I remember when my mother got her first refrigerator. I was so excited because I was used to a refrigerator when I lived with my aunt and uncle. When my mother got a refrigerator, that made me very happy.

My mother was a good cook. She would cook and she would feed us. I said I was hungry at my aunt's house because she could not cook like my mother. My mother was born a cook from South Carolina. She could just make biscuits that would roll in your mouth. My mother would say, "You look like you never get enough." I would eat everything. Sometimes I would eat until I would get sick on my stomach, but my mother would just let me eat all I wanted to eat.

When I was about 12-years-old, my sister Pearl had a baby. When my mother came from the hospital, she told us how beautiful that baby was. We called that baby, Babydoll. My mother had a white crib waiting for Babydoll. It had screens on it and a top on it so that the flies would not land on her.

My mother, my sister, and the baby came home in a red ambulance. When they held that baby up in the air, I declare, she was a beautiful baby doll. She had a beautiful, full round face, black curly hair, and heavy eyelashes. Her eyes were big as the moon and her eyelashes were so long.

My mother held her up and said, "You are my Babydoll." At that very moment, something dropped in my heart. I had come back to my mother when I was nine-years-old. Here it was three years later and Babydoll had come. From that day on, while I know now that it was not true, at the time, I felt as if Babydoll had taken my place. I had never had a chance to be my mother's baby and I knew, now that I would never get the chance to be my mother's baby.

My mother dressed Babydoll up. She would tell my sister Gwen and myself that we better take care of Babydoll. My sister Pearl would go out. Sometimes she would come back and sometimes she would just stay out all night. Gwen and I would have to sit up through the night. If Babydoll cried, we would have to get up and rock her. On Sundays, if we wanted to play, we would have to take Babydoll outside. When my friend Sandra came, Gwen or I would be outside holding Babydoll. I loved Babydoll, but I just felt that something changed in my life.

When I was 13, we moved from 8th Street to Cameron Avenue, but we were still living in a three-room house. We lived in front of the 14th Street Elementary School. Also on the block, there was a gymnasium and Atkins High School. The walk wasn't long. Somehow, even though Gwen was older than I, we both ended up in the eighth grade.

As a child, Gwen knew how to match her clothes. She would fix herself up so nice. On the other hand, I think after Babydoll was born, I just lost myself. I would just put on anything to wear as long as it was clean.

My oldest sister, Fannie, was the one left to take care of us when my mother went to work in the laundry. Fannie saw to it that Gwen and I went to school, that we were dressed. She was responsible for us. She would wash our clothes. We didn't have washing machines and dryers. Fannie would wash the clothes on the rub board. Sometimes, it would be so cold, especially in the morning, that when we hung the clothes on the line, the clothes would freeze.

Fannie would cook for us. She was a good cook. I remember a time when Fannie took a chicken and rung its neck. She cut it, we hung the chicken on the line, the blood would drop, and we had to pick the chicken. That was funny to me to see the chicken fluttering all around the yard.

On the weekends, my mother bought chickens. Fannie was the oldest and she always helped kept us clean and made sure that our hair was combed. Fannie would wash, iron, and cook. On Saturdays, Fannie would kill the chickens so that every Sunday we could have chicken. You could not pay me to kill the chicken. I was afraid and would not do it. I would run. Gwen and I would run away and keep away from Fannie because we did not want anything to do with killing the chickens.

But God

Sometimes me and my sisters would go live with my father, I don't really know why. The man next door had chickens. We would put corn down on the door of the house and lure the chicken to walk into my father's house. We killed the chicken, cooked the chicken, and ate the chicken. That was fun to me. We did things together. We laughed. We had fun. We were a family.

There were days when Sandra, Gwen, and myself would go blackberry picking. I remember one day, my mother told us not to go. I told Gwen, "Let's not go. We're going to get a beating." Gwen said, "Oh no and beating don't hurt no longer than you get it." I said, "Yeah, but it hurts." We went blackberry picking anyway and we got a beating.

I learned something that my mother was doing. I would see the people come to our house and we would be surprised who came. We had a speak easy house. My mother was selling whiskey and the church people would come and buy the whiskey. She would say, "Whoever comes in here, you better not tell who came in here." Some of the same people I saw shouting in church, were the same ones who would come to get a shot of whiskey, but we dare not talk about it.

On Friday nights, we had the red light rent party. We would put a red bulb on the porch. My mother would take the beds down and put a table across the kitchen door. She was like an entrepreneur. My mother would cook fish and chitlins in the wintertime. In the winter and the summer, she would cook chicken, make soup and oyster stew, whatever that weekend called for. Fannie and Pearl would be in the kitchen selling the food.

When my mother took the beds down, we would put up a couple of card tables. People would play pity pat. My mother would buy different kinds of candy bars by the boxes. Gwen and I would sit all night when they would play pity pat. Whenever they played, everybody would have to put a nickel on the table. Everybody put up the nickel and whoever won, if there were five people, they got five bars of candy. Gwen and I would collect the $.25. In the morning, we would have a lot of change for my mother. Gwen and I would be very happy. At that time, I was twelve and Gwen was thirteen.

When people knocked on the door, we would ask them, "What do you want?" They would say, "I want a side of whiskey." We would say, "Momma is tired and sleepy. We'll sell you a whiskey."

At about fifteen, we started tasting the whiskey. My mother had the whiskey in the ceiling in the kitchen. Gwen and I learned to go to the ceiling, get a jug of that whiskey, pour us out some, put some water and sugar in that jug, and put that jug in the back. Then we would put the good jug to the front. When my mother got to the back jugs, the people would say, "Anna, this whiskey's been watered down." My mother would tell them, "I don't put no water in my whiskey." Gwen and I would be looking because we knew that we had put the water in the whiskey. We wouldn't say much because we knew we would get in trouble.

Gwen and I would sell the whiskey, but when Fannie would go to the door, she would say, "My mother is not here." She would not sell the whiskey. Fannie, she was always saved. My daddy would take Gwen and I to the revival meetings and we would get salvation every summer. Gwen, Pearl, and I, we would go every year and get saved at the revival, but it would only last as long as the preacher was preaching. That salvation lasted about one week because everything that you did was a sin at that time.

They would put us on the altar and make us say, "Jesus, Jesus, Jesus." We would say that over and over again and then get up. Sometimes, the old saints would put us back down. They would say, "You're lying. You didn't get nothing. Get back down there." So we played saved every year.

My father would tell us do this and do that, but we would still go out and do the wrong thing. We would come back to the altar and shout again the next year and get salvation again. But I thank God for His mercy, that's why I am here today.

But God

    My brother, Bunk, he was a smart boy, just like my mother. He built a shack on the side of the house. He put a shoeshine stand in that shack, put a coke refrigerator in there and he also had potato chips. Bunk would sell the cokes and potato chips in the evenings. He did not allow you to eat one bag of the potato chips. If you ate a bag of chips or drank a soda, Bunk knew it. He loved that money.

    On Sundays, Bunk would shine shoes and charge $.15. He would send Gwen and I out on Sunday mornings to collect the shoes, early before people went to church. Every pair of shoes that we picked up and took back, Bunk would give Gwen and I a nickel.

    When I was a little girl, people were poor and they didn't own much. But my aunt and uncle, after I left, they bought land and they built a house from the ground. I think they were the first ones in the family living in Winston-Salem that built a brand new house. Most of my family had bought houses that other people had lived in, but my aunt and uncle had enough money to build a brand new house. They were prospering.

    Gwen and I were still going to church. No matter what we did, we still went to church. We went to school sometimes. My mother would get us up in the morning and tell us to go to school. We would go out the back door and go to my father's house and sleep all day.

    One day, my daddy came home. Gwen and I, we didn't have any better sense, we made a fire in the heater, and my father discovered that we had been there. My mother said that we better not do that anymore, we had better stop going over there and stop staying up like that.

    Then there were times when Gwen and I didn't like what was going on at our house and we would go to our father's house and stay. We might stay two or three days. I think about it now. How nobody came to look for us or when we finally came home, my mother would say, "You little women. I guess you been to your daddy's house. Huh?" Sometimes, my mother would look at me and say, "You black just like your ole daddy and you look like your ole daddy." She would say bad things to me and to Fannie. I couldn't understand.

My mother, she was light-skinned; Gwen was brown, my brother, he wasn't dark, dark; and Pearl wasn't dark, dark, but Fannie and I were the darker two. It seemed like we got called black and cursed out more than the others. Gwen would speak up for herself sometimes, but my mother would knock her down in the floor. I was scared to speak up and say things, but Gwen had more nerve than I did.

Life went on. Gwen and I went to Atkins High School. One day, Gwen and I went downtown. We saw these guys. They said, "So what you doing this evening." We said, "Nothing." They said, "You want to go for a ride." We said, "Yeah." They came by and picked us up. We got my cousin, Lina Jane. We went out with them that evening. Gwen was about 16, I was 15.

My mother was sitting on the porch. My mother said, "Where you going and who is that?" Gwen said, "That's a friend." She told me, "Come on." So I took off and followed Gwen to the car. Those guys took us to the woods. An old house was down there and a light was on. They told us, "Come on in." We said, "We're not going in there." They said, "If you don't come in, you're going to walk home." We said, "Well, we're going to walk home."

It must have been about midnight and we started walking. We asked people the way. When it got daylight, people began to tell us which way to walk. Come to find out, we were in a place called Thomasville, North Carolina. We walked from Thomasville to Winston-Salem. It was a long walk. When we got home, my mother said, "I'll deal with you when I get back home this evening." It was time for her to go to work. Of course, we walked in and right out the back door to my father's house. We didn't come back for two or three days. My mother didn't get us for that.

There were times when my mother would come home in the evening, and she would come in singing and the switch would come in the door before she came in. She would ask, "Did you fill that wood box?" We would say no. She would look in the kitchen and say, "You didn't bring no water in this house?" We start running, but she would beat us anyway. She would give us a good beating.

Sometimes, when my mother was washing on that washboard, she would start humming low and then she would come to the next voice, and then the next voice. By the time she got to the third voice, she would call our names. When she called your name and she had hit that high note, we knew that we had better start running or go to our daddy because we knew that we were going to get a beating. Gwen and I went through that. But my brother, he would do what he wanted to do. My mother had spoiled him.

Lula A. Scott

Me at my father's home

Chapter 3

I was very smart in high school, but about the tenth grade, I lost interest. I met a young boy. His name was Billy. He was five years older than me. He was one of the boys who were called the tobacco boys. They would come to Winston-Salem every year to work on the tobacco market. When they came, Gwen picked Herbert and I picked Billy. At fifteen, we started running with the tobacco boys. They would come and buy whiskey. They were working and making good money. Momma would tell them to come. They would buy the food. We liked them.

Gwen and I started hanging out in the street. It was not much to do in Winston-Salem, but when people would come to town, like the Temptations, or other groups to sing, we would go to the concert at the gym and we would just dance. We would go to house parties and Gwen and I would just drink. We were young. I don't know how Momma didn't know that we were drinking the whiskey, but we were drinking whiskey and beer.

One evening, I dressed myself up in Fannie's dress and shoes. By then, she was in college. Fannie was determined to get an education. She decided she was going to Teacher's College. My mother said, "You'll never go to college in my house." But Fannie was determined. She got a job at the Robert E. Lee hotel and she worked to pay for school.

I would stay up at night because I felt sorry for Fannie. My mother would say, "Let that fire go out." But when my mother turned that couch down and went to sleep, I would put a log of coal in the heater so when Fannie came home she wouldn't be cold and she could study by the heater. Although it was hard, Fannie made it through school.

Fannie would tell me to get saved. She would say that Gwen, Pearl, and I needed to get saved. We would say to one another that she needed to hush her mouth and just let us drink our beer and leave us alone. We didn't say that to Fannie. She was our mother and we knew better.

Gwen and I kept on dating the tobacco guys. One day, I dressed up and went up the street and on my way back, a young man grabbed me by my neck. He tried to drag me onto to the school ground where a lady had been killed. She had been thrown on that ground and they never found out who killed her. I was petrified.

When I got in front of our house at the school gymnasium, I told him, "Wait, let me take my shoes off and I'll do what you want me to do." He released me to take my shoes off. When he did, I ran across the street to my house and I called my mother as loud as I could. The dogs were barking. A preacher came out and said, "You turn that girl a loose." My mother said she fell out the chair. She couldn't get the front door open. She came out the backdoor and he ran.

About three months later, that young man was coming back across the street. He must have forgotten what he had done. I told my mother, "Here comes that young man who grabbed me." My mother said, "Hi, son." She baited him and he came in the house.

The guy came in. My mother got him into the living room and took him straight to the bedroom. She said, "I want to talk to you." When he came in the bedroom, I was standing there. My brother, he was a Joe Louis type of looking guy. He came out from under the covers and he asked the guy did he know what he was doing. My brother told him, "I'm going to let you go this time, but when you see my sister, cross over on the other side."

My family was not afraid of fighting. After Pearl had Babydoll, she married a man who was abusive to her. Pearl and her husband were fighting all the time. Pearl would always want to be with her husband. More than once, we had to fight him. We would literally beat him up because he would blacken both of Pearl's eyes. By then, she had five children and he kept fighting her. My brother almost killed him.

One night, Pearl's husband, he hit Babydoll. Well, the family almost killed Pearl's husband that night. He got hit in the head, he got cut, and he got stabbed. He was almost beat to death, but Pearl still stayed with him.

Everybody had to go to court on Monday morning. The family doctor said he had looked in the paper and all my family's names, except Fannie, were in the paper. My mother's name was in the paper because when the police asked my sister Pearl, "Who else should I take?" Pearl said, "Get my mother, too." I said, "You gonna send Momma to jail?" She said, "Yes, take her, too. I didn't send for any of you." From that day on, we learned not to fight for Pearl anymore. We left her alone.

Chapter 4

Let me talk about my father, Troy Bradley. He was born to parents who were not married to each other. My father's father had a wife. He went down the road and dated my grandmother and they had two children. My father had two brothers and three sisters, who were by his father and his father's wife. My father and his siblings were very close, and from what I can understand, my grandfather did not allow his children's mothers to argue or have any kind of dissension between them. The two families were very close. My father worked the farm at my grandfather's house. My grandfather provided for my dad and my Aunt Nedith, who raised me.

My father was a quiet man. He really didn't talk a lot. He was a hardworking man, who worked at RJ Reynolds Tobacco Company for 42 years. He loved his girls. Gwen and I would go and look through the factory window on his pay day. Sometimes, my father would come out and give us money. Other times he would go out the backdoor. Gwen could always find him. She would walk until she found him downtown and then she would get the money. The little money that he gave us we would use to buy socks or whatever, but I would mostly always eat my money up.

My father was a deacon in Mt. Sinai Glorious Church of God. He would sing The Debt I owe, Teach Me Lord How to Pray, and I'm Gonna away and I'm Gonna stay. I would laugh because I knew that sometimes he was a little drunk when he was in church singing. My mother would tell me, my sisters, and my brother all the time, "Your daddy is nothing but a little drunk." My father was not a drunk, but he did drink on the weekends a lot.

I never remember my father abusing us or saying bad things to us. My daddy was a short man, but he was well-dressed. I found out later in life that the women in church really loved him and they would dress up and shout all around my daddy. I really admired those people and I had a lot of confidence in them until I realized that they were not holy and that changed my life. I looked at them and I would always say, "I don't want to be a hypocrite like them."

My mother sold whiskey. One day I walked into the living room and she tried to stop me. But, before I got there, one of the ladies was sitting there with the elders of the church and they were drinking whiskey. That hurt me to my heart to know that they had a form of godliness, but they were not living it.

I learned not to play with God. I always had a repenting spirit. My favorite Bible verse that I learned was on the wall and I remember it to this day, "Fear God, keep His commandments for this is the whole duty of man." I learned to fear God. Not the kind of fear like the boogey man or a ghost was coming, but the correct word was reverence God and respect God.

Sandra, Gwen, and myself would travel all the way to Lexington, North Carolina with the Bishop on Sunday nights. He had a church there and he would take us. Gwen could really sing. She would go to churches and she would sing the solos.

The young guys would be around the window at the church and we throw notes out the window so that we could get a word to them. Sandra's mother, Sis. Garner, soon found out what we were doing, so the next Sunday she said we could not go. Sandra and I were scared so we wouldn't try to get in the car, but Gwen tried to get in. Sister Garner pulled Gwen by her neck and pulled her right out of that car and told us that we could not go with the Bishop again and she meant what she said.

My father would come home. Gwen and I would be at his house and I would tell him what to bring us to eat. He had a little bill at the grocery store where we could get some food. He really tried hard. He kept a three room house and we could always go there and we would always be comfortable.

My father had a kind heart and mind. He didn't teach us to talk about people or run people down. He always had something good to say about people. During the week, my father was always home with us. When he got paid on the weekends, he would go and drink, but he would never stay out all night. My father was good to all of us. That's how I remember my dad, even until the end he was just a good, kind, and loving man.

Chapter 5

My father and mother married when they were very young. My mother worked for 32 years in a laundry. She was very proud, very smart, very hardworking, very kind, and very clean. She would sing a lot. My mother kept her hair beautiful. When I was home with her, she made sure that we were clean.

My mother was very strict. While now I can say that she meant it for our good, I used to say that she was very mean. I didn't understand. But as years went by, I came to understand that at the age of 28, my mother had had seven children. My father would drink on the weekends and when he came home, he would fight my mother.

I also came to know that I had a brother named Samuel Louis. He contracted mumps and had stumped his toe and died. My brother's death hurt my mother very bad. She had five girls and two boys, but after Samuel Louis died, there was only one son, Bunk. My mother loved Bunk and she spoiled him to death.

My mother was raised in South Carolina. She told us that as a young girl, she would have to go to the white peoples' houses and cook and clean for them. When she was little, they would stand her on a bench and at night men would come riding in. As she got older, she understood that they were the Ku Klux Klan. They had white hoods over their heads, but when they removed the hoods, she recognized who they were and they would tell her that she better not tell about what she saw. My mother would stay at the white peoples' homes and prepare the food for them when they came back. The people were not mean to her. God gave her favor as a child.

My mother was sent to Kingstree, South Carolina one day to sell some chickens and she met with my father. They were teenagers. They left and went to Winston-Salem, North Carolina and a relative there took them in, who signed for my mother and father to get married. That was the union that my siblings, Troy, Fannie, Annie, Pearl, Samuel Louis, Gwen, and I came out of. My parents had had a baby every year from the time they had gotten married until my mother was 28-years-old. My brother, Samuel Louis, had died before Gwen and I were born. As children, we went to Sunday School and that helped shape our lives.

I remember my sister Pearl had all kinds of beautiful hair, beautiful socks and ribbons, and I told her that I wanted some of that pretty stuff. Pearl told me to go downtown. She gave me a shopping bag and told me to just pick up what I wanted and put it in the bag. I picked up some navy blue socks and some other things, but I don't remember what. A lady came and asked me what was in the bag. She told me that I could to go to jail and that she was going to call my mother. I don't know why I didn't say don't call my mother, I said, "Please don't tell Sister Ray." She asked me who was Sister Ray. I told her that Sister Ray was my Sunday School teacher. That lady gave me a good talking to and I was so shamed because one of the commandments that I had learned in Sunday School was "Thou shall not steal."

I didn't see my sister Pearl anywhere in the store. When I got out, I found her way down the street. Pearl told me that I should have looked up and looked all around because someone was sitting up hiding, and that I would have seen them. From that one experience, I never stole again.

My mother worked really hard to try to keep all of us together, but somehow my Aunt Sadie got my sister Annie and she raised her in Philadelphia, Pennsylvania. My aunt Nedith got me when I was two-years-old and she raised me in Winston-Salem. While we had a pretty exciting life, I can say this, I know that God had a purpose for our lives in everything.

As I think back over my life, I thank God that I trusted Him at an early age. I thank God that He was directing my life from birth and that the purpose of my life was from conception. My life had been directed like a compass that went out the wrong way, but in the end, the compass put me back on the right track. The light in the lighthouse began to show because Jesus was that lighthouse.

Chapter 6

In February 1956, I found out I was pregnant. In March 1956, Gwen had a baby girl. She named her Cynthia. My mother was taking care of Gwen, she was taking care of the baby, she was taking care of Babydoll, and she was taking care of me.

My mother came in one evening from work and she started that singing. I heard her when she hit the third note. By the time she hit the third note, she said, "Lula, come here." She said it with a voice like you better get in here.

When I came in, she sat me by the table and said, "You pregnant huh?" When she said that, I don't know why the devil came in my mouth and made me say it, but I said, "Are you asking me or are you telling me?" When I said that, my mother picked me up and threw me to the next room and started beating me. She tried to knee me in my stomach and Gwen pulled her off of me.

I jumped up and my mother said, "Where's my gun?" I had the key to the wardrobe. She always kept a .38 in the wardrobe. I threw that key on the table and out the backdoor I went to my father's house. When I got to my daddy's house, I told him what happened and he said, "Don't go back."

The next day, Gwen called me. She said, "Mommy said she's sorry and she wants you to come back." I said I am never going to come back there again. I said, "I'm not coming back." Gwen said, "Lula please." She pleaded with me because we were such good friends. I said, "I'm not coming back." I was seventeen and I never went back to live with my mother again. I went to my father's house and I stayed with him for about two weeks.

I was pregnant by Billy Campbell. I told him that my mother was very angry because I was pregnant. So about two or three weeks later, Billy and I decided to get married. We ran off to Bennettsville, South Carolina. I was too young to get married, but Pearl went with us and she signed the papers.

When I came back home, Fannie tried to have a little gathering to say that Billy and I had gotten married. We had celery sticks and sandwiches. My mother did not participate. The only person who came was Sandra and she brought me a set of bed linens.

Initially, Billy and I moved together in a room that he was renting and stayed there for a while. Later, we moved to an apartment. At that time, you could buy furniture for $399. We bought a living room set, a bedroom set, and paid extra money, and got a stove and a refrigerator. Other people had a wood stove, but we had an electric stove. I was so proud of my three rooms of furniture that consisted of a living room set, an end chair, two tables, and what we called a coffee table. I had a breakfast room set and a bedroom set.

We didn't know if the baby was a boy or a girl, but we bought a crib and set it in the corner of our bedroom. We had running water and a bathtub. I thought I was living high and good.

We lived on the second level and I would stand on the porch in the evening and look for Billy to come across the field. He worked in the hosiery mill. I was seventeen and Billy was five years older than me. He would come home good from work in the beginning and I was so happy to have him.

I knew Billy had another girlfriend before we got married. One day, I met up with him and the girl and asked him who did he want? He told us that he didn't want either one of us. I had completely forgotten about that incident because I was so happy.

Lula A. Scott

Billy started staying out at night and not coming home. When he would come home, if I said anything, Billy would get so angry, so sometimes I would not say anything. But then, being only 17, there would be times when I would say something because I had a lot of fight in me. I had heard how my father treated my mother and I had already made up my mind at an early age that no man would treat me like that.

CHAPTER 7

My baby girl was born, Sharon. I dedicate this part of my book to her, a gift that God gave me; the one thing that I could call my own. While in my womb, I gave Sharon back to God. When I was pregnant with her, I would walk the streets and cry, sometimes late at night. I would hold and rub my stomach, and I would say, "Lord, please let this baby be different from me. Let this child never touch or taste the things of the world." I wanted a baby who would be saved, sanctified, and filled with the Holy Ghost. I always prayed that she would have beautiful legs and I think she did pretty good. She was a very beautiful baby.

Born in October of 1956, it's strange that everything about her birthday was ten. She was born on the tenth day, the tenth month at 10:10 at night. I was so happy when she was born. Billy was not there for her birth. Finally, the next day, he came to see us.

When I brought Sharon home from the hospital, she was so little. She only weighed six lbs. I thought Sharon was a doll baby. I would dress her up in the mornings and I would just look at her. Her father would hold her and we would just look at her. As she grew, she grew more beautifully.

When I took Sharon to my mother's house, my mother always gave the babies a nickname. She looked at Sharon and said, "This is Pudding." From that day on, we began to call my baby Pudding.

After Pudding was born, Billy continued staying out. He would come at 11, 11:30 at night, change his clothes, go out, and stay out all night. I decided one night that I was going to find out where he was going. I got in the car. Billy was so busy getting ready that he didn't even notice that I was laying down in the back of the car on the floor.

When Billy got to his destination and got out of the car, he came back and got a pack of cigarettes and then he went in the house. I watched his silhouette on the shade when he took his clothes off. When the lights went out, I got out of the car and knocked on the door. A lady from came from the opposite side of the house where Billy went came to the door. She was an older woman. I said, "I would like for you to tell my husband to come out." She said, "Your husband didn't come in here." I said, "Oh, yes he did. His name is Billy."

The lady almost convinced me, but something clicked in my mind. I said, "Do you have a daughter named Eloise?" She said, "Yes." When she said that, I pushed her out of my way. I went to the side that I saw Billy go in and I went to the door. I saw him on the side of the bed. He had already put his shirt on and was putting on his shoes.

Billy and I began fighting. By that time, this girl jumped out of the bed, ran down the hall, came up the back way, and bit me in my back. When I turned around to get her, I looked at her and her stomach was big, like she was nine months pregnant. I just walked out.

Billy came behind me and he tried to explain. He said, "Get in the car and I will take you home." I got in the car and I said to him, "When we get home, my father is going to kill you." He parked and began pleading and begged me not to tell anybody. I didn't tell anybody because I knew that if I had told my sisters and my brother what he to me, they would have hurt him real bad.

I remember there was a day when Pearl came to my house and her husband came in and he jumped her and we had an awful fight. I hit her husband with a broomstick because he was breaking my sister's arm. He left, but he told me that he was coming back to kill me. He came back, kicked the door open. I had a wood heater with a pot of boiling water. When he came towards me, I threw that hot water on him and he ran back out of the door. We had to go to court for that.

When we went to court, Pearl's husband said he didn't want to have the warrant for me, he took it down. My sister was sitting there. The judge asked me what did I want to say. I told the judge that Pearl's husband was dating my husband's girlfriend's aunt and my husband was dating Eloise. I said, "I want you to ask my sister and her husband to stay away from my house. I don't want either one of them ever at my house again. They turned my baby's crib over with her in it. My husband was out in the street. It was three or four o'clock in the morning, they came to my house and started that." The judge gave me an order against them and instructed my sister and her husband never to come to my house again.

Chapter 8

I remember one day I was in the house and a boy came and said, "Where's Mr. Billy?" I said, "He's in the house." The boy said, "Tell him Eloise said she had the baby and she wanted him to come to the hospital." Billy left and went to the hospital.

One day, while I was in a corner grocery store, I saw Eloise. She had a baby in her arms. I said to her, "You knew that I was married to Billy and you still got pregnant by him?" She said, "I want to tell you something. I didn't know that he was still married to you. He would spend so much time with me and I came by the apartment and you all had lost the apartment and he told me that you had gone home to your father." I said, "He would be with me until he would go to work in the evening." She said, "Well, when he would go to work in the evenings and on the weekends, he would spend time with me a lot."

All of these things began to add up. When you are young, you don't think about it. And not being married before and not seeing marriage in my family, only my brother and his wife, which was a good marriage, I didn't understand a lot of things. I said to Eloise, "Okay."

As time went on, Billy and I kept fighting, raising sand all the time, and just keeping the devil up. I would go to church and when Billy would come home at night, sometimes I would be on my knees praying. He would say, "All you want to do is go to that church." I would say, "All you want to do is run with the women." Even though he would say that to me, church was good for me. I kept on going to church. I had my baby christened.

Sometimes, I would go out on the weekend. My mother would keep Sharon. Gwen and I would drink. We would have our parties. Billy wouldn't be home so I was worried that by the time I got home, he would be there. We were still having our ups and downs.

Billy worked on the tobacco market and every now and then, he would have to go out of town. One particular time, some friends of mine were going to Atlantic Beach. I went with my girlfriend and her husband. When we got to the beach, I said, "That looks like Billy's car." My girlfriend said, "Oh, no, that can't be him. They went to Virginia." I said, "It looks like his car."

We went on and walked around. About eight o'clock in the morning, I saw his car again. I looked in the car. He was laying in the car and a girl was laying over him. I opened the car door and they jumped up. He said, "Wait a minute." The girl said, "Who are you?" I said, "I'm his wife." She said, "His wife?" Then she told me her name. She said, "I've got two children for him and he's my man." I said, "How is he your man when he is my husband?" I left Atlantic Beach. Billy went one way, I went another.

I had no idea Billy was going to be at Atlantic Beach. When he would leave on the weekends, I always thought he was going to work on the tobacco market, but Billy would go to Whitesville, North Carolina, his hometown. I was never invited to go with him.

Later in the day, Billy and I met up again at Atlantic Beach. Billy said, "My mother and father are here. I want you to meet them." I had on daisy dukes and stick legs. That was the first time I had ever met his mother and his father.

So a few years later at Christmas, we went down to Whitesville to visit Billy's mother and father. He deposited me in the house and left, and I didn't see Billy for another day when he finally came home.

I asked him where he had been and the ruckus started. We came back to Winston-Salem and I never went to his parents' home again.

Chapter 9

Life went on, and Billy and I reconciled. After all, we had our little baby, Pudding, and she was wonderful. She did not do a lot of crying. She would just lay in the bed and look all around. Her father and I would just pick her up and hold her. Pudding would just giggle when I talked to her. When her daddy would pick her up and hold up her in the air, she would just look down in his face and laugh and Billy would let the slobber fall down in his face. He was just so happy about her and he really loved Pudding. When Billy came home at night, and Pudding would be in crib, he would pick her up, wake her, and put her in the air.

When Sharon was a baby, there were no disposable diapers. We used cloth diapers called Birdeye. I would wash Sharon's diapers and socks on a rub board and hang them out on the line to dry. The neighbors would talk about how bright and white they were and how when they saw Pudding, her clothes were never dingy. I would always put fresh clothes on her. I did not have a lot of clothes for her, but what I had, I kept them sparking clean. I kept Pudding very clean and I always had good shoes on her feet.

I remember Pudding loved to suck a bottle. And no matter how her daddy treated me, he always made sure that seven half gallons of milk were in the refrigerator every week. There was always milk for Pudding. I never had to worry where milk was coming from. I never had to wonder where food was coming from. In that way, Billy took care and provided for us.

Pudding would not walk. I would say, "Walk Pudding, please walk. I just want you to walk." After carrying her in my arms, I would go to church on Sundays. It was not a long walk, but it was a pretty good walk. I didn't have a stroller, so I would always have to pick Pudding up and carry her. She was about two-years-old and still crawling on the floor.

My niece Cynthia, she was the same age as Pudding, had made such progress. Cynthia was walking. Sharon was talking, but she was not walking. They would say, "Oh, well, she's not going to walk and she's going to suck a bottle until she's six-years-old." I would say, "Let her have her bottle." I did not have a problem with Pudding having her bottle, but when she started walking, I used to look at her and say, "Why don't you put the bottle down? You're a big girl."

One night I was in the house and I was doing something in the living room. I heard something pattering in the bedroom. I peeked and Pudding was walking around in the floor. I hollered, "Oh, my God, she can walk. She can walk."

When her daddy came home, I told him that she could walk. I told everybody that she could walk. Well, Pudding did not walk again for another two weeks so everybody thought I had a dream and made that up. They would all say, "You were drinking and you made that up." I said, "I was not drinking. The girl can walk." Then one day, Sharon just got up and started walking.

Not only was Pudding a late walker, but she was also late cutting teeth. My next door neighbor, Miss Annie, would always call her Grandma because Sharon would eat and Miss Annie would feed her things and Sharon knew how to gum it down. Soon after she started walking, teeth began busting out in her mouth, but she would still suck that bottle.

One day, I went to my Daddy's friend, Miss Louise's house, and I had Pudding with me. When I came, Miss Louise said, "Pudding don't want no bottle anymore." I said, "What do you mean she don't want a bottle any-more?" She said, "I put hot sauce on the bottle and she won't take it now." I was kind of upset because I didn't mind her sucking her bottle, but everybody else did. But from that day on, Pudding did not want a bottle.

Pudding would play by herself in the floor. She would just laugh and play and walk through the house. A friendly baby, she did not run from anyone. When her aunts and uncles and cousins came, Pudding would always play with them. She would run with them. She would laugh with them.

Pudding, Babydoll, and Cynthia were the three kids who hung together. When we would go to my mother's, which was every day, they would all sit on the steps. In the summertime, they would play and talk in their little children's language. Babydoll was the oldest and she could really talk. Cynthia and Pudding were saying something, I really did not know what they were saying, but the three of them would all be together. They were very close.

Billy and I stayed on Woodland Avenue until Pudding was about two-years-old. When Sharon was three-years-old, we lost the apartment. Well, actually, we were evicted after Billy stopped paying the rent, the electric, and everything else. He even stopped paying on the furniture, which was repossessed. Billy, Sharon, and I moved into my father's house on Jackson. My daddy loved Pudding to death.

In the mornings, Sharon would play. I remember, I brought her some chickens, little baby bitties. I didn't know that she was afraid of the bitties. But then I heard the bitties scream. When I looked out, each one that came by Sharon, she would pick up and choke them to death. She was screaming, "Eee." Sharon killed all three of the little baby chickens because she was frightened by them.

Pudding liked to sing Charlie Brown. One day, my sister Pearl told her, "Don't go outside." Pudding looked at her and said, "Charlie Brown, he's a clown." She skipped through the house and when she got to the door, she again said, "Charlie Brown is a clown." Pudding went out the door, ran down the steps, and Pearl had to catch her.

Pudding would always do things to make me laugh. She loved to hold my face. She would just look at me, like, "Are you really real? Are you really real?" I would just hug her and say, "This is my baby." I always referred to Sharon as "My baby." It was like I had my baby and nobody else mattered.

Sharon and I would go to my mother's every day. One day, on the way back home, I found a puppy. I brought that puppy back, gave him a bottle, and named him Rusty. Sharon would play with Rusty. She would holler, "Oh, Rusty, Rusty, Rusty." He would throw her down and she would just hug on Rusty. She loved Rusty so much.

As a little girl, I would take Sharon to church, that was a main thing for us. When she was about three-years-old, she would hold onto a bench in the church and just shout and dance. When we would go home to my mother's house and my mother would be doing her business of selling liquor, Sharon would get in the corner and start singing, "I'm coming up Lord. I'm coming up soon for you just to hear my tune, tune, tune." She would just sing that song. My mother would say, "I wish that girl would stop singing like that." Sharon would sing whatever she had heard in church.

When we moved to Jackson, there wasn't much to do, so Sharon and I would go to through the brickyard to my mother's house and sit there during the day. My mother sold whiskey and I would stay at her house and sell whiskey for her until she came home from work.

Pudding had a lot of love and care. When we would get to church, they would take her and pass her from arm to arm. Everybody wanted to hold Pudding. Bishop Johnson would say, "Hand me the baby." He would say, "Nurture that baby. Take care of that baby. That baby has a calling on her life."

There was a lady at our church who had made Sharon and I some dresses. Sharon was dressed like me. I just thought we were the cutest thing. We went to church and had our dresses on and everybody was talking about us. Two weeks later, the lady made us another set of matching dresses.

My neighbor called Pudding her goddaughter. She would buy her Roman sandals that buckled. There were three straps on them that came to the ankles like boots. During the week, my neighbor would put the white ones on her and black patent leather ones on Sundays for church.

Pudding had hair that hung down her back and I did not know how to comb her hair. She would cry and put her head on my lap. I would spank her with the comb because I wanted her to sit up. I was having a hard time combing her hair and nothing seemed to help.

While I was careful of what I did around Sharon, I did give her a lot of beatings. To this day, she would say, "My mother would beat me with the switch." I did not know any different. I had been beat with the switch and told if you beat a child with the switch, the child would be a better child. So during that time, everybody beat their children with the switch.

I had a cousin named Lina Jane, she's gone, but I can tell you one thing, she raised a fine bunch of children, just like I did. Lina Jane and I were young mothers, but we were determined that our children would not be like us. Sometimes, I would think that we beat them too much with the switch, but other times I would think to myself, the Bible says spare the rod and spoil the child. Although I believed that we may have given our children too many beatings, I also believe that it helped them. I tell Sharon all the time, I apologize for giving you so many beatings, but I don't apologize for giving you some.

Chapter 10

Billy left Winston-Salem, North Carolina and began working and traveling with the tobacco market. Sharon and I stayed with my father. One day, Billy called me up. I asked him where he was. He said, "I'm at the tobacco market in Orlando and I want you to get the baby and I want you to come." I said, "Oh, I don't know." He said, "I'm sending you a ticket and I want you to come." I said, "Okay, I'll come." My mother said, "You shouldn't go." I said, "That's my husband and I'm going to go."

I got my baby ready and on my way to Orlando, I asked my mother for some money. She wouldn't give me any. I went to my father and I asked him for some money. He said, "I'm not giving you any money to go back down there to Billy." I said, "Well, you all can't stop me. I'm going to go." I got my baby and got on the bus. I had ninety cents in my pocket. When we got into the station I got Sharon, she was two at that time, some milk with the ninety cents.

Sharon and I moved with Billy to Eatonville, a small town made up of all blacks. Established by some influential black people, the policeman was the mayor, he was the judge, and he was the mailman. That one person did everything in that little town.

Billy had a room in a house, and his mother and father had a room in that same house. Sharon would spend time with her grandparents and that way she got to know them.

But God

After moving to Eatonville, I got a job and Sharon went to nursery school. I remember the first day I left her there. When I walked off, it was difficult because I had never left Sharon with anyone. I just did not do that. I believed that Sharon was mine and that she was my responsibility and that I should take care of her.

Billy and I both were working. Although her grandmother was there, I wanted Sharon to be in daycare, but when I left, I could hear her screaming. Sharon was hollering and crying, "Mommy, don't leave me." I went back, but they convinced me to go to work and leave her there.

When Sharon came home from the daycare, she told me that the children were picking with her and they had called her names. The next day, I told her that I was going to remove her from the daycare. I told her to call them whatever they called her back. She said, the other kids said, she was "country." I talked with the teacher. The teacher told me, "Don't worry. The children are picking at her today, but wait, next week, you'll see."

Two weeks later, the teacher said to me, "Guess who was calling the new child a name today?" I said, "Who?" She said, "Pudding." I took Pudding home and said to her, "You know how you felt when the kids were picking on you so don't you make another child feel like that." She said she was sorry.

Pudding always had a soft heart. I always told her, "If anybody hits you, you hit them back." Sometimes, she would give them a lick and sometimes she would bite them depending on what was going on, but she never started a fight. Sharon always had friends who liked her and would always want to be around her.

Chapter 11

In December of 1960, Sharon was four-years-old, Billy and I had a big blowout. Billy's father told him that he shouldn't fight me like that. I called and said I was going home. I went home to Winston-Salem. I was all scratched and beat up. When we got to Winston-Salem, Sharon tried to tell my family that I was choked before I came. They didn't understand what she was saying. I made her hush so that they would not know that I had this big fight before I came.

Sharon and I stayed in Winston-Salem for about two weeks and I told my mother that I was going back to Florida. My mother literally begged me not to go. I said, "I'm going anyway." I told her, "If you never see me no more, just know that I left happy."

I went back to Florida; that was the beginning of the week. That Sunday night, Billy and I got into a big fight. His parents had lived in the same rooming house that Billy and I had lived in, but when I went back to Florida, they said that Billy and I fought so much that they moved to Orlando. His daddy said that something bad was going to happen and he couldn't take it anymore.

After I came back to Eatonville, Billy's parents came to see Sharon and myself on a Sunday. When they left that night, Billy and I got into a big altercation. We were fighting- a bad fight, a bad fight. In the midst of the fighting, he said he was going to kill me. I had been beaten badly time and time again. Billy came at me. I feared for my life. I picked up a kerosene can that was there, threw the kerosene at him. He came towards me. I lit a piece of paper on a heater that was in the room and I threw it at Billy. He caught on fire.

As accurately as I can remember, I ran out the door and Billy ran out after me. Some people put him in his work truck. I got in the truck with Billy. He sat down and put his head in my lap. I said, "You see what this has come to? I didn't want this to happen." I was crying and telling him how sorry I was. At that time, he wasn't on fire and I didn't know how badly he was hurt.

The ambulance came. I remember my baby was running around crying like she didn't know what to do or which way to go. I asked the neighbor to take her and she did. I got in the ambulance with Billy. When we got downtown, the police came and they arrested me and put me in jail.

I remember them taking me through the streets of Orlando, my hands cuffed behind my back. I am not telling this because I want sympathy. I don't want any sympathy. I'm telling this to let you know that there is a consequence for your disobedience; being disobedient to God; being disobedient to my mother. Marrying Billy when she told me not to marry; going down to Florida when she told me not to go there; marrying a man who told me that he did not want me. All of what had happened was a consequence of my disobedience.

I remember as I laying in the jail crying, the police came that night and they said, "He died." When they said he died, I bust out, and I just screamed and cried. I didn't have anybody there. My mother was in North Carolina. I didn't have any friends, only the lady next door who had taken Sharon.

The thing that hurt me the most was being away from my baby. I had never been away from Sharon. That was the one thing that I fretted about most because she was the love of my life. Anything else could have happened but me having to leave my baby and think how was she going to survive was very hard. How was she going to be without her mother?

As I laid on the bed in that jail cell, I could hear Bishop Brumfield Johnson's voice, saying, "It's going to come a time in your life when you can't even pray. If you can just remember to say, 'Lord have mercy,' that would be a prayer." I laid on that bed and began to say, "Lord have mercy." I didn't know who had Pudding. I didn't know what to do. I thought I was losing my mind.

Before I had gotten arrested, I had gotten a job in Winterpark, Florida, working for a doctor and his wife, cleaning their house and taking care of their two boys. I had only worked for the family for maybe like a month. But the next morning after I had been arrested, the police came into the cell and said, "Lula Campbell, somebody wants to see you." I said, "Who could want to see me? I don't know anybody." They said, "It's an attorney here to see you." I said, "I don't have an attorney."

I came out of the cell and the attorney told me his name. I said, "But where did you come from?" He told me that the lady that I had worked for, saw what had happened to me on the television, and had hired him to come the next day to see if he would take my case. That was another divine intervention from God. I didn't know anybody. I didn't know which way to go, didn't know what to do. **BUT GOD!**

I went to court for the hearing. My mother came. One thing about a mother, a mother will show up. In the court, they would not let me talk to my mother. She could only show make gestures at me, throw me kisses and nod her head and smile. She later sent word to me that she was praying and that she was going to finish paying the lawyer.

They said I was going to put me in the electric chair, that I was going to be electrocuted, and at that time, they did electrocute women in Florida quite frequently. I said, "Well, Lord, I'm going to die."

My mother said when she went to go and get Sharon, she said, "I don't want to go. I want to stay with my grandmother." So my mother left Sharon with Billy's mother and father. Thank God because the life that my mother lived and the way she spoiled the grandchildren, Sharon

But God

might not be the person she is today. I was hurt when Sharon didn't go, but even in that, later on in life I have learned what that was all about.

Chapter 12

I stayed in the jail cell from January until September 1961. On my 22nd birthday, I went to court for the trial. My sister Gwen, no matter what, even if she was drinking and I got in trouble, my family would say, "She's coming and she's drunk," but drunk and all, Gwen would always come. We were close and she would always come and see about me.

I was found guilty and sentenced to twenty years. I don't remember, but Gwen said I fainted in the floor. After that, I was sent to Lowell Women's Correctional Institution in Lowell, Florida. I just did not understand and I did not know how Sharon would make it. I would write her letters. She would write me little letters back. I would tell her that I loved her and that I was coming home. I would tell her that I was coming to get her.

I wanted to see Sharon so bad. One day, I was told me that I had a visitor. When I went up to the place, it was Billy's father and he had brought my baby to see me. I thank God that I had a good father-in-law and a good mother-in-law and even with what had happened, they did not turn their backs on me. I know that it had to be a lot of pain with them losing their son, but they were faithful to take care of Sharon.

When I took my baby to the bathroom, she wrote on the wall 20 and she said, "Mommy, you're going to be in here 20 years." She wrote 20 and she said that's how many years I would be there. I told her, "No, four years and I'll be home." By then, I had been told that if I had good behavior, I would be out in four years.

In prison, they put me in the laundry to work where all of the laundry for all of Lowell Correctional Institution. I only weighed 97 lbs. and I had to pull sheets and pillowcases out of this big machine. A lady looked at me and said, "She's too little. She's getting too wet and she's getting pneumonia so we'll have to move her out of here."

I was moved me out of laundry and put in the factory where they made uniforms and clothes. I had to lift bolts and bolts of material and I would be staggering. They looked at me and said, "She's too weak for this. We have to find another place for her."

I was put in a dental office to keep the office clean. There were two white prisoners also assigned to the dental office. Never had there had been a black prisoner in the dental office. I must say that God began to work in my life because every dentist who came was an apprentice and they would teach me everything that they were teaching the dental assistants.

While in prison, I went to school to study for my GED. The first time I took the test, I failed. I came into the kitchen and I was crying. A lady named Miss Abstein looked at me and asked me why I was crying. I said, "Well, they're teasing me, saying I thought I was so smart and I failed the English part of the GED and I didn't get my GED." She said, "I want you to go back and take the test. I want to tell you something, I watch you. You have common sense and mother wit and that is going to take you where education is never going to take you. I want you to hold your head up." That lady encouraged me. I took the test again and scored very high. I thank God for that. I also took typing courses and I excelled in that.

At Lowell Correctional Institution, we had church services on Sundays and I would go. One day, I said to the chaplain, "Wouldn't it be nice to have a Bible study?" He said, "You know Lula, I never thought about that. Do you think it would work?" I said, "Sure, because we want to get out of the dormitory. I want to read and understand the Word better and people will come just to get out of the dormitory." So, the chaplain started a Tuesday night Bible study from what I said.

After the chaplain started the Bible study, I said, "Maybe we could have a choir." My idea was put before the board and we started a choir. Oh boy, could we sing. There was a girl named Bessie who would lead the choir and she could really sing. So we began to have Sunday morning service, Tuesday night Bible study, and a choir. I thank God that He even intervened in that.

After we started the choir, they made us robes and the people in Orlando would invite us to sing at their church. We would go on a chartered bus to the church to sing and the people would cook the best food and we would eat.

I had the respect of everyone in the prison; all the matrons in the dormitory, the guards, the chaplains, and fellow inmates. I studied my Bible and took Bible courses through the mail. I excelled in the Word of God and I would talk to people about the Word and encourage them.

While I was in prison, my mother wrote me and my sister Fannie and her husband would keep money on the books. I always had money I could share with other people. I had plenty of soap and everything that I needed the Lord saw to it that it was provided for me.

I met some wonderful people in prison. Some people said that because they met me, their lives were changed because I was there. I became a better person because I was there. I've told people, those four years meant more to me than some of the years I spent out in the world because I was miserable. I didn't know a lot of things. I had no one to really teach me things. **BUT GOD!**

I said that God sent me to prison for four years for a learning experience. I learned so much. I learned how to take care of myself, respect myself. I learned that I was worth something. I learned how to go home and be a mother. I never mistreated my baby. I always did everything that I thought was right for her, but I learned that I could be even better than that. I learned to knit and I learned how to make hats and send them home to people.

For me, prison was a good experience. I can't say that it was a bad experience. The only thing I can say is that I missed being home, I missed being with my baby, but I did not miss much else.

I guess that's something to say, being in a prison, but it wasn't really like a prison. We lived in dormitories. We had beds that were lined up. We went to the dining room. We were fed on china. We had people to come and serve us while we were eating. We didn't have to wash dishes. We didn't have to wash clothes. They took care of our laundry. So it wasn't a bad experience, but I still missed home.

In 1966, I went before the Parole Board. They said, "There's no way we can turn you down." My cousin was a dentist. My experience in the prison prepared me to get a job. He signed the papers so that I could come home and gave me a job. I was released from prison in four years and went home to Winston-Salem.

Chapter 13

When I was released from prison in 1966, I returned to Winston-Salem, and went back to live with my father. My cousin, Lina Jane, told me that youth department was still working at Mount Calvary. I went on a Tuesday night and I reconnected with the church. They just loved on me and loved on me. They were glad to see me. They said, "Lula is home."

A woman named Mother Cloud was there and they were trying to build a new church and I was so happy. She taught me how to cut up a case of chicken and how to cut up a bushel of greens. That was just everything to me, just to be at church and to be a servant. When I came home, I came with a mind to serve God.

One Sunday, after morning service at church, I went to my friend's house. I was sitting there and all my friends came to see me. They had whiskey. They had beer. They said, "All come on, beer won't hurt you."

I used to love beer. I picked up the beer can and the Holy Spirit said, "Get out of here." I heard it like a voice. I put the beer can down and stood up. They said, "Where are you going?" I said, "I'm leaving. I have evening service and I'm going back to church." I left and I never saw my friend again.

Many years later, after I had left Winston-Salem, I came back and my friend, who had invited me to her house, her obituary was on the radio. I have come to understand why God said, "Come out from among them." He said, "Shun the very appearance of evil." Sometimes, when you leave the world, you try to keep one foot in the world and one foot out. You cannot do that. Sometimes, you're not strong enough. Now, I can go sit with anybody with whiskey and it wouldn't bother me. But at that time, I had not yet arrived.

I say to you, if you are struggling with anything, you need to be with people who are different. You need to be with people who are saved. You need to have people who are on the right road. Don't let your feet slip because you might fall. Even if you are a backslider, God said, "I'm married to you." God is faithful. He is faithful.

When I first got of prison, Sharon was not yet with me. My mother-in-law and father-in-law had moved from Orlando, Florida to Whitesville, North Carolina. I had promised Sharon that I would get her as soon as I got home. She was ten-years-old and even though I wanted to bring her with me, I did not take her out of school. I let Sharon stay in Whitesville until she finished the fourth grade that year.

My uncle took me to Whitesville to get Sharon; my daddy wouldn't go. He said, "You're going to get hurt down there." I said, "I don't feel like that." When we got to Whitesville, my mother-in-law had Sharon ready. I thanked them and I brought her to Winston-Salem. I took Sharon from her grandparents when she was in the fifth grade and I never took her back. I never tried to call. I never tried to say anything to anybody.

After I got Sharon back, I never wrote my mother-in-law. I never said anything. I just brought her with me. I never asked Sharon if she wanted to see them. She never said anything about them, so I never said anything, which was wrong. I had talked to her about everything, except I had not asked Sharon about her grandparents. She told me once, she had wanted to go back to her grandparents and I started to cry. Sharon told me that when she saw me cry, she never said that again. So she never brought that subject up again. But sometimes I did wonder if she wanted to see them.

I've always apologized to Sharon. I've always told her how sorry I was. I've always told her how hurt I was for her. She would always say, "Mommy, I forgive you." She would hug me, tell me not to cry, say, "It didn't do nothing for my love for you, no matter what happened, Mommy. You did it, but I know that you loved my daddy and you loved me. It was just something that happened. You could not control that night and I forgive you." I appreciate that and I love her.

I look at Sharon even now and I say to myself, "I hurt my baby. I hope that she can get over it even though she says she's over it." But I know that your heart must feel something because my heart feels things.

I want people to know that little girl, Sharon, now a woman, has made it in life. When I think about her life now, I think how she never complained. She never said, "Mommy, can we go back. Mommy, this is too hard. Mommy, I'm hungry." I never heard a complaint out of my daughter. And while as a child, I'm sure that she had plenty to complain about, never once did she look sad or depressed.

Chapter 14

When Sharon came back to live with me, I put her in 14th Street Elementary School. Low and behold, she had the same elementary school teacher that I had, Mr. Haines, and he could identify with her because she was a Bradley's daughter. Sharon excelled at the 14th Street Elementary School. You saw no traces of anything that might have affected her mind because of what she had seen. She saw the everything that night. She saw it all and that grieved my spirit to think that she might have something happen to her mentally because of what she had seen. But she was fine. That was the grace of God and the mercy of God and the praying over the stomach when she was in my womb, asking God to sanctify the child holy, asking God to cover her with the blood even before she hit the earth. I believe that faith works. Not making excuses, but I see God in my pain and in my hurt. In Sharon's pain and in her hurt, I see God. Nobody but God, only God could ease your pain.

My cousin Lina Jane's daughters, they loved Sharon. They would come to the house and they would look for her. Sharon would take them in the backyard and build a church with match boxes and they would sing and shout. They would praise God and say I got Jesus all in my head. I would notice that Sharon was never the servant leader. She would always say, "I'm the preacher." Her cousins would sing, but she would always say, "I'm the preacher."

Lula A. Scott

When we came to Winston-Salem, I was working in the dental office and got $30.00 a week. Out of that money, I would pay my tithes, $3.00. I was so happy to pay that in church. God took care of us and Sharon and I were doing very well.

Out of the $30.00, my father wanted $15 and I paid it to him. I say to young people, you can't live anywhere free. My father taught me, you use toilet paper; you use soap and you have to pay $15 because these things have to be bought.

The lady next door, my father's girlfriend, Miss Louise, would take care of Sharon during the day. She didn't charge me anything. On the days that it was cold, Sharon would bring in the wood and coal before I came home and Miss Louise would start a fire. Sharon would have the matchbox and the snails and the birds. She would have a funeral, she would have the flowers. I never saw Sharon play house. I only saw her do church.

I remember one day, Sharon went to school and they told her that they would give her free lunch. Sharon came home and said to me, "Mommy, they said they would give me free lunch, but I don't want it because that's for poor children." It was hard, but I made sure that she ate lunch.

CHAPTER 15

After being home for about a year, my parole officer allowed me to go to Buffalo to visit my mother and Gwen for a week. I was so happy. My mother said, "I want you to move to Buffalo."

When I went back home to Winston-Salem, my sister Fannie, who lived in Philadelphia, told me she was praying. She said that she never prayed so hard in her life that I would not go to Buffalo because she felt if I went there it would be like damnation to me; that I would go back, and something would happen to me. She said, "I laid before the Lord and I didn't want you to go."

That same year, I came to Philadelphia to visit Fannie at Christmas time and I brought Sharon. I laugh about it now. When I got to the bus station to come to Philadelphia, my father said, "Where's your rent money?" I said, "I won't be here." He said, "But you'll be back and I need your rent money." I reached in my pocket and I gave him the $15. I needed it really to travel, but I didn't worry about it.

When we came to Philadelphia, Sharon and I stayed with Fannie and her husband, Rudy. My brother-in-law treated me so good. He welcomed us in his home and took us to the store and brought what we needed.

My mother and my niece, Cynthia, had also come to Philadelphia for Christmas. Everybody gave me money. My aunt Roxie, she bought me clothes, and she also took me to church. My family brought Sharon all kind of clothes. We got everything that Christmas. It was a beautiful Christmas. Sharon and I had such a good time.

After I returned to Winston-Salem, Fannie wrote me a letter. She said, "I need to go back to work and I don't have anyone to keep my children. Would you consider moving to Philadelphia? I won't charge you any money and you and Sharon can stay here with me. I really want you to come."

I was real happy because when I was came to Philadelphia for Christmas, I had met a fellow, John. He was a nice fellow. My sister Annie was married to his brother. After Sharon and I came home, John travelled to Winston-Salem a couple of times to visit us.

In June of 1967, I told Fannie that I would come and I would stay. John came to Winston-Salem to get Sharon and me to take us to Philadelphia. He had brought a Cadillac. Everybody at church was saying, "Oh, Lula is leaving. She's going to get a husband." I said, "Oh, yeah I'm going to Philadelphia and I'm going to get a husband."

Sharon and I stayed in Philadelphia for a few weeks and then John brought us to back to Winston-Salem because I knew in September 1967 I would be moving permanently. It was at this time that I began keeping Fannie and Rudy's baby boy, Eric. He was nine-months-old and just a joy to me. I kept Eric until he was two-years-old and my other nephew, his brother, Gilbert, who was both a terrorist and a sweetheart to me.

At Fannie's house, I would iron, clean, and keep the house, but I never cooked because my sister thought a wife should cook for her own husband. But everything else in that house that I could do, I did. Fannie had made a home and Sharon and I didn't want for anything. When we were with Fannie and Rudy, they took Sharon and me everywhere with them. John, the guy who had brought Sharon and I to Philadelphia, he would come by and take us to dinner.

On the weekends, when Sharon and I were not at Fannie's house, we were at Annie's house with her, her husband, Jimmie, and their children, Kevin, Judy and Mark,. Kevin played the piano, Judy sang, and Sharon and Mark preached. They had church. They would preach and my sister would get the Holy Ghost. We were one big happy family. Annie, Jimmie, and their children would travel and Sharon and I would go with them.

Sharon attended T.M. Pierce Elementary School. By that time, I had started calling her Sharon because one day when she came home from school, she said to me, "My name is not Pudding. My name is Sharon. The teacher said you must not call me Pudding, you must call me Sharon." So I practiced from that day to call her Sharon, not Pudding.

They put Sharon in a class where the teacher called her ignorant because Sharon would answer, "Yes ma'am." Her teacher would say, "You're just ignorant. Sit your country self down. I told you not to say that." Sharon was hurt because she had been taught in the South that saying yes ma'am was manners and it was hard for her to break it. When Sharon came home from school, she told me and we talked about it. Her grades were good, but the teacher kept giving her trouble.

One day, I saw the teacher in the bar drinking whiskey on her lunch hour and I decided it was time for me to move Sharon out of that room. I had her moved out of that classroom and had put into another classroom. The new teacher's name was Miss Wilson. She thought the sun rose and set on Sharon. She just thought that Sharon was the world. Sharon excelled in everything in Ms. Wilson's class. I was very proud of her that she could come to Philadelphia and weave in.

CHAPTER 16

When I left North Carolina, Bishop Brumfield Johnson had told me that there was a mission in Philadelphia, Mount Calvary Holy Church, with two or three little old ladies and that he wanted me to go to that church. He wanted me to be faithful because God was going to do a work. Sharon and I went Mount Calvary Holy Church and moved our membership there. Pastor Ruth Greene was the pastor. It was Sis. Beulah Wells, Sister Dorothy Cody, Mother Nellie Clark, Sis. Rose Quan. Mother Clark, who lived a good distance away, would walk to church and would not even tell us. We would always take her home.

There were also six children at the church. Sharon started a Junior Church and every fourth Sunday evening, we would have a little service. James Cody, one of the few faithful young men, would cut the grass and fix up whatever needed to be done in the church. Sister Wells, Sister Cody, myself, and the young girls would clean the church and keep it like it needed to be. We worked hard. We had Women's Day services and paid the church off in a few years.

The few of us kept the oil on in the church, kept the electric repaired, and we did not let the doors be closed. We were faithful. Pastor Greene typically only travelled to Philadelphia from Long Island, New York only on Sundays. If she did not come, at that time, there were no cell phones, and we did not have a way to find out if she was on her way. So, we put a telephone in the church which allowed Pastor Greene to call us and tell if she was unable to come.

But God

At Mount Calvary Holy Church, we had all night prayer services. The people would come and sometimes they would join the church, but oftentimes, they came and then left. Thank God, in later years, they began to stay. After many years, Pastor Greene became ill and she could no longer pastor the church.

Once a year, Sharon would do a big service and we would do a concert. The three older people would have gowns on because there weren't many young folks so we would have to join in with the young people. We would sing and we would bring a good preacher in and Sharon built the Youth Department from that.

At that time, Sharon was also doing a one-woman show, reciting and performing, and she could really do it. She travelled all over, Philadelphia and throughout New York, New Jersey, Delaware, and North Carolina, doing that one-woman show and it was phenomenal. Sharon wrote and produced these shows on her own. I really think that she could have done Momma, I want to Sing because she wrote that play and they acted it in church.

Sharon would also recite The Creation by James Weldon Johnson. I would dress her in a white gown, put a crown on her head, and put white socks on her feet and she would recite The Creation until people would cry. No one could recite that like that.

On Sundays, Sharon and I would visit Ebenezer Church of God and Christ's Sunday School, but I remained a member at Mount Calvary Holy Church. It was while at Sunday School, it was 1967, I saw this nice gray haired man teaching Sunday School. From the moment I saw him, I thought he looked like Jackie Robinson. I just kind of looked at him and I saw him just kind of look at me.

When I got home, I said to Fannie, "That man up there teaching Sunday School, who is that?" My sister said, "That's funny you would ask me about him. That's Brother Dennis. He is a widower and he has three children." I said, "Umm. There's something about him and he's looking at me." She said, "But you're dating John." I said, "But it is something about him."

The next time I saw Dennis was at his church. The church mother was selling black pepper and she asked him if he wanted to buy a can. Dennis said yes. He turned and looked at me and told the church mother, "Give it to that young lady right there." I said, "Wow, he's giving me some black pepper" and I laughed. Sometimes, I would visit Dennis' church and I even sang on the choir, but I stayed a member at Mount Calvary.

One Saturday, my sister was selling dinners. She called Dennis and said to him, "I'm selling dinners and I know that sometimes you like to buy food for the children." He said, "Yes, I'll come over and buy four dinners from you."

Dennis came and I was just walking around helping my sister fix the groceries and the dinners for him. Fannie said to him, "Brother Dennis, I want to introduce you to my sister." She told him that I was single. He said, "I sure was wondering if you were single."

Dennis' three little children, Marlene, Clyde, and Eddie, were peeking out at me. Eddie and Sharon were the same age. Marlene was a year older and Clyde was four years older. I looked at them and said, "Oh, three children." I introduced Sharon to Dennis. She looked him over and seemed to be satisfied. His three kids seemed satisfied with me.

A few days after that conversation, Dennis came to our house. He stopped by because my sister had invited him. When Dennis came in, my sister was baking a cake. When the cake got done, she asked him if he wanted to stay for peaches and cake. Dennis said yes. I was getting ready to go out on a date with John, but when Dennis said yes, he was staying, I made up a really good excuse why I could not go on my date. Dennis stayed. He and I ate cake and peaches, talked, and laughed.

Before Dennis left, we exchanged phone numbers. But he did not call me. After a week went by, I told myself I'm going to call him just to say hello. I was kind of nervous, but I called him anyway. I said to him, "What were you doing?" He asked me, "Do you really want to know?" I said, "Yes." He said, "I was sitting in this chair and I was really thinking about you." I said, "Me." He said, "Yeah, I was thinking about you." I laughed.

When I got off the phone, my father, who was visiting at my sister's house, said, "Get off of that floor. What's wrong with you?" I said, 'Oh, my goodness. He was thinking about me." My dad said, "Get up girl and stop that clowning like that." I was the laughing stock of the house, but I was didn't care. I was so glad, because I had told God, "If this is the one for me, I would let the other one go."

One day, my brother-in-law, Rudy, took me to see Dennis because the washing machine needed to be fixed. When we got on the porch, Rudy ran back to the car and left me standing on the porch. Marlene opened the door, closed the door, and said, "Daddy, it's a lady at the door." Dennis came and he invited me in. I told him about the washing machine, but I was so nervous.

After that, Dennis started coming around and we would talk. He would just stop by with the children. One day when he came by, I said, "Let's go to Kelly's Corner," which was a store not far from us. We took the four kids and we walked to Kelly's Corner and Dennis and I talked all the way there. Sharon skipped and played with his children. It seemed like everything was going well. We loved to go to Kelly's Corner and eat kielbasas. Sometimes, we would all go to the drive-in movie. We would have so much fun.

One Sunday evening, Dennis called me and said, "You know, one Saturday evening, I'm going to come and take you to the mart." I said, "Where is that?" He said, "I'm going to come and take you and Sharon." Later, Dennis came by with Clyde, Marlene, and Eddie, and Sharon and I got in the car and we went to Jersey's Mart. It was a big store, kind of like Jerry's Corner. We went and ate hot dogs, Philadelphia pretzels, and walked the whole mart over.

If we went to the drive-in, or the chicken shack, or wherever we went, we always took the four children. He never left his children behind and I certainly was not leaving Sharon. I could leave Sharon with Fannie and Rudy or I could have left her with Annie and Jimmie because they would take care of her like she was their own child so there was no problem with that, but Dennis, he just did not leave his children.

I don't ever remember us going on a date without the four children. The only time, we would be without the children, was when he would pick me up to take me to school. I was going to school to on the boulevard to earn a certificate to become a dental assistant. At the time, I was working in a dental office and I wanted to be certified. Dennis would come to my home at night and take me and then later return to pick me up. This went on for a few months. I would be so glad to see him.

John was still coming by to see me, but I was pushing him aside more and more. Annie didn't tell me, but she was praying that I quit John. Although he was her brother-in-law, she said he was not the one for me.

One Saturday night when John came to pick me up to take me out, I said, "I'm not going." He said, "You're not going out?" I said, "No, I'm not going out tonight. I don't want to go to dinner." He knew Brother Dennis, but he didn't see him at the house. John said, "Okay" and went on out the door. I didn't say anything.

Dennis, I, and the children kept going out and he continued to take me to and from dental school. One night when he was bringing me home, I said to Dennis, "I'm going to run this by you. I'm going to move out of my sister's house." He asked me, "So, where are you going?" I told him, "I'm going to rent an apartment." Dennis said, "Oh."

The next time I saw Dennis, he asked me, "So, are you really going to move?" I told him, "Yes, it's time for me and Sharon to move out and be on our own." When I saw him again, we continued to talk about me moving. But on this particular night he came to me and said

But God

to me, "You're not going to move into an apartment, you're getting married." I said to him, "Getting married to who? Are you asking me to marry you?" He said, "Yes." I couldn't believe it.

Dennis had a ring. I was happy and I was sad. I had not told him my past. One day, I thought, I have to tell him. I can't marry him and he doesn't know about my past. So one day when he came, I told him, "I have something that I have to talk to you about." Dennis sat on one side and I sat on the other in the living room. I said, "What I am about to tell you is very disturbing. And when I tell you, if you don't want to marry me I would be hurt, but I would really understand." He said, "Okay."

I began to tell Dennis about my past and I began to weep. The tears were running down my face. When I finished, he just sat and was looking at me and I continued to cry. Then Dennis came and said to me, "If I said this to you, would you understand me?" I said, "What?" He said, "I want to tell you that my brother told me that about you weeks ago." I said, "You already knew?" He said, "Yes." I asked, "What difference does it make?"

I was still crying. I said to him, "You have three children. That means you will be bringing me into their lives and trusting me to be their mother. This is a big thing. Don't you need to think about it?" He said, "No. When my brother told me that, I thought about David in the Bible. You didn't do anything worse than David and God forgave him. I love you and I trust you. I would be glad to bring you home to be the mother of my children." When Dennis said that to me I boohoo cried. I didn't know what to say because I didn't think that anybody, especially a man, would ever receive me. I knew that Dennis was the one for me. He was a saved man who really loved Jesus.

There are times when your fear will overcome you and keep you locked up. I learned that the way to face your fears is to stare fear in the face and confront your fears. If you confront your fears, you can get over them.

I remember being at the Mount Calvary Holy Church and thinking about how much the pastor loved me and the congregation loved me. I had to get up and stand before the whole church and tell my story and how after that, the people loved on me and cared for me for who I was and not who I used to be. That was a good consolation for me. Facing my fear released me.

John, who I had been talking to, he did not know about my past because I had not told him. One day, John called me. I told him that he needed to come over so that I could tell him something. When he came, I said to him, "You know you moved Sharon and I to Philadelphia. You have been a good friend and I have to break up our friendship." He asked me, "What? Why?" He was so sure of himself that he had not even looked at my finger. I held my hand up and it was an engagement ring. He almost fainted in the floor. He could not believe it.

John's mother said, "I can't believe that you are doing that. I thought that you were going to marry him and give me my pretty little girls." I said, "No, Mom-Mom, I'm marrying somebody else. I'm sorry." So we broke it off. John went his way and I went mine.

Dennis and I kept dating, kept talking. I asked Sharon how she felt about him and she said she liked him. I asked her, "Can you get along with his three children?" She said, "I'll get along with them because then I'll have a sister. I never had a sister." She never had a sister that she knew of. Sharon had a sister, but at that time, she did not know that she had a sister.

I married Dennis with Sharon's permission. Long after we married, she told me that she had walked with Dennis down the street one day and told him, "You see that lady that you're getting ready to marry? I want to tell you something. I want to talk to you."

Sharon weighed about 80 lbs., mind you. Dennis might have weighed 180, 200. She's looking up at him, telling him, "If you do anything to that lady, you're going to have to answer to me. I love that lady and you better not do anything to that lady." He told her that he would not do anything to that lady. After I married Dennis, I tried to be the best mother, wife, and friend. He was the best husband, the best father, and my best friend.

My husband was a TV repairman. We had little money, but it was enough to take care of me and the children. We had family vacations to Buffalo, New York or Winston-Salem, North Carolina every summer. We would put the kids in our station wagon and travel to visit either my mother or my father. The kids would look so forward to it. My mother would cook and buy them everything.

One of the vacations, we went to King Stree, South Carolina, my husband's hometown. Well, the kids almost passed out smiling because there was no running water and no toilet. They had to go outside to the bathroom. My cousin took Sharon and Marlene to the filling station to go to the bathroom. They washed up after we warmed the water. They had a good time, but that was an experience they never forgot.

We celebrated Christmas at our house and it was a big thing. I made sure that my children had a Christmas tree from the time I got married and with all the gifts the children were given, it would be so much under the tree that you could hardly see the tree.

Before Christmas, we would always give them money, take them shopping, and let them buy the gifts they wanted to for people. Christmas was a great time for the family. We continued this tradition until 2020 when Covid-19 came, but I still found a way to send out dinners; 25 or 30 take-out trays so that people could have still eat with their family.

After Christmas dinner, Clyde, Marlene, Sharon, and Eddie would open up the gifts my husband and I had brought them and we would open our gifts from the children. Early Christmas' morning, Clyde, Marlene, and Eddie's maternal family would come; two aunts, two uncles, and Grandpop. The kids would get up and come downstairs. Clyde, Marlene, and Eddie would be so happy because that they would bring loads of gifts and Sharon would be included.

Lula A. Scott

Two of my aunts would buy gifts for Sharon and Marlene and one aunt would buy for Clyde and Eddie so no one ever felt left out. We never made a distinction between the children. They were all our children. They were never allowed to say step-children to them. If anyone ever said that to any of my children, they got into a whole lot of trouble.

My sisters would also buy for all of the children and we would take turns having Christmas dinner; going to one house this year and another house the next year. The cousins would get together and we would all have a ball.

As the children became older, each family decided to stay in their own homes and celebrate Christmas, but after church on New Year's Eve, we would get together and have the New Year's breakfast. During the early years of my marriage, for Christmas dinner, Dennis' family would join us, but as the family grew with grandchildren, they came less.

Chapter 17

For so long, it had only been Sharon and I and then we became a part of a blended family. When Dennis and I married and we were raising our four children, I had input with my husband into how we would do things. The first year of our marriage, I told my husband that I would raise the girls and he would raise the boys so that there would be no conflict. We both agreed. My husband was strict and I really did not like for him to be a disciplinarian of the girls. I believed that I had better ideas and I could be more understanding.

Marlene went to Ebenezer, but a lot of times my husband would allow her to go with me to Mount Calvary. I sent her and Sharon to the Youth Convention, dressed them in white dresses, and made sure that they looked the best I could.

Being new to the family, I found out that Clyde, Marlene, and Eddie's maternal family and my husband's family would say negative things about me. Because I was younger than my husband, I believed they questioned how was I going to raise four children and how was I going to treat their niece and nephews, would I treat them different than Sharon.

I tried at first to satisfy all families. I had three families, Clyde, Marlene, and Eddie's maternal and paternal relatives, and my family members, all talking in my ears, and my kids also had other family members talking in their ears. I found out that as long as I tried to satisfy everyone, I was having a really hard time.

One day, I thought I had had all that I could take and the struggle was just too much for me. I went to a neighbor, who was much older than me, and I sat down with her and told her that I was going to have to take my daughter and leave because it was too much frustration. I was doing the best that I could, but I was still having a hard time because sometimes the children would tell things that were not true or they would say things the way they saw them. I just felt that I had given it all that I had.

My neighbor made me some coffee, sat me down, and said, "I want to talk to you. You're young. You married Mr. Scott and the children. You did not marry his former wife's family. You did not marry his family and you did not marry your family. You got to forgot about them and you have to raise the children the way you and Mr. Scott think they should be raised. You need to do your best and stop trying to satisfy everybody else. As long as you and your husband are satisfied, you have to stop worrying about everyone else."

After my neighbor talked to me and consoled me, I made up my mind that I didn't care what the other ones said when they attacked me or came after me, I was just going to tell them to mind their business and stay in their house and I would mind my business and stay in my house. I did it in a nice kind way and I found out that I did not have as much trouble.

In talking to other young women, who would tell me that the first wife was still living or that the dad to their children was living, I found out that they had more trouble than I because the other parent would interfere with the way the children were being raised.

I remember speaking to a young woman, who had married, and the former wife had called the house and spoke to her husband and he had to go and see about the children who were in her care. The second wife was kind of upset. Having learned what I had learned, I told her, "The next time, what you do, is kiss your husband, get up, help him get his clothes on, prepare him some food, tell him, 'By all means, go see about your child and hurry back. I will be here waiting for you.'" After that, she didn't have any more trouble. She had a good relationship with the former wife and the children and it worked out well.

Sometimes when you find yourself fighting against the former spouse or fighting against the other family members, it only brings more trouble to you. When children go and try to start that kind of division between the two families, I found out that sometimes, in their little hearts, they like that kind of attention. But I also said, "Whatever your family member said, that's okay, but you still have to do what I say. I am your mother now and we're going to get along. You need to stop making up things. If you have a problem, you need to come to me. You need to talk to me and tell me what you feel."

As I look back now, I say we're so far ahead in the world today and we're more learned about situations than we were knew back then. We have counseling and tools that are offered to families and parents now. I would suggest that if you are going to get married and you are going to have a blended family, the husband and wife receive counseling or sit and talk things over, lay out a plan as to how they are going to raise the children.

I think it would even be good to talk to family members and let them know that you are bringing a new husband or a new wife into the children's lives and you know that they may have a lot of concerns, but they need to give you and your new spouse a chance to be in their home with the combined family and that you will be able to run your house well. If there is anything they have concerns about from the children, they should come to you and not talk to the children.

The other thing I suggest is that there are times when the child needs counseling. Speaking as a parent who decided to take one of her children to counseling, I know that was one of the best things that could have happened to help my child. But then after only one session, the family interfered and opposed continuing. The family said my decision was "just terrible" and made several negative accusations. Although I did not take the child back, I built upon what I had been told, what I had been taught in that one session and I worked on that with my child. The child overcame that issue.

It was at that point that I realized that my child had been through some things before I entered into the family. If they have a living mother or a living father, those persons have been their idols and you cannot substitute. I realized that there was no one who could have taken the place of that mother, but I could be the best mother for them now. I found that there was no one to satisfy everyone, no matter how hard I tried.

I discovered that with love, kindness, and prayer, I could conquer most things. I found out that you need Christ. You need prayer. You need love. You need understanding. You cannot freak out at everything. There has to be a better way. You have to think things over before you act. You have to weigh wrong from right. You have to listen to yourself when you are talking to your children. You have to take the time to explain things to them, not tell them "Go away." It will not go away, but it will only get bigger, and ultimately destroy your marriage and destroy you.

If the husband and wife can agree, and come into a good agreement, they can win the children over and walk upright before them to make a pleasant home and life for them. When friction comes, sit down and talk to your children, have family meetings. My husband and I would sit down at the table and talk to our children. We did not allow things to just go on believing that it would fix itself. We recognized that some things cannot fix themselves, we needed to fix it.

It is a challenge when you go into a blended family, but I can tell you, all of my children are grown now, in their sixties, and I have grandchildren and great-grandchildren and they have the utmost respect for me and I have the utmost respect for them and they love me as their momma. They give me all kind of accolades and I give them the same. They did not have to receive me the way they did. They could have grown up with the spirit of rejection, but I was determined that they would grow up in the spirit of love. I thank them today.

I hope that this will help you when you enter into a blended family. I hope that you will look to God, who is the Author and Finisher of your faith. I know that I could not have made it, my family could not have made it, my children would not have made it, but I say to you, **BUT GOD!**

Chapter 18

As part of a blended family, Sharon had some ups and downs. She and Marlene had their fights, their hits, and their moves. Two sisters; one was this way; one the other. One had an attitude, one didn't, but even in this middle of that, Sharon hung on. She said, "I love my daddy." I asked her at times, "Do you want us to leave? Is it too hard for you? Is it too much?" The brothers could just eat her, but the sister could not adjust to it. But thank God, when she did adjust to it, now they are the greatest sisters you have ever seen, but it took some adjustment.

After I married Dennis, he, Marlene, Clyde, and Eddie stayed at Ebenezer Church of God, but Sharon and I stayed at Mount Calvary. At 14-years-old, Sharon was called to the ministry. We would go to different churches in Philadelphia. When Sharon would start preaching, I would be so excited, I would jump up and start shouting. Sharon would say to me, "Mommy, can you please wait until I stop preaching before you start shouting?" But my head was so big I didn't notice it then. I was so happy, I would just jump up and shout.

Sharon was invited to preach at Jones Memorial Baptist Church, a well-known church in Philadelphia and the Inquirer, a local newspaper, came and asked me if they could interview Sharon. I said, "Yes, you can do the interview."

When Sharon came home from school, we had music on and the Bible was on the table. Sharon was shy and she didn't really like to talk, but when the people from the Inquirer came in and talked to her,

Sharon told them that she was in the room one night praying and she had an encounter with God and He told her that she was to carry His word and that she was to preach His word.

They interviewed Sharon, Eddie, and me, and they were very pleased. We were so pleased because when we got the Sunday Inquirer, Sharon was on the front page of Section B. Not only that, but a Canadian newspaper picked it up- "Girl, 14-years-old in the United States preaches the Gospel."

Sharon was on the front page of a Canadian paper and after that, churches from everywhere started calling for Sharon to come to preach. She would get a lot of invitations to preach. We went to North Carolina where she preached her first revival for five nights. Boy was it a success. Sharon still meets some of the young people who are now in their sixties; they were in college then; and they are still saved because they came to that revival.

Although my husband and I went to separate churches, on Sundays, we always ate dinner as a family. Dinner was a special time for the family. During the week, every evening when our kids ate dinner, they would sit at the table together and talk and I would listen to what they were saying. This was how I got to know more about my children. Sometimes my husband worked late, but when he came home, we would all have dinner together.

When my children got older, I started working nights at the dental office. When I would come home, I would also tell them goodnight and then they would go to bed. Dennis and I worked together. He always saw to it that they would do their homework.

Every Sunday evening, my husband had Bible study with the children and they had to do a written Bible report. They all excelled in that and Sharon was glad to do it. My children learned the Bible because their father sat down with them in the evenings and he taught them the Bible. I thank God that He was put into their lives and they know who He is.

Lula A. Scott

Before I married, when Sharon was attending Fitzsimon Junior High School, I said to her, You're going to go to college." After I married Dennis, I had put that in all five of my children. That was my word every day, "When you finish high school, you're going to go to college." Sharon and Marlene went to Gratz High School and Clyde and Eddie went to Benjamin Franklin High School.

Sharon did ninth, tenth, eleventh, and twelfth grade at Gratz High School, which was not a good school, although I did not know that at that time. When she was in Gratz, she would stay in her room, do her lessons, and would pray a lot.

After Sharon graduated from Gratz, she said to me, "I'm going to college." I said, "You are?" She said, "Yes. You always said to me that I was going to college. I don't know nowhere else to go." I said, "That's good." Sharon applied, got accepted, and went to Eastern College.

After Sharon's first semester at Eastern College, Mr. Chandler, the financial aid officer, sent for her and said some things that were not appropriate. I found out, called him, and told him, "Don't send for my daughter, send for me." Then I went to Eastern and I said to Mr. Chandler, "If it's about the money, you don't worry about it. Sharon will be back to school. My Father owns cattle on a thousand hills and He will pay her way to school."

Mr. Chandler said, "Well, if she does not have it when she comes in January, then she can't come back." I said, "Didn't I tell you that my Father is rich?" Mr. Chandler looked at me and said, "She's not material for Eastern. She should have gone to a community school." I said, "Don't worry about that, she'll get her grades up."

Then Sharon met Karen Wells, who was a year younger and a fellow student at Eastern College. After graduating from Eastern, Karen went on and got a doctorate degree. I know that God put Dr. Karen Wells in Pastor Sharon's life. Sharon says Karen graduated magna cum laude and she graduated good God laude, but because of Dr. Wells and her instructions and the kind of person she is, she helped my daughter to make it through Eastern College. Sharon has been blessed with the best godsister in the world. Karen has stood by her side, through the thick and the thin.

Before going to Eastern, Sharon did not do a lot of dating or anything. When she went to Eastern, she dated a few times. She had one fellow. She thought he was the cutest, he was the best thing that ever happened. He had a Bible. It was the biggest Bible I had ever seen. Sharon was just so enthused with him, but I was not impressed at all.

One day, Sharon and this guy went away to a big football game. I had brought Sharon the most beautiful rabbit coat. Those coats were very popular at that time. Well, she called me up and told me that he had made fun of her coat. She was so hurt. I said, "I'll tell you what to do. When you get home and you get out of that car, you say goodnight and whatever we had, it's over." She quit him just like that.

Sharon had another guy who she really liked him so much. He came to church on Sunday and I was going to take him to my house for dinner. Sharon was so happy, but then he said to her, "Stick to me when church is over." I told her that I didn't like him. She said, "Mommy, why don't you like him?" I said, "I don't even know him."

On the way home, I asked him, "Where do you live?" He said, "South Philly." I said, "Well, if I put you off at 15th and Market Street, you make it." He said, "Yes." I said, "Well, here we are and you can get out." Sharon said, "But he was going to dinner." I said, "But he doesn't like me."

One day this same guy called Sharon on the phone. He said, "May I speak to Sharon?" I said, "No, you may not." I yelled at him so hard, he hung up. Years later, I told Sharon about what had happened. She said, "You know what? He told me that happened and he didn't come back. He told me it was your mother or somebody. I told him, it couldn't have been my mother." I said, "Yes, it was me. He was bad news for you." Sharon laughed and said, "I'm glad that you ran him away."

I really loved Sharon and only wanted the best for her. One day, we were driving to see my family in North Carolina and I got up my nerve and I looked back in the car and I said, "Sharon, do you ever think about your grandmother and your grandfather and your family?" She looked at me and she said, "Mommy, yes I do." I said, "Well, why didn't you tell me?" She said, "Because you had so much hurt and I didn't want to hurt you." I said, "Hurt me. That hurt you. I wouldn't want to hurt you by not letting you see your grandparents."

I didn't say anymore. When we stopped in Winston-Salem, I said to my husband, "Can you take us to Whitesville, North Carolina tomorrow?" He said, "What do you want to do?" I said, "I'm going to find Sharon's grandparents." He said, "Okay." So we got up that morning and I said, "Sharon, we're going to Whitesville and we're going to find your grandparents." She said, "We're going." I said, "We're most certainly going."

We drove to Whitesville and I did not recognize anything. But as God would have had it we saw a broke down gas station, an old country gas station. I said, "Let's pull in here. This town is not this big and somebody might know where they live."

We pulled into the gas station, spoke to the man, got a conversation going, and I said to him, "I'm looking for some Sheridans." He said, "Sheridans." I said, "Yes. I'm looking for William Sheridan. I'm looking for Louise Sheridan. Anyone by that name?" He said, "Funny, you would ask us that. That family moved to Jersey City. He said William and Louise." I said, "They moved?" He said, "Yes, they're in Jersey City." I said, "That's right next to Philadelphia. Is there anyway or anybody down here, anything?" He said, "You know what? The pastor of their church is here running a revival." I said, "Huh?" He said, "Yes." I said, "Could you get him over here?"

The man called the pastor to the gas station. The pastor saw us. He said, "You Pudding." He grabbed Sharon, hugged her, and said, "This has got to be God. Wait a minute. Let me get on the phone." He got on the phone and put Sharon on the phone with her grandmother. I talked to them. I told her, "We're in Winston, but as soon as we get back I'm putting her on the train and sending her to see you in Jersey City. Be careful how you handle her because she's my jewel." They laughed. They said, "Just send her. Just send her." The preacher said that was all the grandmother ever talked about is that she wanted to see Pudding. I said, "Well, she's going to see Pudding."

I sent Sharon on the train to see them. She saw her grandmother and her grandfather. She saw her aunt, her uncles, and her cousins. Sharon came back and she was so happy. Some years later, her grandfather died and I went to the funeral with Sharon.

I had always thought of Sharon as my baby, belonging only to me. One day, I had a conversation with Karen, she's my goddaughter, telling her about how all I could think about when I was in prison was my baby and how much she missed me. Karen, who I call Godbaby, said something to me that I had never thought about. She asked me, "Did you ever wake up and imagine how Sharon felt? Not only were you gone, but her father was gone. A four-year-old woke up one morning and she didn't have mother or a father." That broke my heart. She didn't say it to me to break my heart. She said it to me to give me a change of thinking about things that had happened. She was not correcting me, just giving me good advice. Godbaby spoke something into my life that day and this is one of the reasons why I wanted to write this book; to help somebody think of the bigger picture.

Chapter 19

When Sharon finished college, the Lord said that she must go to Africa. She went with a Christian group to Liberia and stayed for a few weeks, doing a work there that she was remembered for. When she returned from Liberia to the United States, the Lord spoke again and told Sharon that He was sending her to the mission field in Kenya for two years. I almost died. It broke my heart. I could not think about her going somewhere that was a place I could not get to her for two years.

Sharon left and went to Kenya. After being there a year, things were going on in Mount Calvary and we were in need of a pastor. When the Lord told Sharon that her time was up in Kenya and it was time for her to go home, she cried. The Lord told her, "I need you to go home. I have an assignment for you."

When Sharon came back to Philadelphia, she was asked to be the pastor of the Mount Calvary Holy Church of America. Renamed the Mount Calvary Family Worship Center, in 2023, Sharon celebrated 25 years as the pastor.

The people at the Mount Calvary Family Worship Center admire and respect Pastor Sharon. I must say that she is the greatest pastor that I have ever known. I am not saying that because she is my daughter. I've only been a part of two churches, Mount Calvary and Mount Sinai and sat under great leadership, but she has been the greatest pastor.

But God

Sharon has never done anything to make me shame. Her siblings love her and her cousins have the highest respect for her. Our family has put their arms around Sharon and we do anything for her. All Sharon has to say is do it. We might grumble or complain some behind her back and say, we're not going to do it, but we always do whatever she asks.

As an adult, Sharon married, although sadly after ten years, her husband died. Sharon later remarried and she's doing really good. She married a man that I've known since he was a child. He's a very good man and I know that God is smiling on them.

I just want to say, I love you, Sharon. I love you, Pudding. I love you. I love you. I love you. You will always be my baby and I love you from the depths of my heart. Thank you for being my daughter.

ME AND SHARON (PUDDING)

Chapter 20

To my wonderful son, Clyde, I thank you for being my son. The first day I saw you, you had no smile and I said, "I wonder what happened to your smile." I knew that I would be your mom one day and I thought to myself, when I am your mom, I'm going to put the smile back on your face.

When I met his father, Clyde was very shy, soft-spoken, held his head down, and very seldom looked up. I looked at Clyde, and in my heart, I saw a child who had lost his mother and his friend. I knew that I could not replace her, but I also knew that I would teach Clyde and show him how to smile and love again.

Before I married Dennis, Clyde had never travelled anywhere outside of Philadelphia, except to Greensboro, North Carolina. The summer after we married, we went to Buffalo, New York. Clyde was mostly quiet throughout the trip and did not have much to say. But when we arrived at Nana's house, Clyde opened up a little bit. My mother went into the kitchen and she began to cook everything. She said, "Clyde, come and eat." She noticed that he needed something and she wanted him to talk.

During the trip, we went into Canada with cousins and family and had such a good time. Clyde opened up a little bit more. The next trip, we went to Winston-Salem and he met my brother and my dad. His life changed a little around them. Clyde would talk some around the other children.

Clyde was about thirteen when I married his father. He would hang around me, sit on the porch or come into the kitchen. I found out that he loved to eat and I could really cook. I knew that I could win him somehow by the food.

As time went on, Clyde began to call me Mom. He would say, "My mother said this. My mother said that. My mother said it's time to eat." He said it so many times that the girls said, "You know what? She's our mother, too." That was one of the greatest moments to me, being his mother.

As time went on, Clyde opened up a little more about the things that were going on in his life. I would always ask him if he was okay. He would always tell me yes. We became very close and we would talk about many things. On the outside, he was always neat and clean, but I kept trying to reach the inside of him. I would tell Clyde, "If anything comes up, and you need to run it by me, you can do it." Anything that I saw that disturbed Clyde, I immediately took care of it.

When his father would scold him for something he did not do, I would give Dennis heck when I got in our bedroom that night. My husband would say, "I can't speak to my own son." I would say, "You can't speak to him like that. That hurts, that's called mental abuse."

One day, Clyde sat me down and told me, "When my daddy brought you home, I began to see him relax from some of the discipline he was putting on me. I looked at you one day and I said, 'This lady is alright. She makes things better for me.' He told me, "I didn't have as hard a time as I had been having. When you came, things became much easier."

I told Clyde that I thought his father was having a hard time because his mom had passed away and he was left to raise three kids. I told him that his mother's family was always there in his life and after his mom died, his Granddad moved in and his aunts would always come and whatever part his dad would let them play in his life, they tried and would play it.

But God

I remember that they gave my husband a service at Ebenezer to honor him. He called Clyde up, took him in his arms, and told him, "I'm going to give you something that I haven't been able to give you because I wanted you to be a man. I'm going to hug you." Clyde told his dad how much he loved him. He said, "And I love my mom." Pointing to me, Clyde said, "When my mother died, I never smiled until my mother came again."

Clyde was never disrespectful. He never gave me a hard time. He would just talk to the other children and answer whatever I asked him. If Clyde had trouble at school, I would go because I knew it was a mistake made.

At fifteen, Clyde had a paper route and the people just loved him. As a teenager, there were times when Clyde would not tell about things that had happened to him. After he was grown, he told me that one of the customers had robbed him. I said, "You didn't tell me." He said, "No." He walked from school all the way home and back and he never said a word. He ran out of money for transportation and he would not say he needed more.

After working the paper route, Clyde worked in a candy store. He also got his friend a job working in that same candy store. Clyde was always finding a job. His father would say, "When you go to work, you have to bring some of the money home so that I can save it for you." Clyde was obedient. He obeyed his father and gave him what he asked.

Growing up, my husband would tell Clyde not to fight, so Clyde would not fight. One day he came home and told us that some gang boys tried to attack him. His father said, "If they hit you, you shouldn't run." Clyde went back to school the next day and told the gang boys, "I'll fight you one-by-one." I don't know if that was a good idea, but Clyde fought them one-by-one. When he came home, his fists were all busted up, but he said, "I beat every one of them."

Clyde wanted to go to the prom and I was so happy for him because he was so shy. Dennis made him cut your bush. I was so angry because

Clyde was so sad and upset. But I sent him to the barbershop and he got a nice haircut and he looked so handsome.

Clyde went to the prom with a girl that he met on his paper route. This was a big thing to everyone in the house and we were all just so excited that Clyde was going to the prom. His sisters and his brother were just standing on their heads. He got dressed and we thought he was just the best looking guy going to the prom.

My husband did not allow secular music in the house but that night when the prom was over, I made a prom breakfast for Clyde, his date, and another couple. They came and we played the music and they danced. My little Eddie was looking down the steps and he was laughing. He could not believe that we were playing secular music in the house. We had a good time and Clyde was happy.

My husband was very strict, and even though Clyde was an adult, he still had to obey the house rules. Clyde began to stay out a little later and a little later. Dennis would put the top lock on the door at 12 o'clock. I would stay up and wait for Clyde and take the top lock off.

One night, Clyde pushed it to the max and stayed out very late. It was very cold. When he came in, I gave him heck. I said, "If your father wakes up and you're not in this house and I'm downstairs waiting on you, you're going to get both of us in trouble."

Clyde explained to me that the buses were moving very slow and he wanted to get home because he knew that I was waiting, but he had to walk home and it was very, very cold. I felt bad. Clyde told me that he were sorry. I said, "Momma understands." No matter, I always tried to cover Clyde and I did not want him to get in trouble.

Clyde did not want to go to college. He decided that he wanted to go to a trade school and was trained in electronics, following in his father's footsteps. Clyde got a job, working at Philco Electric Company. At his job, some of the men would tell him things that were not good. They saw that Clyde was quiet and would try to challenge him. But because there was a mother-son trust, Clyde would tell me the things that were being said and I would instruct him.

As an adult, Clyde saw a therapist because all too often, he would not talk about things and I could see the pain in his eyes. Clyde was prescribed medication because he was sad, but the medication made him tired and weak. We went to revival one night at the Garden of Prayer and Clyde gave his life to Christ. I looked up and he was running around the church, saying, "You are sweeter than chocolate."

After giving his life to Christ, Clyde changed. He always knew Christ, but once he made that acceptance, it made a difference. I knew that Clyde loved God and we would talk about God and what He wanted him to do.

I always sat my dinner at the table with my children and I would ask them about them and learn how their day was. One Saturday night, my children were at the table, they were laughing and talking. I was cooking. I heard Clyde express how his dad was treating him. The kids were laughing about his pain. I knew then that he was hurting.

I took Clyde on a Monday and we had our first real talk about how he felt his dad was treating him. The main thing he said was that he would always be accused of doing things that he did not do. And when his father found out that it was not him, that he had made a mistake, he would never say to him. "I was wrong." He would never say "I'm sorry." He would never say "forgive me." That hurt my son badly.

My husband was a very good father, a good provider, but a very strict disciplinarian because of the way he was brought up. I began watching my husband's interactions with Clyde and I found out that my son was right. I never corrected my husband in front of the children, but I began to work with him. I told him, "Clyde is smart."

To fathers, raising their sons, please allow them to have a voice. Tell your sons that you are proud of them, that you love them. Your opinion, your words, your encouragement, matters to your son.

After Clyde graduated from high school, he went to work for GE. A couple of years later, when Sharon went away to college, Clyde was very helpful to her. I soon found out why. A college friend of Sharon's, named Patricia, caught Clyde's eye and he was glad to take them back to school. Clyde would get up early in the morning and pick Sharon and Patricia up. He would hang out with them, eat pizza, and use his JC Penney's card to buy Sharon things. Anything that had to do with Sharon and Eastern College, Clyde you would do it.

After a while, Clyde began to date Patricia and I knew the reason he dated her was because he loved her. Patricia was a very pretty girl and Clyde was handsome, too.

One day, Clyde told me that he was in love. I said to him, "You know that I never judge people and when the subject comes up and I talk to other people about their lives, I don't make judgments because I had a life, too."

I had a talk with the young lady and she assured me that she loved Clyde so very, very much. I told her to make sure because Clyde was my jewel and I was so happy. I said to Clyde, "Okay, you can marry her" and I told Patricia that I gave her permission to marry my son. We made a nice wedding for Clyde and Patricia. It was beautiful and they looked good. We wanted Clyde and Patricia to be happy and to have a good life together.

Clyde and Patricia had a son, Darnell, and then a second son, Daniel, and they were beautiful children. Darnell and I became close. He was going to school up the street from my house. For a while, he would stop past every evening and everybody would call me Mom-Mom, but Sharon taught Darnell to call me Grandma. From that day to this day, he still calls me Grandma.

Darnell and Daniel grew up and gave Clyde six grandsons, who are the joy of his life. Clyde loves those grandsons to the bone and I love the way he has bonded to them. They can always call on Pop-Pop and they know that he will make it happen. Whenever he talks about his grandsons, Clyde has a smile on his face and he makes sure that I know every word that they say.

Darnell drives an eight-wheeler and Clyde thinks that is the greatest thing in the world. He always talks to Clyde about what he is doing and I have to sit and listen to that, too, because Clyde is so proud of Darnell.

Daniel grew up and went to trade school. When 911 came, he and Clyde took courses together and they were very happy. Sadly, too soon, Daniel died at an early age, leaving his three sons and a wife, who is doing a great job raising the boys.

Clyde and Patricia had divorced prior to Daniel's death, but he remained close to his son. Daniel's death was a tough time in Clyde's life, but God sustained Clyde and continues to take him through that situation as Clyde continues to grieve the loss of his son, and rightfully so.

After 17 years of working at GE, Clyde began working at Septa, where he would later retire. He was well respected on that route. Everybody loved him. The day he retired, they gave him such a big send off. He was full of smiles and came home with all kinds of pictures and other things that would remind him of the time he spent with Septa.

Years later after I married Dennis, I said to Clyde, "I'm going to ask you some questions." When your father told you that he was going to marry me, what did you say? Clyde told me, "I feel okay and I feel that's okay. I will have another sister. I miss my mom and I knew that my daddy was getting a wife and I was very happy. My father was very strict on me most of the time, but I saw relaxation when he was with you.

I felt that nothing that I did was right and would satisfy my daddy. People told me that when he got married, it would be a lot of negative things about a new woman coming into the house. Even when you were dating, I always saw a big change in my dad. And then I thought, I'm going to have a new sister and a lot of new family."

I asked Clyde how he felt about life with me because I wondered how he, being the oldest, and having the most memories of his mother, would feel. Clyde said that he felt happy on our first trip to Kelly's Corner and that he was good. "It was only a trip to a dry goods store, but I had a nice time." Clyde said that he saw his father smiling and talking and that every time we were out, he felt happy because his father was more relaxed. He said that he felt that me being with his father was good and everything was going to be alright.

Speaking now directly to you, my wonderful son. You have always made me proud, especially when you told me that I gave you confidence and helped build your self-esteem. I thank you for being my son. I thank you for telling me of the treasures that I deposited in your life. I love when we sit and have talks and you still say "My mom." I thank God because you are still by my side, answering my beck and call. That makes me feel very good.

I also feel good when you say that your father taught you to be a man. You worked more than forty years of your life and that makes me proud. You always took care of your family. You say that your father was hard on you, but now that you are a man, you understand that he wanted to save you from the streets and keep you from the streets. You said that your daddy did what was best for you and it shaped your life.

Clyde, I want you to know that the one thing I want you to do is keep a smile on your face. Your sister, Sharon, says that you're my little Jesus. Always know that I love you and I am so grateful that you are my son.

Chapter 21

To my lovely daughter, Marlene, I want to speak directly to you. I remember the first day seeing you. I thought you were so cute. I remember when we went to Kelly's Corner and you and Sharon were getting along so good. The next time, when I saw you, I came to the house to bring a piece for your dad to fix our washing machine. You opened the door and slammed the door in my face, went running in the house and said, "She's here."

When your dad asked me to marry him, I was concerned about you. I thought this little girl is probably missing her mother and she is probably her daddy's girl. I thought how it must have been hard to lose your mother at such an early age. You would look at me, and when your father and I would take the four of you with us on dates, you began to soften up some. When we told you we were getting married, you had a little struggle, but you eventually accepted it.

The day your father and I married, I dressed you and Sharon just alike. I thought to myself, these are my two little girls, my two happy girls. I would always include you in every plan. You were good.

You and Sharon shared a room for a while. Then it came to me that you might have felt that this was your room and "this girl is taking over." One day, you and Sharon had a fight and you hid Sharon's shoe. When it was time to go to school, I moved Sharon to another room and then it began to be okay. But then there were still times, when I would go to clean your room and move things around, and you would have a fit. You would say, "I had that paper since I was in the fifth grade." You didn't want anybody invading into your privacy. I would work around things as much as I could because I didn't like to see you get upset.

I would always make sure that whatever I did for Sharon, I did for you. You were sisters. You were no longer Marlene and Sharon, you were one. If I brought Sharon a pair of shoes, whether you needed shoes or not, I bought you shoes. When I sent Sharon to the hairdresser, I would send you. But sometimes I would remember you would get into your aunt's ears and they would say things that your hair was not fixed. I would say, "But I sent her to the hairdresser."

You had a mind of your own and you would like to comb your hair the way you wanted to and dress yourself the way you wanted to because that was what you were accustomed to doing and you had to get used to having me as your mother.

Sometimes other family members would get in your ear and tell you things and you would tell them how you perceived things. Sometimes, I would not see it that way, but you thought it was true, so I would accept it. Then one day I decided to take you to the therapist so I could better understand what was going on with you. When we got to the therapist, the first thing that you did was draw a picture of an ugly lady. I laugh now; she was horrible looking.

The therapist told me that was me, not to take it personally, but you had been used to being the little lady of the house and I had come in and taken your place and it would take some time for me to ease myself into your life. So I just decided to be the best mom that I could be.

Finally, one day, you called me Mom and that broke the ice for me and you. You would no longer stand back or go upstairs. You stayed around and when extended family came, everybody was one.

Life began anew and you and I were mother and daughter. I was so happy that we were a family. I remember the greatest compliment that you gave to me, was when I said to me at Christmas time, I didn't have a lot to give you and you said, "Mom, that does not matter, you are my Christmas gift. I have you here with me and that's all I need."

Marlene, I thank you for who you are to me and how you are always there for me and helped me. Even in the midnight hours, the darkest of times, I have called you and you were the first one there. I love you, I adore you, and I am grateful for having you in my life. Love and kisses to my big girl.

Chapter 22

When I married Dennis, Marlene had music lessons and we continued to pursue that interest. I also sent Sharon to learn how to play the piano and she and Marlene went to music lessons together. Marlene excelled, but all Sharon wanted to do was to learn how to play chords. Marlene wanted to learn how to play the piano, so I had the pleasure of attending her music recitals. I would dress her up in beautiful dresses, and watch her play the piano. She was also a good singer. Marlene would go with Sharon to preach and Marlene would sing. Churches would have concerts and Marlene would sing and she was absolutely beautiful.

At home, Marlene would come in the kitchen with me because Sharon would always be in her room preaching and calling on the name of Jesus. She was the one who wanted to be at my side, wanting to know what I needed and what she could do next. Marlene would want to help with the cooking and would be stay in the kitchen. She turned out to be a really good cook.

Even as a young girl, Marlene was kindhearted. She would go with her father on the mission field. I remember one time, when Marlene was about 15-years-old, I left her with my husband's Aunt Fannie. During the night, Aunt Fannie got real sick and Marlene orchestrated things so that Aunt Fannie could go to the hospital. It took five policemen to take her from the home. Marlene remained right by my Aunt Fannie's side. She stood right there and made sure that all went well until my husband and I arrived at the hospital.

As a teenager and young adult, Marlene would confide in me about her little love affairs. Dennis didn't really want to hear that stuff and he was real strict. Marlene would talk to me about her boyfriends and when she would bring one of them home, I stayed up until the boyfriend left and kept an eye on them. If I did not like them, I would run them away.

Academically, Marlene did good in school, but she would always try to be the boss. Sometimes, the guidance counselor would call me and I would have to go to the school and straighten things up for her.

When Marlene graduated from high school, she decided that she did not want to go to college. She got a job right away and she excelled in that. Everything that Marlene did, she excelled in.

One day, Marlene told me that she wanted to go to school to become an X-ray technician and she followed through with her plans. I did not want her walk home alone from the school at night so Sharon and I would sit on the corner and wait for Marlene to get off the bus so that we could walk with her. Marlene became employed as an X-ray technician, a job she stayed com-mitted for several years.

It was while Marlene was working as an X-Ray technician that she met a man who would later be her husband. One night as Marlene was leaving to go to a revival, before she left, she told me that she was going to meet her husband that night. I thought to myself, when you bring this husband home, you are going to have to deal with your dad. When Marlene came home, she told us that she had met Dwight, and after a while, she told us that Dwight was the one and she wanted to marry him. I did not interfere. I just watched them, and watched them, and watched them.

One day, I sat Dwight down and talked to him. I asked him, "Are you sure that you want to marry Marlene?" He said yes. I asked Marlene, "Are you sure that you want to marry Dwight?" She said yes.

So we all agreed. Marlene and Dwight had a beautiful wedding on a Saturday evening.

After they married, Marlene and Dwight stayed at our house a little while and then they moved into their own home. Shortly thereafter, Dwight Jr., who we called DJ, was born. He was our first grandchild and was a little joy.

DJ would come to the house and I would make peanut butter and jelly sandwiches. I would tell him, "This is peanut butter and jelly, but it's love on the sandwich. It's not good if you don't have love on the sandwich." DJ went home and told his mom, "Your sandwich doesn't taste as good as Mom-Mom's cause she put love in it."

I remember DJ wanted some sneakers. I went to JC Penney's to get the sneakers on my account. When I gave the sneakers to DJ, he told me, "The kids are going to call them bobos." I told him, "I don't care what they call them, you tell them that this is the last thing that your grandmother had that she could use to buy you some sneakers. You tell them I couldn't buy name brand sneakers, but I bought sneakers with love. It's a lot of love in these sneakers and they wished they had a grandmother that loved them like that." DJ went to school and he didn't have any better sense than to say it. He was the laughing stock of the school. He said, "I don't care because I know that my grandma loves me."

A little later, Dennis and I went away on vacation to the Pocono Mountains. We took DJ because Marlene was pregnant and about to have her baby. When we came back on Saturday morning, they told us that she had a little girl. We didn't have any little granddaughters in the family; we had only had the boys. Alicia was born and she was the joy.

Alicia, who I call Lee-Lee, when she talks to me, she will say, "Mom-mom, I didn't do that." I would listen to her and give her good advice. Lee-Lee can always talk to Mom-Mom because Mom-Mom will listen to her.

But God

After Alicia was born, Dwayne came, Marlene's youngest. He is a little light to me. He comes to my house and he talks to me about things. When I need to have something straightened out, I can call Dwayne and we would settle things and everything would be alright. I thank God for all of the grandchildren.

It was not long after the kids were born that Marlene moved into her house. Her husband came, but he did not stay long. After he left, Marlene was a single parent. When she moved with the three kids, there were struggles, sometimes even in her marriage.

After Marlene separated from her husband, she took on two jobs so that she would have enough money to make it. Marlene did not ask my husband or me for anything, but we would do whatever we could do to help her and the grandchildren.

After working two jobs, Marlene was hired by the Philadelphia Board of Education. She started out as a bus driver and then advanced to working as a dispatcher in the office. After working more than twenty years, Marlene retired. She is now enjoying her life with her children and grandchildren.

Chapter 23

Eddie was my youngest son. He was so young when his mother died. When I married Dennis, Eddie would call me that lady sometimes. He tried to be hard, but he really wasn't. Eddie was my prank child and he liked to play tricks on me. He would say to Sharon, "Your mom said, so and so and so." Sharon would come and ask me and find out it wasn't true. Eddie was pranking her.

Eddie was very mischievous. He would often get in trouble with his dad and I would have to rescue him. He would still call Sharon by her nickname, Pudding, and tell her how he was going to do the opposite of what his dad told him. Sharon would tell him, "You're going to get in a whole lot of trouble with Dad and he is going to beat you." Eddie would do it anyway.

Eddie loved the girls. He always talked about how he was going to have the girls and he was going to have five children.

Eddie liked to dress up. He loved to wear white shirts, both him and Clyde. Every Sunday, when they went to church, they were dressed nicely. Eddie was very proud of how he dressed for church. He was also happy to play the bongos for the Brockington Singers, a gospel group that also attended Ebenezer.

Eddie also liked to ride horses. He would shine shoes so that he could have money to ride the horses. My father got a kick out of Eddie riding the horses. In the summer, my father would sit on the porch, waiting for Eddie because he knew that he had made the money and would be coming down the street on the horse.

Eddie loved my father and my mother. When we go visit my mother in Buffalo, my mother would sit him at the dining room table and she would just feed Eddie everything. Eddie would cry when it was time to leave her. My mother thought that was the greatest thing.

Eddie loved to work. One summer, he got a job. All four of my children had to work. My husband had a saying, "No work, no eat." I said they would eat because I would sneak the food to them.

When the children got jobs, they were told to save some of the money and give to their father. Well, Eddie was not going to do that. Every job that he got, he did the opposite.

When Eddie was in school, there were times when I had to go and stand up for him. If he was right, I would tell him. And if he was wrong, I would tell him. Eddie learned to give me respect and I always treated him with respect. Eventually, he came to call me Mom and would often say, "I will ask my mother" before he attempted to do things.

There were times when Eddie tried my patience. I never told my children to wait until their father came home. I handled the situation because I thought it was a terrible thing to make kids wait all day and then act like their daddy was the boogey man.

One day, Eddie was about 14-years-old at the time, he really tried me. I told him, "If you come up to me and do that, I am going to stand you up on your head." Eddie was a chunky little boy. He came up to me and I did just what I said. I stood Eddie up on his head. From that day on, Eddie said, "Mommy is crazy."

Eddie attended the Benjamin Franklin High School where he graduated from with honors. He and Sharon graduated the same year. Eddie went to Northeastern College and Sharon went to Eastern College. They had a lot of plans of what they were going to do and how they were going to visit each other at their respective campuses.

Lula A. Scott

When Eddie and Sharon entered college, Dennis went back to work at RCA. Prior to this time, Dennis took courses and learned to fix air conditioners, dryers, and washing machines. A repairman by trade, he was a brilliant man. In the Navy, he had been a pipefitter. He later worked for Bud Company, had a record shop, a TV business, worked at GE, and made a TV for his mother. When people did not have televisions, they would come to his mother's house and watch TV.

In July of 1974, my husband and I went away to take my father-in-law to King Stree, South Carolina to visit with his sister. My husband and I had never left our children home alone, but we decided that they all graduated high school and Clyde and Marlene were old enough and they could stay home with Eddie and Sharon. We gave them a good talking to before we left.

After we left home, I realized that I had left my white dress home, a garment needed for convocation. When my husband and I returned home, Eddie was outside. I said to him, "Go get my dress out of the dryer for me" and he did.

When Eddie returned with my white dress, I asked him, "What are you getting ready to do?" Eddie said, "Sharon is fixing me some food, we're getting ready to eat?" I had cooked food before I left for them to eat. When Eddie told me that, I laughed. It was funny to me because I and my husband had only been gone about ten minutes before we had to return to the house.

My husband and I prepared to leave again. His father told him to never get into anyone's car. We were going away and he especially did not want him in anyone's car while we were gone. I told Eddie, "I know that you and I have had a lot of ups and downs. Eddie, I want you to be good. Momma loves you." Eddie told me, "I love you, too, Momma." I told him again to be good. The last I saw of my son was him going into the house.

On Sunday, Clyde, Marlene, and Sharon went to church, but Eddie decided that he was not going. He returned to the college campus. On

But God

Monday, although his father had told him not to get into anyone's care, he did not listen. He got in the car with a supervisor, who worked at the school, and the supervisor had a seizure while driving and Eddie was killed instantly.

My son Eddie died and my husband and I were away. The police came to our home and told Clyde that his brother had been killed in an accident and he had to go and identify his body. Clyde was so brave. Not only did he identify his brother, but he came back and took care of his sisters until Dennis and I returned the next morning.

The death of my younger son broke my heart. It took me years to go over. I said to myself, if a mother birthed a child and I felt the pain that I felt, I don't know how they could bear it because I could hardly bear that pain.

Eddie was not able to give us the five children that he said he was going to have. We never had any grandchildren from him. But we have so many memories of the things he would do. He would go to work for the neighbor. He would say when he finished, "Here's your receipt, I need to be paid." Eddie would charge her so much for this and so much for that. The neighbor would call me and say, "Eddie gave me a receipt and he's charging me too much money." Eddie would say, "I'm a business man." My husband and I would tell him, "Eddie, you can't charge her like that." He would say "okay" and would adjust the amount.

Eddie loved to play outside with the other children. The kids on the block really loved him; all of the neighbors loved him. It was a great loss when he left us. Although his life ended early, I had a great joy in raising him.

Before Eddie went to away to college, Sharon lead him to Christ. She had a conversation with him and they discussed being born again. Eddie said the sinner's prayer and he accepted Christ as his Savior. His life change was revealed to us when a young lady, who had come to his funeral, told Sharon how she had lead him to Christ and that he gave his life to God. These words gave me peace, knowing that my son had accepted Christ in his life.

In my heart, I still miss my son. I think about him and what he would be doing today. I will always my Eddie.

But God

My son Eddie

CHAPTER 24

My children were all different. There were so many things about each of them that were dear to me. I have three living children who are well-versed in work and have a solid work ethic. Dennis and I never had to worry about them. We knew that if we died, our children would be alright. They would know how to make it. They would not be beggars on the street. They would not be homeless. They would know how to be adults, who could take care of themselves. I am proud of my children and how they know how to function in life.

My children gave me love and I hope that I was able to show and give them love in the ways they needed. A lot of times, my husband and I did not come to our children's rescue in the way they thought we should have. We came in ways that we knew would help them grow, so that when we left this earth, they would be able to stand on their own feet.

Dennis and I agreed that when our children became parents, they would take care of their own children. We also made sure that they had a place to live. If the mortgage was not paid, my husband would make a way. If the water bill was not paid, if they were getting put out of a house, my husband would make sure that there was another house for them to live in. My children learned how to stand on their own two feet and they did a pretty good job with their own children.

I loved my grandchildren, but I did not keep them. When Christmas came, I would buy them whatever I could and then owe Macy's and JC

Penney's my entire check, or should I say, checks for weeks to come. I would buy my grandchildren everything; underwear, socks, coats, anything that they needed. And then the same would happen for their birthdays and at Eastertime. I would make sure they had clothes when school began in September. I would not only make sure that they were well dressed, but also that my grandchildren had food to eat.

While I really loved my grandchildren, my husband and I had made a decision that we would not babysit or ever become any of the grandkids' primary caregiver. As a child, I watched my mother keep her grandchildren and saw that she struggled. She had to work and made my sister Gwen and I care for our nieces when we were teenagers. At that time, I made a decision that when I had grandchildren, I would not repeat my mother's pattern. I promised myself that when I had children, I would raise my own children. I would not send them off to my mother. I would keep them in my care, take them wherever I went and, I would be the parent to my own children. I was their mother. There may have been one or two times when my children stayed with an aunt, but my children were my responsibility.

Lula A. Scott

Me and my children- Clyde, Marlene, & Sharon

CHAPTER 25

My life has been surrounded by people with needs and I thank God that He has used me to meet those needs. Nobody was "too bad" for me. I had a godson who had AIDS and he could come in the house, take a bath, and stay there. I would keep up on him so that he knew he had a place he could always come and nobody would judge him. My husband treated him like a father.

Other young people would come and Dennis would treat them like a father so much so that they would never want to leave. Sometimes, I would say, "You have to go home to your mother now" and some would not even understand.

Some mothers would say, "I don't know what to do with my child." I would say, "Let them come and stay the weekend with my family. We would be alright." They would be so gracious and so glad that I would take the teenagers and I would teach and talk to them. Some of them went on to be ministers and some married preachers. They have a testimony about living in the Scotts' house and they say, "Aunt Lula" or "Mother Scott." I tried to take good care of them.

I thank God because Sharon would go out into the streets and she would witness to prostitutes. She would minister to lesbians. She would bring them home and we would sit at the table. We would eat, we would laugh, we would talk and nobody frowned on them.

Then there is Sister Kim Wells, my best friend, who came along and said, "I'll help take the children to the Youth Convention." We would ravel on the van to the Youth Convention, but then one year, Sis. Kim got a chartered bus and we and our kids went to Washington, D.C. They felt so good about themselves. We put self-esteem in them and let them know that they were good and that God had a plan for their lives.

I thank God because He gave me that kind of vision and until I was 75-years-old, I was still going to the Youth Convention with Sis. Kim Wells. I remember Bishop saying to me, "75-years-old and still travelling with the Youth Department." I thank God because He said, "He will reward you and you will rise up like the wings of an eagle." God gave me favor and I was able to do it. Some of them, even today, although they have left Mount Calvary, they come back, every now and then and give a testimony.

I thank God because even in my neighborhood, I could be a witness and I would look for people who needed help. I would look for the senior citizens. Even though I was a senior citizen myself, I could still cook, clean, and bathe seniors and I would do whatever my hands found to do. I would go into my neighbors' house and I would take care of them.

One of my neighbors, she was blind. I saw a man on her porch with an oxygen tank. I asked her sister-in-law, "Why is that oxygen tank going in there?" She said, "My brother is sick." I said to her, "Would you just give me a key in case something happens in the night, then I could go in and see about them?" She told me yes and gave me a key. I went in the next morning and before I went to work, I bathed her brother. Every evening, my husband and I went in and we would give him a bath and I would feed him until he passed on.

After my neighbor passed, his wife was left alone. Every morning when I got up, seven days a week, I would go in the house. I would say, "I'm here" and I would make her breakfast. When I came home from work, I would make her dinner. When I could not do it, I would send my children in to take care of her until God called her home. I thank God because when you have been through, you know how to be a vessel. I thank God for being a vessel that He could use.

But God

Although my husband gave me an allowance, I worked. Once when I was laid off, I found another job. While it was supposed to only be two weeks, I stayed eleven years. It was really was my mission, taking care of an 82-year-old woman, who was extremely wealthy, but felt she had nothing was worth living for. God gave her hope, watching me.

On Friday evenings, she would say to me, "I envy you, Lula." I would ask her, "Envy me, for what?" She would say, "You're going home to a family and when you come back on Monday mornings and you tell me all the good things that you have done and the places you've been, the only thing that I have is to sit and look at these four walls. I don't have another person until you come back on Monday."

She was a person who did not understand racism, although she was a racist. God used me to teach her, to walk with her, to talk with her and let her know that all people were equal; that there is no color in God. My family was her family. I was her daughter and she loved me and I loved her. We gave each other the love. When she went to be with God, I had already talked to her about God, what it was to love God and to have God love you. I thank God that she understood and she decided.

After she passed, I decided to go to college for two semesters, but I could not pass algebra. It was at that point that I decided to go to school to become a nursing assistant. I went and got the certification. At first, I worked nine years with a couple. During this time, I met a lot of people and I found my ministry there also. I would meet people who did not have food, did not have anyone to go shopping for them, did not have anyone to wash their clothes. They did not even know that there was a person who existed who could love them the way that God loved them. I know that God sent me to them and they came to realize it. I would always do extra because God would point me that way.

I went to work with a couple, both needed help. After working with them, I then worked in hospice care for about six years. I learned about death, the last days, the last hours of people's lives. God taught me how to minister to the dying. He taught me how to lead Jewish people to Christ. He taught me how to teach people who were racist, to love them and let them know that we were kind people. He taught me how to put my hands on them and nurture them and their families. He taught me how to live in their homes, sleep in their beds, eat their food, and still be a servant to them. God said, "You must be a servant first" and I thank God that He used me to be a servant to these people and to give them the strength of God to go through.

After working in hospice, I went into Victim Services for ten years to be used in the courtroom, to sit there with mothers, fathers, sons, daughters, and family and pray for them, love people who had committed crimes and say to them that there is still a God. After sitting beside mothers who had to bury their sons, I could tell other mothers, "It's better to look inside a prison cell than to look in a grave. That mother buried her son and you can still see your son." I was able to tell them about a forgiving God. I was able to work and stand on the corner, the front steps of my job, and talk to drug dealers and they would tell me things about their lives. I would say to them, "You're too young. That's got to be a better way. There is a better way and God is that better way."

Sometimes when the boys would come out of jail, they would come on the corner and began to talk to me. I would pour into them. I could speak to people firsthand about having a door closed and how God could open the door that was shut in your face. I could tell them that after years of trying to get a job, everywhere I would go, because I had a prison record, society would close the door in my face. But I even thank God for that because if I had gotten that kind of job in the beginning, I would not have been able to be used by God.

Sometimes, what you call your lowest place is what God would call your highest. I thank God for being there. I thank God because one day, I did go to a job when I was 65-years-old and I was given a chance to have a real job, a best job of going to court, dressed up in the morning, feel real good about myself, and nobody would throw

But God

up my record in my face. When God shows you mercy and gives you a new heart, then you need to learn how to show other people mercy and say to them that God can create in you a clean heart.

CHAPTER 26

I love all of my children, but there was no greater love than the love I had for my husband. It was reciprocal and unconditional. I knew that my husband loved me a whole lot. Sometimes he would take me in his arms and just hold me.

When I married him, I was slender, although as the years went by, my weight increased. Dennis would sit me on his lap and I would protest, thinking that I was too heavy for him. He would say to me, "The more of you, it's the more of me to love."

I never had to worry about my husband. I trusted him. I loved him. I did not worry about him looking at other women. One day, we were riding along and Dennis said to me, "That lady has on some white looking stockings and she looks nice." The next week, when I got dressed up to go to church, I asked my husband, "How do you like my off white stockings?" He said, "They look good." Even when they went out of style, I kept wearing off white stockings, because I knew that Dennis loved them.

When Dennis and I would go out, we would hold hands. A lady said to me one time in church, "Every time I see you and your husband, you all are always holding hands." I said, "Yep, we hold hands." One day, my cousin said to me, "Why don't you turn that man loose and let him walk?" I said, "Nope, if I turn his hand loose, you might get a hold of his hand." My husband and I would say that holding hands were like holding our hearts.

But God

The ladies who were married at my church, I gave them some instructions. Clean your house, wash and iron your husband's clothes, make sure it's a hot dinner on the table every day. When I told them about how I cared for my husband, they laughed. They said, "Sister Scott, you're telling us too much to do." I told them, "Well, this is how you will keep your husband."

My husband had a garden that was about an acre and that was all he dreamed about was the acre. He made farmers out of me and my children. I laugh about it even now. My husband would come home from work in the evenings and say, "Okay, let's go. We're going to New Jersey to the garden." Everybody knew that we had to get ready, pack up our stuff and go to the garden.

There was an elderly man and his mother who allowed my husband to use the land. We found out that they really needed help. I would clean their house; my husband would cut their grass, and whatever else we could do for them, we did. If anything happened and they needed help, they knew that they could always call us.

The children went happily with us to the garden because they knew when we left, they would be treated to fast food at the A & W. They loved Arby's, especially the honey dipped chicken. They loved McDonalds. Whatever fast food they wanted, as long as they worked on the farm, my husband would buy it for them. When the children got a little older, they did not like going as much.

My husband was a kind man. He loved missions. Dennis would go and take care of the elderly. He would go see the church mothers, take them to the store, and would bring them fresh vegetables from the garden. My husband would always take bags of vegetables and give to members of his church, members from my church, and my aunts and uncles. He would spread it out so that people would have food to eat.

My husband taught me how to pay bills. The first month we were married, he gave me the money to pay the bills. I had never had this type of responsibility. I took the money and spent it on everything but the bills. I bought clothes and everything I thought me and my kids should have. When the bills came and not been paid, I thought my husband was going to get me. But he did not say anything to me about the unpaid bills. He then told me that from now on, he would pay the bills and give me an allowance so that I could have money to buy something for me and the kids. Although I worked, my husband continued to give me money just because he wanted to.

Whenever we went on vacation, I would save money because I wanted to have extra for whatever we needed. On one of our family vacations to Buffalo, I found out that a store was going out of business. I spent money like crazy on anything that I saw that the kids and I could use. And I spent all of the money.

On the way home from Buffalo, the car broke down. I thought, "Oh, my God, what am I going to do?" I had my four kids and my niece from Buffalo, who would visit with us every summer for two weeks, and I had no money left. I sneaked and called my sister and her husband and told them "Y'all are going to have to get some cars or vans or something because we broke down and we don't have any money."

Dennis did not say anything. He called for two taxis. I thought, "Two taxis? What are they going to do when they get here because I don't have any money?" The taxis came, took us to the Greyhound bus station. Dennis walked up to the window and said to the clerk, "Give me five children's tickets and two adult tickets." He never said a word to me about the money. But guess what? Lesson learned. Never spend all of your money. Always keep enough money to get home.

When my children were young, Dennis and I would always take them with us for family vacations. Once they were grown, my husband and I would visit his cousin, Thomasina, and her husband, Dave, in Baltimore, Maryland. Visiting them was one of the things my husband loved most. Two or three times a year, we would back our bags and we would stay with them. When our children were growing up, Dennis and I travelled all over the United States. After 25 years of marriage,

But God

for our anniversary, Sharon and Godbaby sent us on a cruise, something I had never expected to do in my life. My husband had been out on the waters, but I had never been on a ship. From that day until now, I have never forgotten about that trip. We would sit and have lovely conversations about "my cruise." It was my cruise. My husband would just laugh at me.

Lula A. Scott

Me and my husband, Dennis

CHAPTER 27

Dennis made our house, the house of prayer for all people. People came from everywhere and would often stay at our house for three or four nights, sometimes the whole summer, and my husband never complained.

When my father got sick, and the doctors told him that he could no longer stay home alone, there was no one who could take care of him in North Carolina. My father called me. I said to my husband, "What are we going to do?" He said, "We have to go get him." We packed up and went to North Carolina. My sister Fannie also went. We sold everything out of my father's house and brought him to Philadelphia. My father stayed with us for about two years. He got homesick and he wanted to go back to North Carolina.

I made arrangements with my brother, who lived in North Carolina, to take care of my father. I asked him if he was sure and he said yes. My husband and I agreed that my father was much better. His diabetes was under control; he had had good doctors' care; his mind was good. At the time, 86-years-old, my father went back to North Carolina and lived two more years before he died.

After my father left, my sister Gwen was having some problems in Buffalo. She asked if she could come to live with us in Philadelphia. I sat down with my husband and I talked to him and I asked him, "You know that I know that it's hard and every time you look, I'm bringing somebody here to live with us." He said, "What now?" So we talked about it and he said, "Okay." So then Gwen moved to Philadelphia and lived with us.

After Gwen came, I got a call from Buffalo that my mother was living in the house and when the snow came, they could not get her out. The snow in Buffalo is a hard snowfall and it was dangerous for her to remain there. So, I had another conversation with my husband about my mother coming to live with us. He said, "Lula, whatever you do, that will be alright with me." That was the kind of man my husband was. My mother came that year for Christmas and she never returned to Buffalo.

After my sister and my mother came to live with us, my niece Diana, Gwen's daughter, came from Buffalo and she lived with us. After Diana moved to our home, she had a baby and then five years later, Diana had another baby and everybody lived with us. During this time, we had a cousin in Rochester, New York, who was having a hard time so we brought him to Philadelphia and he lived with us for a year. This was the kind of house we had. Every Sunday the house was full of people. We cooked for everyone.

My husband, a gentle soul, would never complain. He and I always looked at giving young people a chance. We would take our children and other young people, who didn't have the money, and go to the Youth Convention. The young people would have the best time. This was our way of keeping them out of the street.

In 2007, my husband became sick with kidney failure and the doctors gave him two months to live. Dennis told the doctors, "I know a Man. I will be alright." The doctor asked him, "Where do you want to die at?" Dennis told him, "Doctor since you said that, you're going to die yourself. If I die, I'll die at home."

I told the doctor, "I'll take my husband home. I'm a hospice person and I'll take care of him myself." After that diagnosis, my husband and I travelled all over the South for two years. Dennis continued doing the things he loved. He still drove and every Sunday, he went to Sunday

But God

School. When he would go, he took a pot, hot dogs, mustard, and hot chocolate and all the kids knew that Deacon Dennis was bringing a hot dog and hot chocolate for them to have. He was a good Sunday School teacher.

After my husband became ill, unlike what the doctors had expected and said, he did not get sick the way they predicted. He did not swell up. He did not need all of the medications the doctors said he should have and he did not have hallucinations in response to the medications he was given.

During the latter time of Dennis' illness, he said to me, "Come here. I want you to sit on my lap." I said to him, "You're too weak." He said to me, "I want you to sit on my lap." So I sat on his lap, looked in the mirror, and we both laughed and then I broke down and started crying. Somehow in my heart, I knew that would be last time I would be able to sit on his lap.

It was during the last two weeks of his life, when my husband got really sick and I really felt bad. At that time, I would go to work and my sister Gwen would take care of him. When I came home from work, I would do whatever I needed to do.

One day, I called Gwen to see how my husband was doing and on this particular day, the Holy Spirit spoke to me and said, "Go home and don't come back." I had a peace in my soul. I cleaned out my drawer and did not come back. Thank God for a good boss. I said to her "I have to quit. I have to go home and I won't be back." She said, "Miss Lula, do what you have to do." I will always be grateful to her.

Ironically, that day, I was being interviewed by a local newspaper. The lady who was interviewing me asked, "Miss Scott, what are you doing?" I told her, "My husband is very sick and I'm going home. I don't think he's going to make it. I think he's going to die. It's my place to be there, taking care of my husband and I'm leaving my job." The lady wrote what an asset I had been to the job and to the community.

I went home and I stayed. My husband died two weeks later. I tell God thank you even now. I had those last two weeks. After 34 years of marriage, I had lost my love, but until this very day, I still have his loving spirit that will be with me always.

Sometimes, I lay in the bed at night and I talk to Dennis and I know that he hears me. I say to you, "Dennis, wherever you are, my heart is still with you." I thank you because you were so good to me and Sharon. You were such a good father and you took care of all of our children. I know that I will see you again one day. Until then, I will always thank you from the bottom of my heart.

Chapter 28

I have had many tears and sorrows, pain and dread, but through it all, I've learned to trust in God. This is the way that I have learned to walk- my trust in God, my strength in God, my learning, and not leaning to my own understanding, not leaning to my own ways, but standing on every promise in God. He said in the Word that His promises are true. The reason I titled my book, **BUT GOD** is because I know, if it had not been for the Lord on my side, I would have never made it.

I thank God that I can be a witness today that God is a deliverer, God will forgive, and God will make you whole again. It was meant to take me out, the things that I went through, and to destroy me. But it ended up being for my good. I feel like God had a compass for my life to guide me through the storm. When the storms were raging and I should have been like Paul, shipwrecked, but I came through on the broken pieces.

Today, I can say, thank God. He took me through at the age of 23 from prison and death row on a journey that I never expected or imaged the things in life that God had in store for me; how many lives He would use me to touch. The love of the people of God would surround me. He would give me people who would love and teach me, be up with me in the midnight hour, listen to my pain, and go through with me. I thank God for them today.

Lula A. Scott

My testimony is that God will use who He pleases. It does not matter what people think, it only matters what God thinks. Sometimes, what you call your lowest place is what God would call your highest.

I thank God for being there. I thank God because one day, when I was 65-years-old, I was given a chance to have a real job, a job of going to court, dressed up in the morning, feeling real good about myself, and nobody would throw up my record in my face. When God shows you mercy and gives you a new heart, then you need to learn how to show other people mercy and say to them that God can create in you a clean heart.

God can and will give you the strength to move on. I wish that someone had talked to me and told me that there was another way to make it. He says, "I know the plans I have for you and it is for your good."

There is help, get out before it is too late. Once you get out, find a good place to be. Give your life to Jesus and God will lead you, guide you, and teach you along the way. Always look for the mercies of God. Morning by morning, new mercies, you will see and you will be able to say, "Great is thy faithfulness, Lord unto me."

God will use who He pleases. It does not matter what people think, it only matters what God thinks. I went from working in prison to working in two dental offices and God used me on those jobs to be a witness to many people.

I am 85-years-old and I have never seen the righteous forsaken. I have my right mind, still standing, still leaning on God, still able to help people. I am telling you, God has a plan for your life.

I hope that reading this book, you will enjoy it and that there will be something that will inspire you and give you a mind to know that God is on your side and that there is nothing too hard for God. Man says no, **BUT GOD** can do anything but fail.

But God

Me with my parents- Anna Bradley and Troy Bradley & siblings- Troy, Fannie, Pearl, & Gwen

Lula A. Scott

Me with my daughter and son, Sharon and Millard

Milton Keynes UK
Ingram Content Group UK Ltd.
UKHW052042140824
446844UK00017B/723

Silence of Secrets

Stella Mace

Copyrights

Copyright © [Year of First Publication] by [Author or Pen Name]
All rights reserved.

No part of this publication may be reproduced, distributed, or transmitted in any form or by any means, including photocopying, recording, or other electronic or mechanical methods, without the prior written permission of the publisher, except as permitted by U.S. copyright law. For permission requests, contact [include publisher/author contact info].

The story, all names, characters, and incidents portrayed in this production are fictitious. No identification with actual persons (living or deceased), places, buildings, and products is intended or should be inferred.

Book Cover by [Artist]
Illustrations by [Illustrator]
[Edition Number] edition [Year of Publication]

Also by Stella Mace

Alex Harper Mystery Series
Shrouded Deception

Mia Conrad Mystery Series
Shattered Echoes

Parker Rose Mystery Series
Small Town Shadows
Small Town Secrets

Standalone
Silence of Secrets

Confession

As I listened to my patient's chilling confession, I realized I was about to be drawn into a deadly game of cat-and-mouse with a cunning psychopath. The evidence was hidden; the crime seemed impossible, and time was running out. This revelation sent shockwaves through my world, marking the beginning of my entanglement in a complex web of mysteries. With every word that came out of Steven's mouth, I was more and more shocked.

Nothing, absolutely nothing, could have prepared me for the rollercoaster of emotions I experienced as Steven narrated his ordeal. When he said he needed to say something he had never told anyone before, I thought he meant opening up about something in his past. I had been excited, thinking I was about to make a breakthrough with Steven, but then he started talking, and I could not stop him.

When I left my house that morning, I looked up to the blue sky, which had been repeatedly grey with clouds the last few days, and breathed in the petrichor that filled the air after last night's rain. I said, "Let's hope today turns out interesting, huh?" My cat Gojo meowed from beside me, and I looked down at her snow-white face, staring in the same direction as I was as if she was contemplating some deep life issues.

I really should be more careful what I wish for.

I should back up a little.

"Come on, Gojo. It's time for work," I said to my cat as we left home that morning. Yes, my cat follows me to work. Gojo likes to leave the house daily, and she's the only cat I've met who likes going out. Besides, when I started my practice three years ago, I quickly learned that seeing a cat around helped some patients relax and made our sessions easier. Many clients had unraveled the darkness of their souls while stroking Gojo's white fur, their eyes closed, breathing in the incense I always have burning, and listening to Gojo purr in their lap or chest, depending on whether they were sitting or lying down.

However, as I did not open the office until 10 a.m. and my first session was not until 12:15 p.m., Gojo and I went out for breakfast. I would leave her in the car, order my fast food, and return to eat in the parking lot. I would also drive to a park and spend the next hour studying the people passing us by based on their appearance, countenance, dress, and other such things.

I liked to pretend this kept me sharp in my profession, but the truth is, besides Gojo and Kat, my singular friend, I had no other friends. My receptionist, Andrea, and I had a professional relationship. We had become acquaintances over the one year she had been working for me. But we were two very different people. This little escapade was my way of getting human contact.

I did not date much, although Kat insists I could be a man-eater if I wanted to. I had classic Nordic features, elevated by my Slavic heritage on my mother's side. This affair resulted in a six-foot-tall frame, blue eyes set in an almond shape, slightly high but definite cheekbones, and an easy jawline. My raven hair framing my face was a source of eternal delight for Kat whenever I allowed her to do it. I have a lithe figure, kept in shape by running every night and every dawn.

When I walked into the office that day, Gojo following behind, I could not have expected my office to become a stage for murder discussions.

"Good morning, boss." Andrea greeted me as usual. I have tried and sadly failed to get her to call me by my first name, Olivia, or at least Dr. Jenson. She bent to pat Gojo, whom she greeted with a lot more warmth than she greeted me.

"Hey, Satoru." She said, using the first name of the character I'd named my cat after. So she can be on a first-name basis with the cat, but not with me.

"Good morning, Andrea; how're you today?"

"Just fine. Your first appointment is in two hours."

"Slow day then?" I asked.

"Indeed. Three appointments all day, all of them well spaced apart."

My first appointment was with Mrs. Johannes and her daughter. She was trying to bridge the gap that opened between them since she remarried after the girl's father's death. It didn't help that she had married the girl's teacher. However, we were finally making progress, and Mrs. Johannes became a better parent. I was confident we managed to steer Vera from doing anything stupid just for shock value and to hurt her mother.

Gojo and I went out to lunch before the third appointment. I asked Andrea to join us as I always did, but she refused, as she always does. She chose instead to have lunch in the next building where her fiancé and one of her friends worked respectively as trainer and yoga instructor. The building was a gym and spa center for rich teen snobs, the kind that Andrea wished she was.

Maybe that was unkind of me, but I see the longing in her eyes every day. I could also see that her fiancé and her friend had more going on between them than just work. But it was not my place to say.

After lunch, I returned to my office to await my 5 o'clock, Steven.

Fifteen minutes before his arrival, I pulled up his file on my computer to re-familiarize myself with him and our progress before the session began.

Twenty minutes later, he came in and took his seat. Immediately, Gojo started rubbing against his legs, begging for pets and rubs. He reached down to pick her up, but she leaped onto his lap and made a perfect loaf with her face buried in her paws.

"So Steven, it's nice to see you back."

Across from me sat Steven, a familiar face I'd known for almost two years. Unlike my other patients, Steven wasn't burdened by the weight of everyday anxieties or relationship woes. He always exuded an aura of quiet control, his demeanor cool as a cucumber. But under that coolness was such deep sorrow as I had never seen in anyone else besides myself. Although his visits were spaced weeks or even months apart, he was one of my favorite patients. There was something in him that I recognized in myself. Besides, he never pretended not to know what I was talking about. He opened up quickly and allowed me to help him.

He would come in confidently but with a troubled aura. Sometimes, I could almost touch the depressive cloud around him, and once he started talking, you could sense the depths of his issues, but when he was done, he would look lighter and happier.

I suspected he only came in whenever it became too much to bear to lease himself a little more time. I have been trying since he booked his first session to get him to come in regularly, but Steven did things his own way. He had told me bluntly, he said, "Doc, I can handle myself quite well, and trust me, I am not going to kill myself. That will inconvenience a lot of people, so I stopped thinking about it. I had my chances in college but failed to do it; it's too late now."

"Nevertheless..." I started to say, but he cut me off.

"Really, doc, I'll come in when I need you."

I knew he was not going to be moved, so I stopped. He booked his sessions days before. Steven never came in without an appointment.

Today, however, something was different. A flicker of fear had replaced the usual calmness in his eyes, his hands clenching and unclenching in his lap, ignoring Gojo altogether. As I settled into my chair, I couldn't help but notice the tremor in his voice as he began to speak.

"Dr. Jenson," he started, his voice barely a whisper, "I need to tell you something. Something I haven't brought myself to say before, not even to myself."

His words hung heavy in the air, and I felt a chill down my back. That should have been my last warning. Gojo sat up, got off him, and walked off—another omen that I failed to register.

I waited for him to speak, and he finally got to it. Taking a deep breath, Steven continued, "I... I think I killed someone."

The stark confession hit me like a physical blow. My mind raced, searching for an explanation, a hint of a joke or something, anything to dispel the dread settling in my chest. But as I looked into his troubled eyes, the raw vulnerability on his face spoke volumes. This wasn't a joke; it was a confession and a plea born of a terrible need—a desperate appeal for release, for absolution.

"Please, Dr. Jenson," he pleaded, his voice cracking, "you have to believe me. I didn't want to do it, but I had no choice."

My professional training asked me to remain objective and to listen without judgment. The sensible part of me wanted to call the authorities and reach out and call the police. Yet, a part of me, the human part, ached for the man sitting opposite me, his world crumbling before my eyes.

"Steven," I began, my voice calm but filled with concern, "tell me everything."

He took another deep breath, his body visibly trembling. Then, in a voice barely above a whisper, he began to weave a tale of manipulation, coercion, and a crime so perfectly executed, so meticulously planned, that he was sure to get away with it.

"There's this man, Mr. Patterson. You may have heard of him. He's quite a popular businessman. He deals in stones and jewelry, mostly diamonds. There's hardly a diamond in this city that doesn't pass through his hands first. I run a small family business, which I inherited from my grandmother. My business is not on a scale to compete with him, and I never tried to. I like being small and intimate.

"I don't deal with wives and girlfriends and daughters of rich assholes who want to show off their wealth when they come into my store. I sometimes send them away, most often to any of Patterson's stores. Heirlooms and family jewels are what I deal with, as well as grandmothers with stones inherited from their own grandmothers.

Sometimes, these older women don't trust banks and don't want this jewelry in their houses, so they come to me. Sometimes, they want to sell something off and come to me. To sell, to exchange things like that. Men who want to craft something unique for their soon-to-be brides. I like the intimate cases and make a decent income as I have only myself to care for.

"Sometimes, I travel to Russia or Israel to get new stones. I travel worldwide to pick up unique things, which I sell off. I also deal in antiques. Over the years, I have built a reputation and a name for myself, such that I've had to expand and train two employees to help me. You must understand, Doc, that my business is heavily built on familial values, and I intend to keep it so."

"Somehow, Patterson gets it in his head that he wants my piece of the business and says he wants to buy me out. He offered me 10 million, a reasonable offer, but see, I love my business. My grandmother raised me after my parents died, and we've done this together all my life. She's 90 now, and seeing me sell out would break her heart. I can take the money, expand into something else, or even start a new business doing the same thing, but it wouldn't be the same. We've done business from the same building for four generations, and I'll be damned before I let a greedy capitalist turn it into an extension of his soulless thievery.

"Let me not bore you with details of how he kept badgering me. But three days ago, I came home from work to find my house broken into. I live with my grandmother and Dr. Jenson, and" here his voice broke. "I found her dead. That is the only proof I have that someone was in the house.

"No footprints, no marks on her, nothing, but I know someone killed her!"

"She couldn't have died in her sleep?" I asked. "She was 90?"

"Yes, she was, but she was a stubborn woman, and she always said she would be holding my hand when she died. I refuse to believe a woman who survived wars and raised a cantankerous young boy on her own would die sitting at the dining table. There was no food before her, nothing to explain why she was sitting there."

"You think she met with some people there?"

"I'm sure of it." Tears were streaming down his face now. He continued. "I loved her, and he killed her."

"And what happened next?"

"Well, that's where it gets complicated. I clearly remember, well, now I'm not sure, but I think I remember coming home to see her dead. After I called the hospital and had her body taken away, I somehow slept off. When I woke up the next day, I had this feeling of dread in me. And I clearly remember having killed my grandmother."

An eerie stillness descended on the room, and I sat up straighter.

"How?"

"I do not know, and the memory is apparent in my head. I'd drugged her tea, and the teacup was on the dining table. Of course, the toxin would not show in an autopsy, and I would have readily turned myself in had I not gotten mail from Patterson."

He showed me a document. It was a bank statement, money leaving his account to a certain Mr. Taskin.

"I don't see the importance of this?" I asked.

Then he showed me the following document, a PDF about Mr. Taskin, a toxicologist. I began to see the implications.

Then he played a video for me.

"Is that Patterson?" I asked when a fat face appeared on the screen. The beady eyes were green, and the nose veiny.

"Yes."

Patterson was saying how it would be a pity if this bit of information made it to the police and how it would be even more of a shame if they found out that some of Steven's clients had suddenly changed their will to leave all their fortunes to him within the last two years and then began to die in the same manner as his grandmother.

The video ended with Patterson telling my patient there was one way to stop this, and this time, he wasn't paying a dime; he wanted a complete handover.

Steven held his head in his palm.

"This is the only reason I know I didn't kill my grandmother. Even now, I'm still unsure, and the memory is very vivid. I can see myself watching her die. Please, I know it sounds unbelievable, Dr. Jenson," Steven said, his voice barely a whisper. "But I'm telling you the truth. You have to help me before he kills again."

Hidden Clues

When Steven stopped talking, the confession settled heavily in the air between us, and I felt a deep fear rising within me. My mind raced, trying to make sense of the scenario he described. I had to admit to myself that it didn't look good for him; even though I could tell he was being truthful, I still had some suspicion. After all, he could be pulling my leg, or he could be lying, and he'd really done it.

I looked at Gojo, who was now sitting by the door eating a piece of chicken. From my receptionist, no doubt.

"Steven," I began, my voice slightly shaking, "you need to tell me everything you remember. Every detail, no matter how small, could be crucial."

"It's all a false memory; how could it help?"

"I think it could; no one can recreate a perfect memory and implant it in someone's head."

He nodded, his eyes shrouded with guilt and uncertainty. "I'll try, Dr. Jenson. But it's all so blurry, I feel like pieces of a puzzle that don't quite fit together."

"Take your time," I urged gently. "Start from the moment you arrived home that night."

Am I now committing to helping him? I asked myself. This is insane! He should go to the police, one side of me yelled. But we both knew he'd be arrested immediately.

And you're sure he really didn't kill the woman? I asked myself again.

Well, what would he stand to gain? He already had the business.

Spite, Liv. Or life insurance. Something clicked! But I held my tongue for now.

He closed his eyes as if trying to retrieve the memories from the depths of his mind. "I... I remember walking through the front door and finding it unlocked. That is strange because I always make sure to lock it. My grandmother dislikes unlocked doors, some leftover paranoia."

"Go on," I encouraged.

"I called out for Grandma, but there was no answer," he continued, his voice shaky. "Then I saw her... sitting at the dining table, the teacup in front of her."

"The teacup," I repeated, my mind racing. "Did you notice anything unusual about it?"

Steven frowned, deep in thought. "It was her favorite cup, the one she used every evening for her tea. But that is odd. I just can't explain it."

"It's odd she had her favorite cup?"

"Sounds strange. But something about that memory isn't quite right."

I made a mental note of this observation, my analytical kicking in. That's the thing with false memories, there will always be gaps, no matter how good you are.

"And then what happened?"

"I... I don't know," Steven admitted, frustration in his voice. "It's like there's a gap in my memory, a blank space where everything goes dark until I'm poisoning her tea."

I could sense his distress, his desperation for answers. "Steven, let's try something," I suggested, leaning back in my chair; there was a slight crick in my neck. "Close your eyes and focus on that moment. Picture the scene in your mind as vividly as you can."

He followed my instructions, and his brow furrowed in concentration. I watched him closely, noting shifting emotions on his face as memories seemed to flicker across his face.

"Dr. Jenson," he whispered after a moment, his eyes still closed, "I... I remember the smell of almonds."

"Almonds?" I repeated. "That could be important. Did your grandmother have any almond-scented products in the house?"

Steven shook his head, his eyes still closed. "No. It's... it's strange."

I made a mental note to look at this further, as my mind was already trying to form connections and theories. After three tries and coming up blank, I pushed those thoughts aside for now, focusing on Steven and the task at hand.

"Steven, I want you to try to remember," I urged gently. "Think back to that moment, to the teacup, to the smell of almonds. What else do you see? What else do you remember?"

He fell silent. Minutes ticked by as we sat in the quiet office, the only sound coming from Gojo as she aggressively attacked the already dead and fried chicken. You would think that after eating the large piece of meat, she wouldn't have dinner, but I could already hear her screaming in my ears as soon as we got back home.

Finally, Steven opened his eyes, "I... I remember nothing else. I'm sorry, doc."

I reached out a hand to him, "Steven, it's okay," I said softly. "You're doing great. Just take a deep breath and try to relax. I sense we won't be making any more progress tonight. You've done a lot better than I expected."

He nodded, his shoulders sagging with some measure of relief. We sat in silence for a while longer.

"Dr. Jenson," Steven said into the silence, his voice barely a whisper, "what... what do I do now? How do I prove that I didn't... that I couldn't have...?"

Gojo looked at me then as if asking the same question. Honestly, I had been asking myself the same question. How can he prove that he didn't do it? If indeed he didn't do it.

I met his gaze, my mind racing with possibilities. "We'll figure it out together," I said firmly. "But first, we need to gather more information, more evidence."

I glanced at the clock on my desk, noting the time. "Steven, I have a few more questions for you," I said, pulling out a notepad and pen.

I want you to try to remember everything you can about that night before you went home—every detail, no matter how small. The entire day would be helpful."

For the next hour, we went into Steven's day, making a recreation of his entire day before he went off. He recounted everything he could remember, starting with the moment, to the clients he saw that day, the lunch he had, and finally, heading home in the evening to the chilling discovery of his grandmother's lifeless body.

Throughout our conversation, my cat Gojo sat perched on the windowsill, her round never leaving us as she cleaned herself after her meal. But she soon saw a bird outside and forgot about us.

As we talked, I couldn't shake the feeling of unease that settled in the pit of my stomach. Steven was right. Something about the entire day didn't quite add up; it didn't quite fit the puzzle. I had at first thought the mind trick was the work of some highly skilled psychologist, but I was beginning to see the sloppy workmanship.

For starters, he seemed to have met a high number of new clients that day. I immediately realized someone was trying to keep him at work until a certain time, but they didn't know when exactly.

Finally, as the afternoon sun began to wane and shadows lengthened in the office, I closed my notepad.

"Steven, we don't have a lot to work with here. However, I'm going to do everything I can to help you, to uncover the truth."

He looked at me, his eyes filled with gratitude and relief. "Thank you, Dr. Jenson," he said, weeping into his hands. I... I don't know what I would do without your help."

I smiled at him. Inside me was saying, "Yeah, thanks for the weight of the world on my shoulders."

Outside me said, "We're in this together, Steven. Now, let's get to work."

As I drove home, I thought about the murder. I could hear Gojo moving around in the car, but my mind was too far away to pay attention.

I knew that finding my way through the maze of misleading clues and false leads would be a herculean task. But I was determined to uncover the truth, to unravel the web of deception surrounding Steven's grandmother's death.

I also could not deny that I was a little excited. This was perhaps the most exciting thing that has ever happened to me, and a part of me enjoyed myself. Morbid, I know.

After serving Gojo her dinner, I headed to the bathroom for a warm shower. Momentarily, all thoughts of Steven and Patterson were out of my mind as I savored the heat and the water running down my body, my hands following.

When I was done, I threw on a sports bra and shorts, which left most of my long legs exposed, and headed out for my evening run. An hour later, I returned home and took another shower, this one longer as I drank in the feeling of the hot water and my hands on my skin. Years of strict skincare had left my skin baby-smooth. The way it feels under my hands was a source of eternal delight to my senses.

Finally, I stepped out, dried off, and threw on a large t-shirt and panties. I packed my hair in a loose bun and wrapped it in a silk scarf for the night. I headed to the living room, where Gojo had finished half her dinner and was waiting for me to shake the bowl to make it full again. I shook it, sat down to my dinner of egg fried rice from the Chinese deli three blocks away, and turned on the TV, my phone in my left hand.

The night passed, and Gojo and I soon retired to my bedroom.

The next morning, the murder did not look any clearer. Then, I got an idea while pouring my cereal, which was about the most cooking I did in my kitchen. I called it a kitchen only because that's what the room had been designated for. There was nothing to say this was a kitchen, except for the sink.

I didn't cook; I hated cooking. So my cupboard was filled with cereal boxes upon cereal boxes and snack boxes, chocolate boxes, candy, and the like. I also had a coffee maker, some odds and ends, and a magnificently extravagant water bong. While I was pouring my morning cereal, I had an idea. I decided to focus my efforts on Mr. Patterson. If there was any connection between his business dealings and the events of that fateful night, I was determined to find it.

I knew he did it, and the mail he sent Steven proved he had tied it all nicely to Steven, but there must be something that tied Patterson to it. No matter how little, I should find something about him. But where to start?

I wasn't a police detective, and I didn't have a warrant, and I couldn't get one.

I started by visiting his stores, posing as a curious customer interested in purchasing diamonds. The employees greeted me warmly, eager to showcase their products and expertise. As I browsed through the dazzling displays of jewels and gems, I discreetly asked about their boss, Mr. Patterson. However, one or two things caught my eye.

"Mr. Patterson? Oh, he's a nice businessman," one employee commented, but I sensed a hint of unease in his voice. His eyes were roaming the store as if looking for onlookers. But he keeps to himself mostly, doesn't interact much with the staff."

I went to three more stores, and I heard about an employee who was fired years ago. "Strangest thing, she had a fall from her story building not long after being fired," the girl showing me a pair of earrings said.

"Oh my god, that's horrible."

"Oh, not so much," I was shocked by her disregard for human life. Then she said, "The foolish girl managed to land on an ambulance that was there to get an old woman who'd had a stroke. She survives with not so many injuries."

"Oh," I said. "Still, the way she had blithely spoken about the jumper was disturbing.

"Do you know where I can find this girl?"

"What do you want her for?"

"Morbid curiosity."

She looked at me suspiciously, then shrugged. "Her name is Janice Waters, but she moved away after the accident. Last I heard, she's in Cuba or something."

I heard the first mention of an employee falling sick or having an accident, but not the last. I couldn't find Ms. Waters, but I found several of the others. Many were reluctant to talk, but I found a middle-aged woman who had been wheelchair-bound ever since she got run over. She seemed to have a vendetta against Patterson and claimed he had ordered the hit on her.

When I asked why, she said because she had stumbled upon some rumors of shady dealings, whispers of clients disappearing mysteriously after doing business with Mr. Patterson. My heart raced at the mention of disappearing clients, a slight resemblance to Steven's grandmother.

"Did you ever notice anything unusual or unexplained happening when you worked there?" I probed further, careful not to arouse suspicion.

The woman did not take time to debate whether to share her secrets.

"Well, there was this one time," she began, glancing around as if to ensure no one was listening. But it was just us in the building. "I saw Mr. Patterson meeting with a group of shady characters in the store. But it wasn't his office; it was a different office hidden behind the backroom. But that was not the suspicious part. I was cleaning that night, and no one should have been around. The odd thing was, as they walked towards the office, they were exchanging briefcases, and it all seemed very... clandestine. Passing it between hands so smoothly. I saw

Mr. Patterson open the secret door, and they all went in, then he caught me staring."

"Did you hear anything they were saying?" I pressed, my mind racing with possibilities. I calmed the eager look in my eyes.

The employee shook her head, his expression troubled. "No, they were speaking in hushed tones. But it didn't look like a regular business transaction if you know what I mean."

"So, there is more to Mr. Patterson than met the eye; who knew?" I said to myself in my car.

Over the next few days, I continued my investigation, visiting each of Mr. Patterson's stores and questioning the former employees I could find. I heard whispers of unexplained occurrences, missing inventory, and strange disappearances of other employees. One employee mentioned a peculiar incident where a valuable diamond suddenly went missing from the store's inventory, only to reappear mysteriously the next day. Another spoke of strange noises coming from the basement late at night, as if someone were working down there in secret.

Each piece of information added to the growing puzzle, but none of it provided concrete evidence of Mr. Patterson's involvement in Steven's grandmother's death. It was frustrating, to say the least. As I sat in my office one evening, poring over the notes and documents I had gathered, Gojo jumped onto my desk, scattering the papers. I nearly snapped, but I calmed myself. Gojo isn't my problem. She cocked her head as she looked at the papers. Her left forepaw raised tentatively, her green eyes gleaming with curiosity. Then she smacked a stray paper with her paw.

"Stop it." But she looked into my face and smacked it again. She started pushing against my hands for rubs, and I stopped working.

"You know, Gojo," I said softly, scratching behind her ears. "We're getting closer; I can feel it. I feel like we just need that one piece of evidence to connect it all together."

Patient's Past

As I sat in my office, the weight of the evidence against Mr. Patterson was heavy on my mind, and I couldn't shake the feeling that there was more to this story than met the eye. The pieces of the puzzle were falling into place, but they formed a picture that was far more complex and sinister than I had anticipated.

From what I gathered, Mr. Patterson was a shrewd businessman with a penchant for secrecy. His past employees spoke of him in hushed tones, mentioning rumors of shady dealings and unexplained disappearances, which only added to the air of suspicion that surrounded him. It was beginning to look like Patterson was more than just a businessman, which would explain his viciousness.

But as I reviewed the information I had gathered, a nagging thought tugged at the edges of my mind. Why was Mr. Patterson so intent on going after Steven with such viciousness? What could have prompted him to target a small family business with such relentless determination?

I decided to ask Gojo. But she only ignored me, choosing to groom herself as she waited for my next appointment.

I knew that to unravel the mystery, I needed to go deeper into Mr. Patterson's past. There had to be a connection, a link, something that tied him nicely to Steven's grandmother's death and the events that had unfolded since. Maybe that's hoping for too much, but I couldn't let the woman's death go unpunished.

With a sense of determination, I began to piece together what I learned about Mr. Patterson. He was a self-made man, rising from humble beginnings to become a successful businessman in the world of diamonds and jewelry.

But after speaking to five former employees and one particularly scared former associate, it was obvious there was something else, something hidden beneath the surface—something oily, dirty, and smelly, something that squirmed and stunk.

I recalled snippets of conversations I had had, mentions of a troubled past, and a history of shady dealings. Could it be that Mr. Patterson had a darker side, one that he was desperate to keep hidden? Or was this just the people who didn't like him talking? Yes, he was a ruthless businessman, but aren't most successful businessmen and women required to be vicious? Especially those who prefer to do business on a large scale.

I pulled out my laptop and began to search, scouring the internet for any mention of Mr. Patterson's past, using keywords from my conversations with his detractors. It was a tedious process, sifting through news articles and business reports, most of them useless. There were so many Patterson's in the world. Why are there so many Patterson's in the world?

And then, buried deep within the archives of a long-forgotten local newspaper, I found it. An article detailing a long-forgotten scandal involving Mr. Patterson and a notorious crime syndicate. All hail the immortal internet.

According to the article, Mr. Patterson had once been involved in a series of illegal activities, ranging from money laundering to extortion. He had managed to evade prosecution because no evidence, concrete or even remote, could be linked to him. He'd finally established himself as a respectable businessman in the trade of diamonds and jewels, but the stain of his past lingered, a shadow that followed him wherever he went.

As I read through the article, a chilling realization dawned on me. Could it be that Mr. Patterson's vendetta against Steven was rooted in this dark chapter of his past? Was he seeking revenge for some slight, some long-forgotten betrayal? Then I had another thought. Could this vendetta be against Steven's grandmother and not Steven himself? Was my patient just collateral damage?

I had thought of looking into the death of Steven's parents, but maybe I was being too fantastic.

The pieces of the puzzle were beginning to fall into place, forming a picture that was both terrifying and illuminating. Mr. Patterson was not just a ruthless businessman; he was a man driven by past demons and a thirst for vengeance.

Steven's grandmother was Henrietta Gundel, a Hungarian Jew. I went back to Mr. Patterson's former associate, Mr. Jorges, and started asking about any association with someone named Gundel.

He looked at me through thinly slitted eyes for several minutes before speaking.

"You lied to me earlier."

The game was up. "Yes, Mr. Jorges, I did."

"Patterson has done something again, hasn't he?"

How did he know that? And wait, again? What did he mean again?

"What do you mean again?"

Mr. Jorges sighed. Then, he told me the story of Gundel, Jorges, and Patterson, which ended in Gundel deciding that he was better off alone as he was before, Jorges getting nothing but escaping with his life, and young Patterson, a rich man who could afford to open five diamond stores at once.

A deal that had soured their relationship and left a bitter taste in Mr. Patterson's mouth.

"He was too wily for me, but he never could outsmart Gundel. You just can't trick the man." Mr. Jorges seemed to take pleasure in this fact. "Of course, Akiva died, and Henri took over. You know we called her Henri, short for Henrietta. She and Patterson used to be a thing, that was until Akiva came along. He was a better man all around and treated her better. After she took over, he tried again. She was even smarter than her husband, and Tim soon learned that he could do nothing there. He left her alone, thank heavens."

"Tim being Mr. Patterson?"

"Tim being Mr. Patterson." He affirmed.

Could this failed deal have been the catalyst for Mr. Patterson's vendetta against Steven and his family? Was he seeking revenge for a perceived betrayal, a chance to settle an old score?

It had been two weeks since Steven's chilling confession, two weeks of relentless pursuit of the truth in the fog of uncertainty. As each day passed, the increasing weight of the mystery pressed down on me, the elusive threads of the clever crime slipping through my fingers like wisps of smoke every time I thought I had something. Digging up Tim's past was all well and good, but I needed something to clear up the present, especially since I didn't know when he would try to frame Steven again.

More deaths could mean the chair for Steven whenever Patterson decided to send his so-called clues to the police. Because I knew Steven Roseblood-Gundel, he would not sell out.

Since that confession day, I had made it mandatory for Steven to come in every Wednesday and Friday for our sessions. These sessions were no longer the usual therapy discussions, but even then, they'd still been relaxed. But recently, they had taken on a new urgency, a desperate attempt to dislodge anything new from the false memory that haunted Steven. Patterson had reached out and given a week before the next person died.

But despite our efforts, the real memory of the night his grandmother died remained elusive, hidden behind in a haze of confusion and doubt. With each growing day, Steven's mind seemed to be a battleground of conflicting emotions, the guilt of a crime he believed he had committed warring with the nagging sense of doubt that spoke of a different truth. And that was what was muddling up his mind even worse than the trick. It was also fragmenting his sanity.

It hurt and angered me to see.

As Steven entered my office today, I couldn't help but notice the bags under his eyes and the weariness lined into every part of his face.

The burden of his guilt seemed to weigh even more heavily on him, casting a dark cloud over his once-confident demeanor. He looked like he was shrinking, too, maybe.

"Good afternoon, Steven," I greeted him softly, gesturing for him to take a seat. "How have you been feeling since our last session?"

Steven sank into the chair, his gaze fixed on the floor as if unable to meet my eyes. "Not good, Dr. Jenson," he admitted, his voice barely above a whisper. "The guilt... it's eating me alive."

Gojo padded to him, but he couldn't even bring himself to acknowledge her. I wondered if she would get insistent. Gojo tended to get loud when she wanted something.

I nodded sympathetically, my heart aching for the turmoil he must be going through. "I understand, Steven. But we need to stay focused. We're making progress, even if it may not seem like it."

I had told him some things I'd found out but admitted they still didn't help us solve his grandmother's death.

I could see the doubt flicker in Steven's eyes, the uncertainty that gnawed at the edges of his mind. He wanted to believe in his innocence, to trust that the memory of his grandmother's death was nothing more than a twisted illusion.

"Today, I want us to try something different," I said, my voice gentle but firm. "Today, we're going to talk about your past before you took over the business."

Steven shifted in his seat, his eyes flickering with a mix of apprehension. And was that shame? This was about to be interesting.

I leaned forward, waiting for him to begin.

"I used to run with a group," Steven started, his voice low and hesitant. "We called ourselves 'The Misfits', stupid name. But then, we were stupid kids. We were a bunch of misfits, drawn together by our shared sense of rebellion and defiance. Or maybe they were. I was just being stupid."

I nodded encouragingly, urging him to continue.

"We used to hang out in abandoned buildings, graffiti-covered alleys, old malls, things like that. Anywhere we could escape the monotony of our lives," he continued, his gaze distant as if lost in memories. "We were young and foolish, chasing adrenaline highs and the thrill of breaking the rules. I, in particular, was rebelling against my grandmother, who was determined to shape me into something straight."

"Tell me about the others," I prompted gently, wanting to delve deeper into Steven's past.

Steven's eyes darkened slightly as he spoke of his former comrades.

"There was Jake, the charismatic leader of our group," he began, his voice tinged with admiration and resentment. "He had a way of making you believe that anything was possible, that the rules didn't apply to us."

I could sense the conflicting emotions in Steven's voice as he spoke of Jake. It was clear that their relationship was complicated; whatever had gone wrong probably had to do with Jake. Groups like these usually start out as a bunch of kids doing stupid things, but then one of them always gets involved with the wrong crowd, and soon, it's all of them—if they're stupid enough.

"There was Sarah. She was sensible. She never got into trouble with us. But there was Lily," he continued, a small smile tugging at the corners of his lips. She was the heart of our group, always looking out for everyone, always ready with a joke to lighten the mood. She was the funniest, prettiest woman you've ever seen."

I couldn't help but smile at the image of Lily, the glue that held 'The Misfits' together. Steven clearly had feelings for her.

"But things changed," Steven said, his voice growing somber. "We started getting into more dangerous activities, pushing the boundaries further and further. And it was always Jake starting it."

I leaned forward, my curiosity piqued. "What kind of activities?"

Steven hesitated for a moment, his eyes flickering with uncertainty. And then, with a deep breath, he spoke.

"We started getting involved in petty crimes," he admitted. " We broke into stores and buildings, stealing insignificant items—nothing too serious at first. I would feel guilty and leave some cash behind every time."

I listened in silence as Steven told me of their descent into the world of crime, the rush of adrenaline, and the thrill of danger.

"But then one night," Steven continued, his voice filled with regret, " we decided to break into a bigger store. Actually, Jake decided. Lily was high and agreed, so I followed Lily."

He laughed. He definitely still had feelings for her. "We thought it would be easy, that we could get in and out without anyone noticing," he said, his voice trembling with emotion. But things went wrong. Terribly wrong."

I could sense the guilt and remorse in Steven's voice as he spoke of that fateful night.

"What happened?" I asked softly, urging him to continue.

Steven took a deep breath, his hands trembling slightly. "We... we were inside the store, grabbing whatever we could. I kept telling Jake we should leave, but he yelled at me to keep stuffing the bag he brought. And then the alarm went off."

Even Gojo was listening now as if interested in the story.

"We panicked," he continued, "we tried to run, but the police were already outside. We were caught red-handed."

I listened in stunned silence as Steven recounted the events of that night, the fear and desperation palpable in his voice.

"We were arrested and charged with burglary and theft," Steven said, his voice filled with shame. "I... I couldn't believe it. I had never been in trouble with the law before."

I reached out to touch his hand, offering what little comfort I could.

"Thankfully, the store owner didn't press charges. My grandmother had intervened somehow. It was a wake-up call," Steven said, his voice growing stronger. "I realized that I needed to change, to leave that stupidity behind."

"I left 'The Misfits', determined to start anew," Steven said, his voice filled with resolve. "I went back to school, got my degree, and eventually took over my grandmother's business."

"You don't know anything about how the others turned out, do you?"

"Jake never stopped. Not until he'd been to jail and back."

"And Lily?"

"I haven't heard from her in a long time."

"You don't think, doc," Steven said, his voice growing troubled. "I can't help but wonder if my past has come back to haunt me. Jake always seemed to be oddly interested in my family's business. He had a thing for jewels."

"I doubt it."

It was highly unlikely.

Regardless, I decided to visit Steven's former comrades. It may have been nothing, and it most likely was, but I wanted to hear what his friends thought about Steven.

My first stop was Jake, the leader of 'The Misfits'. I heard he worked as a bartender at a dive bar on the outskirts of town. As I walked into the dimly lit establishment, stale beer and cigarette smoke filled my nostrils. Typical place for Jake.

The bar was sparsely populated, with a few patrons nursing their drinks in silence. Jake stood behind the bar, a rag in hand, wiping down the counter. His eyes flickered with recognition as I approached, and a small smirk played at the corners of his lips.

"Hey there, sweetheart," Jake said, his voice smooth and charming. "What can I get you?"

Yeah, keep trying. Not gonna work, but keep trying.

I smiled warmly, "Just a beer, thanks," I replied, taking a seat at the bar.

As Jake poured me a drink, I struck up a casual conversation about the city, asking about local attractions and places of interest. All the while, I watched him carefully, searching for any sign of recognition when I mentioned Mr. Patterson's name.

Jake was wearing a ring that was very obviously fake. Painted on silver and a fake emerald. But I nevertheless asked if he'd gotten it from one of the big stores. He lied and said yes. He's a big customer.

"Oh, you must know Mr. Patterson, then? He's the biggest dealer in this city, and that's what Tracy says anyway. She's kind of super obsessed with stones."

To my surprise, Jake's demeanor shifted slightly, a flicker of unease crossing his features. "Patterson?" he repeated, his voice guarded. "Can't say I know the guy."

I was willing to bet my money that Jake was still involved in crime.

I raised an eyebrow, feigning curiosity. "Really? I heard he was a big shot in the business world, dealing in jewelry and stones. That looks like something from one of his stores. You know, Tracy's dad, actually he's her stepdad, he's taking her shopping tomorrow. Actually, he won't be there, just her driver, but it's his credit card, so he's basically taking us shopping."

Jake shrugged nonchalantly, but I could sense the tension in the air. "Yeah, I guess I've heard the name around," he muttered, avoiding my gaze.

I pressed on, determined to get more information. "Really? You've met him?"

Jake's eyes narrowed slightly, a glint of suspicion in his gaze. "Why are you asking about Patterson?" he asked, his tone sharp.

I leaned in closer, lowering my voice conspiratorially. "I'm just curious, that's all. I heard he owns most of the jewelry stores in this city, and I wanted to know if the rumors were true. That's so boring, though."

Jake hesitated for a moment, weighing his options. And then, with a sigh, he leaned in closer. Really? Did he fall for it? I wasn't even convinced of my acting. "Alright, fine. Yeah, I know Patterson," he admitted, his voice barely above a whisper. "We... we used to do some business together."

My heart raced with excitement as I listened, eager to hear more. "Business? What kind of business?" I asked, my voice filled with curiosity.

Jake glanced around nervously before leaning in even closer. "Let's just say he's not exactly a Mr. Nice Guy," he whispered, his eyes darting around the room.

I leaned back, feigning shock. "Really? What kind of stuff was he involved in?"

Jake hesitated, clearly torn between revealing too much and holding back. "Just regular business, but he's a mean shark. I used to work for him."

"Really?" I gave him eyes and looked him over, lingering on his exposed tattoos. "I guess you're not a nice guy either."

"Oh yeah, darling, I'm a bad boy; you can call me a misfit."

I rolled my eyes internally. Of course. "You ever feel like you just don't fit anywhere?"

"Exactly!"

"See, that's why I come to bars like this. My friend, Tracy, she's in a club uptown, but it's so boring. I like edgy things." Jake was nearly drooling then; it was time to make my escape. I asked for another beer, and while Jake was gone, I went to my phone's settings and hovered my finger above the select ringtone button. Jake returned, and in three seconds, I pressed it.

The phone rang a sample of the tone, but that's all I needed. "Sorry, it's Tracy."

I faked a phone call, slammed a twenty on the table, and hurried out, screaming, "Oh my gosh, she drank too much again?"

As I left the bar, I couldn't help but feel a surge of excitement.

My next stop was Lily, the heart of 'The Misfits'. I had heard that she now worked as a waitress at a cafe in the city center. As I entered the bustling cafe, the aroma of freshly brewed coffee and baked goods enveloped me—heaven.

Lily greeted me with a warm smile, her eyes bright and welcoming. "Hi, what can I get you today?"

I smiled back, adopting the role of a curious journalist doing a piece on local businesses. "Just a coffee, please," I replied, taking a seat at one of the cozy tables.

As Lily poured me a steaming cup of coffee, I struck up a casual conversation about the cafe, asking about their specialties and popular menu items. All the while, I watched her carefully, searching for any sign of recognition when I mentioned Mr. Patterson's name in reference to the store I was looking at in the next street.

To my surprise, Lily's demeanor remained the same, "Patterson? Yeah, he owns the store." she repeated, her voice tinged with uncertainty. "Why do you ask?"

I sighed dramatically. "My brother has tasked me with finding the best ring to propose to his girlfriend with."

Lily nodded slowly, a smile on her face. A romantic. "Yeah, you'll find something nice in there. He's got stores all over London."

I briefly wondered about her and Steven.

I finished my coffee and left. Lily knew nothing.

My last stop was Sarah, the quiet and mysterious member of 'The Misfits.' The one even Jake had been protective of and never took on their thrill-seeking adventures. She now worked as a librarian downtown. As I entered the grand building, the smell of old books and dust filled my nostrils. Oh yeah, this is a place for my soul.

I couldn't decide which one I liked better, coffee or books.

Sarah greeted me with a polite smile, her eyes curious. "Hello, how can I help you today?"

I smiled back, adopting the role of a history enthusiast doing research on the city's past. "Just looking for some information on the city's history," I replied, taking a seat at one of the study tables.

As Sarah fetched a stack of old books for me again, I struck up a casual conversation about the library, asking about their rare collections and historical archives. I started talking about how my friends and I were book and history nerds, and we had regular meetups to discuss books and the like. The discussion lengthened, and we started exchanging stories about friends. She told me something of her old friends, giving a similar account to Steven's. She had apparently dated Jake until that night they'd gotten caught.

He'd tried to come back to her life with a jeweled ring as a present, but she could tell right away he'd stolen it. Jake had claimed he'd been given it by his new boss, Mr. Patterson. I asked if Jake might have visited others; perhaps he had a grudge against any of the others.

Sarah's eyes widened slightly, a flash of recognition crossing her features. "You... you mean with Steven?" she asked, her voice barely above a whisper.

"Why would he have a grudge against Steven? He sounds nice. A little like my cousin, though."

"Steven was a rich kid, and he was going to inherit some family business. Jake was always bothering him about it, to spend more. However, Steven, although he was as restless as the rest of them, was not quite stupid. Besides, have you seen that grandmother of his? Oof, she's scary—like a dragon."

"I like her."

"Yeah, she bailed them all out after that incident. We didn't see much of Steven after that. She cut off Jake's funding for weed and whatnot, which made him mad."

Interesting, I thought to myself. Here was a former friend with a thing for precious stones who was mad at Steven and had dealings with Mr. Patterson. Curiouser and curiouser.

The Unseen Threat

My hands trembled slightly as I gripped the steering wheel, the excitement of the revelations making me excited. Sarah's confession about the stolen ring and Mr. Patterson's possible connection to Jake was a bombshell. This may not be such a sinister plot after all; it may just be a petty vendetta. At least, that's what I was getting from Mr. Jorges' story.

Because I was still far from the truth, the image of Steven's face, etched with despair and confusion, haunted me. The thought of him being framed for a crime he didn't commit, his very life hanging in the balance, fueled my determination. I had to act swiftly, expose Mr. Patterson's web of lies, and clear Steven's name.

Reaching his shop, I found him pacing restlessly, a storm brewing in his eyes. The air crackled with tension as I entered.

"Steven," I began, my voice betraying a nervousness I tried to mask. "We need to talk."

He halted, his gaze searching mine. "Is it about the case? Did you find anything new?"

I hesitated; it was a delicate thing to tell him that his grandmother, both his grandparents, may have been involved with Patterson. The burden of a truth threatened to spill. Taking a deep breath, I decided honesty was the only course of action.

"Steven," I said, my voice softer now, "there's something you need to know. It's about Mr. Patterson and your family."

His eyes narrowed, a flicker of apprehension crossing his features. "What about him?"

"There's a connection, Steven. A deep-rooted one that goes back to your grandparents, but especially your grandmother." I braced myself for the impact as I revealed the truth I pieced together.

"Mr. Patterson," I continued, my voice an indistinct murmur, "was involved in a deal years ago. A deal that tarnished his reputation made him rich and, more importantly, entangled him with your grandmother, Henrietta Roseblood."

Steven stared at me, his face a mask of disbelief. "My grandmother? But how?"

I explained everything, the details I gleaned from Mr. Jorges. As I spoke, I saw the pieces click into place in his mind, and a horrifying realization dawned on him.

"He... he never let it go," Steven finally whispered, his voice hoarse. "He hates my grandparents for something."

"It appears that way," I said, my heart heavy with empathy. "His vendetta isn't just about business; it's personal. And he's using you, Steven, to exact his revenge."

Silence descended upon the room, thick and suffocating. Steven ran a hand through his hair, his face etched with a mixture of anger and despair.

"But why?" he finally asked, his voice barely a whisper. "What did my grandmother do that was so bad?"

I shook my head. "Besides rejecting his advances? That, I don't know yet. But uncovering the truth is paramount. We need to understand what transpired between Mr. Patterson and your grandmother all those years ago."

Steven's eyes lit up with rage. "I can't let him win, Dr. Jenson. We have to fight back."

I placed a hand on his shoulder, offering silent support. "We will, Steven. But we need to be strategic. Confronting him directly might be unwise."

"So, what do we do?" His voice held a hint of desperation.

"I have an idea," I said, my voice firming with resolve. "We dig deeper into Mr. Patterson's past and his connection with your grandparents. Perhaps the answers lie in those hidden bits of their life."

I had to dig deeper into the past, but how? One evening, after a particularly boring day, I found myself staying back in my office, staring at Steven's patient file. A thought struck me: a plan of action that might hold the key to unlocking the past.

Reaching for my phone, I dialed Steven's number.

"Dr. Jenson?" he answered, his voice weary.

"Steven," I began, taking a deep breath. "There's something I want to discuss. It might seem unconventional, but hear me out."

"What is it?" he asked, a hint of apprehension in his voice.

"We've been searching for answers in Mr. Patterson's past," I explained. "But what if the key lies closer to home? What if your grandmother..." I hesitated, searching for the right words.

"What if my grandmother what?" Steven prompted, his voice laced with curiosity.

"What if she documented something, some record of what transpired between her and Mr. Patterson?" I suggested, my voice tentative.

A long pause followed, filled with the crackle of the phone line. Then, a scoff escaped Steven's lips.

"Dr. Jenson, with all due respect, my grandmother wouldn't keep something like that lying around. Besides, I helped clean out her attic after she passed. There was nothing of the sort."

Disappointment washed over me, but I refused to give up. "Steven, I understand your skepticism. But sometimes, the most valuable information can be hidden in plain sight. Perhaps there were letters, old documents, anything that could shed light on their dealings."

"Honestly, Doc," he sighed, "there wouldn't be. My grandmother was a meticulous record keeper, but mostly for business purposes. Besides, even if there was something like I said, I would have found it."

The conversation reached an impasse. Steven's certainty was a formidable wall, yet I couldn't shake the feeling that there might be more to the story.

"Steven," I began cautiously, "think about it. Your grandmother was a shrewd businesswoman. Perhaps she anticipated something like this, some future conflict with Mr. Patterson. Maybe she left behind some kind of record, a safety net in case things went south."

Silence again, heavier this time. I could almost hear the wheels turning in his mind.

"Look," I continued, my voice gentle but firm. "I'm not asking you to ransack your entire house. But maybe, just maybe, there's a box tucked away in a corner, a forgotten file cabinet in the basement, something you might have overlooked. It wouldn't hurt to let me take a look."

Another pause, longer this time. Then, a reluctant sigh escaped Steven's lips.

"Alright, fine," he conceded. "...I'll glance around," Steven finished, his voice laced with a hint of defeat. "But I truly doubt there's anything to be found."

A sliver of hope flickered within me. "Thank you, Steven. Even a cursory look could prove invaluable."

The following days were a tense waiting game. Every fiber of my being yearned for Steven to call and report some hidden trove of documents, a missing puzzle piece in this complex equation.

Then, one afternoon, my phone rang. It was Steven, his voice tinged with a tremor of disbelief.

"Dr. Jenson," he stammered, "you won't believe this."

"What is it, Steven?" My heart pounded in my chest.

"I found something," he said, a hint of awe creeping into his voice. "In the attic, tucked away in an old trunk... there are letters. Letters from my grandmother to a man named Jorges. And some... legal documents."

A surge of excitement coursed through me. "Can you meet me at my office right away?" I asked, barely containing my eagerness.

"On my way," he replied, the phone clicking off.

Moments later, Steven burst into my office, a stack of aged papers clutched tightly in his hand. His eyes shone with a mixture of trepidation and a spark of newfound hope.

"These..." he began, his voice thick with emotion, "these are from my grandmother's time before she married grandpa. Now these are business letters, some personal letters addressed to Jorges, and some legal contracts. Many of them are dated after my grandpa died."

I carefully took the papers from him. "Let's see what we can find," I murmured, laying the documents on my desk.

The first few letters were filled with business talk. First, Akiva and Henrietta discussed potential acquisitions and market trends with a certain Jorges. However, as I went further, a shift in tone became apparent.

"Jorges," one letter read, the urgency apparent in the forceful strokes of the handwriting, "the situation with Mr. Patterson is untenable. His demands are outrageous, and I refuse to be bullied any further. We need a plan, a way to extricate ourselves from this mess."

Another letter, dated a few months later, hinted at a potential solution.

"I have secured the necessary evidence," Henrietta wrote. "Proof of Patterson's underhanded dealings. This should be enough to leverage a fair agreement and finally sever ties with him. I'll make sure he knows your continued safety is in his best interest."

The legal documents further solidified the narrative. One was a non-disclosure agreement, heavily redacted but clearly outlining a settlement between the involved parties. Another appeared to be a property transfer, a deed signed by Mr. Patterson relinquishing ownership of a specific asset. Frustratingly, they did not mention in detail what this asset was, but I could get a sense of how Patterson suddenly became rich. Such a crook.

"This is incredible," I breathed, my voice filled with a mixture of awe and trepidation. "These documents paint a very different picture."

Steven leaned closer, his eyes scanning the papers with newfound intensity. A flicker of understanding dawned on his face.

"So, Mr. Patterson wasn't just some disgruntled business partner," he stated, the realization settling in. "He was caught doing something wrong, and my grandmother had the proof."

"It appears that way," I concurred. "This changes everything. We have leverage now, a weapon to use against Patterson in his web of lies."

I could practically see a wave of new determination coursing through Steven. The defeated man I had spoken to days ago was replaced by a resolute individual, ready to fight for his future.

"We need to get this to the authorities," he declared, his voice firm. "This is evidence of Mr. Patterson's wrongdoings. He can't frame me anymore."

Relief washed over me. The truth, though buried for years, had finally surfaced. The road ahead wouldn't be easy, but with these newfound revelations, Steven had a fighting chance.

"We can't rush into this, Steven," I cautioned. "We need to present a solid case. These documents require careful analysis and verification of their authenticity. Involving a lawyer would be the most prudent course of action."

Steven nodded slowly, the fire in his eyes tempered by reason. "You're right. We need to be strategic."

After Steven left, the office fell into a hushed stillness. I sat at my desk, the stack of old papers scattered before me like pieces of a puzzle waiting to be solved. The fading light of the setting sun cast long shadows across the room, adding to the solemn atmosphere.

Gojo meowed from somewhere in the building. She was probably calling for me so we could go home. But I remained seated, looking at these bits of the past lives of four friends who had turned to foes.

As I sifted through the documents once more, my eyes caught on a different name. I reached for a particularly worn letter; its edges yellowed with age. The ink was faded, but the words were clear, detailing a business transaction between Henrietta and Patterson. Again, there was mention of a valuable asset, something that seemed to hold great importance to both parties.

My curiosity piqued, and I looked further into the papers. Carefully, I spread them out on the desk, each image a glimpse into the past. There, in the center of one photograph, stood Henrietta Roseblood, her eyes sparkling with steel. Beside her, the man I now recognized from the letters as Jorges, his expression grave and thoughtful.

In another picture, they were joined by a third figure—Mr. Patterson. His presence seemed to cast a shadow over the group, his eyes beady and calculating.

Turning back to the papers, I noticed a reference to a lawyer—a certain Mr. Brown. He had been involved in their business dealings until Jorges and Henrietta suddenly cut him off. There was nothing in the papers that mentioned him again; I just started seeing another attorney's name dealing with Mr. Jorges and Henri.

After gathering the papers and photographs, I planned to visit Mr. Brown to hear what he had to say.

"Gojo? Let's go grab dinner."

The streets were still bathed in the soft glow of streetlights as I made my way to Mr. Brown's office. The air was crisp with the promise of autumn, leaves crunching beneath my feet as I walked up the lane to the office. The lawyer's office was located in a quaint building on the outskirts of town, its exterior adorned with ivy crawling up the walls.

As I entered the building, the scent of old books and polished wood greeted me. The reception area was cozy, with plush armchairs and a mahogany desk where a middle-aged receptionist sat, typing away on her computer.

"Good morning," she greeted me with a warm smile. Do you have an appointment with Mr. Brown?" I had arrived very early—it was just 7 a.m.

I shook my head, flashing her my most charming smile. "No, I'm afraid not. I'm actually a journalist, doing a piece on local businesses and their histories. I was hoping to have a chat with Mr. Brown about his work with a client of his, a Mr. Gundel."

The receptionist nodded, her interest piqued. "I'll see if Mr. Brown is available. Please have a seat."

I settled into one of the armchairs, my heart pounding with anticipation. As I waited, I took in the surroundings—the walls lined with shelves of leather-bound books, the soft glow of a lamp casting a warm light over the room.

After a few minutes, a tall, distinguished man entered the room. Mr. Brown was in his late fifties, with silver hair and a sharp gaze that seemed to miss nothing. He wore a tailored suit that spoke of wealth and sophistication.

"Good morning, I'm Mr. Brown," he said, extending his hand with a polite smile. "How can I help you?"

I rose from my seat, shaking his hand firmly. "Fahey Colen," I introduced myself. "I'm an investigative journalist, currently working on a piece about the local business scene. I've heard some intriguing rumors about Mr. Gundel and his business dealings, and I was hoping you could shed some light on the matter. I gather you used to be his attorney."

Mr. Brown's expression remained neutral, though I detected a flicker of wariness in his eyes. "I see. What specifically would you like to know?"

I leaned forward, my voice dropping to a conspiratorial whisper. "Well, Mr. Gundel has been mentioned in connection with a rather... shall we say, murky business deal from the past. Something about a partnership gone wrong, allegations of underhanded tactics, that sort of thing."

Mr. Brown's brows furrowed slightly, but he maintained his composure. "I'm afraid I can't discuss the specifics of my client's cases. Attorney-client privilege, you understand."

I nodded, feigning understanding. "Of course, I completely respect that. But perhaps you could speak to Mr. Gundel's reputation in the business world? Was he known for taking risks, or perhaps engaging in ventures that were... less than above board?"

Mr. Brown hesitated for a moment, his gaze flickering to the window as if contemplating his response. "Mr. Gundel was a savvy businessman," he finally said, choosing his words carefully. "He was always looking for opportunities to expand his portfolio, sometimes taking on ventures that others might consider... unconventional."

I leaned in closer, my interest piqued. "Unconventional in what way, if I may ask?"

Mr. Brown sighed as if reluctant to divulge too much. "Oh, what the hell? The man is dead now, and he gave me a lot of grief. Let's just say he wasn't afraid to get his hands dirty. There were rumors of backdoor deals, secret partnerships, that sort of thing. But nothing was ever proven, of course."

I nodded, scribbling notes in my notebook. "And what about his relationship with a certain Mr. Patterson? I've heard they were once involved in a rather lucrative deal that went sour."

At the mention of Mr. Patterson's name, Mr. Brown's demeanor shifted imperceptibly. "Ah, yes, Mr. Patterson," he said, his tone guarded. He and Mr. Gundel did have some business dealings in the past—a partnership that seemed promising at first, but... well, things took a turn."

My heart quickened at the mention of their partnership. "Could you elaborate on that? What exactly went wrong?"

Mr. Brown hesitated, his eyes avoiding mine. "I'm afraid I can't go into details. It's a sensitive matter, you understand."

I pressed on, determined to extract any information I could. "But surely, as a respected lawyer and the attorney acting as a go-between, you must have some insight into the nature of their business relationship. Was Mr. Patterson known for his... aggressive tactics, perhaps?"

Mr. Brown sighed, rubbing his temples as if weary from the conversation. "Look, Miss Colen, I understand your curiosity. But I can't speak ill of my clients. It's not my place."

I leaned back in my chair, studying him carefully. "I appreciate your discretion, Mr. Brown. But surely you can understand the importance of uncovering the truth, especially when it comes to matters of public interest."

He met my gaze, his eyes hardening with resolve. "I'm sorry, Ms., I've said all I can on the matter. Now, if you'll excuse me, I have clients to attend to, and I must prepare for them."

I nodded, hiding my disappointment behind a polite smile. "Of course, Mr. Brown. Thank you for your time."

I walked back to my car, thinking about what Mr. Brown had said and what he hadn't said.

I returned to my office, my mind buzzing with thoughts and the encounter with Mr. Brown lingering in my mind. There was a palpable tension in the air as if the very walls of the room were whispering secrets that I had yet to uncover.

As I stepped into the office, my receptionist, Andrea, greeted me with a smile that seemed a touch forced. Something about her demeanor seemed off, but I couldn't quite put my finger on it. She handed me a small package wrapped in plain brown paper.

"Dr. Jenson, this arrived for you earlier," she said, her voice cheerful but lacking its usual life. "I signed for it, I hope that's okay."

I took the package, noting the lack of a return address or any indication of its sender. The only thing adorning the front was my name, written in neat, block letters.

"Thank you, Andrea," I said, offering her a smile in return. "Is everything alright? You seem a bit... distracted."

Her smile faltered for a moment before she quickly masked it with a shake of her head. "Oh, it's nothing, just a busy day. You know how it is."

I nodded, though a nagging feeling of unease settled in the pit of my stomach. "Well, thank you for handling this. I'll take a look at it."

As Andrea busied herself with some paperwork, I settled at my desk and carefully unwrapped the package. Inside, nestled among layers of tissue paper, was a small, ornate box. It was exquisitely crafted, with intricate designs etched into the silver surface.

Curiosity piqued, I opened the box to find a single piece of paper folded neatly in half. I unfolded it, revealing a message written in elegant script:

"Curiosity killed the cat, Ms. Olivia Jenson. Be careful where it leads you."

A chill ran down my spine as I read the ominous words. Who could have sent this? And what di–before I could ponder further, the shrill ring of the phone broke the silence of the office. I picked it up, my heart still pounding from the unsettling message.

"Andrea," I answered, trying to keep my voice steady.

"Dr. Jenson, I... I just wanted to let you know that we have a new appointment scheduled for Friday at 2 PM."

"Oh? Who is it for?"

"It's for a Mr. Timothy Patterson," Andrea replied.

My blood ran cold at the mention of the name. What was he doing scheduling an appointment at my office?

"Are you sure about the name, Andrea?" I asked, my voice barely above a whisper.

There was a brief pause on the other end of the line before Andrea replied, her voice scornful. "Yes, Dr. Jenson. Mr. Timothy Patterson. The appointment is confirmed. Do you wish me to cancel it?"

"No. Friday then."

I thanked her and hung up the phone, my mind racing with possibilities.

The day of Mr. Timothy Patterson's appointment arrived with heavy anticipation. Every passing minute felt like an eternity as I sat in my office, my mind consumed with thoughts of what Patterson was going to say.

When Mr. Patterson finally arrived, my heart skipped a beat as he stepped through the door. He was impeccably dressed, exuding an air of confidence that sent a shiver down my spine. His gaze swept over the room, lingering on me for a moment before settling into the chair across from my desk.

Mr. Timothy Patterson was a man of imposing stature, a figure that seemed to fill the room with his mere presence. His frame was not one of athleticism or grace but rather of excess and opulence. He indulged in the pleasures of life without restraint, and it showed in every inch of his corpulent form.

His face was round and pudgy, with small, calculating eyes that seemed to miss nothing. Thick jowls framed a mouth that was perpetually set in a smug smirk as if he knew some secret that the rest of the world was not privy to. His chin disappeared into the folds of his neck, a testament to years of unchecked indulgence.

Mr. Patterson's attire only accentuated his larger-than-life presence. He favored expensive suits tailored to accommodate his generous girth yet somehow always managed to look slightly disheveled. His ties were always silk, adorned with ostentatious patterns that spoke of wealth and power. As he moved, it was with a slow, deliberate grace, as if every step was a calculated display of his dominance. He exuded an aura of authority, a man accustomed to getting what he wanted without question.

Despite his formidable appearance, there was an unsettling charm about Mr. Patterson. His voice was smooth and honeyed, with a hint of a cultured accent that spoke of privilege. He had a way of speaking that drew people in, a subtle manipulation that left them hanging on his every word. But beneath that charm lay a darkness, a ruthlessness that lurked just beneath the surface. It was in the way his eyes would narrow imperceptibly when he spoke of his past, a fleeting glimpse of the true nature hidden behind his facade.

"Good afternoon, Dr. Jenson," he greeted, his voice smooth and controlled.

"Good afternoon, Mr. Patterson," I replied, my voice steady despite the unease coursing through me. "Please, have a seat.

As the session began, Mr. Patterson said nothing about my investigation into his past. Instead, he spoke at length about his mental health, detailing his struggles with anxiety and stress. I listened intently, every fiber of my being on high alert for any hint of malice or deception. As the session progressed, it became clear that Mr. Patterson was genuinely seeking help. He spoke of his fears and insecurities, his vulnerabilities laid bare before me. He was playing a different game here.

Still, I couldn't shake the feeling of fear that lingered in the air. Finally, the session came to an end, and Mr. Patterson stood to leave after giving Gojo one last pat. My heart raced as I watched him, waiting for some sign of the danger I was convinced lurked beneath the surface.

To my surprise, he simply thanked me for the session, his expression unreadable. "Thank you, Dr. Jenson," he said, his voice cordial. "I appreciate your time. I will return next week."

"You're welcome, Mr. Patterson," I replied, my voice tight with tension.

As he turned to leave, Andrea, my receptionist, greeted him with a warm smile. "Have a nice weekend, Mr. Patterson," she said, her voice cheerful.

Mr. Patterson paused, his gaze flickering over Andrea for a moment before a paternal smile crossed his lips. "And you too, Miss," he said, his voice softening. "You're such a nice lady and pretty, too. Take care of yourself, my dear. I would be very sad if anything happened to you."

The hairs on the back of my neck stood on end as I watched him leave, his words echoing ominously in the air. It was a subtle warning disguised as a well-wish.

The ringing of my phone shattered the silence of the morning, the shrill sound cutting through the air like a knife. I picked it up with a sense of unease, a feeling of impending dread settling over me like a heavy shroud.

"Dr. Jenson," Andrea's voice came through the line, thick with tears and barely contained anguish.

"Andrea, what's wrong?" I asked, my heart pounding in my chest.

"I... I won't be able to make it to work for a while," she choked out, her voice trembling with emotion.

"Why? What's happened?" I pressed, my concern growing with each passing moment.

There was a long pause, the silence on the other end of the line heavy with unspoken grief. Then, in a voice barely above a whisper, Andrea spoke.

"They... they found them," she managed to say, the words coming out in a choked sob.

"Found who, Andrea? What's going on?" I urged, my heart clenching in my chest.

"My... my fiancé, Gary, and... and my friend, Lisa," she struggled to say, the weight of her words almost too much to bear. "They were... they were found dead."

The world seemed to stop spinning as her words sank in, a cold dread settling in the pit of my stomach.

"Oh, Andrea," I murmured, my voice filled with genuine sorrow. "I'm so sorry. What... what happened?"

"They were... they were at our apartment," Andrea's voice cracked, tears flowing freely now. I was... I was babysitting for my sister. They were supposed to just hang out and watch some movies. But... but someone broke in."

The horror of the situation unfolded before me, the image of Andrea's beloved fiancé and her friend lying lifeless in their own home. I could hear the pain in her voice, the rawness of her grief threatening to consume her.

"There... there was a struggle," Andrea continued, her voice trembling with emotion. "They... they were found... naked. And... and there was a condom still on Gary..."

The words hung in the air, heavy and suffocating. My mind reeled at the implications, the sheer brutality of what Andrea was telling me.

"Oh, Andrea," I whispered, my voice thick with emotion. "I can't even begin to imagine..."

"They were... they were cheating on me," Andrea's voice broke, a gut-wrenching sob escaping her lips. "How could they... how could they do this to me?"

Tears streamed down my own cheeks as I listened to Andrea's heart-wrenching pain. The betrayal, the loss, the sheer injustice of it all was almost too much to bear.

"Andrea, I... I don't know what to say," I struggled to find the right words, anything to offer her even a sliver of comfort. "I'm here for you. Whatever you need, I'm here."

"I... I don't know what to do," Andrea's voice was a broken whisper. "I can't go stay in the apartment. I can't... I can't bear to see..."

"Take all the time you need, Andrea," I said, my voice gentle and soothing. "Don't worry about work. Just focus on taking care of yourself right now."

"Thank you, Dr. Jenson," Andrea's voice was barely audible now, the weight of her grief pressing down on her like a suffocating blanket.

"Call me anytime, Andrea," I reassured her, my heart aching for her pain. "I'm here for you."

A Dangerous Alliance

I threw on a sweatshirt and sweatpants and rushed out of my home, yelling to my cat that I would be back later. I quickly filled her bowl on my way out. On my way to Andrea's apartment, my heart was pounding in my chest, and dread lay heavy on my shoulders.

The drive to her place felt agonizingly long, each passing moment filled with a sense of urgency and apprehension. When I arrived, Andrea's sister met me at the door, her eyes red and swollen from tears. I had to pass the police, who had been called to the scene. The police were crawling about the room, looking for clues.

"Dr. Jenson, thank you for coming," she said, her voice trembling with emotion.

"Of course," I replied, offering her a reassuring squeeze on the shoulder. "How... how is Andrea holding up?"

Her sister's eyes welled up with fresh tears, and she shook her head, unable to speak. Without another word, she led me inside.

Inside the apartment, it was eerily quiet, the air heavy with the weight of grief and loss. Andrea sat on the couch, her head buried in her hands, her body shaking with silent sobs. My heart broke for her, the depth of her pain palpable in the air. The place had been trashed a little from the break-in, and I could see some bloodstains on the living room floor. And a pair of panties, which Lisa obviously discarded.

"Andrea," I said softly, approaching her with a gentle touch on her shoulder. "I'm here for you. Whatever you need, I'm here."

She looked up at me with tear-filled eyes, her expression a mix of anguish and disbelief. Without a word, she reached out and clutched onto me, her grip tight and desperate.

I held her close, offering what little comfort I could in the face of such devastating loss. We sat like that for what felt like an eternity; the only sound in the room was the quiet hitching of Andrea's breath. After a while, Andrea's sister joined us; together, we sat in silence, each lost in our own thoughts and grief.

As I comforted Andrea, my eyes scanned the room, searching for any sign of anything that could tell me who had done it and if that person was Patterson or sent by him. As it occurred to me, Patterson had intended the attack to be on Andrea to get to me, but she had been babysitting at the time, and her cheating partner had been caught instead.

Tears streamed down Andrea's cheeks as she reached out a trembling hand towards the photograph of herself, Gary, Lisa, and two other friends on the mantle. "How... how could they do this to me?" she whispered, her voice filled with pain and betrayal.

As Andrea was taken aside by one of the detectives, I saw an opportunity to slip away unnoticed. I made my way back to the room where Gary and Lisa's bodies lay. My heart pounded in my chest as I approached the bodies. I could feel the physical presence of death in this room. Gary lay sprawled on the floor, his eyes wide open in a frozen stare of terror; his member was still wrapped. Lisa was nearby, her body contorted in a grotesque twist of agony. The sight was enough to make my stomach churn, but I pushed aside the wave of nausea that threatened to overwhelm me.

Bending down beside Lisa's body, I carefully examined her hands. There, under her nails, I found what I was looking for - flecks of skin and dried blood. My hands trembled as I reached for a small, clear bag in my pocket, intending to collect a sample. But before I could do so, a voice behind me made me freeze.

"What do you think you're doing?"

I turned slowly to see the detective in charge, his expression stern and suspicious. Panic surged through me as I tried to think of a plausible excuse.

"I... I was just..." I stammered, my mind racing for a believable explanation.

The detective's eyes narrowed, his gaze fixed on the evidence bag in my hand. "Don't move," he ordered his voice firm.

With a sinking feeling in my chest, I knew I had been caught. The detective approached, his footsteps echoing in the silent room.

"What exactly are you doing?" Detective Reynolds's voice was firm, and his eyes pierced mine with suspicion.

"I... I was just trying to gather evidence," I stammered, my mind racing for a plausible explanation. "I believe there might be more to their deaths than meets the eye." I was still bent over Lisa's body.

His eyebrows furrowed in disbelief. "And you thought it was a good idea to tamper with a crime scene?" His tone was incredulous, and I could feel the righteous anger.

"I... I didn't mean to tamper," I protested. "I was trying to help, to find out what happened to them."

Detective Reynolds's expression hardened, his features set in a stern mask. "You realize this is a crime scene? Touching anything without authorization is a serious offense."

"I know, I know," I said quickly, "But I had to see for myself. I found skin and blood under Lisa's nails. It could be from their attacker, a clue to their killer's identity."

Detective Reynolds's gaze shifted to the evidence bag in my hand, his expression unreadable. "That may be," he said finally, his voice measured. "But that doesn't excuse your actions. We have protocols in place for a reason."

"I understand," I said, my voice barely audible. "I just... I wanted to help."

"You could have compromised the evidence," Detective Reynolds said sternly, his tone brooking no argument. "You're lucky I didn't arrest you on the spot."

"I'm sorry," I said, my voice barely a whisper. "I just... I wanted to find out the truth."

Detective Reynolds regarded me for a long moment, "Well, now you'll have to explain yourself down at the station," he said finally.

My heart skipped a beat at his words, "Please," I pleaded, desperation creeping into my voice. "I was just trying to help. I'll do whatever you ask, just... please understand."

But Detective Reynolds was unmoved, his expression hard as he gestured towards the door. "Let's go, Dr. Jenson. We have a lot to discuss."

I was led out of the room. Outside, Andrea was waiting, her eyes wide with shock and disbelief. "Olivia, what's going on?" she asked, her voice trembling.

"I... I'll explain later," I all but whispered. "I just... I'm sorry."

"She was found with the bodies," Reynolds said. That sounded worse than what I had actually done, and everyone took it that way, judging by the number of heads that turned to me.

Andrea's expression immediately turned to anger and betrayal. "Sorry? Sorry, that doesn't cut it, Olivia," she said, her voice filled with hurt. "You've always been a creep. I always felt you were creepy, always talking to your cat, but this? I will not be returning to work. Find yourself a new receptionist."

"I was just trying to help," I protested, feeling the weight of guilt and responsibility settle heavily on my shoulders.

"Help?" Andrea's voice rose in amazement. "You call this help? Look at what you've done!"

Tears welled up in my eyes as I looked at Andrea, the weight of her words hitting me like a physical blow. "I... I know," I said, my tears streaming down my cheeks. "I'll make it right, I promise." Andrea shook her head, her expression hard.

"No, Olivia," she said firmly. "I don't want to hear it. You've crossed a line."

As the police car rumbled along the darkened streets towards the station, I couldn't shake the sense of dread that gnawed at my insides. I had crossed a line, but I also knew that I couldn't undo what had been done.

With Andrea's words echoing in my mind, I realized the gravity of the situation. My investigation and behavior today had not only jeopardized my career but also resulted in the tragic deaths of Gary and Lisa. The guilt weighed heavily on my conscience, a constant reminder of the consequences of my actions.

As we neared the police station, I made a decision. I needed help and expert advice to navigate this dangerous terrain. But who could I trust? Who would believe my story, despite the damning evidence against Steven? A risky idea began to form in my mind, a gamble that could either save me or seal my fate. I knew I had to take the chance.

Once inside the station, I was escorted to a small interrogation room. Detective Reynolds sat across from me, his expression stern and unwavering. His gaze bore down on me.

"Dr. Jenson," he began, his voice serious. "You are aware of the severity of the charges against you?"

I nodded, my throat dry with apprehension. "Yes, Detective. I understand."

He leaned forward, his eyes searching mine. "Then explain to me, in detail, exactly what happened tonight."

Taking a deep breath, I launched into my account of the events at Andrea's apartment. But Detective Reynolds remained unmoved, his expression cold and calculating. "Tampering with evidence is a serious offense, Dr. Jenson,"

"Detective," I said, my voice trembling slightly. "There is more to this than meets the eye. I... I need your help."

He raised an eyebrow, skeptical. "Help? What kind of help?"

I hesitated, knowing that what I was about to say could either save me or damn me further. "I need your expertise, Detective," I said finally. "But not here, not officially."

His brow furrowed in confusion. "What do you mean, not officially?"

"I mean," I said in a low voice, "that I need you to interrogate me alone, off the record. And I'll tell you everything."

Detective Reynolds regarded me for a long moment, his gaze piercing. "And why should I do that?" he asked, his tone guarded.

"Because," I said, my voice steady despite the turmoil within me, "I have information that could help you solve a case—a case that is much bigger than this."

His eyes narrowed in suspicion. "What case?"

I took a deep breath, steeling myself for what was to come. "The case of Timothy Patterson," I said, watching his reaction carefully.

Detective Reynolds's eyes widened in surprise, a flicker of interest crossing his features. "Patterson? What does he have to do with any of this?"

"Everything," I said, my voice low and urgent. "He's the key to everything that's been happening."

He agreed, and I proceeded to tell him about Steven's case. At first, Detective Reynolds was skeptical, and his disbelief was evident in his expression. But as I laid out the facts before him, his demeanor began to change. A furrow appeared between his brows, his lips pressed into a thin line.

"This... this is quite a lot to take in, Dr. Jenson," he said finally, his voice measured. "Are you sure about all of this?"

I nodded. "Yes, Detective. I'm sure."

He leaned back in his chair, his gaze fixed on me intently. "And what about this warning you mentioned? From Patterson himself?"

I recounted the encounter with Patterson after his therapy session, the subtle threat in his words sending a chill down my spine.

Detective Reynolds listened intently, his expression unreadable. "This... changes things," he said finally, his voice low.

"I know," I said, "But we need to act fast. Patterson is dangerous, and I fear for Steven's safety."

Detective Reynolds nodded, a grim determination settling over his features. "I'll need to verify this information," he said, his tone firm. "But if what you're saying is true..."

"It is," I interjected, my voice urgent. "Please, Detective. Steven needs your help."

He regarded me for a long moment, weighing his options. Finally, he nodded. "Alright, Dr. Jenson. I'll do as you ask. But this stays between us, understood?"

I nodded, a wave of relief washing over me. "Thank you, Detective. Thank you."

After I laid out all the evidence and details surrounding Timothy Patterson's involvement in the tangled web of deceit, Detective Reynolds sat back in his chair, a thoughtful expression crossing his features. I could see the wheels turning in his mind, weighing the gravity of the situation against the evidence I had presented.

"This is a lot to take in, Dr. Jenson," he finally spoke, his voice grave. "But I need to make one thing clear. This homicide case is my priority."

I nodded. "Of course, Detective. I understand."

He leaned forward, his gaze intense. "However, I do believe there is merit to your claims. If what you're saying is true, then Patterson is involved in something much larger than we anticipated."

I held my breath, waiting for his decision.

"I'll need some time to verify the evidence you've provided," Detective Reynolds continued, his voice measured. "But I'll do it off the record, as you requested."

Relief flooded me, mixing with gratitude. "Thank you, Detective. Thank you for giving this a chance."

"But," he continued, holding up a finger, "this doesn't mean you're off the hook. You'll still need to cooperate fully with the investigation, and you'll be under strict supervision."

"I understand," I said, nodding eagerly. "I'll do whatever it takes to help."

Detective Reynolds stood from his chair and said, "Alright then. I'll need you to come down to the station tomorrow morning to give a formal statement. And in the meantime, stay out of trouble."

"I will," I promised.

As Detective Reynolds led me out of the interrogation room, we were met by a group of his colleagues. Their expressions ranged from curiosity to suspicion as they examined me.

"What's going on, Reynolds?" one of them asked, a note of skepticism in his voice.

Detective Reynolds cleared his throat, his gaze steady. "This is Dr. Olivia Jenson," he began, gesturing towards me. "She's just a civilian with a morbid interest in crimes. I've decided to let her go for now."

The skepticism in the room was thick, and I could feel their eyes boring into me.

"I'll vouch for her," he said, meeting each of their gazes in turn. "But let's keep an eye on her, just in case." There was a moment of tense silence before his colleagues finally relented, nodding in reluctant agreement.

"Alright, Reynolds," one of them said, his tone begrudging. "But if anything goes wrong, it's on you."

Detective Reynolds nodded, his expression resolute. "Understood."

With that, he escorted me out of the station, the weight of the evening's events still heavy on my shoulders. But for the first time since this nightmare began, I felt a glimmer of hope.

As we stepped out into the cool night air, Detective Reynolds turned to me, his gaze intense.

"We have a lot of work to do, Dr. Jenson," he said, determined.

After the tumultuous events of the previous days, Detective Reynolds and I met at my office to discuss Timothy Patterson and his nefarious activities. Steven, understandably anxious and eager for answers, was also present, ready to retell his story.

The atmosphere in the room was tense as we gathered around my desk; the evidence spread out before us like pieces of a dark puzzle waiting to be solved. Detective Reynolds took a moment to glance over the documents I had gathered, his brow furrowing in concentration.

"Alright, let's start from the beginning," Detective Reynolds began, his voice commanding attention. "Steven, I'd like you to tell me everything you know about your grandmother's dealings with Mr. Patterson."

Steven took a deep breath, "Nothing, actually."

It was I then who he turned to. As Steven spoke, I watched Detective Reynolds closely, noting the subtle shifts in his expression. He listened intently, occasionally nodding for me to continue or asking clarifying questions.

Detective Reynolds leaned forward, his eyes focused. "And what about you, Steven? Did Mr. Patterson ever approach you directly?"

Steven shook his head, a frown creasing his brow. "No, not directly. Not until recently did he seem interested in our family's business. Especially the jewelry aspect."

Detective Reynolds turned his attention back to the documents, his expression thoughtful. "And what about the incident with 'The Misfits'?" he asked, referring to the night that had changed everything for Steven and his friends.

Steven hesitated, the memories of that fateful night still fresh in his mind. "It was a mistake," he said, his voice filled with regret. "We were young, reckless... and Jake's obsession with my family's wealth didn't help."

I could see the pain in Steven's eyes as he recounted the events of that night, his friend's betrayal, and the rift it had caused them.

Detective Reynolds listened silently, absorbing every detail. "And do you believe Mr. Patterson had a hand in this?" he asked, his voice low and measured.

Steven shrugged a helpless gesture. "I can't say for sure," he admitted. "But it wouldn't surprise me. Jake seems to have a connection to him after we drifted apart."

Detective Reynolds turned to me, his gaze piercing. "I'll need your full cooperation on this, Dr. Jenson. We're entering dangerous territory, and I can't guarantee your safety."

I met his gaze, my determination matching his. "I understand, Detective. I'll do whatever it takes to bring Mr. Patterson to justice."

Detective Reynolds turned to me with a serious expression. "Dr. Jenson, I need your professional opinion on Timothy Patterson," he began, his gaze piercing. "Based on everything we've uncovered, what kind of man are we dealing with here?"

I took a moment to gather my thoughts, considering everything I had learned about Mr. Patterson's actions and motivations.

"Well, from what we know," I started, my voice measured, "Mr. Patterson exhibits traits of narcissism and a deep-seated need for control. He thrives on power and manipulation, using others as pawns in his game."

Detective Reynolds nodded, his brow furrowing in concentration. "Go on."

"He also displays a lack of empathy," I continued, my mind racing as I constructed a profile of the man. "His actions, especially towards those who oppose him, show a callous disregard for human life. He sees others as tools to be used and discarded at will."

"Sounds like a dangerous man," Detective Reynolds muttered, jotting down notes as I spoke.

"He is," I affirmed, my voice firm. "But there's more to it than just a thirst for power. Mr. Patterson's need for control stems from a deep-seated insecurity, a fear of losing everything he has built."

Detective Reynolds raised an eyebrow, intrigued. "So, you're saying he's driven by fear?"

"Yes," I confirmed, leaning forward in my chair. "Fear of failure, fear of being exposed for the fraud he truly is. His recent actions are a desperate attempt to maintain the illusion of success and power."

The detective absorbed my words, his expression thoughtful. "And what about the crime scene?" he asked, changing the subject slightly. "What can you tell me about what you saw?"

I closed my eyes, the images of the gruesome scene flashing behind my eyelids. "It was a brutal attack," I began, my voice faltering slightly. "There were signs of a struggle, defensive wounds on the victims' bodies."

The detective leaned back in his chair, a deep frown marring his features. "This was a targeted attack," he said, more to himself than to me. "But why? What was the motive?"

I pondered the question, my mind racing through the possibilities. "It was to be a warning," I suggested, the pieces clicking into place. "A message to me"

Detective Reynolds nodded slowly, the pieces of the puzzle coming together in his mind. "So, we're dealing with a man who will stop at nothing to protect his secrets," he concluded, his voice grim.

"Yes."

The Ticking Clock

I swirled the ice in my lukewarm coffee, the clinking seeming to echo in my ears. Detective Reynolds, his brow furrowed in concentration, let out a low whistle as he turned the page of the crime scene photos.

"Interesting contusion on the back of the man's head," he muttered, his voice barely above a whisper. "Blunt force trauma, most likely delivered from behind. Suggests the attacker might have surprised him."

I leaned in, peering at the close-up shot. A dark bruise marred the otherwise pale skin, its jagged edges hinting at a rough, uneven object used as a weapon.

"Could it be the same object used to subdue the woman?" I questioned, the thought sending a shiver down my spine.

Reynolds nodded slowly. "The possibility exists. The lack of any murder weapon at the scene points towards something readily available, something the attacker could have easily concealed."

He tapped a finger on the photo, his eyes narrowing. "Another detail—the woman's purse is open, yet nothing seems to be missing. Doesn't strike me as a robbery gone wrong."

"True," I concurred. "The brutality of the attack suggests something more personal, a motive fueled by rage or vengeance."

"Envy, lover's spat."

"Or a paid hit," I said. A beat of silence followed, thick with meaning.

"There's something else," Reynolds spoke. He flipped to the final page of the photo set, revealing a close-up of a small, silver object clutched tightly in the woman's hand.

Before he could continue, my phone buzzed on the desk, startling us both. I glanced at the caller ID and saw Steven's name flashing on the screen.

"Excuse me," I said to the detective, stepping away to answer the call. "Steven, what's wrong?"

"Olivia, something's come up," Steven's voice sounded urgent on the other end of the line. "I need to talk to you right away."

I furrowed my brow, concern washing over me. "Where are you?"

"At the coffee shop down the street from your office," he replied. "Please, it's important."

I glanced at Detective Reynolds before nodding to myself. "I'll be there soon," I said into the phone before ending the call.

Returning to the detective's side, I explained the situation. "Steven needs to see us right away. He's at the coffee shop down the street."

Detective Reynolds nodded, his eyes serious. "Let's go. We can discuss the rest on the way."

We hurried to the coffee shop, which was just a short walk away. As we entered the bustling cafe, I spotted Steven sitting at a corner table, his expression grave. He stood up as we approached, a sense of urgency in his very steps. The aroma of freshly brewed coffee filled the air as we gathered around the small table in the corner of the cozy coffee shop. The place was bustling with activity, and the sound of chatter and the clinking of cups created a comforting background hum. I took a sip of my steaming latte, the warmth seeping into my bones as I listened intently to Steven's story. He unfolded the letter with trembling hands, the paper crinkling softly under his touch.

"It arrived in the mail yesterday," Steven explained, his voice filled with a mixture of confusion and fear. "No return address, just a message about one of my older clients."

I leaned forward, studying the letter with furrowed brows. It detailed the life of one of Steven's previous clients, a man named Robert Simmons. The obituary mentioned his sudden and mysterious death, with the date of the murder listed as two weeks from the sending date of the letter.

"This is... unsettling," I murmured, my mind racing with possibilities. "Why would someone send you this?"

Steven shook his head, his eyes wide with disbelief. "I have no idea. Robert was a difficult client, but I never imagined..."

Detective Reynolds, seated across from us, listened intently. He was a sturdy man with a no-nonsense demeanor, his sharp eyes taking in every detail of our conversation.

"What was your relationship with Robert Simmons?" the detective asked, his voice gruff but not unkind.

Steven sighed, running a hand through his hair. "He was a client of mine a few years back. Troubled, to say the least. He had a history of divorce, but nothing that would suggest..."

I glanced around the coffee shop, taking in the warm, inviting atmosphere. The soft glow of the overhead lights cast a comforting aura over our table, providing a brief respite from the darkness of our conversation.

"Let's go over everything you know," Detective Reynolds suggested, his eyes meeting mine. "Starting with Mr. Patterson."

I nodded, setting my latte aside and pulling out the documents we had gathered. Steven laid out the letter detailing Robert Simmons' death, his hands trembling slightly.

"We know Mr. Patterson is behind the attack on Steven," I began, "But we need to clearly understand his motives. This sounds a lot more serious than just him wanting your business. And now, this letter..."

"It's a deadline. If you don't give him what he wants, he kills the man."

The detective's expression darkened, his jaw clenched in frustration. "He could easily incriminate Steven," he finished, his voice heavy with concern.

Silence. I glanced around the coffee shop, the soft murmur of conversation providing a backdrop to our tense discussion.

"We need to stay one step ahead of Patterson," I said, breaking the silence. And we need to be prepared for whatever he throws at us."

Steven nodded, his eyes determined. "Agreed. But what about this letter?"

The detective leaned forward in his chair, his expression thoughtful. "We need to prevent Robert Simmons' death," he said, his voice firm.

Detective Reynolds laid out the results of the forensic analysis on the small table of the coffee shop.

"These are the prints we found at the crime scene," the detective began, pointing to the images on his tablet. "They belong to the deceased, Andrea, as well as one Jake Hail."

Steven clenched his jaw, his fists tightening around his coffee cup. "Jake," he muttered, the name dripping with disdain.

"You know him?" Reynolds asked.

"Old friend, we are no longer in contact."

"I should hope so. He's been in jail for robbery and assault."

I leaned forward, studying the prints on the screen. "And Andrea's prints?" I asked, my voice steady.

The detective shook his head. "We ruled out Andrea. She had an alibi for the entire night of the murder."

I breathed a sigh of relief, grateful that Andrea was not a suspect. I knew she couldn't do it, but there was a niggling doubt, and she had plenty of motive. "What about the DNA samples?" I inquired, already anticipating the answer.

The detective's expression darkened. "We're still waiting on the results, but I can bet they'll match with Jake's."

Steven's eyes flashed with anger; his voice edged with frustration. "So, it was him. Jake killed them."

Detective Reynolds nodded, his gaze serious. "It seems that way, which brings us to the next step. Finding and arresting him."

I looked up, meeting the detective's eyes. "I would like to ask Jake a few questions," I said, my voice firm.

The detective hesitated, his brow furrowing in thought. "That's... unorthodox," he admitted. "But given the circumstances, I suppose it can be arranged."

Steven's gaze turned to me, and his eyes were filled with hope and desperation. "Please, Olivia," he pleaded. We need to know why he did it."

I gave a nod, my determination intensifying. "I promise to keep it short," I told him. "But we need to understand his motives."

"He was most likely hired help; this reeks of Patterson."

Rubbing his hand through his hair, the detective sighed. He gave in and said, "Okay." "I'll arrange for you to speak with Jake. However, I will be present in case."

As we packed up our things and left the coffee shop, the city bustled around us, completely unaware of the seriousness of our situation.

"I will notify you as soon as the bastard is taken into custody." Detective Reynolds said.

I nodded, feeling a surge of thankfulness within. "Thank you, Detective. We appreciate your help."

He acknowledged with a nod of his head and turned to leave.

Steven looked up at me, his gaze sweeping over mine. His voice was full of emotion as he said, "Thank you, Olivia. For everything."

I touched his shoulder, providing reassuring support without words. "We'll get through this," I assured him, my voice steady.

Steven nodded once more and moved away in the other direction. Even though I was by myself on the pavement, my distaste for Jake persisted. For Steven, the man had been a friend for a very long time, but in an instant, he became an enemy.

Trail of Deception

Detective Reynolds' call came in the late afternoon, pulling me away from the stack of paperwork on my desk. His voice was brisk and to the point.

"Dr. Jenson, we need you down at the station. There's been a development."

I grabbed my coat, heart racing with anticipation and dread. The drive to the station was a blur of thoughts, each one racing through my mind in a dizzying whirl.

When I arrived, Detective Reynolds was waiting for me, his expression grave. He wasted no time in getting to the point.

"I can only allow you to watch the interrogation," he explained, leading me down the dimly lit hallway towards the interrogation room.

I nodded, the gravity of the situation settling heavily in my chest. As we entered the observation room, I could see Jake sitting across from Detective Reynolds and his partner, a defiant glint in his eyes.

The interrogation was tense, Jake putting on a tough guy act, refusing to say anything without a lawyer present. I watched, silent and vigilant, as the detectives pressed him for answers, their questions sharp and relentless.

Finally, Detective Reynolds called for a break, and his partner stepped out of the room to make a call. As they left, the detective leaned in close to me, his voice a low whisper.

"If the door happens to be open, and no one is looking," he murmured, "you might have a few minutes alone with Jake."

I nodded, a surge of determination coursing through me. This was my chance, my opportunity to get the answers we needed.

As the detectives stepped out, I slipped into the interrogation room, the door clicking shut behind me. Jake's eyes flicked towards me, a mixture of surprise and defiance in his gaze.

"Well, well, well," he sneered, leaning back in his chair. "Who do we have here?" So he recognized me.

I ignored his taunts, my voice steady as I spoke. "I know Patterson paid you," I stated, watching for any flicker of reaction in his eyes.

Jake's expression remained impassive, but I could see a hint of wariness in his gaze. "And what if he did?" he countered, a challenging edge to his voice.

"He paid you to kill Gary Lyoll and Lisa Wynder," I pressed on, my eyes never leaving his.

"Fuck you." He gave a bitter laugh.

"Patterson paid you to kill Andrea, but you got Gary and Lisa instead, am I right?"

A flicker of something crossed Jake's face, too quick to catch. "Prove it," he demanded, his voice low and dangerous.

I leaned in closer, my voice barely above a whisper. "I have evidence," I stated, watching as realization dawned in his eyes.

For a moment, silence hung heavy in the air, the weight of the confession settling between us. Then, Jake let out a bitter laugh, the sound echoing off the walls of the room.

"And what good does that do you?" he spat, his voice laced with venom.

I held his gaze, my voice firm. "It might not hold up in court," I admitted, "but it's enough to know the truth."

A dangerous glint entered Jake's eyes, a smirk twisting his lips. "The truth?" he scoffed. "You think you know the truth?"

I leaned back, studying him carefully. "I know enough," I replied, my voice unwavering. "I know you did it because you know Patterson is trying to ruin Steven."

At the mention of Steven's name, Jake's demeanor shifted, anger flashing in his eyes. "That bastard," he growled, his voice low and guttural. "He deserves everything that's coming to him."

I pressed on, my voice urgent. "Was Steven's grandmother part of this too?" the question hanging heavy in the air.

Jake's expression darkened, a shadow passing over his features. "No," he replied, his voice tinged with bitterness. "But I wish she was."

My heart skipped a beat, the implications of his words sinking in. "You weren't there when she was killed?" I pressed.

Jake shook his head, a bitter laugh escaping his lips. "No," he admitted, his voice filled with regret. "But I would have wished to be there."

Jake's words settled over us like a shroud. "Yeah, I did it," Jake finally admitted, his voice barely above a whisper. "I killed them both. But it wasn't just me."

I studied him carefully, the weight of his confession settling heavily in my chest. "Why?" I asked, hanging between us.

Jake's gaze hardened, his eyes locking with mine. "Because they were in the way," he replied, his voice cold and unyielding. "Because they deserved it. I don't know. I got money and an order."

"You're despicable."

"Looks like you're having a bad day, Miss Tracy's Friend."

The interrogation room reeked of stale coffee and nervous sweat. Detective Reynolds, a man sculpted from granite with a face etched with years of chasing shadows, loomed over the metal table like a predator sizing up its prey. Across from him sat Jake, the suspect. A bravado flickered in his eyes, but the tremor in his hand betrayed the fear gnawing at him.

I joined Reynolds outside the room. My heart hammered a frantic rhythm against my ribs, mimicking the frenetic buzz of the fluorescent lights overhead. The air hung heavy with tension, thick enough to slice with a knife. The only sound was the ragged rasp of my breathing. Reynolds turned towards me, his gaze connecting with mine. No words passed between us, yet a silent understanding crackled in the air.

"Alright, Olivia." His voice cut through the tension, low and gravelly, like gravel grinding against asphalt. "Hit me with everything."

I took a shuddering breath, willing the nervous tremor in my voice to subside. "Jake cracked," I blurted, adrenaline overriding my composure. "He admitted he was hired to rough up Andrea, but things went sideways."

Reynolds' brow furrowed like thunder rolling across the horizon. "Sideways, how?" he demanded, his voice a guttural rasp.

"He wasn't alone," I continued, my voice gaining strength with every word spoken. "The memory's hazy for him. Blackout drunk, maybe." I darted a glance toward the interrogation room, where Jake flinched under the scrutiny.

A burly figure, Detective Miller, Reynolds' partner, slammed his fist on the table, the metal groaning in protest. "And who the hell are you?" he growled his voice like sandpaper on wood.

Reynolds shot him a steely glare that could curdle milk. "Consultant," he said smoothly, deflecting the heat. "External. Working a parallel case that might have some overlap."

Miller grunted, unconvinced, but returned his attention to the interrogation room. Just then, the door creaked open, admitting a man who could have been a bulldog in a pinstripe suit. He swaggered in with an air of entitlement, his movements purposeful. This was Jake's lawyer, Mr. Thorne, his gaze flickering to me with suspicion before settling on Reynolds.

A low murmur rippled through the observation room, filled with other detectives and officers who had gathered to witness the interrogation. Whispers swirled like smoke as they speculated about the case and my presence. I ignored them, my focus solely on the scene unfolding before me.

The interrogation resumed a verbal assault with Reynolds and Miller as the relentless attackers. They bombarded Jake with questions, meticulously picking apart his flimsy alibi. Each question landed like a hammer blow, chipping away at the facade he'd tried to construct. Jake wilted under their relentless pressure, his bravado withering faster than a flower in a furnace.

"Alright, Jake," Reynolds said finally, his voice surprisingly gentle considering the intensity of the preceding exchange. "Let's rewind. Tell us about the night of the attack."

Jake squirmed in his seat, his eyes darting around the room like a trapped animal searching for an escape. "Let's say hypothetically, someone was hired to scare Andrea," he mumbled, his voice barely a croak. "But things..." he trailed off, his voice choked with unspoken terror.

Reynolds leaned forward, his eyes burning into Jake's with the intensity of a blowtorch. "Things went south?" he pressed, his voice a low growl.

"Didn't expect someone else," Jake confessed, a tremor running through his voice. "Lost it when they saw the other person."

A flicker of understanding passed between Reynolds and Miller. A silent conversation played out in their eyes, shared knowledge that sent a jolt of anticipation through me.

"Go on," Reynolds urged, his voice laced with steel.

Jake swallowed audibly, his throat working like a rusty hinge. "Attacked them," he whispered, his face pale as a ghost. "Didn't mean to... just snapped."

"Olivia mentioned an accomplice," Reynolds stated, his tone devoid of emotion. "Who was it, Jake?"

Silence stretched, thick and suffocating. Jake's bravado crumbled entirely, replaced by a terrified confusion. "Hypothesis, detective. Hypothesis."

Reynolds' expression hardened. "Are you sure about that?" he asked, his voice dripping with skepticism.

Jake shook his head, defeated. "Maybe... maybe there was someone else. Maybe not," he mumbled, his voice barely above a whisper.

A wave of despair washed over him. Mr. Thorne, his lawyer, finally stirred, his voice sharp as he cut through the tension. "Mr. Reynolds, perhaps a break is in order. My client clearly needs some time to recollect his thoughts."

"Not yet, Mr. Thorne," Reynolds countered; his retort was cut short by Mr. Thorne's sharp interjection. "On what grounds, Detective? My client is clearly under duress. You've been grilling him for hours without a shred of concrete evidence."

A tense silence descended upon the room. Reynolds locked eyes with Mr. Thorne, their gazes locked in a silent battle of wills. The other detectives in the observation room leaned forward, captivated by the unfolding drama.

"We have his confession, Mr. Thorne," Reynolds finally said, his voice low and steady. "He admitted he was hired to attack Ms. Johnson."

"Hired?" Mr. Thorne scoffed. "That's hearsay. You have no proof of any such arrangement. And even if you did, my client maintains his innocence. He doesn't remember any such event."

"Convenient amnesia," Miller snorted from across the table, his voice laced with sarcasm.

Mr. Thorne ignored him, turning his full attention back to Jake. "Remain silent, Jake," he instructed in a firm whisper, his voice barely audible. "Don't answer any more questions until we've had a chance to discuss this further."

Jake, his face pale and drawn, looked from Mr. Thorne to Reynolds, a flicker of defiance flickering in his eyes. He seemed to teeter on the edge, unsure whether to follow his lawyer's advice or cooperate with the detectives.

Sensing his hesitation, Reynolds pressed on. "We can offer leniency, Jake," he said, his voice surprisingly gentle. "If you cooperate and tell us everything you know, we might be able to work out a deal."

"A deal?" Mr. Thorne sputtered, his voice laced with indignation. "There's no deal to be made here, Detective. My client is innocent!"

"Then why the amnesia?" Reynolds countered, his gaze unwavering. "If he has nothing to hide, why can't he tell us who his supposed accomplice was?"

A bead of sweat trickled down Jake's temple. He darted a nervous glance toward Mr. Thorne, his defiance waning with each passing second. The lawyer, sensing his client's weakening resolve, leaned in closer, his voice urgent.

"Don't be a fool, Jake," he hissed. "They're trying to manipulate you. Don't say anything that could incriminate yourself. We'll fight this in court."

But the seed of doubt had been sown. Jake looked from his lawyer back to Reynolds, the promise of leniency dangling before him like a carrot on a stick. The fear in his eyes was slowly morphing into a desperate hope.

Finally, he spoke, his voice barely a whisper. "I... I want to talk," he choked out, the words tumbling over each other.

Mr. Thorne slammed his hand on the table, his face contorted in fury. "Objection! My client is clearly under duress and incapable of making rational decisions!"

Reynolds ignored him, a triumphant glint in his eyes. "Good decision, Jake," he said, his voice warm. "Now, tell us everything."

Mr. Thorne opened his mouth to protest, but Reynolds cut him off with a steely glare. "We'll resume this conversation later, Mr. Thorne. Right now, your client has something to say."

Defeated, Mr. Thorne slumped back in his chair, his face a mask of thunder. The detectives in the observation room murmured amongst themselves, the tension slowly giving way to a sense of anticipation. As Jake began to speak, his voice shaky but resolute, I leaned forward, eager to hear the truth spill from his lips.

Jake took a shuddering breath, his eyes darting nervously towards his lawyer's impassive face. Ignoring Mr. Thorne's silent disapproval, he continued his voice, which was barely a whisper.

"It all started a few weeks back," he began, his voice raspy. "A guy named Mark approached me at a bar. Seemed shady, but the money was good. He wanted me to rough up a woman, scare her a little. Andrea Johnson, he said. Said she owed someone a lot of money, and this was a way to collect."

Reynolds leaned forward, his gaze unwavering. "Did he say who this 'someone' was?"

Jake shook his head, his brow furrowed in concentration. "No name. Just that this message needed to get delivered, he gave me an address, a picture of Andrea, and a description of the place. Said there'd be a package inside I needed to leave behind."

"What kind of package?" Miller asked, his gruff voice breaking the silence.

"Didn't say," Jake mumbled. "Just a small box wrapped in brown paper."

A chill ran down my spine. This detail matched what Andrea had reported—an attacker leaving a mysterious package.

"So, you went to her house?" Reynolds prompted.

"Yeah," Jake continued, his voice picking up a shaky rhythm. I broke in through a back window, just like Mark said. The place was dark and quiet. I figured Andrea was alone. But as I crept in, I heard... noises."

He choked back a sob, his face contorted in a grimace of disgust. Miller grimaced, seemingly understanding the implication.

"Someone else was there?" Reynolds asked, his voice devoid of emotion.

Jake nodded, his eyes filled with a haunted look. "A couple. I didn't expect that. They were... intimate. My first thought was to get the hell out of there. I didn't want any trouble."

"But you didn't," Reynolds pressed, his voice firm.

Jake's gaze darted towards his lawyer again, a silent plea for support. But Mr. Thorne remained silent, a grim expression etched on his face.

"Just then, my phone buzzed," Jake continued, his voice barely audible. "It was Mark, his voice tight with panic. 'Don't leave! You need to finish the job!' he yelled. Said leaving witnesses wouldn't look good for me or him."

Frustration and anger bled into Jake's voice. "He never mentioned anyone else being there! I saw red. Didn't care anymore. Just wanted to get it over with and get out."

He wiped a bead of sweat from his brow, his confession gaining momentum. "So, I grabbed a lamp from a side table and used it to threaten them. The guy, Gary, whom I think she called him, tried to fight back. The woman, Lisa, screamed. It was all a blur—fear, adrenaline, fury. I ended up... hurting them."

His voice broke, his confession turning into a choked sob. Reynolds waited, the silence in the room heavy with the weight of his words.

"I didn't mean to kill them," Jake rasped, his voice raw with emotion. "But they fought back, wouldn't let me leave. And then... I saw their faces. Panic set in. Mark had warned me—no witnesses. So..."

He trailed off, unable to finish the sentence, the gravity of his actions hanging heavy in the air. I could only imagine the horrific scene that unfolded, the desperate struggle for survival.

"So you... killed them?" Miller finally asked, his voice gruff but laced with a hint of grim understanding.

"I... I didn't want to," Jake stammered, tears welling up in his eyes. "But they saw me. I had no choice."

A heavy silence descended upon the room. Reynolds leaned back in his chair, his face an unreadable mask. Mr. Thorne, defeated, remained silent. The detectives in the observation room exchanged solemn glances, the weight of the confession settling upon them all.

Jake's confession painted a horrifying picture—a simple scare tactic gone terribly wrong. The image of a terrified couple fighting for their lives against a desperate man was etched into my mind. At that moment, I felt a surge of conflicting emotions—anger towards Jake for his brutality, but also a flicker of sympathy for the fear that had driven him to such violence.

Reynolds finally broke the silence, his voice low and serious. "Tell us about the package, Jake. What was in it?"

But Jake did not know. He could not remember where the package went. I shared a look with Reynolds. The package was for me and indirectly for Steven. Jake did admit that he'd taken the job because of the man Mark and said it was a way to get back at his old friend, Steven.

The Sinister Plan

After Jake's interrogation concluded, Detective Reynolds ushered me out of the room, his expression unreadable. I couldn't shake the weight of Jake's confession from my mind, the haunting realization of the darkness that lurked within him. As we stepped out into the station, I caught sight of Steven pacing anxiously in the waiting area. I'd told him Jake was in detention but hadn't expected him here. His face was a mask of tension and worry, and my heart ached at the sight of him.

"Steven," I said as I approached him. "We need to talk."

He turned to me, his eyes wide with apprehension. "What happened, Olivia? What did Jake say?"

I took a deep breath, steeling myself for the difficult conversation ahead. "Jake confessed to the attack on Andrea, my receptioni– former receptionist." I began, my voice trembling slightly. "But there's more... he admitted to the murders of Gary and Lisa. And that he'd known it was somehow related to you."

Steven staggered back as if I had physically struck him, his eyes filled with disbelief and horror. "No... no, that can't be true," he whispered, his voice barely audible.

"I'm so sorry, Steven," I said, reaching out to touch his arm and offering what little comfort I could. I know this is a lot to take in."

He shook his head, his eyes filled with tears. "How... how could he do this? I trusted him, Olivia. Grandma welcomed him into our home..."

The anguish in Steven's voice tore at my heart, his pain palpable in the air between us. "I don't know, Steven," I admitted, my voice thick with emotion. "But we have to focus on getting justice for your grandmother and for Gary and Lisa."

Steven nodded, his jaw clenched with determination. "I want to see him," he said, his voice firm. "I want to confront Jake myself."

I hesitated, torn between my role as a therapist and the need to support Steven in his quest for closure. "Steven, I understand your anger," I began, my voice gentle but firm. "But going alone to the jail... it's not safe. Jake is a dangerous man."

"I don't care," Steven interrupted, his eyes flashing with defiance. "I need to see him, Olivia. I need to hear it from his own mouth."

I sighed, knowing that I couldn't dissuade him. "Alright," I relented, my heart heavy with worry. "But I'm coming with you. We'll go together."

The drive to the jail was tense, the silence between us heavy with unspoken fears and emotions. I could feel Steven's anger radiating off him in waves, his hands clenched tightly on the steering wheel.

As we arrived at the jail, Steven's resolve seemed to harden, his jaw set in a determined line. We made our way through the cold, sterile corridors, the sound of our footsteps echoing ominously in the empty halls.

Finally, we reached the room where Jake was being held. Steven pushed open the door without hesitation, his eyes blazing with fury as he confronted the man.

Jake slumped in a chair, his eyes empty as he stared back at us. His demeanor was chillingly calm, a stark contrast to the turmoil raging within Steven.

"Steven," I said, gently touching his arm to temper his rage. Let's hear what he has to say first."

Steven nodded tightly, his jaw clenched with tension as he glared at Jake. "Why, Jake?" he demanded, his voice laced with anger and betrayal. "Why did you do it?"

Jake remained silent for a moment, his gaze locked with Steven's. Then, finally, he spoke, his voice low and chilling.

"Because I was paid to," he said, his words like a dagger to the heart. "Patterson offered me money to attack Andrea, but when I arrived at the house... I found Gary and Lisa instead."

Steven's eyes widened in shock, his fists clenched at his sides. "Paid to attack Andrea?" he repeated, his voice barely whispering.

Jake nodded, a cruel smirk twisting his lips. "And when I saw them together... I couldn't resist," he admitted, his voice dripping with malice. "It was supposed to be a simple job, but things got out of hand."

Steven's hands trembled with barely contained rage, his eyes blazing with fury. "You... you killed them," he whispered, the words heavy with disbelief and horror.

Jake's smirk widened, his eyes glinting with malice. "And I'd do it again," he taunted, his voice filled with venom. "For the right price."

The room seemed to close in around us, the air thick with tension and anger. Steven took a step forward, his fists clenched at his sides.

"Steven, no!" I exclaimed, grabbing his arm and pulling him back. "We can't let him get to you."

But Steven shook off my grip, his eyes locked with Jake's. "You're a monster," he spat, his voice filled with loathing. "And you'll pay for what you've done."

With that, Steven turned on his heel and stormed out of the room, leaving me alone with Jake. I could feel the weight of his gaze on me, his eyes boring into mine with a chilling intensity.

"You shouldn't have come here, Olivia," Jake said, his voice low and menacing. "You're meddling in things you don't understand."

I held my ground, refusing to show any sign of fear. "I'm here for justice," I said, my voice steady despite the unease churning in my stomach. "And I won't rest until Gary and Lisa's killer is brought to justice."

"Well then, ain't this mission accomplished?"

"We both know you are just a tool. The crude murder weapon swung by the reaching hand of Patterson."

Jake's laughter echoed in the empty room, a cold, cruel sound devoid of genuine humor. "You think you can stop him?" he taunted, his eyes glinting with malice. You're just a therapist, Olivia. What can you do?"

I squared my shoulders, meeting his gaze head-on. "More than you think," I replied, my voice filled with determination. "And I'll do whatever it takes to bring him down."

With that, I turned and left the room, the weight of Jake's threats hanging heavy in the air behind me. As I made my way out of the jail, I couldn't shake the unease that clung to me like a shadow. The drive back to my office was filled with a tense silence, the events of the day weighing heavily on my mind. Steven was silent beside me, his jaw clenched with anger and grief. When we finally arrived back at the office, I could see the toll that the confrontation with Jake had taken on him. His shoulders slumped with exhaustion; his eyes filled with a haunted look.

"Steven," I said, touching his arm. "I'm so sorry."

He looked up at me, his eyes filled with pain. "I just... I can't believe it," he whispered, his voice cracking with emotion. "Petty theft is one thing, but how could he do something like that?"

I didn't have an answer for him, only the shared weight of grief and anger that hung between us. We sat in silence for a long time, each lost in our own thoughts.

Eventually, Steven spoke. "I need to talk to the others. They should know what's happened to him."

The Therapist's Gambit

I was at home, thinking about the case while distractedly eating my dinner, which was ramen.

Steven was the key witness, the man who'd seen Patterson's ruthlessness firsthand. Now, fear had driven him into hiding, leaving me to navigate this treacherous path alone. He had stopped coming for his sessions, and the deadline for Mr. Robert's death was approaching.

"Except I'm not entirely alone," I murmured, a smile tugging at the corner of my lips. Gojo blinked in response, her tail twitching in agreement.

"The documents," I breathed, a surge of determination washing over me. "We need to find what Detective Reynolds slipped me."

I ransacked through the files, searching for the manila envelope Reynolds had discreetly passed me after the interrogation. Frustration threatened to cripple me again, but I persevered. Just as exhaustion threatened to win, my fingers brushed against the smooth paper.

There, nestled amongst the other documents, lay the manila envelope. A rush of exhilaration coursed through me. This could be it, the weapon I needed to expose Patterson.

Gojo, who'd been napping on a legal pad, stretched languidly at the sudden noise. She sauntered over to the edge of the desk and peered down at the envelope, her head tilted inquisitively.

"Patience, Gojo," I chuckled, carefully retrieving the documents. "First, we need to decipher what Reynolds gave me. Then, we might just have ourselves a little surprise for Mr. Patterson."

The rain lashed against the windowpanes, relentless drumming that mirrored the frantic rhythm of my thoughts. Tonight, the light from my desk lamp struggled to pierce the shadows clinging to the corners of the room. The files sprawled across my desk seemed to writhe and twist, a tangled mess of deceit spun by Mr. Patterson. Gojo sat regally on the windowsill, her eyes reflecting the city lights distorted rain.

"Mr. Patterson," I muttered, the name a bitter taste on my tongue. Jake's confession, the muscle hired to silence Andrea, felt like a hollow victory. It was just one piece of a much larger puzzle, a puzzle with a missing picture and jagged edges. Who was Mark, the shadowy figure who'd pulled Jake's strings? I knew the real purpose behind silencing Andrea. Debt collection was just a flimsy motive for an idiot like Jake.

Patterson was a man who moved through the world like a shark, leaving a trail of devastation in his wake.

Frustration gnawed at me. Gojo, sensing my turmoil, thumped her tail rhythmically against the windowsill before, with a graceful leap, she landed on the desk. Immediately, her white fur created a stark contrast to the dark ink scrawled across the files.

The financial records swam before my eyes—transactions, investments, shell companies. A labyrinth designed to obscure any trace of wrongdoing. But somewhere, there had to be a chink in his meticulously constructed armor.

"There!" I exclaimed, a flicker of hope igniting in my chest. It was an anomaly—a series of seemingly insignificant payments to an offshore account meticulously spaced out over a period of months. It wasn't much, but it was a start—a thread dangling in the vast tapestry of Patterson's financial dealings.

Gojo nudged the file with her head, her inquisitive meow echoing in the quiet room. Following the money—that was Detective Reynolds' advice, his voice gruff but kind in my memory.

A low rumble of thunder echoed outside, mirroring the sudden jolt of adrenaline coursing through me. The offshore account could be the key to unraveling Patterson's web. But prying into offshore accounts was no easy feat. I needed leverage, a way to pressure the authorities into cooperating.

By the time the first rays of dawn peeked through the blinds and painted the room in a soft, bruised-purple light, I was tired. The remnants of the night's investigation lay scattered across my desk—financial records, old interview transcripts, and the manila envelope from Detective Reynolds, from within which all these had come. Exhaustion gnawed at my bones, but sleep felt like a distant luxury.

Gojo, who'd slept on my desk, woke up and stretched languidly on the desk, her white fur catching the first slivers of sunlight. She let out a soft meow, a gentle reminder that even warriors needed rest. I forced a smile, scratching her behind the ears.

"Just a little longer, Gojo," I promised, my voice hoarse from disuse. "What I really need is a plan."

The confession had been a breakthrough, of course, but it left more questions unanswered than it satisfied. Mark remained a shadow figure, an unknown. And while the offshore account was a potential lead, cracking it would be a bureaucratic nightmare.

Steven, the crucial witness, was now a ghost, his fear keeping him out of reach. Without him, building a strong case against Patterson felt like trying to scale a mountain with one hand tied behind my back.

Discouragement threatened to engulf me, but then a memory surfaced, a fragment of a conversation with Steven. He'd mentioned a hunch—a feeling that Patterson wouldn't stop. He was a predator, and predators, according to Reynolds, always returned to the scene of the kill. Besides, we knew who his next target was.

Naturally, a cold dread settled in the pit of my stomach. I couldn't afford to wait and see if his game played out. I needed to force Patterson's hand, to draw him out and expose his vulnerabilities. But how?

I scanned the documents on my desk, searching for an answer hidden between the lines. An idea, audacious and risky, began to take shape. It would be a public spectacle, a direct challenge that would force Patterson to either react or expose his fear. It was a gamble, but one I was willing to take.

The first step was Steven. I needed to get him back on board, to remind him that he wasn't alone in this fight. Grabbing my phone, I dialed his number, my heart pounding a frantic rhythm against my ribs. The call went straight to voicemail.

"Steven," I said, my voice firm despite the knot of worry in my throat. "It's Olivia. I know you're scared, but you can't hide forever. We need to talk. Meet me at the cafe at noon. Please, don't let fear win."

I hung up, the silence in the room thick with uncertainty. Would he come? The answer held the key to my plan.

Next, I needed to alert the press. A well-placed anonymous tip about Patterson's actions. The thought of going public sent a shiver down my spine. Patterson was a powerful man, and drawing unwanted attention could backfire spectacularly. But the alternative—remaining silent and hoping for the best—felt far too passive.

But I must protect Steven.

I booted up my laptop, fingers hovering over the keys. Finding an anonymous way to contact the media was a hurdle, but one I was determined to overcome. With a deep breath, I began my search, the rhythmic tapping of the keyboard a counterpoint to the frantic drumming of my heart.

Finally, after countless dead ends and frustrating detours, I found a potential lead—an investigative reporter known for her tenacity and fierce commitment to truth. She was a college student doing her MBA, but she'd been a journalist since high school. Composing the anonymous email was a tense affair. I kept it brief and to the point. The screen glowed with the draft of the email I was about to send, a gamble.

Subject: Wealthy Jeweler Involved with Underworld Deals

Dear Ms. Rodriguez,

This message comes to you anonymously, but the information I possess is of great public interest. It concerns a prominent figure named Mr. Timothy Patterson, a known London jeweler.

I have reason to believe that Mr. Patterson's businesses may pose a security threat, and he may be involved in criminal activities. In the past, his business practices have left a trail of disgruntled former associates and employees. Some have been inexplicably fatally injured or disappeared. Some survivors, I believe, would be willing to come forward and share their experiences.

I am in possession of a list of these individuals, people who may hold crucial information about Mr. Patterson's questionable business dealings. These testimonies could expose a pattern of intimidation and potentially illegal activity.

Due to the sensitivity of the matter, I must remain anonymous at this time. However, if you are interested in pursuing this story further, I can provide you with a secure way to access the aforementioned list.

Sincerely,

A Concerned Citizen

Rereading the email, I weighed the potential benefits against the risks. Exposing Patterson publicly would raise his hackles, but the promise of a list of disgruntled ex-employees could be a powerful motivator for an investigative journalist like Ms. Rodriguez.

With a deep breath, I hit send, the message hurtling through the digital void and landing in the inbox of a woman who could potentially become my greatest ally.

Leaning back in my chair, I let out a long sigh. The first steps of my plan were in motion—an anonymous tip about a security threat, a desperate plea to a reporter, and an unsettling wait for a response. The world outside seemed to blur, the rhythmic patter of rain against the windowpane a soothing lullaby.

Suddenly, the sound of the doorbell pierced the quiet, jolting me awake. Gojo shot up from her nap, and her eyes narrowed in suspicion. Who could be visiting at this ungodly hour? With a cautious glance at the peephole, my heart lurched. It was Steven, his face drawn and pale, worry etched deep into his lines. He looked like a man on the verge of collapse.

It wasn't noon yet.

Gojo arched her back and hissed, a low rumble emanating from her throat.

"Gojo, it's okay," I soothed, gently stroking her fur. "It's Steven."

Steven offered a watery smile, his eyes filled with a haunted look. "Olivia," he croaked, his voice hoarse. "I got your message. I... I had to come."

Relief washed over me, mingled with a surge of protectiveness. "Come on," I said, guiding him towards the couch. "Let's get you some dry clothes and a hot cup of tea."

As Steven settled down, his trembling subsided with each sip of tea. He needed reassurance and a plan, and I needed his cooperation for this to work.

The doorbell shrilled a harsh counterpoint to the tense silence. This time, it was Detective Reynolds, his trench coat a dark silhouette against the doorway. I'd texted him as soon as I came up with this plan. His presence, gruff and reliable, offered a sliver of comfort.

"Olivia," he greeted, his gaze flitting between us. "I didn't expect to see you here," he said to Steven.

I explained the situation, gesturing towards the empty coffee mug. "We need to talk about a plan."

"What do you have in mind?" Detective Reynolds asked, his gruff demeanor masking a flicker of curiosity.

I leaned forward, my voice dropping to a murmur. "Patterson craves control. He feels untouchable. What if we gave him a reason to doubt that?"

Intrigue sparked in Detective Reynolds' eyes while Steven's brow furrowed in confusion.

"I can meet with him," I continued, my gaze unwavering. Alone, in a secluded location. We can use it as an opportunity to gauge his reaction and see if my threat can truly rattle him."

A collective gasp filled the room. Steven shot to his feet, his face pale. "Olivia, that's insane! It's too risky!"

"It's also our best shot," I countered, my voice laced with a quiet determination. Think about it, Steven. He wouldn't expect me to have gone as far as I have. The element of surprise could be our advantage."

Detective Reynolds steepled his fingers, his expression thoughtful. "It's a gamble, Olivia. A high-stakes one. But if it works..."

"If it works," I finished, my voice gaining strength with each word, "we might just get him to back down."

The plan was audacious, a tightrope walk between bravery and recklessness. But as I looked between Steven's worried gaze and Detective Reynolds' considering nod, a sliver of hope ignited within me. This was our chance, a desperate gamble to bring Patterson to his knees.

Detective Reynolds and I dissected the audacious plan. Steven, his face a mask of worry, paced the room. His damp clothes were beginning to smell. I got up and turned the heat up. Gojo, who suddenly remembered him, walked around his feet.

"Olivia," Detective Reynolds began, his voice gruff but laced with concern, "this is not some James Bond shit. Going in alone... it's risky as hell."

"I know," I admitted, meeting his gaze. "I'll be going with Gojo, so I'm not alone."

"Not funny," Reynolds said.

"Oh, I wasn't joking. I need Gojo to keep me calm."

"This isn't a smart plan," Reynolds complained.

"But it's the only way to catch him off guard. He really wouldn't expect me, and that element of surprise could be our biggest weapon."

Steven stopped his pacing, his eyes pleading. "But why you? Let me go. He threatened me, not you."

"Because, Steven," I said gently, "he sees you as a loose end, someone to silence. He could damn it all to hell and just shoot you or something. Me? I'm the one with all the information on him. He will want to know what I really know before doing anything rash. And you're kind of looking rattled already. I need to project confidence. And if the detective goes, well, it's all up in smoke."

A flicker of understanding dawned in Steven's eyes. "So, you're the bait?"

"In a way," I replied. "But this isn't just about luring him out. This is about getting him to crack, to show his hand. I need him to do something irrational."

Detective Reynolds leaned forward, his eyes gleaming with a steely resolve. "Alright, let's say you do manage to lure him out. What then?"

I outlined my plan, "First, location. It can't be somewhere public or easily accessible. We need a place where I have some control, somewhere with an escape route if things go south."

We brainstormed for a while, discarding parks and cafes as too open. Finally, Detective Reynolds suggested an abandoned warehouse on the outskirts of the city, a place he knew was being prepped for demolition. It was isolated, with only a single, easily monitored entrance. But he knew a secret way in and out.

"Perfect," I breathed, a sense of relief washing over me. "Now, safety measures."

Detective Reynolds nodded, his gaze unwavering. "I'll have an undercover team stationed nearby. They'll be discreet but close enough to intervene if needed."

"But Gojo?" Steven piped up, his voice tight with concern.

I reached down to stroke Gojo's fur, her deep rumble a comforting presence. "She'll be with me, yes. She may not be a police dog, but she's got several things in her point."

A small smile tugged at the corner of Detective Reynolds' lips. "Alright then, let's talk about what you'll say to Patterson."

"I'll play on his fear," I declared. "He thinks he's untouchable, that his crimes are buried in the past. I'll use the threat of going public, of exposing everything, to rattle him."

Steven looked troubled. "But wouldn't that put more of a target on your back?"

"Perhaps," I admitted. "But it will also make him desperate. That's when we might see his true colors."

We spent the next hour meticulously crafting my conversation with Patterson. I would feign a change of heart, claiming I no longer cared about Andrea's death and just wanted things to go back to normal. I'd dangle the carrot of Steven dropping the lawsuit and me ceasing my investigation, all on one condition: Patterson leaves Steven's business alone.

"It's a gamble," Detective Reynolds cautioned. "He might call your bluff."

"He might," I agreed. "But desperation can be a powerful motivator. If he truly believes I'm his way out of this mess, he might just agree."

Of course, the plan had holes. There was no guarantee Patterson would fall for it. He could choose violence instead of negotiation. But it was the best, and perhaps only, option we had. I packed a small first-aid kit, a hidden panic button linked directly to the police, and a miniature voice recorder disguised as a pen.

Gojo nudged my hand with her nose. "Don't worry, girl," I whispered, scratching behind her ears. "We'll be okay." But she meowed loudly.

"Shit! I've not fed her."

Three days later, I was on my way to rendezvous with Patterson.

Steven, unable to shake his worry, insisted on driving me to the abandoned warehouse. The silence in the car was thick, punctuated only by the rhythmic hum of the engine. Finally, he broke the silence.

"Olivia," he began, his voice husky, "if anything happens..."

"Don't even think about finishing that sentence," I interrupted him gently, placing a hand on his arm. "We've planned for every scenario we can. You'll have Detective Reynolds and his team watching my back, and Gojo will be with me. Besides, I'm not about to let Patterson win."

He squeezed my hand briefly, saying nothing. As we pulled up outside the deserted warehouse, a wave of apprehension washed over me. The building loomed before us, a skeletal silhouette against the sun. Broken windows gaped like empty eyes, and the air hung heavy with the scent of dust and decay.

Taking a deep breath, I forced a smile. "This is it, Steven. Showtime."

He nodded curtly, his jaw clenched tight. "Stay safe, Olivia. Promise me you'll call off the whole thing if it feels wrong."

"I promise," I lied, unable to burden him with the truth. There was no turning back now. This was the only shot we had.

We said our goodbyes, his hand lingering on mine a moment too long. Then, with a final, worried glance, Steven drove away. I watched the taillights disappear into the distance, a knot of worry tightening in my stomach. Alone, I turned towards the warehouse, Gojo padding silently at my side. She chirped inquisitively. I had no answer for her.

"I hope we'll be alright, Gojo."

The air inside was thick with dust motes dancing in a single shaft of sunlight that pierced through a hole in the roof. The silence was oppressive, broken only by the crunch of broken glass underfoot. Following Detective Reynolds' instructions, I made my way to a small, semi-enclosed office space on the second floor. The walls were crumbling, but it offered a modicum of privacy and a potential escape route through a broken window leading onto a fire escape.

Taking out the hidden microphone, I clipped it to my shirt, hoping it would capture the entire conversation. Gojo, sensing my nervousness, whined and nudged my hand once again. I knelt down, burying my face in her fur and drawing strength from her unwavering loyalty.

"Alright, girl," I whispered, stroking her head. "Let's do this."

I sat down, arranging my papers of 'evidence' before me. I wanted Patterson to feel like he was in my consulting room when he arrived. The metallic clang of the warehouse door echoed through the dusty emptiness. My heart hammered against my ribs, a frantic drum solo against the sudden silence. When they came in, I was surprised. This wasn't Patterson.

Disappointment battled with adrenaline. A stooge, then. They were testing me, gauging my reaction before unleashing the real threat. Whoever it was, they'd made a grave mistake underestimating me. A burly man filled the doorway, his face obscured by the shadows. He wore a worn leather jacket and a sneer that stretched across his scarred face. His eyes, however, held a flicker of uncertainty, a chink in his otherwise menacing facade.

"Dr. Jenson?" he rasped, his voice gravelly.

"That's me," I replied, my voice betraying none of the fear churning in my gut. Gojo took a step forward, then returned to my side.

"Where's the muscle?" he scoffed, regaining some of his bravado. "Expecting some kind of hero show?"

"No show," I countered, my voice firm. "Just a conversation. Is Mr. Patterson too afraid to face me himself?"

He chuckled harshly, humorless. "Don't flatter yourself, doll. The boss-man just likes to delegate," Gojo hissed at him.

"Easy, girl," I murmured, stroking Gojo's head to calm her. "He's just a messenger."

"My name is Mark."

"You hired Jake."

"Hmm, I assure you, I know no Jake. That was another Mark."

His sneer cut through the dusty air of the abandoned warehouse, his scarred face twisted into a mocking grin. But behind the bravado, I could sense the flicker of uncertainty, a primal fear lurking beneath the surface.

"I must say, Dr. Jenson," he rasped, his voice dripping with disdain. "You're something of a surprise. I was expecting someone... different."

I met his gaze head-on, refusing to let his taunts rattle me. "I'm exactly where I need to be," I replied, my voice steady despite the pounding of my heart. Gojo, sensing the tension, stayed close at my side, her tail flicking with nervous energy.

Mark chuckled, a grating sound that set my teeth on edge. "So, what's this all about? Patterson said you had something to discuss."

"Oh, we do," I said, my voice cool and calculated. "I have information. Damning information. About Mr. Timothy Patterson."

His smirk faltered for a moment before he regained his composure. "Is that so? And what kind of information might that be, Doctor?"

I leaned forward, my eyes boring into his. "Let's just say I know about his little... side hustle. The ones he'd rather keep hidden from the public eye."

A flicker of panic crossed Mark's face before he masked it with a snarl. "You're bluffing," he spat, taking a step closer. "Patterson is untouchable. You think some therapist with a cat can bring him down?"

"Believe what you want," I replied, my tone icy. But I have evidence: records of shady transactions, connections to criminal elements, and a trail of broken lives left in his wake."

Mark's sneer returned, his confidence seemingly restored. "And what do you want, Doctor? Money? Fame? Or are you just looking for a way out of this mess you've gotten yourself into?"

I shook my head, a ghost of a smile playing on my lips. "I want one thing, Mark. For Patterson to leave Steven alone. To drop the lawsuit, cease the threats, and disappear from his life forever."

His laugh echoed through the empty warehouse, a cruel sound that sent shivers down my spine. "You're a fool, Doctor. Patterson doesn't negotiate with amateurs."

"Then let's see how he reacts when I go public," I countered, my voice ringing with determination. "The press would love to sink their teeth into a story about a wealthy jeweler with a dark past."

Mark's facade cracked just a fraction, revealing the fear that lurked beneath. "You wouldn't dare," he growled, his fists clenched at his sides.

"Try me," I shot back, my resolve steeling. "I have nothing to lose, Mark. But Patterson? He has everything to lose."

The standoff between us crackled with tension, the air thick with unspoken threats and hidden agendas. Mark, sensing the weight of my words, took a step back, his eyes darting around the dimly lit room.

"You're playing a dangerous game, Doctor," he warned, his voice low and menacing. "Patterson doesn't take kindly to threats."

"Then he shouldn't have given me a reason to threaten him," I retorted, my voice ringing with defiance. "Now, here's how it's going to go. You tell Patterson that I have the evidence, and I'm not afraid to use it. If he wants to avoid a scandal, he'll leave Steven alone. Otherwise, he can deal with the consequences."

Mark clenched his jaw, his fists trembling with suppressed rage. "You think you're so clever, don't you? But you have no idea who you're dealing with."

"I know exactly who I'm dealing with," I shot back, my voice ringing with authority. "And I'm not afraid of him."

For a moment, it seemed as though Mark would lunge at me, his anger barely contained. I slipped my hand inside my bag to the gun Reynolds had given me.

Face to Face

Mark paced like a caged animal, his shadow contorting on the peeling brick wall with each restless stride. He was a study in controlled tension, his knuckles white as he gripped the worn leather satchel slung over his shoulder.

I sat across from him, pretending to be calm amidst the storm. My gaze wasn't accusatory, just steady and unwavering. We were playing a silent game of chicken, each waiting for the other to make the first move.

"You know," I began, my voice laced with a hint of amusement, "silence can be deafening. Wouldn't you agree, Mark?"

Mark flinched, his eyes darting towards the shadows at the edges of the room. He cleared his throat, the sound rough and uneven. "There's nothing left to say, Dr. Jenson. You lost."

"Lost?" I chuckled, dryly, humorless. "Quite the opposite, Mark. I believe you're the one at a crossroads."

His jaw clenched, the muscle jumping beneath his skin. "You don't know what you're talking about."

"Oh, I think I do," I countered, leaning forward slightly. "You see, desperation has a tell, Mark. That twitch in your fingers, the way you keep glancing at the door. It speaks volumes."

Silence stretched between us, thick with unspoken accusations. He knew I knew. My words had pricked the carefully constructed dam holding back a torrent of anxieties.

"There's no point," he finally muttered, his voice barely a whisper.

"On the contrary," I countered, my voice gentle but firm. "There's always a point, Mark. Especially when lives are at stake. Lives Mr. Patterson seems quite comfortable holding in the balance."

A shiver ran through him, and for the first time, I saw a flicker of something akin to fear in his steely gaze. "Don't bring him into this."

"You already have, Mark," I replied, my tone unwavering. "By being here, by keeping his secrets. You're an accomplice, willingly or not."

The anger flashed hot in his eyes, a momentary defiance before fading into a resigned slump. He slumped into the rickety chair opposite me, his shoulders slumping. The bravado was gone, replaced by a deep exhaustion.

"It's not that simple," he mumbled, defeated.

"Perhaps not," I conceded, "but pretending nothing's wrong doesn't make it go away. It just allows Mr. Patterson to continue his charade."

He let out a frustrated sigh, the sound heavy in the silence. "He has everyone fooled. Power, influence... he controls everything."

"Or does he control you, Mark?" I pressed gently. "Is that why you're here? Because you finally see the truth for what it is?"

The leaky pipe in the abandoned warehouse was by now a metronome of dread, its rhythm a counterpoint to the frantic hammering of my heart. Mark shifted uncomfortably across from me.

"Mr. Patterson," he began, his voice tight, "is a man of... vision. He sees the bigger picture, the potential in every situation."

I raised an eyebrow, a silent question hanging in the air.

"He's not afraid to take risks," Mark continued, a defensive edge creeping into his voice. "He knows that sometimes, unconventional methods are necessary for success."

"Success," I echoed, the word dripping with skepticism. "Is that what you call it, Mark?"

He flinched at the use of his first name, a flicker of vulnerability betraying his carefully constructed facade. But he quickly recovered, straightening his back.

"He's a leader," Mark asserted, his voice gaining a touch of defiance. "He inspires loyalty and dedication. He knows how to motivate people."

I leaned forward, narrowing my eyes. "Or manipulate them, wouldn't you say?"

His gaze darted away for a fleeting moment, a telltale sign of discomfort. "No, not manipulate. He... incentivizes results."

"Incentivizes," I repeated, the word dripping with sarcasm. "Is that what you call silencing dissent with threats and intimidation?"

Mark's jaw clenched, and a muscle in his cheek twitched with suppressed anger. He remained silent, the weight of my accusation hanging heavy in the air.

"Look, Dr. Jenson," Mark finally said, his voice strained, "the world of business isn't always sunshine and rainbows. Sometimes, tough decisions need to be made."

"And who gets to decide how 'tough' these decisions need to be, Mr. Patterson?" I pressed, my voice unwavering.

He hesitated, a flicker of doubt crossing his eyes. He opened his mouth to speak, but the words seemed to catch in his throat.

"Is it because he promises you a piece of the pie?" I continued, my voice laced with a hint of pity. "A chance to be part of something bigger than yourself? Or are you simply afraid of what might happen if you step out of line?" My words hung in the air, sharp and piercing.

He didn't answer, but a flicker of something passed through his eyes, a silent admission that resonated louder than any words.

"Look, Mark," I continued, deciding to attack him directly. "You still have a choice. You can be a pawn in his game, or you can choose to break free. Speak up, tell the truth about what you know, and together, we can expose him. Think about it: all the blood on your hands is because of one man's greed. Does your wife and lovely children know what you do for a living? Do they know the bread and wine you feed them is the flesh and blood of innocent souls Patterson has cut down?"

The silence stretched for an eternity, thick with the weight of his decision. His gaze flickered across the room.

Finally, with a deep breath, he spoke. "There's evidence in here," he stammered, pointing to his head. "Financial records, emails... proof of his underhanded dealings."

A surge of triumph swelled within me. This was it. The key to bringing Patterson down. "Excellent, Mark," I said, my voice steady despite the tremor in my heart. "They could be the key to bringing him to justice."

Suddenly, a sharp crack echoed through the warehouse. The world went still. Mark crumpled to the floor, a crimson stain blooming across his chest. His hand, frozen in mid-motion, still pointed to his head.

My scream died a silent death in my throat. I ducked under the table, my gaze darted around the room, searching for the source of the attack. There were no visible entry points to me. It was as if the bullet had materialized out of thin air.

Panic clawed at my throat, icy and suffocating. Fear, sharp and primal, shot through me. I was alone, a lone target in this desolate warehouse. Squeezing my papers in my bag and scooping a scared Gojo up, I ran out of the stale office. I turned to the stairs but came face to face with Patterson. He was flanked by three gunmen, their faces masked, their hands gloved.

Cobwebs, heavy with dust, draped across the exposed beams high above, casting grotesque spider-legged shadows that danced on the uneven concrete floor. A single bare bulb cast a sickly yellow glow, illuminating Mark's crumpled form a few feet behind me, a crimson stain blossoming across his chest like a grotesque flower.

Across from me stood Mr. Patterson. In the harsh light, he looked like a carefully cultivated charismatic leader. His eyes, devoid of warmth, glittered like obsidian chips, reflecting the warped image of the warehouse back at me. A thin smile played on his lips. It wasn't a smile of triumph but one of chilling amusement like a predator savoring the fear in its prey.

He was dressed impeccably, a contrast to the grime and decay that surrounded us. His tailored suit, a deep charcoal, seemed to absorb the dim light, making him appear even more imposing. Every inch of him screamed control, power, a predator perched at the apex of the food chain.

My hand instinctively tightened around the gun in my bag. Go for the chest, Reynolds had said. But fear, a primal instinct buried deep within, threatened to paralyze me. My breath came in short, shallow gasps, the only sound breaking the oppressive silence besides the relentless drip, drip, drip.

Gojo, sensing my fear, stirred within my bag. Her tiny white paw nudged against the zipper. I reached in, my fingers brushing against her soft fur. The warmth of her tiny body grounded me. At that moment, I knew I couldn't let fear win. I had to fight for myself, for Steven's grandma, Gary, and Lisa, and now for Mark and for the countless others Patterson had likely silenced.

Slowly, I straightened my spine, forcing my gaze to meet Patterson's. A flicker of surprise, a momentary crack in his facade, crossed his face. He had expected fear, a whimpering surrender. Instead, I met his gaze head-on, my own eyes burning with a steely resolve.

The silence stretched, thick and suffocating. It was a battle of wills, a silent scream echoing in the warehouse's emptiness. Patterson's smile faltered, replaced by a flicker of something akin to respect. Perhaps he recognized the spark of defiance in my eyes, the unwavering determination to see this through.

He took a slow, deliberate step forward, the movement predatory, calculated. I held my ground, my grip tightening on the gun. Each beat of my heart echoed in my ears, a drumbeat against the oppressive silence. The air crackled with unspoken threats, and the warehouse was a pressure cooker on the verge of exploding.

Then, with a sigh that spoke volumes, Patterson stopped. He tilted his head slightly, studying me with an intensity that made my skin crawl. Was he gauging my strength, my resolve? A cruel smile played on his lips once more.

He spoke, his voice a low purr that sent shivers down my spine. "So, Dr. Jenson," he began, his voice dripping with a false sincerity, "it seems we've stumbled upon something rather... inconvenient."

The words were laced with a veiled threat, a reminder of the power he wielded, the lives he could extinguish with a flick of his wrist. Yet, there was also a hint of curiosity in his voice, a morbid fascination with the cornered prey that dared to fight back.

I swallowed the lump in my throat, my voice surprisingly steady when I finally spoke. "You underestimate me, Mr. Patterson," I said, each word carefully measured. "The truth will come out, one way or another."

A sharp laugh escaped his lips, devoid of humor, a chilling sound that echoed through the warehouse. "The truth," he scoffed, "is a malleable thing, Doctor. Easily manipulated, rewritten to suit one's needs."

"The truth," I countered, my voice unwavering despite the tremor in my heart, "is a stubborn thing, Mr. Patterson. It has a way of wriggling free, no matter how tightly you try to control it."

A glint of something akin to anger flickered in his obsidian eyes. "Control," he repeated, the word dripping with disdain. "You misunderstand, Doctor. I don't seek control. I orchestrate. I ensure the right notes are played, and the proper narrative unfolds."

His words sent a shiver down my spine. He spoke of manipulating lives like a conductor directing an orchestra, a chilling metaphor that laid bare his ruthless pragmatism.

"And what happens," I pressed, my voice laced with a dangerous calm, "when the music sheet gets ripped, Maestro? When the discord becomes too loud to ignore?"

A slow, predatory smile spread across his face. "Then, dear Doctor," he drawled, his voice dripping with a false sympathy, "one must improvise. A touch of persuasion here, a well-placed silence there. The symphony continues, albeit with a slightly altered score."

He took another deliberate step forward, the polished leather of his shoes whispering against the grimy concrete floor. I held my ground, my grip tightening on the bag strap and gun until my knuckles turned white. Every fiber of my being screamed at me to run, but I knew flight wouldn't save me.

"Let's cut to the chase, shall we, Doctor?" He stopped mere inches away from me, his cologne, a cloying mix of power and entitlement, filling my nostrils. "You have something that... inconveniences me. Now, a woman as intelligent as yourself must understand the precariousness of such a situation."

His voice held a thinly veiled threat, a reminder of the bullet that had silenced Mark just moments ago. The image of his lifeless body flickered at the edge of my vision, a stark reminder of the stakes involved.

"And what exactly is the nature of this inconvenience, Mr. Patterson?" I asked, my voice steady despite the tremor running through me.

He chuckled, a dry, humorless sound that echoed through the warehouse. "Ah, the thrill of the unknown," he purred, his eyes glinting with predatory amusement. Let's just say, Doctor, your little investigation has ruffled a few feathers. The feathers belong to people who could very well clip your wings if you're not careful."

He leaned in closer, his breath warm against my cheek. "So, tell me, Doctor," he continued, his voice almost inaudible, "are you willing to play along? Perhaps we can find a way to... rewrite the narrative, shall we say?"

His words were laced with a false promise, a dangling carrot meant to lure me into compliance. But I saw through his façade. This wasn't about negotiation; it was about asserting dominance, about crushing any potential resistance.

"There's no rewriting the truth, Mr. Patterson," I countered, meeting his gaze head-on. "The evidence speaks for itself."

He threw his head back and laughed, a harsh, guttural sound that bounced off the warehouse walls. "Evidence," he scoffed, wiping a mock tear from his eye. "Such a quaint notion, Doctor. In the grand scheme of things, a mere detail easily manipulated or conveniently forgotten."

His words were a challenge, an attempt to break my resolve. But as he spoke, a flicker of something akin to fear crossed his eyes, so fleeting it could have been a trick of the light. Yet, it was enough. It confirmed my suspicion: the evidence held within the satchel was more than just an inconvenience; it was a genuine threat to his carefully constructed world.

"Perhaps," I conceded, my voice laced with a dangerous calm, "but some details have a nasty habit of sticking around, Mr. Patterson. Like the stench of corruption that clings to you like a cheap cologne."

My words hung heavy in the air, a silent accusation that seemed to prick his carefully cultivated image. A muscle in his jaw clenched, and for a fleeting moment, the facade of composure wavered.

"You're a clever woman, Dr. Jenson," he said, his voice tight with contained anger. "But cleverness alone won't save you in this game."

He straightened his tie, a gesture that reeked of regaining control. "Now," he continued, his voice regaining its earlier smooth cadence, "let's be reasonable. You hand over whatever little trinket you've unearthed, and we can forget this little... misunderstanding ever happened."

His offer, although laced with thinly veiled threats, was tempting. Part of me, the rational part, screamed to take the easy way out, to walk away from this potential death sentence. But the other part, fueled by a fit of righteous anger and a fierce determination for justice for Mark and countless others, drowned out the voice of reason.

"Justice," I spat, the word a defiant challenge hanging heavy in the air. "Justice isn't on the menu tonight, Mr. Patterson. You may control the orchestra, but you don't control the conductor of your conscience."

My words struck a nerve. A flicker of something akin to fury momentarily replaced the practiced charm in his eyes. But it was quickly masked by a chilling smile.

"Conscience," he scoffed, the word dripping with disdain. "A foolish notion for the foolish, Doctor. In the real world, power dictates the narrative, not some abstract moral compass."

The silence stretched, thick and suffocating, broken only by the relentless drip, drip, drip of the leaky pipe. My heart hammered against my ribs, a frantic drumbeat echoing in my ears. Terror, icy and suffocating, clawed at my throat, threatening to paralyze me. Especially since I was staring down three guns. But I forced myself to breathe, slow and deep, focusing on the rise and fall of my chest, anchoring myself in the present.

"Power," I countered, my voice raspy but firm, "is a fickle thing, Mr. Patterson. It can crumble in the face of truth, just like a house of cards built on lies."

He took a slow, deliberate step back, his eyes narrowing as if reassessing me. "So be it, Doctor," he said, his voice laced with a dangerous calm. "If that's the game you want to play, then by all means, play."

The guns all moved closer. Where were Reynolds's policemen?

"The game has already begun, Mr. Patterson," I declared, my gaze unwavering. "And the truth will be the winning hand."

A slow, predatory smile spread across his face. "We shall see, Doctor," he purred, his voice dripping with a chilling amusement. "We shall see."

He took another step back, his hand slowly reaching towards his pocket. My breath hitched, and every muscle in my body tensed in anticipation. Was this it? Was he about to call my bluff?

But then, a sudden movement from within my bag startled him. Gojo had pushed her way out of the zipper opening. She perched on the edge of the bag.

For a fleeting moment, a flicker of surprise crossed Patterson's face, a chink in his otherwise unreadable armor. It was a split second, barely perceptible, but it was enough. In that instant, I saw an opportunity.

"Gojo!" I called out and, whispering an apology to the cat, threw her at Patterson's face.

She let out a hiss and clawed him. It was a pathetic defense, I knew, but it was enough to distract Patterson for the crucial moment I needed.

I extracted the gun and pointed it at Patterson's head as he batted Gojo away. He froze. "You dare!" he roared, his voice a guttural growl.

"Don't make any sudden moves," I warned, my voice surprisingly steady despite the tremor in my hand. To his men, I said, "One wrong step, and this bullet finds a new home in your boss."

Just then, the warehouse was plunged back into darkness. One of the men shot the single bulb, leaving us shrouded in an inky blackness. A terrified scream ripped from my throat, a sound of pure terror and surprise.

The darkness enveloped us like a heavy shroud, suffocating and oppressive. My heart pounded in my chest, each beat a thunderous echo in the silence of the warehouse. I could feel Patterson's presence looming before me, a menacing force that sent shivers down my spine.

"You think you can just waltz in here and threaten me?" I screamed, my voice echoing in the darkness. "You have no idea who you're dealing with, Patterson."

His laughter was a chilling sound, a dark symphony that seemed to fill the entire warehouse. "Oh, I know exactly who you are, Dr. Jenson," he taunted, his voice dripping with malice. "A desperate woman clinging to her last shreds of hope."

I felt anger rise within me, a defiant fire that burned bright despite the darkness that surrounded us. "Desperate, maybe," I admitted, my voice steady despite the turmoil churning inside me. "But I'm not going down without a fight."

Patterson's presence seemed to loom larger in the darkness, a shadowy figure that threatened to consume me whole. I could feel his hot breath against my cheek, his hands grasping at my arms with bruising force.

"You really have no idea what I'm capable of," he hissed, his voice low and dangerous. "I'll make you regret this, Jenson. I'll make you pay for every moment of this, your foolish defiance."

I could feel the panic rising within me, a primal fear that threatened to overwhelm my senses. But I forced myself to stay calm and focus on the task at hand. I had Patterson in my grasp, and I wasn't about to let him slip away.

"Regret?" I scoffed, my voice filled with a defiance I didn't quite feel. "I don't think so, Patterson. You're the one who's going to regret underestimating me."

"I'll make you regret this, Dr. Jenson. You and that pathetic excuse for a patient of yours."

The mention of Steven sent a jolt of fear through me, the image of his terrified face flashing before my eyes. I couldn't let Patterson get to him, couldn't let him hurt anyone else.

"I won't let you touch him," I said, my voice barely above a whisper. "I won't let you hurt anyone else after today."

Patterson laughed, the sound echoing through the darkness like a sinister melody. "Oh, you think you can stop me? You're just a lonely psychologist, Jenson. What can you possibly do?"

His taunts cut through me like a knife, each word. But I refused to back down, refused to let him see the fear that gnawed at my insides.

"I have the gun," I said, my voice stronger now despite the tremor in my hands. "And I'm not afraid to use it."

There was a tense silence, broken only by the distant sound of footsteps echoing through the warehouse. I held my breath, waiting for the moment when Detective Reynolds and his team would burst in and save me.

"You're bluffing," Patterson's voice was a sneer, his confidence unwavering. "You don't have the guts to pull that trigger."

"Try me," I challenged, my finger tightening on the trigger. "I'll do whatever it takes to stop you."

For a moment, there was a palpable tension in the air, a silent standoff between predator and prey. Then, with a sudden movement, Patterson lunged forward, his hands reaching for me.

Instinct took over, and I reacted without thinking. I grabbed hold of him, my fingers digging into his flesh as I held on for dear life. Our bodies collided with a thud, the force of his momentum sending us both stumbling backward.

I could hear Patterson's furious shouts, his curses ringing in my ears as we grappled in the darkness. Adrenaline surged through my veins, lending me a strength I didn't know I possessed.

"Let go of me, you bitch!" Patterson snarled, his voice filled with rage.

But I held on, my grip unyielding as I fought to keep him restrained. "Not a chance," I spat back, my voice filled with a determination born of desperation.

"If I hear one more footstep, I'll blow his brains out!" I yelled into the warehouse for his men's benefit.

"Let go!" he roared, his voice echoing through the warehouse.

But I held on. I had him, and I wasn't about to let him slip away now. Suddenly, there was a commotion from outside the warehouse, the sound of voices and footsteps growing louder by the second. I felt a surge of relief wash over me, knowing that Detective Reynolds and his team were finally here.

"Drop the gun, Dr. Jenson!" Reynolds' voice cut through the chaos, his tone firm and commanding.

I hesitated for a moment, torn between the desire to hold on to Patterson and the knowledge that help was finally at hand. In the end, I made my choice. I released my grip on Patterson and dropped the gun to the ground. The warehouse was flooded with light as Reynolds and his team burst in, guns drawn and ready. Patterson lay on the ground before me, defeated and broken. I could see the fear in his eyes, the realization dawning that he was no match for the forces arrayed against him.

"You're finished, Patterson," Reynolds said, his voice cold and unforgiving. "It's over."

But even as Patterson was dragged away, his protests echoing through the warehouse, unease settled over me. The darkness had shown me just how far I was willing to go, how deep I was willing to sink to protect what I knew was right.

As the blinding light flooded the warehouse, illuminating the chaotic scene before me, I felt a surge of relief wash over me. But before I could fully process the situation, before I could even begin to lower my guard, the tranquility of the moment shattered like glass. A sudden eruption of gunfire echoed through the warehouse, the deafening roar of the bullets drowning out all other sounds. Instinct took over, and I dove for cover, my heart pounding in my chest as adrenaline surged through my veins.

The air was thick with smoke and the acrid stench of gunpowder, the haze obscuring my vision as I struggled to make sense of the chaos unfolding around me. Patterson's men were everywhere, their faces masked as they unleashed a hail of bullets upon us. I could hear shouts and cries of pain as my people fell around me, their bodies crumpling to the ground as Reynolds and the police returned fire. Panic clawed at my throat, threatening to overwhelm me as I fought to stay focused, to keep my wits about me in the midst of the madness.

Through the smoke and the confusion, I caught sight of Patterson lunging towards me, his eyes blazing with a feral intensity. But before I could process it, Patterson was upon me, his fingers closing around the pen mic in my shirt in a vice-like grip. I felt a surge of panic course through me as he tore the pen mic from my shirt, a triumphant sneer twisting his lips. I could feel his hot breath against my cheek, his foul scent invading my senses as he loomed over me like a malevolent specter. Fear clutched at my heart, threatening to paralyze me as I struggled to find the strength to fight back.

Before I could even begin to formulate a plan, Patterson was torn away from me by his men, their hands closing around him with brutal force. I watched in horror as they dragged him shielded towards the exit. In the chaos of the firefight, I could see Detective Reynolds and his team returning fire, their guns blazing as they fought to repel Patterson's men. One of Patterson's men fell to the ground with a thud, a crimson stain spreading across his chest as he lay motionless on the cold concrete floor. But even in death, his comrades showed no sign of retreat.

I struggled to stay one step ahead of the onslaught. The warehouse seemed to spin around me, a dizzying blur of chaos and violence as I fought to make sense of the madness that surrounded us. Where was Gojo?

And then, just as suddenly as it had begun, the gunfire ceased, leaving behind an eerie silence that hung heavy in the air. I cautiously peeked out from behind my makeshift barricade, my breath catching in my throat as I surveyed the aftermath of the battle. Patterson was nowhere to be seen, his escape facilitated by the firefight's distraction. I cursed under my breath, frustration boiling within me as I realized that he had slipped through our fingers.

Finally, I saw Gojo cowering in a corner. My heart broke, and I berated myself for putting her in danger. I scooped her up and joined Detective Reynolds and his team as we regrouped amidst the warehouse's wreckage. Patterson may have won this battle, but the war was far from over.

A Desperate Escape

The rhythmic clack of my keyboard created a comforting background noise, and the soft glow of the desk lamp cast a warm pool of light over the papers on my desk.

It had been a long day, filled with endless phone calls, meetings, and a long list of candidates applying to be my receptionist. My mind buzzed with information about the candidates. And it often went back to snippets of conversations and clues about Steven's case. Both of them were swirling around like a tornado in my head. We were getting closer, inching ever closer to unraveling the mystery that had consumed me for weeks.

The pieces of the puzzle were finally starting to come together, and they were revealing a chilling picture of corruption and greed.

A sudden, bone-jarring crash shattered the tranquility of the office. My heart leaped in my chest, adrenaline immediately pumping through my veins as I whirled around in my chair to face the source of the disturbance. The office door splintered inwards, showering the floor with splinters of wood. My eyes widened in shock as a figure, shrouded in black, materialized from the doorway like a specter from the shadows. Moonlight glinted off a wickedly curved blade held in a gloved hand, sending a shiver down my spine.

For a moment, time seemed to stand still as we stared at each other, the intruder's eyes gleaming with a predatory glint. Panic surged through me, threatening to overwhelm my senses, but years of training and experience kicked in, steeling my nerves.

"Who are you?" I demanded, my voice steady despite the rapid thud of my heart against my ribs.

The figure said nothing, but the cold, calculating look in their eyes spoke volumes. They were here for a reason, and I don't think it was for a friendly chat. Every nerve in my body screamed at me to run, to flee from the danger that loomed before me. But I knew that wasn't an option. I was cornered, with nowhere to go.

Slowly, deliberately, the intruder began to advance towards me, the blade glinting ominously in the dim light. Panic threatened to consume me, but I forced myself to remain calm and to think clearly despite the fear that clawed at my throat.

"What do you want?" I asked, my voice betraying none of the terror that gripped me.

The figure said nothing, their silence a chilling echo in the stillness of the office. I could feel the weight of their gaze upon me, a tangible presence that seemed to suffocate the air around us. And then, without warning, they lunged forward, the blade flashing in the lamplight. Instinct took over, and I threw myself to the side, narrowly avoiding the deadly strike.

Adrenaline surged through me as I scrambled to my feet, my mind racing with a thousand thoughts. I needed to defend myself, to protect myself from this unknown threat. With a surge of strength, I reached for the nearest object – a heavy paperweight – and hurled it towards the intruder. It struck them square in the chest, sending them stumbling backward with a grunt of pain.

Seizing the opportunity, I dashed towards the door, my heart pounding in my chest. But before I could reach safety, a strong hand closed around my arm, yanking me backward with brutal force. I cried out in pain as the intruder spun me around to face them, their eyes blazing with a feral intensity. The blade hovered menacingly at my throat, a deadly promise of the fate that awaited me if I dared to resist.

"Give me the files," they hissed, their voice a low, menacing growl.

I could feel the cold metal of the blade pressing against my skin, a chilling reminder of the danger that lurked just inches away. Fear gripped me like a vice, threatening to paralyze me as I struggled to find the strength to resist. But then, a surge of anger and defiance rose up within me, banishing the fear that threatened to consume me. I would not go down without a fight. With a fierce determination, I met the intruder's gaze head-on, my eyes blazing with a fire of their own.

"I'll never give you what you want," I spat, my voice dripping with venom.

The intruder's eyes narrowed, a cruel smile twisting their lips. "We'll see about that," they taunted, their voice laced with malice.

My heart lurched in my chest, a primal instinct of danger flashing through me. This wasn't a random break-in; it was a targeted attack. The realization sent a surge of adrenaline coursing through me, replacing fear with a steely resolve. Without hesitation, I lunged for the nearest object that could serve as a makeshift weapon - a heavy medical textbook resting on my desk.

The worn leather cover offered scant protection, but it was a weapon, nonetheless. Gripping it tightly in my trembling hands, I swung with all my might. The book connected with a sickening thud against the attacker's shoulder, momentarily disrupting their charge. A muffled grunt of pain escaped the figure as they stumbled back, the glint of the blade mere inches from my face.

A scream tore from my throat, a raw, primal sound of desperation and fear. Chaos erupted in the small office as we grappled with each other, the intruder's blade flashing dangerously in the dim light. Papers fluttered like confetti, swirling around us in a cinematographic fashion. A prized framed degree crashed to the floor, its glass shattering with a million mournful tinkles. The metallic tang of blood filled the air as a deep gash bloomed on my arm, sending a spike of pain through me. But there was no time for self-pity.

Having no other choice, I fought back, desperation lending me a fierce determination. The attacker was skilled, their movements swift and calculated. I dodged and parried as best as I could, the weight of the textbook becoming heavier with each swing. A glancing blow struck my side, the blade slicing through fabric and skin. Pain flared along my ribs, hot and searing. I gritted my teeth against the agony, refusing to let it weaken me. I couldn't afford to falter; my life depended on it.

In a moment of desperation, I aimed a swift kick at the attacker's knee. It connected with a satisfying crunch, eliciting a cry of pain. Seizing the opportunity, I pushed with all my might, sending the figure stumbling backward. They recovered quickly, their dark eyes glinting with malice. With a growl of rage, the attacker lunged forward once more, the blade slashing through the air with deadly intent. I ducked and weaved, narrowly avoiding the lethal edge.

Time seemed to blur as we fought, the room spinning around us in a dizzying whirl. Adrenaline pumped through my veins, heightening my senses to a razor-sharp edge. Every move, every breath was a calculated risk. Then I saw my chance. As the attacker's blade arced towards me once more, I twisted to the side, letting it sail past harmlessly. I brought the textbook down with all my strength, aiming for the figure's wrist.

There was a sickening crack as bone met leather, and the blade clattered to the ground. The attacker let out a cry of pain, stumbling back and clutching their injured hand. It was my turn to seize the advantage. With a fierce determination, I pressed forward, my movements fueled by a primal instinct to survive. The attacker stumbled, their footing unsure as they tried to evade my relentless assault.

I was relentless, my blows raining down with a relentless fury. The textbook became an extension of myself, a weapon of retribution against the one who sought to harm me. With a final, decisive blow, the attacker crumpled to the ground, defeated. Panting heavily, I stood over them; the textbook still clutched tightly in my trembling hands.

The office was silent now, save for the ragged sound of my breath and the distant wail of sirens. Blood dripped from my wounds, mingling with the shattered glass and torn papers on the floor. I was bruised and battered but alive. The adrenaline that had fueled me moments ago now ebbed away, leaving behind a bone-deep weariness. I sank to my knees, the weight of the ordeal crashing down on me.

There was no time to rest. The attacker lay at my feet, unconscious but still dangerous.

I scrambled towards the open window, thankful that I had not brought Gojo with me that day. After that episode at the warehouse with all the guns, I was loathe to bring her anywhere until this Patterson business was settled. Urgency lent wings to my movements, propelling me forward despite the searing pain that came from my wounds.

As I reached the window, my heart pounded in my chest like a drumbeat, signaling a tribal village of impending danger. With a desperate heave, I flung it open, the hinges protesting with a resounding clang that echoed through the night. The cold rush of wind slapped against my face, whipping strands of hair across my vision.

Without hesitation, I clambered onto the fire escape, the metal grating cold and unforgiving beneath my hands. The dizzying drop below threatened to steal my breath, a yawning abyss of uncertainty. But there was no time for hesitation.

I cast a quick glance over my shoulder, dread coiling in the pit of my stomach. Fear, sharp and primal, clawed at my throat, threatening to overwhelm me. But I couldn't afford to succumb to panic. With gritted teeth, I pushed myself forward, even though each step was a struggle against the burning ache in my muscles.

The city lights below blurred. I couldn't help but wonder if anyone would notice if I disappeared into the night, swallowed whole by the chaos that threatened to consume me. The fire escape creaked and groaned beneath my weight as I descended, each step a precarious dance on the edge of oblivion. The wind howled around me, a haunting chorus of the night.

I risked a glance downwards, the vertigo-inducing drop sending a jolt of terror through me. But there was no turning back now. The alternative, the thought of what awaited me if I stayed, spurred me on. Behind me, the footsteps grew closer, the ominous sound of pursuit echoing in the narrow confines of the fire escape. Panic threatened to overwhelm me, a suffocating grip that tightened around my chest.

I reached the next landing, my heart hammering in my chest. With trembling hands, I fumbled for the latch of the gate leading to the next flight of stairs. It swung open with a rusty protest, revealing the dark descent that lay ahead. A surge of adrenaline coursed through me as I plunged downwards, each step a heart-stopping leap into the unknown. The wind whipped around me, tugging at my clothes and hair like ghostly fingers.

Finally, mercifully, I reached the ground floor. The alleyway stretched before me, a narrow passage of shadow and uncertainty. I could hear the distant wail of sirens, a glimmer of hope in the darkness. Without pausing to catch my breath, I sprinted towards the car park, the cold pavement rough beneath my bare feet. I made it, but the attacker was after me, so I turned into an alley.

I hurtled into the narrow alley, the rough pavement unforgiving beneath my footsteps. The darkness enveloped me like a suffocating shroud, the only illumination the distant glow of city lights filtering through the maze of looming buildings. Years of late-night jogs through these labyrinthine alleyways had burned their paths into my memory like the grooves of an old record. But tonight, familiarity offered little comfort as desperation lent wings to my feet.

Every overflowing dumpster, every shadowed nook, and cranny became a potential hiding place, a fleeting refuge from the relentless pursuit at my heels. I darted around corners with reckless abandon, the urgent need to escape driving me forward. The echo of my pursuer's footsteps reverberated off the grimy walls, a relentless drumbeat of menace that spurred my frantic sprint. My lungs burned with exertion, each breath a searing agony in my chest.

The usual cacophony of the city faded into a distant murmur tonight, drowned out by the hammering of my own heart in my ears. Adrenaline pushed me on, sharpening my senses to a razor's edge. I risked a glance over my shoulder, my heart skipping a beat at the sight of the shadowy figure in pursuit. Their silhouette loomed large against the dimly lit alley, a specter of danger and relentless determination.

I pushed myself harder, my muscles screaming in protest as I hurtled past rusted fire escapes and graffiti-covered walls. The chill of the night air bit at my skin, mingling with the sheen of sweat that coated my brow. A flicker of hope ignited within me as I recognized a familiar turn ahead. The alley widened slightly, offering a fleeting glimpse of escape. With a surge of determination, I pushed myself to go faster, to reach that narrow passage of freedom.

But fate had other plans.

As I rounded the corner, a shadow detached itself from the darkness, blocking my path. My heart lurched in my chest, dread coiling like a serpent in the pit of my stomach. Instinct took over as I skidded to a stop, my pulse thundering in my ears. I darted to the side, searching desperately for an alternate route, but the alley offered no escape. The figure stepped forward, their features obscured by the shadows. A glint of metal caught the faint light, and my blood ran cold. A weapon gleaming with deadly intent.

"You can't run forever."

Annoyingly, they were correct. But I can try. So I ran in the other direction.

I stumbled through the darkness, my breath coming in ragged gasps as I fought against the pain pulsing through my battered body. Every step was a struggle, every movement sending waves of agony coursing through me. But I couldn't stop. Not now. Not when my life depended on it.

My surroundings blurred into a haze of shadows and indistinct shapes as I ran, my senses dulled by exhaustion and fear. I had no destination in mind, no plan beyond putting as much distance between myself and my pursuers as possible. The city streets stretched out before me like a labyrinth, each alleyway a potential trap, each corner hiding unseen dangers. But I pushed on, driven by a primal instinct for survival.

And then I saw it—the old safehouse where Reynolds had told me I would be safe, if only for a while. I stumbled towards the looming structure, my legs threatening to give out beneath me with every step. The ground seemed to sway beneath my feet, the world spinning dizzily around me as I fought to stay upright.

Finally, I reached the shelter of the warehouse, collapsing behind a stack of rotting crates with a relieved sigh. My body trembled with exhaustion and pain, every muscle screaming in protest as I curled into a tight ball, seeking refuge from the storm raging both outside and within.

My breaths came in ragged gasps, the sound echoing in the cavernous space around me. I strained to hear any sounds of pursuit, any hint of danger lurking in the shadows. But all I heard was silence. A wave of relief washed over me, mingling with the dull ache pulsing through my battered body. For the moment, at least, I was safe. Safe from the relentless pursuit of my enemies, safe from the violence and chaos that had consumed my life.

But even as I allowed myself a moment of respite, I knew it wouldn't last. They would come for me, of that I had no doubt. With trembling fingers, I fumbled for my phone, the screen illuminating the darkness with a harsh glare. Tears welled up in my eyes as I punched in Detective Reynolds' number, my heart hammering in my chest.

It rang once, twice, before he answered, his voice cutting through the silence like a lifeline.

"Olivia? Is everything okay?" His voice was filled with concern, and I couldn't hold back the flood of emotions threatening to overwhelm me.

"Detective Reynolds," I choked out, my voice a raspy whisper choked with fear. "It's... it's not okay. Someone... someone attacked me. They're trying to silence me."

There was a sharp intake of breath on the other end of the line, followed by a tense silence. I could almost hear the gears turning in his mind as he processed my words.

"Where are you now?" he asked his voice firm and steady.

"In... in the warehouse," I replied, my voice trembling. "The one you told me about. I... I don't know what to do, Reynolds. I'm scared."

"Okay, listen to me," he said, his tone commanding. "I'm going to send backup right away. Stay where you are and keep your phone with you. Can you do that?"

I nodded, even though I knew he couldn't see me. "Yes, yes, I can do that."

"Good," he said, a note of relief in his voice. "Now, tell me what happened. Start from the beginning."

I took a deep, shuddering breath, the memories of the attack flooding back with vivid clarity.

"I was... I was working late in my office," I began, my voice shaking. "And then... then I heard a crash. The door... the door burst open, and there was... there was someone there. A figure clothed in black."

I could feel the panic rising in my chest, threatening to choke me. But I forced myself to continue, to recount the horror of what had happened.

"They had a knife," I said, the words tumbling out in a rush. "They... they came at me, and I... I fought back. I hit them with a book, but... but they cut me. I managed to... to escape through the window, and I ran. I ran until I found this warehouse."

There was a long pause on the other end of the line, the silence heavy with unspoken questions.

"Olivia," Detective Reynolds said finally, his voice gentle. "I need you to stay calm. Backup is on the way, and they'll be there soon. You did the right thing by calling me."

I nodded, even though he couldn't see me. "Okay, okay. I'll wait for them."

I sat in silence for a moment; the only sound was the raggedness of my breathing, which was slowly returning to normal.

The screech of tires announcing Detective Reynolds' arrival was the sweetest music I had ever heard. I hid in a corner as he came in to be sure it was him. He stopped when he saw me.

"Christ! Let's get you checked out by a medic," Detective Reynolds said. "We need to make sure you're okay."

I nodded numbly, my thoughts still spinning with the events of the night. Outside, I was greeted by a team of paramedics. Apparently, Reynolds had called ahead.

"Jenson, are you alright?" one of them asked, rushing forward to assess my injuries.

I nodded, the pain in my body suddenly more pronounced now that the adrenaline had begun to fade. "I think so. It's just a scratch," I said.

I looked again and realized it was Jim. "Hey, Jim." Jim was a guy I knew from somewhere.

The paramedic inspected the wound, his brow furrowing in concern. "We'll need to clean and bandage this up," he said, his voice gentle. "Just a scratch indeed."

As he worked, Detective Reynolds stood by my side, his presence a silent comfort as I endured the pain of my injuries being tended to.

Relief and then exhaustion crashed over me as strong arms helped me into the waiting police car after Jim and his team finished with me.

"Dr. Jenson, are you okay?" Detective Reynolds's voice was filled with concern as he settled into the driver's seat beside me. His eyes searched mine, seeking reassurance.

I nodded weakly, the events of the night still replaying in my mind like a horror movie I couldn't escape. "I... I think so. I just... I can't believe this happened."

Detective Reynolds's hand found mine, squeezing it gently. "I'm just glad you're safe," he said, his voice soft.

I managed a weak smile, grateful for his comforting presence. "Me too."

Wow, Olivia! What's happening here? That was my internal voice yelling at me.

The journey to the station was a blur of flashing lights and distant sirens. My mind was still reeling from the adrenaline-fueled chaos of the past hour, the memory of the attacker's blade inches from my face, sending new shivers down my spine.

As we pulled up to the station, Detective Reynolds helped me out of the car. We made our way inside, the fluorescent lights buzzing overhead like a chorus of angels. Detective Reynolds led me to a quiet corner of the station, away from the prying eyes of my colleagues.

"Are you sure you're okay?" he asked, his voice filled with worry.

I nodded, my eyes meeting his. "I'm shaken, but I'll be fine. Thank you for getting here so quickly."

He smiled with a tired but genuine expression. "I promised I'd keep you safe, didn't I?"

I couldn't help but smile back, grateful for his unwavering support. "You did."

Cool your jets, Liv. I warned myself.

Unraveling the Truth

Three days after the attack, I was back at home, my office still under repairs from the chaos of that fateful night. Sitting at my desk, I squinted at the computer screen, the harsh glare failing to penetrate the fog of exhaustion clouding my mind. Despite the physical safety of my own home, the trauma of the attack lingered, haunting my every thought.

I'd spent the entire night chasing cryptic digital breadcrumbs – IP addresses and bank transactions, all leading to the shadowy figure known as Mr. Taskin. The deeper I delved into the digital labyrinth, the more elusive he seemed, slipping through my fingers like smoke. But finally, after hours of relentless searching, a sliver of success emerged from the darkness.

The money trail led to a single account held under the name William Williamson. Although it was a common enough name, something about it was distinct. I reached for my phone, dialing Detective Reynolds' number. As the line rang, my mind raced with a thousand questions, each one more pressing than the last. But before I could voice them, Alex's voice crackled through the receiver.

"Olivia, is everything okay?" His tone was laced with concern, reflecting the bond that had formed between us after the attack.

"I think I've found something," I said, my voice barely above a whisper. "The money trail leads to a man named William Williamson. I think he's our Mr. Taskin."

There was a pause on the other end of the line, the weight of my words hanging in the air like a heavy fog. "I'll look into it," Alex said finally, his voice tight with determination. "In the meantime, stay safe. I don't want anything else happening to you."

I nodded, even though I knew he couldn't see me. "I will," I promised.

As I hung up the phone, I felt a sense of guilt.

The discovery of William Williamson was just the beginning; factoring in the attacks, I knew I was close. I could feel it in my bones.

Three questions needed to be answered: where the toxin came from, how Steven's memory was corrupted, who did it, and what Patterson's real motive was.

It was clear that Patterson felt he had unfinished business with Steven's grandparents.

I wasted no time. A quick internet search revealed there was only one William Williamson in the city; I found an address on the outskirts. Armed with this single lead, I climbed behind the wheel of my car, the engine purring to life beneath me. Gojo tried to come with me, but I had to leave her behind.

The drive out of town was a blur, the city gradually melting away into the darkness of the night. I hoped this was not just another dead end.

As I pulled up in front of the house, a chill crept up my spine. The neighborhood was eerily quiet, the only sound the soft whisper of leaves rustling in the breeze. There were few houses or even buildings around. I checked the address again, confirming that I was indeed at the right place. The house loomed before me, its windows dark and uninviting. There was no sign of life, no flicker of movement behind the curtains. With a deep breath, I stepped out of the car, my senses on high alert.

The front door creaked ominously as I pushed it open, the hinges protesting with age. The interior was dimly lit the air heavy with the musty scent of neglect. Dust motes danced in the faint beam of light that filtered through the windows.

"Hello?" I called out, my voice echoing through the empty house. There was no response, just the eerie silence that seemed to envelop everything.

I moved cautiously through the rooms, my footsteps muffled by the worn carpet beneath my feet. The house seemed frozen in time as if its inhabitants had suddenly vanished without a trace. A sound from upstairs made me freeze. It was faint, barely audible, but it sent a jolt of fear through me. Someone else was in the house.

Heart pounding, I made my way up the creaky staircase, each step echoing loudly in the silence. The hallway upstairs was shrouded in darkness, the only light coming from a cracked door at the end. With trembling hands, I pushed the door open, revealing a dimly lit room. And there, sitting at a desk, was a man hunched over a computer screen.

"William Williamson?" My voice sounded small and shaky in the stillness.

The man looked up, his eyes widening in surprise. "Who are you?" he demanded, his voice harsh.

"I'm Dr. Olivia Jenson," I said, trying to keep my voice steady. "I'm investigating a case, and I believe you might have information that could help."

Williamson's eyes narrowed, suspicion flickering in their depths. "What case?" he asked, his tone guarded.

I took a step forward, my gaze unwavering. "The case of Steven Roseblood-Gundel," I replied, watching for any reaction.

For a moment, there was silence as Williamson studied me, his expression unreadable. Then, with a sudden movement, he reached for something on the desk. Instinct took over as I dove to the side, narrowly avoiding the object hurtling towards me. It was a small statue.

"You shouldn't have come here," he growled, raising a fist.

I launched myself at Williamson, tackling him to the ground. We grappled and fought, but he was a frail man. I won easily.

"Tell me what you know?"

Surprisingly, he crumbled immediately.

"Alright, alright!" Williamson wheezed, his voice like dry leaves rustling in the autumn wind. His bony frame crumpled under me, his once crisp suit now wrinkled and dusty. Releasing him, I watched with a mixture of surprise and suspicion as he scrambled back, his eyes wide with terror. He looked more like a frightened rabbit than a criminal mastermind.

"Everything," I repeated, my voice firm but laced with a hint of suspicion. "Starting from the beginning."

Williamson took a ragged breath, patting his rumpled clothes self-consciously. "It's... Patterson. Timothy Patterson. We grew up together, you see. Childhood friends, cousins. Both full of ambition, both dreaming of making it big." A bitter smile, like a wilted flower clinging to a barren stem, twisted his thin lips. "We even started a company together. A small startup, they were all the rage back then. We were young, cocky, and thought we were going to change the world."

A tremor ran through his hand, and he clenched it into a fist. "But Timothy, he had a... darker side. Always chasing risk, always pushing boundaries. He saw the potential for more, for faster growth. We started cutting corners, taking on riskier projects, promising more than we could deliver."

Williamson's voice dropped to a conspiratorial whisper. "I started noticing things—missing funds, shady deals brewing in the background. I confronted him, of course, naive fool that I was. He scoffed and said it was all part of the game, the ruthless game of big business. That's when the trouble began."

He ran a hand through his thinning hair, the strands clinging to his scalp like cobwebs. "One particularly ambitious project went belly-up. Millions of investor money vanished, and the authorities started circling. Timothy, ever the snake, pointed the finger at me. He forged documents and cooked up stories about my mismanagement, my supposed gambling debts. I had never been to Vegas in my life. Still haven't."

The whisper rose to a choked sob. "I was blindsided. My own friend, the person I trusted the most, turned on me in a heartbeat. The company collapsed, taking my reputation with it. Newspapers plastered my face across their front pages, calling me a fraud, a thief. Investors lost everything, and I... I became a pariah. I ran, refusing to go to jail for something I didn't do. So I was forced to live in the shadows, a ghost haunting my own life."

Williamson's eyes, brimming with unshed tears, locked with mine. "He took my name, you see. After that, he used it to distance himself from scandal. Every shady deal, every criminal operation he orchestrated, he did it under the name of 'Williamson,' the disgraced ex-entrepreneur. It was the perfect smokescreen, keeping him clean while I rotted away here."

A flicker of anger, hot and fierce, ignited within me. "He used you," I stated, my voice tight with fury.

"Used me, destroyed me," he echoed, his voice cracking. "But that's not all. He kept tabs on me and made sure I stayed quiet. Once, I tried to reach out to an old friend to tell him the truth. But before I could, a 'warning' arrived. He sent me a kneecap from the man. He was forced into a hospital stay with no explanation. The message was clear: stay silent or disappear."

Williamson's shoulders slumped, defeat etched on his face. "For years, I lived in fear, a prisoner in my own city. Take my advice, leave. If he knows you've been here, you're dead. And you'll be one more ghost to haunt my conscience."

"I'm not leaving. He framed a friend of mine. I need Patterson to be brought to justice."

"He's too big."

"The bigger they are."

"The harder they fall?"

He looked at me. Really looked for the first time. I saw a desperate hope flickering in his eyes. Finally, he said, "I can help you bring him down, but you have to protect me. If Timothy finds out, I talked...."

"I understand," I said, my voice calmer now. "You're scared, but I won't leave you alone."

"What do you need?"

"I need to find Mr. Taskin, he is supposed to have sold an untraceable toxin to my friend."

Williamson hesitated for a long moment, his weathered face a mask of conflicting emotions. Finally, with a shaky breath, he spoke. "There's... someone. A man named Dr. Thorne. A brilliant toxicologist, but also... well, let's just say he operates outside the usual ethical boundaries. Timothy approached him a while back, looking for someone with a particular skill set."

"A skill set involving deadly toxins?" I pressed.

"Exactly," Williamson rasped, his voice barely above a whisper. "Thorne wasn't cheap, of course. Timothy promised him a hefty sum, enough to disappear comfortably somewhere exotic. I remember very well, after all, I was the one who had to recruit him."

The pieces were starting to fall into place, forming a horrifying picture. "And Dr. Thorne?" I asked, my voice barely audible.

"He has a secluded lab, a place off the grid," Williamson continued, his voice gaining a hint of urgency. "It's somewhere outside the city limits, near an abandoned quarry. I remember seeing the address scribbled on a napkin during one of their meetings."

He fumbled in his pocket, his hands trembling visibly. "Here," he finally rasped, handing me a crumpled piece of paper. "It's not much, but it's all I have. Go there, see for yourself. If Timothy's truly behind cooking up this toxin of yours, that's where it'll be."

Taking the paper, I unfolded it carefully. The address, scrawled in messy handwriting, stared back at me. This could be the key to dismantling Patterson's web of deceit or a dead end leading me even deeper into danger.

"But how can you be sure?" I questioned, my gaze fixed on the address. "This could be another one of his lies, a way to set you up. Or" I looked at him suspiciously. "You could be setting me up."

Williamson's eyes widened in alarm. "No, no! I wouldn't... Look, there's more. Remember the Davies incident? The woman who accused

Timothy of embezzlement? Timothy... well, he took care of her permanently. And guess who supplied the poison that caused the 'heart attack'?"

My breath hitched. "You're saying..."

"Dr. Thorne," Williamson finished, his voice dropping to a barely audible level. "It wasn't the first time they worked together, and it won't be the last if we don't stop him."

A heavy silence descended upon the room, broken only by the ragged gasps of Williamson's labored breathing. The weight of his confession settled on me, a chilling reminder of the lengths to which Patterson would go to maintain his power.

But within the darkness, a spark of determination ignited. "Alright, Williamson," I said, my voice tight with resolve. "I believe you. And together, we're going to bring him down. But first, we need to get you to safety. The police can offer you witness protection, a new identity..."

Williamson's face contorted in a grimace. "No. The police... they're compromised. Timothy has his fingers everywhere. He'll find me no matter where I go."

Fear flickered in his eyes, a fear that transcended his personal safety. "There's only one person I trust," he continued, his voice barely a whisper. "Someone Timothy wouldn't suspect. Someone who's been investigating him for a while now, a woman."

He trailed off, his eyes darting nervously around the room. Then, leaning in close, he spoke a name so softly it was almost swallowed by the dusty silence of the abandoned building.

Henrietta Roseblood.

"She's dead now. Patterson killed her and is framing her grandson."

Williamson lurched forward, and a long string of cusses and curses flowed from him. They were so violent that I turned crimson like a Regency-era lady hearing her first bad word from the roguish and impertinent driver her father had just hired.

When I left, he was quiet. His gaze was turned to the ceiling, and he was still.

The address Williamson gave me led me on a journey beyond the city's sprawl. Towering skyscrapers faded into a distant memory, replaced by a deserted realm where nature reigned supreme. The asphalt road turned into a dusty track, its surface surrendering to the relentless march of encroaching vegetation. Sunlight, filtered through a dense canopy of leaves, cast a dappled, disorienting light on the overgrown path. The city's cacophony of car horns and sirens was replaced by the song of birds and insects. The calls of animals. The air thrummed with their buzzing serenade.

Williamson's instructions were sparse, a cryptic trail of breadcrumbs leading me deeper into this forgotten realm. He'd mentioned a specific landmark – a skeletal, moss-covered oak tree, its once-proud form split down the middle by a vengeful lightning strike. After what felt like hours of navigating the twisting path, pushing through tangled undergrowth that threatened to snatch at my clothes and snag on my backpack, the telltale oak materialized ahead. Its gnarled, skeletal figure stood like a silent guardian, its jagged silhouette a dark scar against the verdant backdrop.

Pushing through a curtain of clinging vines, heavy with dew and the scent of decay, I emerged into a hidden clearing. A single, dilapidated building squatted in the center, like a forgotten sentinel reclaimed by the wilderness. Its once-vibrant paint peeled in long, sad strips, revealing weathered wood beneath. This wasn't the abandoned factory I'd envisioned, no towering brick walls or ominous smokestacks belching black plumes into the sky. It was a ramshackle, long structure more akin to a long-deserted hunting lodge, its windows boarded shut and a heavy layer of dust clinging to its neglected exterior.

A single plume of smoke curled lazily from a rusty chimney, the only sign of life in this isolated place. It hung in the still air, a wispy beacon amidst the verdant embrace of the forest. This wasn't the scene from a generic industrial thriller; it was more unsettling, more enigmatic. There was an unsettling stillness to the place, a sense of nature reclaiming what man had abandoned. Yet, the lone plume of smoke hinted at hidden activity, a chilling contrast to the serene exterior. Ditching the flashlight in favor of a more natural camouflage, I shoved the backpack deeper under my layers, the cold metal of the crowbar a reassuring weight against my hip. Taking a deep breath, each one punctuated by the rhythmic drumming of my heart against my ribs, I approached cautiously. Each step crunched on the bed of fallen leaves, the sound echoing in the unnatural silence. The sweet, cloying smell grew stronger with each step, a sickly prelude to whatever horrors might lie within. Squinting towards the building, I noticed a single, boarded-up window ajar at the back. This might be my only way in.

Pushing aside the warped wooden board with a soft groan, I squeezed through the narrow opening, blinking as my eyes adjusted from the dappled sunlight to the unexpected scene before me. Gone was the image of a dusty, cobweb-filled laboratory; instead, I found myself staring into a space that resembled a page torn from a high-end interior design magazine.

Polished concrete floors gleamed under the soft glow of strategically placed recessed lighting. Walls were adorned not with peeling paint but with floor-to-ceiling displays of vibrant orchids, their delicate blooms contrasting sharply with the stark modernity of the environment. A sleek, minimalist sofa in pale grey leather sat nestled amidst a sea of plush green ferns, a geometric coffee table anchoring the space with its gleaming chrome base and tempered glass top.

Disbelief warred with caution as I crept further inside. This wasn't a lab; it was a luxurious living space designed to impress. Every detail, from the strategically placed artwork depicting bioluminescent creatures to the strategically placed bowls of exotic fruits overflowing with color, screamed of a man with an appreciation for the finer things in life, a stark contrast to the image of a mad scientist I'd conjured in my mind.

Confusion threatened to paralyze me, but the insistent hum that had guided me from the outside, coupled with the cloying sweetness that was now overpowering, propelled me forward. Navigating the unexpected obstacle course of potted plants and designer furniture, I finally reached a doorway hidden behind a cascading curtain of what appeared to be genetically modified spider plants - their leaves unnaturally elongated and bioluminescent, casting an eerie greenish glow on the surroundings.

Taking a deep breath, I pushed the door open, steeling myself for the horrors I expected to find. Instead, I was greeted by another surprise. This wasn't a cramped, cluttered lab filled with bubbling beakers and hissing contraptions. It was a modern marvel of medical technology.

The room was spacious and bathed in a cool, sterile blue light emanating from strategically placed panels embedded in the ceiling. Stainless steel counters ran along two walls, gleaming under the light. Instead of dusty test tubes, these surfaces were populated with an array of high-tech equipment – sleek, computer-controlled instruments with blinking lights and digital displays displaying complex data streams. Holographic displays pulsed in the air, showcasing molecular structures and intricate chemical formulas. A lone robotic arm, sleek and silver, hovered over a glass containment chamber filled with a swirling green liquid. The air was thick with the smell of almonds, but it was mixed with a faint, antiseptic odor. In fact, the whole house smelled of almonds.

There was also a giant glass case filled with colorful, venomous snakes.

This wasn't the lair of a mad scientist; it was the playground of a genius, albeit a twisted one. Dr. Thorne, it seemed, wasn't content with just creating poisons; he reveled in the aesthetics of their creation.

A shiver ran down my spine, a cold counterpoint to the sterile environment. This lab spoke of a meticulous mind, a man as obsessed with presentation as he was with his deadly creations. The danger here wasn't the dusty lab coat and maniacal laughter I'd envisioned; it was the calculated brilliance housed within this meticulously crafted environment. The hunt for evidence had taken an unexpected turn, but the stakes had never been higher.

I took pictures, knowing this was not a man I wanted to confront on my own. However, if I can get a sample and get Alex to analyze it, maybe they will find it in Steven's grandmother, and then this man can be arrested.

I slipped in, taking care not to touch anything. There were dozens of vials in the lab, and there was no way to know which one was the right one. So, I stole as many as I could. In a minute, I was out of the lab and on my way back to Williamson's place.

After leaving Williamson's, I went back home to bathe and change, then headed to the station. Soon, I was sitting in Reynolds's cramped office. Immediately after he sat down, I recounted the harrowing events of the past days.

"Alex," I began, my voice wavering slightly despite my efforts to keep it steady. "I found something. Something big."

"What is it, Olivia? What did you find?"

Taking a deep breath, I launched into the story, every detail spilling from my lips in a rush. I told him about William Williamson and his connection to Timothy Patterson, the shady deals, the missing funds, and the framing. I told of the abandoned cabin with the hidden lab and the chilling realization of Dr. Thorne's involvement.

As I spoke, Alex's expression moved between emotions. It went from concern about my recklessness to disbelief of Williamson's story and then hardened into a steely resolve. "This is huge, Olivia," he said, his voice low and urgent. "If what you're saying is true, then we have to act fast. This is massive."

I nodded, my heart pounding with a mixture of fear and determination. "That's not all," I continued, reaching into my pocket and pulling out the stolen vials. "I managed to get these from Dr. Thorne's lab."

"I thought his name was Taskin?"

"Apparently, Taskin is a false identity."

Alex took the vials from my outstretched hand, examining them closely. "What are these?" he asked, his voice barely above a whisper.

"They're samples of the toxins he's been working on," I replied, my voice trembling slightly. "I need you to test them. See if any of them match with anything that can be found in Steven's grandmother."

Alex nodded, his jaw set in a determined line. "I'll get these to the lab right away," he said, slipping the vials into a secure evidence bag. "We'll need to do another autopsy on Mrs. Roseblood-Gundel to be sure."

"I'm sorry, Steven," I said silently. "I wish there was another way."

Alex placed a comforting hand on my shoulder, his eyes filled with understanding. "You did well, Olivia," he said softly. "We'll get to the bottom of this, I promise."

I nodded, grateful for his support. "Thank you, Alex," I said, my voice barely above a whisper.

"We'll need your statement, of course," Alex said, reaching for a pad of paper and a pen. "Can you walk me through everything one more time?"

I nodded, taking a deep breath to steady myself. I recounted the events once more. It was easy, and every detail was burned into my memory with excessive clarity. As I spoke, Alex jotted down notes.

"And then I found the lab," I finished, my voice trailing off. "That's where I found the vials."

Alex nodded, his jaw clenched with determination. "We'll get this tested right away," he said, standing up from his desk. In the meantime,

I'll have officers posted outside your apartment—just to be safe. And this time around, no more skulking about, and I mean it."

I smiled coyly.

"I mean it, Dr. Jenson. If everything Williamson said is true, then Patterson is a much more dangerous man than we ever thought."

"I can't promise."

"You will have to. And keep it this time."

"I'll try."

"I'll take it."

"Thank you, Alex."

"Stay safe, Olivia," Alex said, his voice filled with concern. "We'll get to the bottom of this soon. I can feel it."

With that, I left the office. As I walked out into the city, I remembered with alarm that today was our deadline. As if on cue, Steven called me. I already knew what he was going to say.

"Simmons is dead. You got a mail again."

"I did," Steven confirmed.

"We're very close, Steven. I found the toxicologist. Alex is analyzing the samples I took from his lab. He'll let me know when something comes up."

"Alex?"

"Oh, I meant Detective Reynolds."

"Right."

The call ended.

Three days later, I got the call I had been expecting from Reynolds.

"Olivia," Alex's voice came through the line, urgent and tense. "We've got the results."

My heart skipped a beat as I listened, the world narrowing down to the sound of Alex's voice. As he spoke, my breath caught in my throat, the weight of his words settling over me like a heavy blanket.

"There's a match," he said, his voice filled with grim certainty. "We found a toxin in the woman. I mean, we weren't looking before because it was practically untraceable. The toxin found in Mrs. Roseblood-Gundel's system matches one of the samples you brought in."

"We've got him," I whispered, tears almost dropped from my face.

"We've got him," Alex confirmed, his voice filled with grim satisfaction. "Now we just need to arrest Dr. Thorne. Let's hope he hasn't flown the coop since discovering your theft."

I nodded, even though he couldn't see me. "Do you need me to come with you?" I asked eagerly.

"No," Alex replied firmly. "This is police business. You've done your part, Olivia. Let us handle it from here."

Reluctantly, I agreed. "Alright, but keep me updated. I need to know that he's caught."

"I will," Alex promised before hanging up.

Hours dragged by as I paced the living room of Steven's apartment. Steven sat on the couch, his eyes fixed on the TV screen, but I could tell he wasn't really watching. His fingers drummed nervously against the armrest.

Finally, my phone buzzed in my pocket. I snatched it up eagerly, my heart pounding in anticipation.

"Hello?" I answered, trying to keep my voice steady.

"Olivia," Alex's voice came through, and I could hear the exhaustion in his tone. "We've got him. Thorne is in custody."

A wave of relief washed over me, so overwhelming that I sank onto the nearest chair, my legs suddenly weak with relief.

"Oh, thank goodness," I breathed, tears of relief finally spilling down my cheeks.

"He's being taken to the station now." Alex finished. He hung up.

After hanging up, I turned to Steven.

"We did it," I said.

Steven's eyes met mine, his expression a mix of relief and gratitude. "Thank you, Olivia," he said, his voice thick with emotion.

I reached out, squeezing his hand tightly. "We're not done yet," I said, determination flooding through me. "But we're one step closer."

We heard nothing more the entire day until the next morning when Alex called me. He was leaving the station and wanted to update me, so I told him to come to my apartment. I called Steven, and he was soon there. Steven was sitting across from me, trying to pay Gojo attention, when a knock came. Steven rose with a jolt, his hand instinctively reaching for the remote on the table. What good would that do?

"Easy," I murmured.

I took a fortifying sip of coffee. When the door creaked open, Detective Reynolds was revealed in the doorway. His usually impassive face held a hint of urgency that sent a jolt of nervous anticipation through me.

"Detective," I greeted him, rising from my seat. "Any news on Thorne?"

He stepped inside, his gaze scanning the room before settling on me. "Yes, Dr. Jenson. I wanted to fill you both in on what happened last night."

Steven pulled out a chair for Reynolds, who sat down with a sigh. He took a deep breath, his eyes locking with mine. "We arrived at Thorne's cabin," he began, his voice tight, "but the place was deserted. He'd already cleared out."

Frustration crackled in the air. "Cleared out?" Steven's voice rose, his fists clenching at his sides. "He knew we were coming?"

"Seems so," Reynolds interjected, holding up a hand. "We found a moving company packing up his lab in a hurry. There were tire tracks from a garage, but the trail quickly went cold. No vehicle tracks, no witnesses, just...nothing."

"How'd you find him? A chase?" Steven asked.

"Not quite," Reynolds replied, a flicker of something akin to a smile gracing his lips. "While searching through Thorne's belongings, we stumbled upon a torn page with part of a name on it, Williamson."

My heart skipped a beat. "The address," I breathed, a surge of hope coursing through me. "So you went to the address I told you?"

Reynolds's face glowed slowly, satisfied. "I took a chance, Dr. Jenson. And it paid off."

He paused for dramatic effect, then continued. "When we arrived at the address, your friend, Mr. Williamson, was just being bundled into a car by a couple of thugs."

Steven let out a sharp bark of laughter, devoid of humor. "Patterson was cleaning up all loose ends."

"Apparently," Reynolds confirmed. "We apprehended everyone on the scene, not without a bit of a struggle, mind you. But they're all in custody now."

Relief washed over me, a wave so powerful it threatened to pull me under. "You caught them," I said, the words tumbling out in a rush. "All of them?"

"Every last one," Reynolds confirmed, his gaze steady. "It wasn't an easy feat, but you provided a valuable lead, Dr. Jenson."

Steven leaned forward, his voice laced with a newfound determination. "So, what happens now?"

Reynolds leaned back in his chair, steepling his fingers. "With everyone in custody, we can formally charge them with abduction," he explained. "This gives us the time we need to build a stronger case against Thorne, especially now that we have the toxin that killed your grandmother in our possession."

"So Steven can be cleared?" I asked hopefully.

"Not quite. Thorne made it, and someone administered it. Could still be tied to you, Steven."

"But you have him."

"Unless he tells us who bought it from him, I'm afraid there's not much we can do. Especially since Patterson already sent his evidence to the police. My captain is giving me a lot of trouble as it is. They want to arrest Steven but I have managed to stall them with reports on this case. But if Thorne doesn't give up, Patterson, they'll eventually arrest you."

"Except Thorne can't identify Steven."

"If what Williamson told you is true, then he won't be able to identify Patterson either. He would identify Williamson."

"Damn it!" I swore.

"Simmons," Steven said.

"What?" Alex and I asked.

"How did Simmons die?"

"I don't know yet," Reynolds confessed.

"Oh, oh, oh! Do an autopsy. I'm sure Steven has an alibi for Simmons' death; if the same toxin is found or another toxin Thorne made, doesn't that clear Steven?"

"Somewhat. Yeah, we'll do that. But what would really make me happy is a direct link to Patterson. I looked Williamson up, and he was right; his reputation is in shambles. Nothing he says will hold up in court. This Patterson guy is nuts."

Nuts! That was when it clicked. "Almonds."

"What?" Reynolds asked me.

"Steven," I started excitedly. "You said you perceived almonds when your grandmother died?"

"Yes. It was strange."

"Did you smell almonds in Thorne's cabin?" I asked the detective.

He thought for a moment; then his face lit up. "God, the smell was everywhere!"

"That's it. Thorne was on the scene. That's your angle. Apply enough pressure, and Thorne cracks and confesses he was on the scene. That clears Steven."

"It doesn't give us Patterson." Steven pointed out.

"No, but at the very least, we can stop Thorne. And with Williamson compromised, Patterson will either slink away or make a mistake." Detective Reynolds pointed out.

"He already has," I said. "He killed Simmons. Thorne was there again, I'm sure; that's why he wasn't at home when I came calling. He and those goons. If Thorne won't crack,"

Reynolds picked up my line of thought. "One of them will give him up."

Into the Abyss

I pushed open the door to my office, bracing myself for the mess that awaited. The repairs were ongoing after the break-in. I could still see some shattered glass twinkling on the floor. Someone had come to vandalize the place even after I escaped from the attacker. There goes my deposit. With a heavy sigh, I stepped inside. This shouldn't take long.

The door creaked open, revealing a battlefield. Furniture lay slain, and files littered the floor like fallen soldiers. The first thing that greeted me was the smell of fresh paint; I'd decided to repaint it in an effort to make the place look as different as possible from before the attack. It seemed to mix with some lingering scent of fear. Clearing my schedule and informing my clients about my extended absence was my priority today. I needed to focus on the case, which I felt was nearing an end, and after that, my recovery. Both physical and mental.

I righted my chair and sat, then pulled up my client list on the computer. Just as I hit send on the last email, a sound from the doorway made me freeze. My heart hammered in my chest, the hairs on the back of my neck standing on end. Hadn't I told those repair guys to take a breather? Was that one of them?

The person walked in measured steps, coming definitely towards me. My heart rate spiked, and I berated myself. Alex warned you not to go out without informing him! Without thinking, I reached for the small handgun Reynolds had insisted I start keeping after the break-in. Slowly, cautiously, I turned in my chair, the gun held steady in my trembling hands. And there he was, standing in the doorway, a smile on his lips...

"Hold it right there," I rasped, my voice a touch shakier than I'd like to admit. In the doorway stood none other than Mr. Patterson, a nonchalant smile plastered on his face. It was a smile that didn't quite reach his eyes.

"Dr. Jenson," he purred, his voice smooth as butter. "There is no need for theatrics, I assure you. I am just here for a friendly chat."

There was something unsettling about his casual demeanor, something that made my alarm bells ring despite the gun nestled reassuringly in my hand. "Mr. Patterson," I replied, forcing a semblance of composure. "What a... surprise."

He raised an eyebrow, amusement flickering in his eyes. "Surprise? Well, Doctor, according to my calendar, it's our scheduled session time. Therapy thrives on trust, wouldn't you agree?"

The audacity of the man! I wanted to scream, to throw him out on his perfectly tailored backside. Instead, I placed the gun on the desk between us, a silent challenge. "Mr. Patterson," I said, my voice laced with a dangerous sweetness, "well, you must admit, this is an unexpected pleasure. To what do we owe this... impromptu visit?"

Ignoring my thinly veiled hostility, he sauntered over and sank into the chair opposite me. "Doctor, really," he drawled, leaning back with an air of misplaced relaxation. "Check your calendar. Our sessions are scheduled for right now." His voice dripped with an infuriating sense of entitlement.

I gritted my teeth. Fine.

"Therapy does indeed thrive on trust and transparency, Mr. Patterson. Perhaps it's time we delve a little deeper into the source of your... anxieties."

"Intriguing, Doctor," he said, his voice taking on a silken edge that sent shivers down my spine. "But what makes you believe there's anything beneath the surface but a desire for progress?"

I leaned forward, my gaze unwavering. "Oh, I don't doubt your desire for progress, Mr. Patterson," I said, my voice deceptively calm. "But there's always more to the story, wouldn't you agree? Underlying issues that might be hindering you, uhm, well-being." I'd lost all fear of him at this point. All I had left was a deep, deep loathing.

"I assure you, Doctor," he continued, his voice tightening, a telltale sign of his carefully constructed facade cracking, "I have nothing to hide."

"Then you won't mind answering a few questions," I said, my tone pointed. "Starting with your connection to Jake and the rest of his old friend group, 'The Misfits.'"

"I have no idea what you're talking about," he said, his voice low and dangerous.

I tilted my head, a small smirk playing at the corners of my lips. "Oh, I think you do," I said, my voice dripping with disdain. "Especially considering Jake's sudden interest in Henri's business, his love for precious stones... and the fact that he claimed to have received a gift from you."

Patterson's mask slipped, a flash of anger crossing his features. "That's preposterous," he said, his voice was icy.

I leaned forward again, my eyes boring into his. "Is it, Mr. Patterson? Or is there more to your relationship with Jake and his little gang than you're letting on?"

The ball was in his court now. Let's see how he played his hand.

"I have no knowledge of this, Jake or his friends. I cannot believe you would think I would associate myself with common criminals."

How had he known Jake was a common criminal? I certainly hadn't mentioned it.

He leaned forward, her voice a low growl. "Mr. Patterson, your carefully curated facade might fool others, but not me. As your therapist, I can say something in you betrays your hunger for control."

A muscle twitched in his jaw, betraying the simmering rage beneath. "Control? Doctor, I assure you, I manage my affairs quite efficiently."

"Then why frame Steven for his grandmother's death?" I challenged, my voice steady despite the tremor in my hands.

He scoffed a brittle sound. "Steven? Frame him? What a ludicrous accusation, Doctor. The poor boy was clearly traumatized by the incident."

"Indeed," I agreed, leaning forward and lacing my voice with concern, feigning a level of professional detachment I did not possess. "The loss of a loved one, especially under such circumstances, can have a profound impact on the psyche. Tell me, Mr. Patterson, how has Mrs. Roseblood-Gundel's passing affected you?"

His gaze flickered for a fleeting moment, a flicker of something I couldn't quite decipher. "Naturally, it's a tragedy," he said smoothly, regaining his composure. "A woman of great taste and... resilience."

"Resilience," I echoed, the word hanging heavy in the air like a question mark. "Mrs. Roseblood was known for her strong spirit, wasn't she? And much loved by her grandson."

"She was," he admitted, a hint of a sigh escaping his lips.

"And yet," I pressed on, my voice barely above a whisper, "according to reports, Steven claims to have poisoned her."

A tense silence stretched between us, thick with unspoken accusations. His eyes, however, betrayed a flicker of something akin to annoyance, a subtle crack in his carefully constructed mask.

"Steven," he finally said, with a slight dismissive wave of his hand, "is a grieving child. His mind is likely clouded by grief and trauma. Don't you agree, Doctor?"

"Trauma can indeed distort memories," I conceded, keeping my voice neutral. "But there have been... inconsistencies in his account. Discrepancies that raise questions."

"Inconsistencies?" He raised an eyebrow, a flicker of something like genuine surprise in his eyes. "Do elaborate, Doctor."

I took a deep breath, steeling myself for the inevitable pushback. "There's the matter of the specific type of poison used – a toxin not readily available and requiring specialized knowledge for acquisition."

He leaned back in his chair, steepling his fingers in a picture of studied nonchalance. "Dr. Jenson," he said, his voice smooth as silk, "are you suggesting I have knowledge of such... esoteric substances?"

"Perhaps not directly," I countered, "but your... associates are known to dabble in unconventional solutions." My voice trailed off, hoping to see a reaction.

"My associates?" He laughed. "Doctor, I pride myself on keeping a select social circle."

"Indeed," I pressed, "a circle that excludes... certain individuals who might possess a specific skill set, shall we say?"

He stiffened, the carefully cultivated mask finally showing cracks. "Doctor," he said, his voice low and dangerous, "are you questioning my judgment in choosing my acquaintances?"

"I'm simply trying to understand, Mr. Patterson," I replied, my voice steady despite the nervous tremor in my hands. "Why surround yourself with people who operate... on the fringes?"

Silence fell between us, thick with unspoken tension. His gaze burned into me, an attempt to force me back down. But I held his stare, refusing to be intimidated.

Finally, he spoke, his voice carefully measured. "The world is a complex place, Doctor. There are... challenges that require unconventional approaches. Sometimes, unorthodox solutions are necessary to achieve a greater good."

His words hung in the air, cryptic and unsettling. He wasn't denying his association with fringe elements, but he was obfuscating the true nature of their dealings.

"Unconventional solutions," I repeated, my voice laced with apprehension. "What kind of solutions, Mr. Patterson?"

He offered a tight smile devoid of warmth. "That, Doctor," he said, his voice regaining its earlier smoothness, "is a conversation best left for another time. I would like to hear about Steven; I worry about him."

"Perhaps," I said flatly. "But before we delve deeper into Steven's psyche, Mr. Patterson, there's something else I'd like to discuss."

He raised an eyebrow, a hint of suspicion flickering in his eyes. "Oh? And what might that be, Doctor?"

"It's about your... past," I began cautiously, choosing my words carefully. "Specifically, your relationship with your cousin, Mr. Williamson."

He took a moment to school his expression back into practiced neutrality. "Williamson? That's a rather... distant memory, Doctor. Why dredge up the past?"

"Because the past often shapes the present, Mr. Patterson," I countered, my voice firm. "And sometimes, unresolved issues can manifest in unexpected ways."

He leaned back in his chair, silence settling between us. I could practically feel the wheels turning in his head, calculating his next move. Finally, he spoke, his voice carefully measured. "Williamson was a... troubled individual, Doctor. He made poor choices, choices that ultimately led to his downfall."

"Indeed," I agreed, keeping my gaze locked on his. "But from what I understand, those choices involved a rather substantial investment you made in his failing business venture. An investment that, unfortunately, went sour."

A muscle twitched in his jaw, betraying the carefully constructed facade. "Business is a risky proposition, Doctor," he said through gritted teeth. "Sometimes, even the soundest investments go bad."

"Of course," I acknowledged, leaning forward slightly. "But some might say that your swift and rather ruthless acquisition of Williamson's remaining assets after his downfall, as you put it, was a tad opportunistic, wouldn't you agree?"

He shot me a sharp look, the simmering anger finally bubbling to the surface. "Opportunistic? Doctor, I assure you, I simply seized an opportunity that presented itself. Business is a game of survival, and the weak inevitably fall by the wayside."

"Survival of the fittest, as they say. But wouldn't you agree, Mr. Patterson, that sometimes, the ruthless pursuit of power can have... unintended consequences? Consequences that perhaps extend far beyond the boardroom?"

A long silence stretched. "Unintended consequences," he repeated, "Doctor Jenson, are you suggesting I'm some kind of... villain in a morality play?"

"Not at all, Mr. Patterson," I countered, my voice calm and measured. "But the human psyche is a complex thing; it's put together from experiences that are both positive and negative. Sometimes, unresolved conflicts from the past can manifest in the present in ways we don't always recognize."

My gaze held his, unwavering. "Perhaps the loss of your investment in Williamson's company, coupled with the perceived betrayal of trust, triggered a deep-seated need for control. A need to ensure that such a situation never repeats itself."

He scoffed, but the sound lacked its usual conviction. "Control? Doctor, I assure you, I simply possess a healthy respect for the realities of the business world."

"Indeed," I conceded, "but a healthy respect for reality and a compulsive need for control are two very different things. Control can be a powerful defense mechanism, Mr. Patterson. It allows us to feel a sense of security and predictability in a world that can often feel chaotic and unpredictable."

"But sometimes, a rigid need for control can negatively impact our relationships and our overall well-being. It can lead to isolation, paranoia, and even a sense of entitlement."

A sardonic smile. "Entitlement? Doctor, I believe I've earned the success I've achieved through hard work and shrewd business acumen."

"Success is a multifaceted concept, Mr. Patterson," I said gently. "Financial prosperity is certainly one aspect, but it's not the only one. Healthy relationships, a sense of purpose, and a capacity for empathy are equally important for overall well-being."

He remained silent, his gaze fixed on a point somewhere beyond the ransacked office. I knew I was pushing him, venturing into the murky depths of his psyche, but it was necessary. Steven's well-being, and perhaps the safety of others, depended on discovering his psychological Achilles heel. "Perhaps," I continued, my voice carefully measured, "the events surrounding your relationship with Mr. Williamson triggered a sense of vulnerability you weren't comfortable with. Maybe the ruthless pursuit of control is a way to protect yourself from experiencing that vulnerability again."

The words hung heavy in the air, a challenge wrapped in a question. His jaw clenched, and for a moment, I thought he might storm out of the session. But instead, he took a deep breath, his voice tight with suppressed emotion.

"Vulnerability," he finally spat out, the word laced with a bitterness that surprised even me. "Is that what this is all about, Doctor? Some Freudian notion of unresolved childhood issues manifesting in… ruthless business practices?"

"Not necessarily," I replied, shaking my head gently. "But our early experiences do shape our worldview, Mr. Patterson. They influence how we perceive threats, how we navigate conflict, and how we build relationships."

"And what exactly are you suggesting my early experiences were, Doctor?" he challenged, his voice laced with a dangerous edge.

I held his gaze, refusing to back down. "That's something we can explore together, Mr. Patterson. Therapy is a journey of self-discovery, a process of peeling back the layers and uncovering the core beliefs that motivate our actions."

He leaned back in his chair, a contemplative look clouding his features. The anger had receded, replaced by a cautious curiosity, a flicker of vulnerability I hadn't seen before.

"Self-discovery," he murmured, the word tasting foreign on his tongue. "It all sounds rather... nebulous, Doctor. I'm a busy man, and frankly, I don't have time for navel-gazing."

"Therapy isn't about navel-gazing, Mr. Patterson," I countered gently. "It's about understanding the root causes of our behavior, the internal forces that drive us. It's about recognizing unhealthy patterns and developing healthier coping mechanisms."

Another long silence followed.

Patterson's voice, dripping with a dangerous calmness, sliced through the tension. "Darkness, Doctor. You see it everywhere, don't you? Lurking in every corner, a phantom menace only you can discern." His gaze held mine, a challenge glinting in its depths. "Perhaps you should consider a more reflective surface, Doctor. A mirror might reveal a more concerning truth."

His words struck a raw nerve, a shard of truth piercing the carefully constructed facade I presented to the world. Years spent buried deep within, battling the darkness myself, had honed my instincts. But now, those same instincts were turning on me, his accusation landing a heavy blow. For a fleeting moment, the lines between doctor and patient blurred.

"Me?" I stammered. He leaned forward, a predator stalking its prey. "Yes, you, Doctor. Obsessed with chasing shadows, clinging to whispers and rumors. Are you so different from the very people you judge?"

His words were a twisted echo of my own anxieties, the self-doubt that gnawed at me in the quiet hours. Was I becoming consumed by this case? Was my relentless pursuit of justice morphing into something...unhealthy?

"Justice," the word dripped with sarcasm. "Tell me, Doctor, have you ever truly questioned your own motives? Have you ever wondered if your crusade isn't fueled by something a little...darker?"

He wasn't just deflecting; he was attacking, painting me as the obsessed one, consumed by the very darkness I sought to expose.

I forced myself to breathe, to find my center. "I'm a therapist, Mr. Patterson," I said, my voice regaining its strength. "My purpose is to guide you towards self-discovery, to help you understand the motivations behind your actions."

"And who guides you, Doctor?" He slammed the question back, his voice laced with a dangerous challenge. "Who helps you navigate the darkness that festers within your own psyche? Who watches the watchers?"

My voice rose, the carefully constructed therapist crumbling under his accusations. "Don't try to turn this around on me, Mr. Patterson. We're not here to dissect my psyche, and we're here to dissect yours!"

He wagged a finger playfully. "Ah, but Doctor, how can I dissect mine when you're so busy projecting your own shadows onto everyone around you?"

"Projecting? I'm not the one who ruthlessly eliminates anyone who stands in my way!"

"Ruthless? Is that how you characterize... decisive action?"

"Decisive action!" I scoffed. "You call ruining someone's life, then preying on their grief, decisive?"

"Grief is a messy business, Doctor. Sometimes, a little encouragement is necessary to move on."

"Encouragement? You call framing a grieving child encouragement?"

"Enough of this charade, Doctor. You've gotten more than you bargained for. This session is over."

"Don't you walk away from me! We're not finished here, Mr. Patterson."

"We are. Now, get out."
"It's my office!"
"So it is."
He quietly walked out.

A Race Against Time

My fingers trembled as I straightened my rumpled blouse, the silence of my office in Patterson's absence pressing down on me like a suffocating weight. His words, full of venomous justifications, had chipped away at the carefully constructed facade I'd seen, revealing a ruthless manipulator beneath the veneer of a respectable businessman.

Exhaustion gnawed at me. Self-doubt, a serpent I thought I'd long vanquished, coiled around my heart, squeezing tight. Had I been too rash? Could I have pushed him further and gleaned more information before the session devolved into a heated exchange?

A glance at the clock told me it was late afternoon, the sun already dipping below the skyline, painting the sky in vibrant hues of orange and purple. Time, it seemed, was a relentless tide, threatening to drown us all in its wake.

Time was now playing a cruel game with us. Reynolds's boss had given us a mere three days – seventy-two precious hours – to find a definitive link between Dr. Thorne and Patterson. If we failed, the wheels of the legal system would begin to turn. They'd move forward with the case against Thorne and order Steven's arrest based on the anonymous tip they received. It was a prospect that gave me a headache.

Adding to the pressure, there was the gnawing worry about the journalist I'd contacted. I'd sent her a carefully worded email outlining the situation, attaching anonymized reports and interview notes. A part of me hoped for a miraculous breakthrough, a bombshell revelation that would expose the truth and exonerate Steven. But a larger, more cynical part knew that hope was a fragile thing, easily shattered by the harsh realities of the world. A world that Patterson seemed to control.

I sank into my chair, the plush leather offering little comfort. Frustration gnawed at me. The session with Patterson had yielded little in terms of concrete evidence, but it had served a different purpose. It had shaken me to my core, forcing me to confront the darkness that lurked within the human psyche, a darkness I'd spent years battling in my patients but rarely acknowledged in myself. Perhaps Patterson's twisted words held a grain of truth. Was my relentless pursuit of justice fueled by something... darker? An unhealthy obsession born from unresolved personal demons?

The thought sent a shiver down my spine. The line between empathy and obsession was a thin one, easily blurred. But dwelling on self-doubt wouldn't help Steven. I forced myself to take a deep breath, focusing on the task at hand. There had to be something I'd missed, a detail, a clue hidden somewhere in the labyrinthine maze of the case.

The city lights bled through the blinds, casting an unwelcome orange glow on the stacks of files sprawled across my desk. Fatigue gnawed at the edges of my consciousness, a persistent ache that hours of coffee couldn't fully banish. Disappointment gnawed at me, too, a bitter aftertaste from the cryptic text message. It offered a glimmer of hope, then snatched it away, leaving me with more questions than answers.

With a sigh, I pushed myself back from the desk, the screen burning into my retinas. Every dead end, every unanswered question, was a brick wall in the path to getting Steven out of this mess. I needed a new approach, a fresh angle.

I looked around, but Gojo wasn't there. She was probably sleeping in a corner.

I reached for my phone, the familiar weight a grounding presence in the chaos swirling within me. Two rings, then three, before a gruff voice filled the receiver. "Reynolds."

"Detective, it's Olivia Jenson."

"Dr. Jenson," he acknowledged, his voice devoid of its usual warmth. "What can I do for you?"

The guarded tone in his voice did little to ease my apprehension. "It's about Dr. Thorne," I began cautiously. "Has there been any progress on his case?"

A beat of silence followed, heavy with unspoken tension. "Not much, Doc," he finally said. "He's lawyered up, sticking to his story of being an independent researcher. We haven't been able to find any concrete link between him and Patterson."

Disappointment washed over me, a cold wave threatening to drown the embers of hope I'd managed to kindle. "No surprises there, I suppose," I muttered, more to myself than to Reynolds.

"Look, Doc," he said, his voice softening a touch, "I know this is tough, but we're doing everything we can. We've got forensics working overtime on the stuff we found in Thorne's apartment. Maybe something will turn up there."

"I understand," I said, forcing a note of optimism into my voice. "But time isn't exactly on our side, is it?"

"Three days," he confirmed, his voice grim. "That's all we have before my Captain and the D.A.'s office move forward with their case against Thorne."

Three days. The stark reality hung heavy in the air, a countdown clock ticking relentlessly towards an uncertain future. "Have you been able to talk to Mr. Patterson's friends or acquaintances? Anyone who might have known about Dr. Thorne, or perhaps, about any... disagreements she might have had with anyone?" It was a long shot, but I grasped at any straw in the swirling current of desperation.

"We're checking all leads," Reynolds replied. "But so far, nothing concrete."

Frustration bubbled up within me. "There has to be something we're missing. A detail, a connection... anything!"

"I know you're invested in this, Doc," Reynolds said, a hint of sympathy in his voice. "But sometimes, these things take time. We just gotta keep digging."

He was right, of course. But time was a luxury we didn't have. Steven's life was hanging in the balance, and every passing hour felt like a betrayal.

"Alright," I said, deflated. "Keep me posted if anything turns up. And Detective?"

"Yeah, Doc?"

"Thanks for everything. I appreciate you guys looking into this."

He grunted a noncommittal response and then ended the call. I stared at the phone in my hand. That conversation had been stiff. I wondered what that was about.

The call with Reynolds left a bitter taste in my mouth. I could have sworn we were on friendly terms. With a sigh, I sent a quick text to Reynolds requesting a meeting for the following day. Maybe another conversation, a fresh set of eyes on the case, could spark a new lead.

Stepping outside, the cool night air was a welcome change from the stale atmosphere of my office. At this hour, the city was alive with a different kind of energy. Streetlights cast a warm glow on the sidewalks, painting long, wavering shadows that danced beside me as I began my nightly jog.

Starting slow, I eased into a comfortable rhythm, my legs churning against the pavement. The familiar route took me along the banks of a bay, the shimmering water reflecting the city lights like scattered diamonds. A gentle breeze carried the scent of freshly cut grass from the nearby park, with the faint aroma of roasted peanuts from a street vendor a few blocks down.

The path bustled with activity. Young children, their faces flushed with exertion, chased each other around a makeshift football pitch, their laughter echoing through the quiet night. An elderly couple, their steps slow and synchronized, walked hand-in-hand, their silhouettes dwarfed by the towering office buildings across the river. Here and there, groups of teenagers lounged on park benches, their animated chatter punctuated by bursts of laughter.

A sleek black Labrador bounded past me, its tongue lolling out in a joyous grin, the happy barks echoing off the nearby buildings. A young man jogged in the opposite direction, his headphones firmly in place, his brow furrowed in concentration.

As I rounded a bend, the familiar aroma of freshly baked bread from the artisan bakery on the corner flooded my senses. The sight of golden-brown loaves piled high in the window was a source of constant comfort, a reminder of simple pleasures. Next door, the curry house exuded an exotic blend of spices that always made my stomach rumble.

The rhythm of my feet pounding the pavement became a meditative mantra, allowing my thoughts to settle into a steady flow.

As I continued my run, the bay narrowed, giving way to a quaint alleyway adorned with colorful flower boxes overflowing with petunias and marigolds. A young couple, their faces illuminated by the glow of a streetlamp, stood locked in a passionate embrace, oblivious to the world around them. The sight, filled with a quiet intimacy, tugged at a corner of my heart, a bittersweet reminder of a love I'd long ago chosen to leave behind.

Taking a deep breath, I paused for a moment, allowing the panorama to sink in. The city, often portrayed as gritty and industrial, held an unexpected beauty in the hush of the night, a kaleidoscope of sights, sounds, and smells that whispered stories of lives lived, dreams chased, and love found.

As I jogged back towards home, my body was pleasantly tired, and a sense of calm had settled over me. The worries hadn't vanished entirely, but the run had cleared my head, providing a much-needed perspective shift. Exhaustion was a welcome sensation this night of restless sleep.

Reaching for my phone, I scrolled through my contacts till I found Kat. My oldest friend is the one constant in a life filled with fleeting professional relationships and guarded interactions. The phone rang twice before a cheery voice filled my ear. "Olivia! How's the most brilliant therapist in the City doing?"

A smile tugged at my lips. "Brilliant is a bit of an exaggeration, Kat. But I'm hanging in there."

"Well, whatever you're hanging in there for, I hope it doesn't have you working late into the night again," she said, concern threading its way through her voice.

I chuckled. "There might have been a particularly challenging session today, but all is well now."

The truth was tempting, and the urge to confide in Kat and unload the burden of the case was strong. But something held me back. Perhaps it was the fear of tainting our friendship with the darkness that clung to the case. Or maybe there was a part of me still grappling with the revelations from the session with Patterson, unsure how much was truth and how much was manipulation.

Instead, I steered the conversation toward more familiar territory. "How about you? How's the exciting world of research assistantship treating you?"

"Oh, you know," Kat replied, her voice dropping to a mock whisper, "the usual. Mixing chemicals, conducting tests, trying not to blow myself up in the process."

I laughed. "Sounds thrilling."

The conversation flowed easily, with a comfortable rhythm of shared experiences and inside jokes. We talked about a funny meme circulating online (Kat cackled), our plans for the upcoming holidays (vague for both of us), and the latest disaster unfolding on our favorite reality TV show (trainwreck, we both agreed). For a while, the worries of the case faded into the background, replaced by the comforting familiarity of friendship.

"Ugh, Professor Davies is the worst," Kat groaned, launching into a tirade about her absent-minded supervisor. "The man forgets his own head in the morning. I swear, the other day, he left his lunchbox in the fume hood overnight."

"Sounds like you need a vacation," I sympathized. "Maybe a tropical island with a bottomless supply of Mai Tai's?" (Her go-to cocktail)

"Don't even tempt me," she sighed. "But hey, at least my job doesn't involve delving into people's deepest traumas all day. You must hear some crazy stuff."

"You wouldn't believe it," I admitted, a hint of envy creeping into my voice. "But at least my job has some meaning, you know? Helping people navigate the parts of themselves they didn't know about..." I trailed off, unsure how much to reveal.

"Hey, Liv," Kat said, her voice softening. "You don't have to be a superhero all the time. It's okay to ask for help if you need it. You know I'd do anything for you."

I knew she meant well, but her concern was a constant undercurrent in our conversations. But this case needed a more delicate touch, something beyond the reach of our usual conversations.

"I appreciate it, Kat," I said, my voice sincere. But I know what I'm doing. Trust me." The firmness in my tone surprised even me.

A beat of silence followed, then a sigh. "Alright, alright. But promise me you'll be careful, okay?"

"Always," I replied, though a part of me knew it wouldn't be easy.

We exchanged quick goodbyes, and I crashed into my bed, not bothering with a shower or even undressing. I jumped back up when my back met something squishy. I turned the phone's torchlight on and was met by a most disapproving look.

"You scared me!"

Gojo just stared on. Then she lay back down. I crawled in next to her. The instant my head hit the bed beside her, she got up and walked out of the room.

Asshole.

The next morning, I headed to my rendezvous with Reynolds. He'd asked to meet at a restaurant on the way to the precinct. Across the small table from me, Detective Reynolds sat nursing a lukewarm cup of coffee, his usual gruff charm replaced by a stoic indifference. My fingers tapped impatiently on the worn leather surface.

"So," I finally began, unable to hold back any longer, "any progress on Dr. Thorne?"

Reynolds took a long sip of his coffee before answering. "Still digging through the stuff at his apartment," he mumbled, barely audible.

Frustration bubbled up within me. "Alex," I pressed my voice tight with urgency, "we're running out of time. Did the forensics team find anything?"

He finally tore his gaze from the window, a flicker of something akin to annoyance crossing his face. "They're working on it, Dr. Jenson," he said, his voice clipped.

Dr. Jenson?

"But what about the neighbors?" I persisted. "Did you manage to speak to anyone who knew Thorne, or perhaps, anyone else Williamson might have confided in?"

He sighed a long, exasperated sigh. "Look, Doc," he said, his voice softening a touch, "we're doing everything we can. But sometimes these things take time."

"Time is a luxury we don't have, Detective," I countered, my voice sharp with suppressed anger. "Steven's life is hanging in the balance, and all I'm getting is bureaucratic platitudes."

Reynolds held my gaze for a long, uncomfortable moment. "You think I enjoy this, Doc?" he finally said, his voice low and flat. "You think I want to see an innocent man thrown behind bars?"

"Then show me you don't," I retorted, "Show me you're actually fighting for him."

He leaned back in his chair, pinching the bridge of his nose. When he spoke again, his voice was laced with a weariness that went beyond the demands of the case. "Look," he said, "I might not always show it, but I'm on your side. This whole thing... it doesn't sit right with me."

My anger subsided, replaced by a flicker of hope. "Then why the... standoffishness, Detective?"

He let out a humorless chuckle. "Standoffishness?"

"Yes," I confirmed, the word tasting heavy on my tongue. I mean, the way you've been acting since my visit to the station—like you'd rather be anywhere but here."

He hesitated for a moment, then ran a hand down his face, a gesture that spoke volumes of the frustration simmering beneath the surface. "Let's just say," he began, his voice low, "my partner and the lieutenant aren't exactly thrilled with my... unorthodox methods in pursuing this case." He put the last words in air quotes.

Unorthodox methods? A wave of indignation washed over me. "Unorthodox methods?" I echoed, my voice incredulous. "You mean listening to my insights, following leads? That doesn't fit into your neat little boxes. The only reason we've gotten this far is because of my efforts!"

He raised a placating hand. "Whoa there, Doc," he said, his voice calm. "I'm not downplaying your contribution. You've been invaluable. But you gotta understand, they have a point. Protocol exists for a reason."

"And what about justice?" I snapped. "Does that not take precedence over some bureaucratic checklist?"

Reynolds sighed again. "Look, I get it. You're invested, and rightfully so. But sometimes, you gotta take a step back and let the system work."

"The system that is about to condemn an innocent man?" I countered, my voice shaking with anger. "Forgive me if I have little faith in its 'workings.'"

He stared at me for a long moment. Finally, he spoke. "Alright, Doc," he said, his voice softer now. "I apologize. You're right. This whole thing has me on edge, and it came out wrong. I shouldn't have taken it out on you."

The apology caught me off guard, disarming the anger that had been simmering within me. "Thank you," I said, the words a reluctant murmur.

"I have to get to work. If you find anything new, call me."

Later that day, my phone buzzed in my pocket. Glancing at the screen, I saw it was Reynolds. A slight smile touched my lips.

"Dr. Jenson," Reynolds' gruff voice filled my ear. "Just wanted to fill you in on what transpired at the station after the arrests. Call it a peace offering."

"Anything good?" I asked, hope in my voice.

"Good?" he scoffed. It was more like a lawyer's convention. All six of those goons we arrested with Throne had individual lawyers present during their interrogations."

My smile disappeared. Six lawyers? Patterson wasn't playing around. This wasn't just about protecting Dr. Thorne anymore; this was about building a wall around the entire operation. "So, did they manage to get anything out of them?"

"Not much, thanks to the suits hovering over them like vultures," Reynolds grumbled. "Thorne, the spineless coward, readily admitted to selling his toxins to several people, including your client, of course. Basically, implicated Steven right off the bat."

A new wave of frustration. "Damn it!" I exclaimed. "And the almond scent evidence?"

"Not enough on its own, according to the law, their lawyers, and everyone else," Reynolds sighed. "Apparently, it could be trace elements from other sources, such as food, laundry detergent, or anything. It's circumstantial at best. They need a stronger link."

"So, we're back to square one?" I asked, disappointed.

"Not entirely," Reynolds said, a hint of excitement creeping into his voice. "Two of the guys we arrested mentioned that they usually followed Thorne whenever he had a job to do."

"Did they say anything about going to Mrs. Roseblood-Gundel's house or Mr. Simmons' apartment?" I pressed, my pulse quickening with anticipation.

"They mentioned visiting both locations," Reynolds replied, "but they swear Patterson wasn't with them on either occasion. Apparently, he operates behind the scenes, the puppeteer pulling the strings."

"And none of them admitted to knowing Patterson?" I asked.

"Not a peep," Reynolds confirmed. They all claim it was just Thorne they dealt with, and Throne only knows Williamson."

We were so close, yet so far. We had a motive, a connection between Dr. Thorne and the crimes, but without a solid link to Patterson, everything remained circumstantial.

"Look, Doc," Reynolds said, his voice softer now, "I know this is frustrating, but we're not giving up. If they don't budge, maybe we can find another way to make them talk. "

I immediately thought of something. "Can you interrogate them again? But this time, let them do the talking. Ask them to describe the event of Steven's grandmother's death to you. They've already admitted to being there, so it shouldn't be a problem."

"What am I looking for?"

"I don't know yet, but get them to be as detailed as possible if they can recall exchanged words better. Do the same with the second death, too, and the attempted kidnap. Someone must have given Throne the instructions to go kidnap Williamson. Patterson broke his own protocol there. I told you he's made a mistake."

A big one.

Breaking Point

The harsh fluorescent light of the bathroom assaulted my reflection, highlighting the wreckage etched boldly onto my face. Sleep, once a restorative refuge, had become a luxury I couldn't afford. In its place, a relentless parade of anxieties gnawed at my sanity, chipping away at the edges of my composure. The past few weeks had blurred into a relentless pursuit, a desperate chase against a looming deadline that seemed to inch closer with each passing hour.

The vibrant therapist who greeted her clients with a warm smile each morning was a fading memory. The woman staring back at me now was a stranger, a gaunt figure with haunted eyes burdened by the weight of a collapsing world. The lines around my mouth etched deeper with each sleepless night, spoke of a struggle far exceeding the confines of a single case.

Twenty excruciating hours remained before the D.A.'s office moved forward with their case against Dr. Thorne. The clock, a relentless metronome, ticked away in my head, a constant reminder of the dwindling time and the mountain of doubt threatening to bury me alive.

Steven's face, pale and drawn from his recent ordeal, haunted my waking hours. His trust, so readily given during our sessions, felt like a weight around my neck, a constant reminder of the responsibility I'd so eagerly embraced. But the initial confidence, the unwavering belief in justice that had fueled my initial steps, had eroded with each passing day.

Doubt, a serpent coiling tightly around my heart, squeezed tighter with every passing hour. Was I failing him? Was I chasing shadows, tilting at windmills while Steven's future crumbled around him? The unanswered questions echoed in the sterile silence of the room, a relentless chorus of despair. Every negative article in the local paper and every dismissive glance from a colleague who viewed my involvement with suspicion fueled the growing inferno of doubt within me. Had I already failed him?

Yet, where was the progress? We had the murder weapon, Dr. Thorne's deadly concoctions, readily available for purchase by anyone with the means and the malice. But Patterson, the mastermind behind the curtain, had one up on us. He had masterfully woven a web of deceit, manipulating Dr. Thorne into a self-incriminating confession that implicated Steven as one of his clients.

And without a solid link to Patterson, everything remained a web of circumstantial whispers. The forensics team had yielded nothing substantial from Dr. Thorne's cabin. We were grasping at straws, and the weight of that knowledge pressed down on me with suffocating intensity.

The frustration, a bitter cocktail of helplessness and anger, threatened to spill over. I slammed the medicine cabinet shut, the jarring sound echoing in the small space. A single tear escaped, tracing a glistening path down my cheek. Was this it? Was this where my valiant fight for justice would end – defeated, ostracized, and ultimately, a failure?

The memory of my conversation with Kat, a beacon of normalcy in the storm raging within me, flickered at the edge of my thoughts. Her words, laced with concern, echoed in my ears: "You don't have to be a superhero all the time. It's okay to ask for help if you need it."

But who could I turn to? Detective Reynolds was tightly constrained by the limitations of the system.

Back in the living room, the exhaustion that gnawed at the edges of my consciousness finally claimed me. Collapsing onto the worn sofa, I reached for my phone, the familiar comfort of the worn leather a fleeting solace. Ordering food seemed like the most insurmountable task at the moment. With a sigh, I dialed the familiar number of the local Chinese deli.

"Golden Dragon, how may I help you tonight?" A polite, slightly bored voice filled my ear.

"Hi," I began, my voice raspy. "Can I place an order for delivery?"

"Absolutely! What can I tempt you with this evening?"

I hesitated. My usual order of kung pao chicken suddenly held no appeal. "Actually," I started, then changed my mind. "Maybe I'll look at the menu again, just in case there's something new."

A slight pause followed, then a hint of amusement crept into the voice on the other end. "Of course, ma'am. Our menu is quite extensive, so take your time."

I scrolled through the online menu on my phone, each picture of steaming noodles and succulent meats failing to spark any appetite. The exhaustion that enveloped me seemed to extend to my taste buds.

"Are you having trouble deciding?" The voice cut through my internal struggle.

Shame washed over me. "Yes, yes, I'm fine," I stammered, embarrassed by my indecisiveness. "Just... not sure what I'm in the mood for, I guess."

"Ah, I see," they said politely. "Perhaps you'd like some recommendations? We have several popular dishes that our customers love."

The thought of someone making a decision for me held a strange appeal. "Sure," I conceded, relief washing over me. "What would you recommend?"

"Well," they continued, "if you're looking for something light but flavorful, our won-ton soup is always a hit. It's a classic for a reason."

The thought of warm broth soothing my insides held a faint appeal. "Alright," I conceded, "wonton soup it is. And maybe..." I trailed off, scanning the menu again.

"And?" they prompted patiently.

A wave of guilt washed over me. I was holding up this person's time with my indecisiveness. "Actually," I began, feeling utterly defeated, "forget it. I think I'll skip dinner tonight."

A brief silence followed, and then a slightly concerned tone entered their voice. "Are you sure, ma'am? Food is good for the soul, especially on a tough day."

I bit back a choked sob. "It's been a tough day," I confessed, surprised by my own vulnerability.

A pause, then a gentle understanding, softened the voice. "We all have those days, ma'am. But a good meal can make things feel a little better, even if just for a while. Trust me."

Her words resonated with me. Perhaps they were right. Maybe a warm meal, however simple, could offer a momentary respite from the storm raging within.

"Alright," I conceded, forcing a smile into my voice. "You've convinced me. Wonton soup and... let me see... how about the vegetable spring rolls?"

"Excellent choices," they replied, their voices tinged with relief. "Is there anything, a drink?"

"Just water, please."

A few minutes later, after confirming my address and placing the order, I hung up the phone, feeling a flicker of gratitude. It was a small victory, perhaps, but a victory nonetheless.

As I waited for the delivery, I tried to engage with Gojo. Usually, her playful antics and soft purrs were a guaranteed stress reliever. But tonight, her attempts to weave around my feet and nudge her head against my hand fell on deaf ears. My mind was a whirlwind of worry, the clock a relentless drumbeat counting down the remaining hours.

Gojo, sensing my distress, eventually gave up and retreated to her favorite napping spot on the window ledge, bathed in the pale moonlight. The TV played on in the background, an unwelcome distraction, the images flashing by without registering in my mind.

Unable to bear the suffocating atmosphere of the living room any longer, I sought refuge in my home office. Picking up a random client file, I tried to focus on work, a distraction from the storm raging within. But the words on the page blurred, the meaning lost in the fog clouding my mind. Each page felt like a herculean effort, a fight against the overwhelming urge to surrender to the crushing weight of it all.

The minutes stretched into an eternity as I waited for a call. From the delivery person or from Detective Reynolds. Or a reply to the anonymous mail to the journalist. Hell, I'd had even taken a call from Steven.

The rhythmic ticking of the clock, previously a source of relentless pressure, faded into the background as a different kind of storm brewed within me. A wave of dizziness washed over me, momentarily blurring the already illegible words on the page. My breath hitched, and a forgotten memory, a painful echo from the past, surfaced in vivid detail.

I was five years old, a tiny wisp of a girl dwarfed by the towering carousel horses and the throngs of laughing people in the bustling amusement park. The vibrant colors, the blaring music, and the sweet aroma of cotton candy had initially filled me with a sense of wonder. But the wonder quickly dissolved into a suffocating panic as my tiny hand slipped from my mother's grasp.

Everything became a kaleidoscope of unfamiliar faces, their laughter grating against my ears. The world seemed to tilt on its axis, the spinning teacups and the swaying swings blurring into a dizzying spectacle. Disoriented and terrified, I called out for my mother, my voice swallowed by the cacophony. Tears streamed down my face, blurring my vision even further.

Minutes, stretching into eternity in my mind, passed in a haze of panic. Each passing moment amplified the fear, the feeling of utter helplessness, a tightening vice around my chest. Just when I felt like I might crumble, a familiar voice cut through the chaos.

"Olivia! There you are!" My mother's voice, a beacon of warmth and security, pierced the fog of fear. Relief was so potent that it almost knocked me to my knees. It washed over me as I saw her familiar form striding towards me. She knelt down, her arms outstretched, and in that moment, the world around me ceased to exist.

Held in my mother's warm embrace, the fear receded, replaced by a comforting sense of safety. As she held me close, wiping away my tears and whispering soothing words, the park's cacophony faded into a gentle hum. The world, once a menacing labyrinth, felt manageable again.

The memory, a bittersweet cocktail of childhood vulnerability and maternal comfort, lingered in my mind, resonating with the present in a way that sent shivers down my spine. In that crowded amusement park, I was a helpless child lost in a sea of strangers. Now, in the relentless pursuit of justice for Steven, I was once again lost, adrift in a sea of uncertainty and doubt.

The parallels were chilling. The suffocating chaos of the amusement park mirrored the overwhelming pressure of the case, the cacophony of emotions churning within me echoing the discordant symphony of the looming deadline, Steven's hopeful face, and the ever-present weight of doubt.

Just as my mother had been my anchor in that terrifying moment, I craved a similar comfort, a beacon of unwavering support. But the landscape of my life had shifted, leaving me adrift in a sea of professional distance and carefully constructed boundaries. My colleagues, while well-meaning, offered only clinical empathy, unable to truly understand the emotional rollercoaster I was on.

Reynolds, with his gruff demeanor and surprising understanding, could have emerged as a lifeline in this storm. His determination mirrored my own, and his frustration with the roadblocks paralleled my growing sense of helplessness. Yet, even he, bound as he was by the constraints of protocol and procedure, couldn't offer the unyielding support I craved.

The memory of my mother's unwavering presence intensified the feeling of isolation that gnawed at the edges of my being. At that moment, I yearned for the unconditional love and support that only a parent could offer. But my parents were gone, their absence an ever-present ache within me.

Tears, hot and unchecked, streamed down my face. For the first time in weeks, I allowed myself to truly feel the weight of the situation, the fear of failure, the crushing despair that threatened to consume me whole. The carefully constructed façade, the mask of unwavering strength I wore for the world, crumbled, revealing the raw vulnerability beneath.

As I buried my face in my hands, the memory of my mother resurfaced, a gentle whisper in the storm. Her voice, a memory echoing across the years, seemed to say, "Olivia, breathe. You are not alone. You have the strength to find your way out of this, just like you always have."

"But this is different, Mama," I whispered. This was the big world. Miracles don't happen out here.

The memory, a bittersweet comfort, felt like a turning point. The raw outpouring of emotion, a cleansing purge, seemed to have shifted something within me. The despair, though not entirely banished, receded, replaced by a sliver of determination. Perhaps, I thought, the answer to my predicament wasn't in chasing shadows but in finding my own center, the unwavering core that had seen me through difficult times before.

Taking a deep, cleansing breath, I wiped away my tears. Although the clock continued its relentless ticking, a reminder of the dwindling time, the oppressive gloom that had threatened to consume me had lifted a fraction. The memory of my mother, a beacon of unwavering support in a moment of childhood terror, had served as a potent reminder of my own inner strength.

Sitting up straighter, I glanced again at the open file on my desk. The words, once blurred and meaningless, seemed to hold a sharper focus now. But I didn't need the distraction anymore. I took out the folder I'd created for Steven's case. The case details and the complexities of Steven's situation weren't going to vanish. But my approach, I realized, needed to shift.

The frustration with Reynolds, the constant nagging feeling of hitting brick walls, was a product of my own desperation. I'd been chasing a silver bullet, hoping for a single piece of evidence to crack the case wide open. But what if, instead of focusing on one earth-shattering revelation, I looked for a different angle, a way to chip away at the carefully constructed facade Patterson had built?

Perhaps the answer wasn't hidden in the murky past of Dr. Thorne or buried deep within the secrets of Mrs. Roseblood's anxieties. Maybe the truth lay in the seemingly innocuous details, the discrepancies in Patterson's carefully constructed narrative. I was the one who'd said he had made a mistake. Time to identify it.

With renewed purpose, I rose from my chair and began to pace the room. My mind, no longer clouded by despair, crackled with a newfound energy. I meticulously reviewed the case files, highlighting seemingly insignificant details and searching for any inconsistencies or contradictions.

The police report on the scene at Mr. Simmons' apartment, for instance, mentioned a single set of footprints leading away from the back door. But Dr. Thorne readily admitted to visiting Mr. Simmons with six of his associates. Where were the additional footprints then? A minor inconsistency, perhaps, but could it be a clue, nonetheless? I wrote it down. But then I got a notification.

My dinner was here. I left the room. It was time for dinner and maybe one or two episodes of something funny. That should free my mind.

In the Eye of the Storm

The insistent buzzing of the doorbell tore me from a dream where everything was nice, and sunlight dappled through the leaves of a towering oak tree. I grumbled, disoriented, and shuffled towards the front door, my hair a tangled mess and my eyes gritty with sleep. It was barely past seven on a Saturday morning, far too early for unannounced visitors.

Peeking through the peephole, I was surprised to see Detective Reynolds standing on my porch. He looked harried, his usually sharp suit slightly rumpled, a dark circle smudging the skin beneath his tired eyes. I swung the door open, a question already forming on my lips.

"Detective Reynolds? What brings you here so early?" My voice was husky from sleep.

"Dr. Jenson," he greeted, his voice clipped. "No time for pleasantries. We need to get you down to the station. Now."

My drowsiness evaporated instantly, replaced by a jolt of apprehension. "The station? What's happened?"

"Let's just say," he replied, his gaze darting nervously over his shoulder, "we might have a lead on Patterson. A big one."

Intrigue battled with concern. A lead on a Saturday morning? This had to be serious. "Alright," I conceded, grabbing my purse and keys. "Let me just throw on some clothes that don't scream 'pajama party.'"

While I changed, Reynolds paced the living room, his energy crackling like static electricity. He stopped abruptly, his back to me. "There's one thing you need to know before we head in," he said, his voice low.

"What is it?" I asked, pulling on a sweater.

He turned around, his face etched with worry. "I had to pull some serious strings to get you cleared to be present at the questioning. Staked practically my entire career on it with Captain Denver."

A wave of guilt washed over me. "Reynolds, you shouldn't have done that. It was reckless."

He shook his head, his jaw set in a stubborn line. "Look, I trust you, Olivia. More than you know. This lead could be our shot at bringing Patterson down, and frankly," he continued, his voice low, "I don't trust anyone else in this department to handle it with the... sensitivity it requires."

Sensitivity? I wasn't sure what he meant by that, but the determination in his eyes was undeniable. "Alright," I conceded, placing a hand on his shoulder. "Thank you. I won't let you down."

The drive to the station was filled with a tense silence. Reynolds kept his eyes glued to the road, his knuckles white-knuckled around the steering wheel. I could feel the weight of his gamble pressing down on him, the potential consequences hanging heavy in the air.

"You sure you're okay with this?" I finally broke the silence, unable to bear the tension any longer.

He glanced at me, a flicker of a smile gracing his lips for a brief moment. "Honestly? No. Captain Denver is going to have my head on a platter if this goes south. But sometimes," he continued, his voice low, "you gotta take a chance for what you believe in."

I nodded, understanding washing over me. He wasn't just doing this for his career; he believed in Steven's innocence as much as I did. Suddenly, the weight of responsibility felt heavy on my own shoulders. I couldn't let him down either.

As we pulled into the station parking lot, the imposing brick building seemed to loom over us, casting a long, ominous shadow. Reynolds took a deep breath, his face hardening into a mask of professionalism.

"Buckle up, Doc," he said, his voice grim. "This is going to be a bumpy ride."

Inside, the atmosphere was thick with hostility. The air crackled with tension as soon as we stepped off the elevator. Detective Miller,

Reynolds' partner, stood by the coffee machine, a dark scowl etching his features. He eyed me with undisguised disdain as we approached.

"So, this is your 'secret weapon'?" he drawled, his voice dripping with sarcasm. "The shrink who thinks she can solve a murder case?"

I kept my chin held high, refusing to rise to the bait. "Detective Miller," I replied, my voice firm. "Dr. Jenson."

"Let's just hope you don't screw this up," he muttered under his breath, turning away to grab his mug of coffee.

Just then, Captain Denver emerged from his office, his face a thundercloud. He looked at Reynolds, his voice laced with barely contained anger.

"Detective Reynolds," he bellowed, "What in tarnation is the meaning of this? Bringing a civilian into an interrogation room? You said you were bringing a consultant; she's a shrink, for fuck's sake, Reynolds!"

Reynolds squared his shoulders, his voice calm but firm. "With all due respect, Captain, Dr. Jenson is responsible for the progress we've made so far. Remember, these are the six thugs you brought in yesterday, the ones you have not been saying anything useful? Well, it was her suggestion to have them describe the events instead of us asking them what we think we know."

Captain Denver's scowl deepened. "And? She's still a shrink. You think some fancy mind games are going to get them to confess to something they might not have even done?"

"Not necessarily," I interjected, stepping forward. "But if you let them talk without fear of incrimination, something will definitely jump out to you. Oh, they'll lie, but there are six of them. Remember, Captain, a confession isn't always the truth, but it can lead us to the truth."

Captain Denver studied me for a long moment, his expression unreadable. He finally sighed, the tension in the room easing slightly. "Alright, Reynolds," he conceded grudgingly. "You get your way this time. But if this psychologist of yours messes things up, remember your badge is on my desk."

Relief washed over me, a cool counterpoint to the simmering tension. "Thank you, Captain," Reynolds said, a flicker of gratitude crossing his face.

Miller, however, wasn't finished. He sauntered over, his eyes narrowed. "So, Doc," he drawled, leaning in close. "Do you think you can hypnotize the truth out of a suspect? Maybe use some fancy mind control techniques?"

"Detective Miller," I replied, cool as a cucumber, "my methods are based on research, reason, and logic, not parlor tricks. However, observing these men's behavior, their body language and their responses to certain questions can provide valuable clues about their involvement in this case."

My knuckles whitened as I gripped the edge of the observation table. Detective Reynolds ushered Eddie, the first suspect, into the interrogation room. Eddie, a wiry man with nervous eyes constantly darting around, fidgeted in his chair. A lawyer, a stern woman with a sharp bob and a steely glare, sat beside him, her lips pursed into a thin line.

"Alright, Eddie," Reynolds began, his voice deceptively calm. "We just want to get a baseline picture of the scene at Mrs. Roseblood's house the night of the incident. Nothing incriminating, understand? Just the environment itself."

Eddie's lawyer immediately bristled. "Objection! We've already established my client was not involved. These questions are irrelevant."

Reynolds raised a placating hand. "Relax, counselor. We're simply trying to reconstruct the timeline. Think of it as setting the stage, not assigning blame. Now, Eddie," he turned back to Matty, his voice a soothing murmur, "you mentioned being there that night. Can you tell me, was it a large house or a more modest one?"

Eddie hesitated, glancing nervously at his lawyer. The lawyer shot him a warning look, mouthing, "Don't answer."

Sensing the tension, Reynolds leaned forward with a disarming smile. "Listen, Eddie. We understand this is a stressful situation. But cooperating with us on these basic details could be very helpful. It might even clear things up faster, wouldn't you agree?"

Eddie chewed on his lip, his eyes flickering between Reynolds and the lawyer. The lawyer opened her mouth to protest again, but Reynolds cut her off.

"Think of it like this," he continued, his voice confidential. "If you help us piece together the scene, it could potentially eliminate any misunderstandings, right? The quicker we have a complete picture, the quicker everyone can go home."

The lawyer's stern expression faltered slightly. The promise of a quicker end seemed to have a subtle effect on Eddie. He glanced at his lawyer again, a flicker of hope in his eyes.

The lawyer sighed, her voice softer now. "Alright, Eddie. Answer the detective's questions, but only about the general environment, nothing specific."

With a barely audible nod, Eddie turned back to Reynolds. "It wasn't a huge house," he mumbled. "It was more on the... average side, I guess."

"Average," Reynolds echoed, jotting down notes. "And the lighting? Bright and cheery, or a bit more subdued?"

"Subdued, definitely," Eddie mumbled. "Like the curtains were mostly drawn shut."

"Subdued," Reynolds repeated, writing furiously. "And the smell, Eddie? Was there a particular scent in the air? Fresh flowers, maybe, or something a bit... stale?"

Eddie's brow furrowed. "Can't really say there was any particular smell, detective. Just... old house smell, I guess."

"Old house smell," Reynolds muttered, a thoughtful crease forming on his forehead. "Interesting. And the sounds, Eddie. A bustling street outside, or more of a peaceful neighborhood?"

"Quiet," Eddie replied, his voice barely a whisper. It was really quiet. I didn't hear much of anything, just... stuff happening around the house."

"Stuff happening?" Reynolds pressed, leaning forward.

The lawyer shot in, her voice sharp. "Detective, I believe we established my client didn't witness anything pertinent."

Reynolds held up a hand, a disarming smile playing on his lips. "Of course, counselor. Just trying to get a sense of the atmosphere. You know, the creaks and groans of an old house can be quite... unsettling, wouldn't you agree, Eddie?"

Eddie's nervousness seemed to intensify. He cast another furtive glance at his lawyer, who was glaring at Reynolds. "Uh, yeah," he mumbled, "I guess so."

"Especially," Reynolds continued, his voice dropping to a conspiratorial whisper, "if there's someone... unexpected... moving around."

Eddie's eyes widened in alarm. The lawyer slammed her hand on the table.

"Objection!" she barked. "You're clearly trying to coerce a confession!"

"Relax, counselor," Reynolds soothed, his smile widening. "Just painting a picture, that's all. Now, Eddie, tell me, was there anything else you heard that night? Maybe a... muffled conversation, or perhaps a door creaking open?"

Eddie swallowed hard, his gaze darting around the room. "I, uh, I can't really say for sure, detective. Maybe some creaking floorboards, like I said, but..."

"But what?" Reynolds pressed, his voice gentle yet insistent. "Don't leave us hanging, Eddie," Reynolds finished his voice, a soothing murmur that contrasted sharply with the lawyer's steely glare. "Any little detail could be helpful, you see. Think of it like putting together a puzzle – the more pieces we have, the clearer the picture becomes."

Eddie chewed on his lip, his eyes flickering between the detective and the lawyer. The lawyer opened her mouth to interject, but Reynolds cut her off again, this time with a playful wink.

"Besides," he added, his voice dropping to a conspiratorial whisper, "wouldn't you feel better knowing you helped clear things up? The sooner we understand the situation, the sooner everyone can go home, right?"

The lawyer's stern expression softened slightly. The promise of a quicker resolution seemed to have an effect on Eddie. He finally spoke, his voice barely a whisper.

"Well, there might have been... a muffled conversation, like you said. I couldn't really make out the words, though. Just hushed voices coming from somewhere deeper in the house."

"Hushed voices, huh?" Reynolds leaned back in his chair, a triumphant glint in his eyes. "Interesting. And where would you say these voices were coming from? Upstairs, maybe?"

Eddie hesitated again, glancing nervously at his lawyer. "I, uh, I can't be sure. Just somewhere down the hall, I guess."

"Down the hall," Reynolds repeated, scribbling furiously in his notepad. "And how about the time, Eddie? Roughly what time did you arrive at Mrs. Roseblood's house?"

The lawyer's eyes narrowed. "Objection! Time of arrival is irrelevant to my client's lack of involvement."

"Just trying to establish a timeline, counselor," Reynolds countered, his voice calm but firm. "Every detail helps paint a clearer picture."

Eddie, emboldened by the promise of a faster end, answered before his lawyer could protest further. "Uh, it was around... eight, maybe eight-thirty?"

"Eight-thirty," Reynolds muttered, noting the time down. This was the first discrepancy – Steven had mentioned arriving closer to nine. He decided to push it further.

"And how long did you stay, Eddie?"

"Not long," Eddie mumbled. "Maybe half an hour, an hour at most."

This was another inconsistency. Steven had said they were there for a significant amount of time. Reynolds decided to play devil's advocate.

"An hour, huh? It seems like a long time for a brief meeting, wouldn't you agree? Especially considering you said the house was quiet, no party or anything going on."

Eddie's eyes darted around the room, his nervousness escalating. "Well, it wasn't exactly a meeting," he stammered. "It was more like... waiting around. Doc Thorne said there was a delay, that's all."

"A delay," Reynolds repeated, his voice laced with a hint of skepticism. "And what time was this delay? Did Dr. Thorne give you any indication of how long you might have to wait?"

Eddie shook his head, his voice barely audible. "No, sir. He just said there was a change of plans, and we should hang tight."

"Change of plans, huh?" Reynolds leaned forward, his voice dropping to a conspiratorial whisper. "Now that's interesting, Eddie. From what we understand, Dr. Thorne doesn't exactly strike one as the kind of guy who makes a lot of... last-minute changes, am I right?"

Eddie's mouth worked silently for a moment, his eyes wide with a mixture of fear and confusion. The lawyer slammed her hand on the table again.

"Enough!" she barked. "This line of questioning is clearly designed to coerce a false confession! We will not tolerate these tactics any longer!"

Reynolds held up his hands in mock surrender. "Alright, alright, counselor. We'll move on for now. But just remember, Eddie, the sooner you cooperate, the sooner we can all go home."

Eddie's lawyer cleared her throat, her voice regaining its sharpness. "My client isn't obligated to participate in any speculative exercises, detective."

"Of course not, counselor," Reynolds conceded with a slight bow. "But perhaps Eddie can simply confirm or deny a few basic observations. For instance, was there a fireplace in the room you were in?"

Eddie hesitated, then mumbled, "Yeah, I think so. It was in the corner, but it wasn't lit or anything."

"Not lit," Reynolds repeated, scribbling in his notepad. "Interesting. So, the overall atmosphere wasn't exactly warm and inviting, then?"

"No, sir," Eddie mumbled, shaking his head. "More like... cold and stuffy, I guess."

"Cold and stuffy," Reynolds echoed, a hint of a triumphant glint in his eyes. He continued with his questions, each one seemingly innocuous yet carefully chosen to paint a picture of the scene without directly mentioning the events of the night. He inquired about the type of flooring (worn wooden planks), the presence of any pictures on the walls (none that he could recall), and even the type of curtains (heavy drapes in a floral pattern).

The lawyer continued to object sporadically, but with each objection, Reynolds managed to reframe his questions, appealing to Eddie's desire for a quicker resolution. He subtly hinted at the possibility of charges being dropped or leniency being shown if they cooperated, all the while staying within legal boundaries.

As the interrogation progressed, Eddie's initial defiance waned. He began to answer more readily, providing details he might not have considered crucial. He mentioned a faint scent of dust and mothballs hanging in the air, a stark contrast to the image of a bustling household. He described a chipped porcelain lamp on a side table, casting an uneven glow across the room.

The seemingly insignificant details began to paint a picture – a picture of a neglected house shrouded in an air of neglect and disuse. It wasn't a definitive image of what happened that night, but it was a start, a potential chink in the story they were presenting.

Finally, after nearly an hour of questioning, Reynolds leaned back in his chair, a satisfied smile playing on his lips. "Alright, Eddie, that's all we need for now. Thank you for your cooperation. It's been a big help."

Eddie, visibly relieved, mumbled a thanks and looked expectantly at his lawyer. The lawyer, however, remained silent, her gaze fixed on Reynolds with a mixture of suspicion and grudging respect.

They brought in the next man.

Mark, unlike the jittery Eddie, exuded an air of practiced calm. A seasoned lawyer, Ms. Davis, flanked him, her sharp eyes a constant challenge. Reynolds, however, began with the same approach – a picture of the scene at Mrs. Roseblood's house. Mark, cautious but composed, described the house as average-sized with subdued lighting due to drawn curtains. He mentioned worn furniture and a lack of prominent artwork on the walls, confirming Eddie's basic description.

The turning point came when Reynolds shifted the focus to sounds. Mark acknowledged the creaking floorboards, a detail Eddie had also mentioned. Reynolds, subtly hinting at inconsistencies, stressed the possibility of someone moving around unseen in the darkness. This tactic chipped away at Mark's composure, evident in his hesitant replies and darting eyes. Ms. Davis, sensing the shift, tried to deflect, but Reynolds offered a deal - the more details Mark provided about the environment, the clearer the picture, potentially clearing up any "misunderstandings." Stuck between cooperation and fear of revealing too much, Mark fell silent.

Next came Butch, a hulking man with a shaved head and a defiant air. He readily admitted to being at Mrs. Roseblood's house but claimed it was just a quick chat. Reynolds, unfazed, persisted with the scene description. Butch, in his gruff voice, painted a more vivid picture – the house was run-down with mismatched furniture and loose floorboards. He described the environment as noisy, with the howling wind rattling the windows and the groans of the house echoing like screams.

When questioned about the lighting, Butch confirmed it was dim, barely enough to see. The lawyer interjected, but Reynolds spun it as painting a complete picture. Butch's responses diverged from Eddie and Mark in one key detail – the smell. He mentioned a musty smell with hints of dust and mothballs, adding a new element to the description. Reynolds capitalized on this inconsistency, highlighting how their stories differed. As the interrogation progressed, similar to Mark's situation, Reynolds subtly hinted at potential problems if their descriptions didn't align. The pressure visibly affected Butch, his initial bravado replaced by nervous fidgeting. He fidgeted much like Tommy.

Tommy, a younger man with nervous energy, was accompanied by an equally nervous-looking legal defender. The same line describing the scene began the interrogation. Tommy was eager to please and seemingly unaware of the implications, so he readily provided details. He described the house as small and cluttered, with flickering fluorescent lights and old, uncomfortable furniture. He mentioned a dusty carpet and a faint smell of cigarette smoke, adding further details that differed from the others.

Reynolds capitalized on Tommy's eagerness, peppering him with questions about sounds and movement within the house. Tommy, oblivious to the trap, mentioned hearing muffled voices at times and a loud thump from another room. The lawyer objected, arguing these details weren't about the environment, but Reynolds countered by claiming it helped with the atmosphere.

Tommy, unaware of the potential significance of his responses, became increasingly agitated, fearing he messed up. This played into Reynolds' hands, creating a crack in their unified front and highlighting potential inconsistencies in their stories. Unlike Eddie and Mark, who maintained a guarded stance, Tommy's eagerness became a vulnerability that Reynolds exploited.

The fifth member of the group was Sarah, a woman with a sharp mind and a skeptical demeanor who walked into the room with an air of defiance. Her lawyer, a confident woman with a no-nonsense attitude, mirrored her energy. Reynolds, aware of the shift in dynamics, changed his approach.

He began by acknowledging Sarah's intelligence and stating his desire for truthful information. He then presented her with a hypothetical scenario – two individuals providing different accounts of the same environment. He asked her opinion on the consequences of such inconsistencies. Sarah, intrigued by this tactic, engaged in a verbal sparring session, arguing it could be due to faulty memory or different perspectives.

Reynolds then presented specific discrepancies between the accounts, highlighting the differences in lighting, smells, and sounds described by the others. Sarah, surprised by the details but still skeptical, parried each inconsistency with alternative explanations. However, the seeds of doubt were sown. The interrogation ended without any clear breakthrough, but unlike the others, Sarah's skepticism kept Reynolds from chipping away at their story as easily.

My stomach churned as Detective Miller loomed over me, his shadow stretching across the desk like a bad omen. "Anything yet, Doc?" he rumbled, his voice laced with a barely concealed impatience.

"Not yet, Detective," I replied, forcing a smile that felt brittle on my lips. My gaze darted back to the room, the sterile glow doing little to dispel the growing sense of dread in the room.

Miller snorted. "Not yet? We're running out of time here. Less than ten hours until that warrant goes hot, and Reynolds' badge gets a permanent vacation."

He slammed his hand on the desk, and the sudden noise made me jump. "He gambled on you, Doc. He gambled big time. Don't let him down."

I gritted my teeth, the pressure building with every passing minute. Miller, bless his heart, was a good cop and a loyal friend to Reynolds.

"I'm doing the best I can, Detective," I said, my voice tight. "These interviews are extensive, and inconsistencies take time to identify."

Miller scoffed. "From what I saw in that observation room, those guys were sweating bullets. Any half-decent shrink could pull a confession out of them in five minutes flat."

"It's not that simple, Detective," I sighed, the frustration bubbling over. "Confessions under pressure can be unreliable. I need to find discrepancies, subtle shifts in their narratives that expose the cracks in their story."

Miller threw his hands up in exasperation. "Look, Doc, I appreciate your fancy shrink stuff, but time is ticking. If we don't nail something down soon, your friend Steven gets arrested, and Reynolds..." he trailed off, his face grim.

I knew what he wasn't saying. Reynolds would be ostracized. A single, desperate gamble on my expertise would tarnish his career and reputation.

"I understand the pressure, Miller," I said, my voice softer now. "Believe me, I do. But there's no shortcut here. Rushing this could ruin everything."

The last of them was in the room now, and I sent a prayer up for anything useful.

"Alright," Reynolds began, his tone firm but encouraging. "Let's rewind. Take me back to that night, step by step. Start from the moment you enter the house."

Matty, a skinny man with eyes that darted around the room like a cornered animal, took a deep breath. His voice, barely a whisper, painted a picture of Mrs. Roseblood's house – a cluttered haven filled with the dusty relics of a life well-lived. But beneath his description, a subtle unease lurked.

"There was something...off," he mumbled, his voice barely audible. "The air felt thick and heavy like a storm was brewing just beneath the surface."

Reynolds pressed on, his questions like scalpels, dissecting Matty's account. "Anything out of place? An overturned lamp, a broken window – anything that seemed unusual?"

Matty shook his head slowly, his brow furrowed in concentration. "Not at first. We went into the living room. That's where Mrs. Roseblood was."

He described the worn furniture, the faded floral wallpaper, the dusty lampshades – details that seemed mundane on the surface but held the potential to be crucial pieces of the puzzle. As he spoke, my own mind raced, comparing his narrative to the others. Were there inconsistencies? Glaring omissions? Anything that hinted at a deeper truth?

Suddenly, Matty stopped mid-sentence, his voice laced with a tremor that sent a jolt through me. "There was another person there," he mumbled, his gaze flickering away from Reynolds' stony stare.

Revelations

A wave of adrenaline washed over me. This was it. The detail we'd been searching for, the missing piece that could potentially crack the case wide open. Just as Reynolds was about to lean in and press for more details, a sharp voice cut through the tension.

"Objection, Detective," a gruff male voice boomed from the corner of the room. It was Matty's lawyer, a man in a sharply tailored suit with a determined expression.

Reynolds turned towards him, a flicker of annoyance crossing his face. "On what grounds, Mr. Cobb?"

"My client is under no obligation to answer questions that could potentially incriminate him," Mr. Cobb countered, his voice firm and unwavering. "He has already provided a detailed account of the evening's events."

Reynolds sighed, his shoulders slumping slightly. He knew Mr. Cobb was right, but Matty's nervous demeanor and the possibility of a crucial lead gnawed at him.

"Look, Mr. Cobb," Reynolds said, his voice softening slightly. "We're just trying to get a clear picture of what happened that night. If your client has nothing to hide, cooperating with our questions would be in his best interest."

Mr. Cobb's lips pursed in a thin line. "My client will cooperate fully, Detective," he replied, his voice laced with a hint of skepticism. "But we'll proceed at our own pace, and any questions that could be considered self-incriminating are off-limits."

A tense silence descended upon the room. Reynolds exchanged a frustrated glance with me, and the momentum of the interrogation temporarily stalled. It was clear Mr. Cobb wouldn't budge easily, and we needed a new approach.

Turning back to Mr. Cobb, he adopted a conciliatory tone.

"Alright, Mr. Cobb," he said, his voice calm and measured. "Perhaps we can approach this from a different angle. Let's focus on the details of the house itself. Can your client describe the layout, the furniture, anything that struck him as out of the ordinary?"

Mr. Cobb studied Reynolds for a moment, his gaze calculating. Then, with a curt nod, he turned back to his client. "Alright," he said. "You can answer the Detective's questions, but remember to stick to the facts. No speculation, no assumptions."

Matty visibly relaxed, a flicker of relief crossing his face. The interrogation continued, albeit at a slower pace, with Mr. Cobb acting as a constant watchdog, ready to pounce at any perceived threat to his client's rights.

As Matty recounted his story, his voice grew hesitant, his eyes flickering nervously towards his lawyer. He described the living room, the worn furniture arranged around a crackling fireplace, the dusty bookshelves lining the walls. But when Reynolds asked about the hallway leading to the other rooms, Matty's memory seemed to falter. "There was a hallway, I think," he mumbled, his voice barely above a whisper. "But it was dark; I didn't see much in there."

Reynolds pressed on gently, his voice laced with a hint of intrigue. "Can you tell me, was there anything reflective in the living room? A large mirror, perhaps, or a polished surface?"

Matty furrowed his brow, concentrating deeply. Mr. Cobb, ever vigilant, straightened in his chair, his gaze fixed on Reynolds.

"I... I can't recall any mirrors," Matty stammered. "Maybe a picture frame with glass, but nothing big."

"What about the position you were sitting in?" Reynolds continued, his voice calm but persistent. "Could you see the television from where you were?"

Matty hesitated, then nodded slowly. "Yes, it was on a stand facing the couch. We were all sitting there, talking to Mrs. Roseblood."

A surge of excitement coursed through me. This was it. The missing piece clicking into place.

"And since the other person was facing Mrs. Roseblood," he said, his voice barely a whisper, "for a brief moment, did you happen to see their reflection... in the television screen?"

Matty's eyes widened a fraction, a flicker of fear replacing his initial confusion. He stole a glance towards Mr. Cobb, who remained silent, his expression unreadable.

"I..." Matty stammered, his voice barely audible. "I might have... for a second."

Reynolds leaned in further, his voice barely above a murmur. "Can you describe what you saw? Anything you remember about the reflection?"

Matty's Adam's apple bobbed rapidly in his throat. His hands, clenched into fists on his lap, began to tremble. He darted another furtive glance at Mr. Cobb, who remained impassive, but a flash of something close to concern flickered in his eyes for a brief moment.

"It was just... a glimpse," Matty finally managed, his voice barely a whisper. It was like a flash of movement out of the corner of my eye."

"And what did you see in that glimpse?" Reynolds pressed gently, his voice calm but laced with an undercurrent of urgency.

Matty hesitated, his brow furrowed in concentration as if trying to recapture the fleeting image from the recesses of his memory. "He was tall," he said slowly, his voice barely audible. "Not overweight, but broad-shouldered. A big man, but not imposingly so."

A sliver of hope pierced through the tension in the room. This was it. The detail we'd been searching for, the physical description that could potentially corroborate the other witnesses' accounts and shatter the carefully constructed alibi.

"Can you elaborate on his appearance?" Reynolds prompted, his voice barely above a murmur. "What was he wearing? Did you catch any details about his face?"

Matty closed his eyes for a moment as if willing himself to remember more. "He was well-dressed," he finally said, his voice trembling slightly. He was wearing a sharp suit in a dark color. I couldn't make out the details, but it looked expensive."

He paused for a moment, then continued, his voice barely a whisper. "His face, that's what I remember most clearly. Cold. Like he wasn't interested in us at all. Just calculating."

A shiver ran down my spine. Matty's description perfectly matched Olivia's image of Patterson—a ruthless businessman with an icy demeanor. The pieces were falling into place, revealing a far more sinister truth than we had initially anticipated.

"And his eyes?" Reynolds asked, his voice barely a murmur. "Can you describe his eyes?"

Matty took a shuddering breath, his eyes fluttering open. "Dark," he whispered, his voice laced with a tremor of fear. "Cold and dark. Like... like he could see right through you."

Timothy Patterson.

I pivoted towards Captain Denver, my voice barely a whisper that vibrated with barely contained excitement. "Captain, is that enough? Can we bring Patterson in?"

Denver, a stoic mountain of a man with a perpetually furrowed brow that seemed permanently etched into his expression, finally cracked a smile. It was a rare sight like a glacier experiencing a heatwave – unexpected, almost unnatural, yet undeniably genuine. "Enough to bring him in for questioning, yeah," he rumbled, "But holding him? That's a different story altogether."

Disappointment pricked at me, but Denver held up a hand, silencing my protest before it could fully form. "Look, Doctor," he said, his voice softer than I'd ever heard it, softer even than the murmur of the air conditioning humming in the background. "We don't have probable cause for arrest yet. Not enough to make anything stick. But if Matty can ID Patterson in a lineup – "

"He can," I interrupted. "He might be a weasel, a squirrelly little rodent of a man, but he wasn't lying about that part. I saw it in his eyes, the flicker of recognition, the jolt of fear."

Denver's gaze held mine for a long moment, assessing, calculating. Then, with a slow nod, a silent acknowledgment of my conviction, he conceded, "Alright. We'll bring Patterson in. You get some rest. You look like you could use it."

Rest? The last thing I wanted to do was sleep.

The interrogation room had transformed into a battleground, but this time, the war was amongst themselves. I'd requested all six goons be placed in the same room, a tactic Captain Denver raised a skeptical eyebrow at.

"Why stir the hornet's nest, Olivia?"

"Chaos, Captain," I countered, a sly grin tugging at the corner of my lips. "Their practiced little defense crumbles under the pressure of a crowded room. Six egos, all vying to save their own asses – their lawyers will have a hell of a time wrangling them."

Denver considered it for a moment, then, with a reluctant nod, conceded, "Alright, Olivia. But you're on crowd control duty."

The effect was nearly immediate. Reynolds lied about what they'd all told him, and the room erupted into a din of shouts and accusations. Fingers were pointed, alibis crumbled, and the carefully constructed facade of innocence they'd presented during their individual interrogations disintegrated before our eyes.

Butch was the first to crack. He roared over the din, his voice shaking with a mixture of fear and indignation. "I didn't hear nothin'! The old bat and the suit were whisperin' like lovers."

A tense silence descended upon the room, broken only by the ragged breaths of the other goons. Butch, oblivious to the sudden shift in the atmosphere, continued blustering, "Though I did catch a snatch of their conversation. Somethin' about 'tellin' where it is' or tearin' some poor bastard named William apart."

The room exploded once more, this time with a different kind of tension. Eyes darted nervously, accusations changed into desperate pleas for innocence, and the carefully constructed web of lies began to unravel.

"William? You heard somethin' about William?" the scrawny man squeaked.

Butch, emboldened by the attention, puffed out his chest. "Yeah, that's what I said! The suit was talkin' about tearin' him apart if the old broad wouldn't spill the beans about somethin'."

My mind raced, piecing together the fragmented information. Williamson. Henrietta. A hidden item Patterson desperately wanted. The threat of violence.

"Who's William?" I boomed, my voice cutting through the noise.

Silence. Six pairs of eyes locked on me, each holding a different emotion – fear, defiance, confusion. But none of them spoke.

"Look," I said, my voice and demeanor toughening. "We all know you weren't there to serve tea and crumpets. Spill it. Who's William? What does Patterson want?"

"How should we know?" Sarah asked.

True, they wouldn't.

With less than half a day left on the clock before the warrant for Steven's arrest would be acted on, the pressure was immense. We had a confession – shaky, incomplete, but a confession nonetheless – that placed Patterson at the scene of the crime. We had a potential motive – a hidden item, a secret Williamson and Henrietta possessed that Patterson desperately craved. Yet, it wasn't enough. It wasn't the slam-dunk evidence we needed to pin the murder on the ruthless businessman.

Frustration gnawed at me, but giving up wasn't an option—not with Steven's life hanging in the balance. I needed a Plan B, a desperate Hail Mary pass if everything else crumbled around us. My gaze darted to my phone, to Steven. I needed to talk to him, to warn him of the potential storm brewing on the horizon. With a deep breath, I punched in his number, the familiar ringtone a jarring contrast to the tense silence of the room.

"Steven," I answered my voice tight with suppressed urgency.

"Olivia, what's going on? Is there any news?" His desperation mirrored the turmoil churning within me.

"There's been a development," I hedged, carefully choosing my words. "The investigation has taken an unexpected turn. We might not be able to clear your name before the warrant expires."

Silence. It was a heavy, suffocating silence that stretched for what felt like an eternity. Then, a shaky breath. "What does that mean?"

"It means you might need to leave the country, Steven," I said, the words tasting like ash in my mouth. The thought of him, innocent and alone, running from the law, filled me with a sense of sickening dread.

"Leave the country? But... but I'm innocent!" His voice, laced with a mixture of fear and defiance, ripped at my already frayed nerves.

"I know, Steven," I said, my voice softening. "And we're working on proving that. But there's a chance... a very real chance... that things might not go our way."

I explained the situation with Patterson's lawyer and the potential for a legal quagmire that could delay things for weeks, months, or even. I painted a picture of the worst-case scenario, the one where Steven had to disappear to vanish into thin air while we continued our fight for his innocence.

There was another silence after that, longer and heavier than the first. Then, a deep breath, a quiet resignation, settled into his voice. "Alright, Olivia. What do I need to do?"

Relief washed over me, warm and welcome. Steven trusted me, even in the face of this terrifying uncertainty. "Pack a small bag, essentials only," I instructed. "Passport, a few changes of clothes, toiletries. Anything sentimental you can't bear to part with."

"And then?"

"And then," I said, my voice tight with unshed tears, "we'll figure it out. Choose a country without extradition."

Hanging up the phone, the reality of the situation hit me with a force that left me breathless. Steven, a fugitive. But then, the image of Patterson's cold, calculating eyes flashed in my mind. It may come down to this.

I knocked on Mr. Jorges' door, my heart pounding with anticipation. After my previous visit, where he revealed crucial information about Tim Patterson's past dealings with Steven's family, I hoped he might shed more light on the mysterious William Williamson.

Mr. Jorges opened the door, his expression guarded but not unwelcoming. "Dr. Jenson, what brings you back?" he asked, stepping aside to let me in.

"Thank you, Mr. Jorges," I replied, stepping into his office. "I hope I'm not intruding, but I was hoping we could speak further about Tim Patterson and his past associates."

Mr. Jorges gestured for me to take a seat, his eyes curious. "Of course, Doctor. What do you want to know?"

I took a deep breath, gathering my thoughts before speaking. "I'm particularly interested in a man named William Williamson. Do you know anything about him?"

Mr. Jorges furrowed his brow, deep in thought. "William Williamson... the name sounds vaguely familiar, but I can't say I know much about him."

I felt a pang of disappointment but pressed on. "Did he have any dealings with Tim Patterson or your late cousin, Henrietta Gundel?"

Mr. Jorges shook his head slowly. "Not that I recall. But now that you mention it, there was something about Patterson and his cousin, Williamson, around the same time he was partners with Gundel and me."

My interest piqued, I leaned forward. "His cousin?"

"Yes, William Williamson was Patterson's cousin," Mr. Jorges confirmed. "They were close, or so I thought. But then, things soured between them."

I felt a surge of curiosity. "What happened?"

"It was a messy affair," Mr. Jorges explained, his voice grave. "Patterson had a falling out with Williamson over some business deal gone sour. From what I heard, Patterson not only cheated Williamson out of a considerable sum of money but also framed him for something he didn't do."

The pieces of the puzzle began to click into place in my mind. "And this happened around the same time as Patterson's partnership with Gundel and yourself?"

Mr. Jorges nodded solemnly. "Yes, it was during those turbulent years when we were all in business together. Henri, that's what we called Henrietta Gundel; she was the one who uncovered Patterson's deception. She had a nose for these things and could smell a rat from a mile away."

"And how did she react?" I asked, leaning in closer, eager for more details.

Mr. Jorges sighed heavily, a shadow passing over his face. "Henri was furious, as you can imagine. She confronted Patterson about it and demanded he make things right with Williamson. But he refused, claiming it was just business."

"Did she believe him?" I inquired, my mind racing with possibilities.

Mr. Jorges shook his head firmly. "No, she saw through him. She knew he was lying and capable of much worse. That was the beginning of the end for our partnership with Patterson. Henri made it clear that she wanted nothing more to do with him or his dirty dealings."

I sat back in my chair, processing the new information. "So, Henri confronted him about William?"

Mr. Jorges nodded. "That's right. She didn't back down and demanded answers from Patterson. She wasn't about to let him ruin William's life without a fight; she actually managed to get him to let the man live.."

I couldn't help but admire Henri's strength and determination. "But why would Patterson agree to spare William? What changed?"

Mr. Jorges shrugged helplessly. "I wish I knew, Doctor. Maybe she had some sort of hold over him."

I grabbed my coat. "Thank you, Mr. Jorges. I'll keep you updated on any developments."

I hurried back to the police station, my gaze barely leaving the time. I made my way to the front desk, where Officer Reynolds stood, his expression grim.

"Any updates on Patterson?" I asked, trying to keep my voice steady despite the knots of worry tightening in my stomach.

Officer Reynolds shook his head, his jaw set in a tight line. "He's in interrogation room three. But he's not talking. Refuses to say a word, even after the witness positively identified him."

I frowned, "Any idea why he's being so stubborn?"

Officer Reynolds shrugged helplessly. "Your guess is as good as mine, Doc. But whatever he's hiding, he's determined to keep it to himself."

I recounted the meager information gleaned from Jorges. Their faces perfectly mirrored my disappointment; I took another glance at the time.

"Any breakthroughs?" he asked, a simmering urgency threading through his voice.

I shook my head, suppressing the bubbling frustration. "Not much, sir. But there's someone I think I need to talk to."

Reynolds' eyebrows shot up in surprise. "Who's that?"

"Dr. Thorne," I replied without hesitation. "He might have some insight."

Captain Denver pondered my request for a moment, a contemplative crease forming on his brow. Finally, he nodded in agreement. "Alright, Jenson. You have the go-ahead. But tread carefully."

A wave of gratitude washed over me as I strode towards the holding cells. My mind buzzed with anticipation. Thorne had always exuded an air of someone concealing depths unseen. An unshakeable feeling tugged at me, insisting he held a crucial piece of the puzzle.

The sterile silence of the holding area was shattered as I arrived at Thorne's cell. He sat alone, his posture stoic yet guarded. As I approached, his gaze flicked towards me, a mixture of curiosity and wariness coloring his eyes.

"Detective... what was it again?" His voice was measured, betraying no hint of recognition.

"Dr. Olivia Jenson," I corrected, offering a polite smile. "Psychologist."

A flicker of surprise crossed Thorne's features. "A psychologist? Intriguing. What brings you to my humble abode, Doctor?"

"I need to ask you a few questions, Dr. Thorne," I replied, my voice firm yet respectful. "If you don't mind."

"Go ahead," Thorne conceded, leaning back against the cold steel wall.

"Let's start with a man named Tim Patterson. Does the name ring a bell?"

Thorne furrowed his brow, stroking his chin thoughtfully. "Patterson... the name carries a faint echo, but I wouldn't say I know him personally."

Undeterred, I retrieved a photograph of Patterson from my pocket, extending it towards him. "Perhaps this will jog your memory?"

Thorne scrutinized the photo, his brow furrowed in concentration. After a long moment, he shook his head. "I'm afraid it doesn't, Detective. Sorry to be of no help."

A sigh escaped my lips, disappointment stinging my throat. If Patterson wasn't on Thorne's radar, it seemed unlikely he'd have any valuable information for us. Just as I considered conceding defeat, another name surfaced in my mind.

"What about William Williamson?" I pressed, my voice laced with newfound urgency. "Do you recognize that name?"

Thorne's expression remained stoic, devoid of any change. "Williamson... doesn't ring a bell."

I persisted, placing a photograph of Williamson in front of him. "Take a closer look, Dr. Thorne."

Thorne examined the photo with meticulous detail. Then, his eyes widened in recognition. "Wait... that's Taskin."

My heart hammered against my ribs at his words. "Taskin? You're sure?"

"Positive," Thorne said with a grim nod. "I not only knew him on a professional level but I was also entrusted with his medical well-being."

Surprise washed over me. "Medical well-being? What do you mean?"

Thorne leaned forward, his voice dropping to a hushed whisper. "Williamson, or should I say Taskin, isn't exactly the picture of health. He's battling a terminal illness. Doesn't have long left."

The weight of his words settled in my gut like a lead weight. The timing of Williamson's illness seemed too convenient to be a coincidence, especially in light of Patterson's recent activities. Every instinct screamed that these seemingly disparate threads were woven into a much larger tapestry.

"When did you discover this?" I asked, my voice barely above a whisper.

"A few months back," Thorne replied solemnly. "By now, he should have a couple of weeks, tops."

A shiver danced down my spine as the implications of Thorne's revelation sank in. I understood now. Everything was starting to click into place. "Dr. Thorne, your information has been invaluable. Thank you."

The smile on my face puzzled him.

The Final Showdown

Exiting the sterile confines of the holding cell, I found the detectives locked in a tense debate. Captain Denver, his brow furrowed in concern, was the first to spot me.

"Well, Jenson? Anything useful from Thorne?" he inquired, the urgency in his voice a tangible entity in the stale air of the station.

"More than we anticipated, sir," I declared, a spark of newfound conviction burning in my eyes. "I believe I may have a way to crack this case wide open."

Miller, playing the pragmatist, scoffed. "A psychologist cracking a high-profile smuggling case? Now that's a first for the history books."

I ignored his jibe, turning directly to the captain. "Captain, I need your permission to speak with Patterson alone."

Denver's jaw clenched. "Alone? Absolutely not, Jenson. That's a high-security suspect. Interrogation needs to be conducted by a trained officer, preferably with a partner present."

"I understand your reservations, sir," I countered, my voice firm yet respectful. "But trust me, with the information I've just obtained, I can get him to talk. It'll be quicker and more effective this way."

Miller, leaning against the wall with arms crossed, snorted. "You do realize this isn't going to be a therapy session, Doc. We need hard facts, not his childhood traumas."

His skepticism stung, but I refused to be deterred. "Look," I said, my voice rising a notch, "I know what I'm doing. Williamson, or should I say Taskin, is terminally ill. Thorne believes he has mere weeks left. This sudden operation – it doesn't make sense. There's more to it than meets the eye. And a therapy session is exactly what we need right now."

Surprise flickered across Denver's face at the revelation. "Thorne mentioned this illness?"

I nodded curtly. "Yes, sir. And it changes everything. Patterson wouldn't be risking his neck for a dying man. There's something bigger at play here, and I have all the answers, but first, I must talk to him." My voice trailed off, the implication hanging heavy in the air like a storm cloud.

A tense silence descended upon the group. Denver exchanged a troubled glance with Miller, then back to me. Doubt lingered in his eyes, but a flicker of something else flickered there, too – a grudging acceptance. The weight of the investigation, the pressure to crack the case, was clearly bearing down on him.

"Alright, Jenson," he finally conceded, his voice laced with a sigh. "You have ten minutes. But I want eyes on you at all times. Reynolds set up a one-way observation window."

Reynolds grumbled under his breath but complied. Ten minutes. It wasn't much, but it was enough. I nodded curtly at the captain. "Thank you, sir. I won't let you down."

I entered the interrogation room, my heart pounding with a mixture of apprehension and determination. Patterson sat at the table, his demeanor as cold and calculating as ever. But I refused to let his icy stare intimidate me as I took a seat opposite him.

"Dr. Jenson," Patterson greeted me, his voice dripping with disdain. "To what do I owe the pleasure?"

Ignoring his sarcasm, I cut straight to the chase. "Mr. Patterson, I need to speak with you alone."

Patterson's eyebrows shot up in surprise. "Alone? And why would I agree to that?"

"Because this is our last therapy session," I replied calmly. "And I'm afraid your lawyer won't be able to join us."

Patterson's lawyer, a stern-faced man in a tailored suit, bristled at my words. "I'm sorry, Detective, but I'm required to be present for all official proceedings."

I met his gaze evenly. "This isn't an official proceeding, Mr. Jenkins. Just a conversation between me and Mr. Patterson."

Patterson leaned back in his chair, a smirk playing at the corners of his lips. "Very well, Jenkins. You can go join the police in observing the session."

Jenkins hesitated for a moment, clearly reluctant to leave his client alone with me. But ultimately, he acquiesced, rising from his seat and shooting me a distrustful glance before exiting the room.

As soon as the door closed behind him, I turned my attention back to Patterson. "Now that we're alone, let's cut to the chase, shall we?"

Patterson regarded me with curiosity and suspicion. "What do you want, Detective?"

"I'm your psychologist, Mr. Patterson, and I am here for one last therapy session. Before you are headed to jail."

"You think I am headed to jail?"

"Oh, I know it. See, I know everything because I see everything. I have seen everything; you showed me everything."

"Have you gone senile woman?"

I smiled and looked at the watch for nine minutes. "Oh no. I assure you, I am fully in control here, and you will accord me the respect I am due as your psychologist, Mr. Patterson."

"What do you want playing Detective?" he spat, the word laced with a desperate attempt to regain control.

"Detective? My, Mr. Patterson, haven't you been paying attention these past... what was it? One hour? Two? Time truly does lose all meaning in these sterile confines, doesn't it?" I replied my voice a honeyed drawl that seemed to grate on him. "No, no, today you get Dr. Olivia Jenson, your very own therapist, for this final, cathartic session."

He scoffed, his tone humorless. "Cathartic? You think spilling my guts to some shrink is going to change anything?"

A slow, unsettling smile spread across my face. "Oh, Mr. Patterson, spilling your guts wouldn't even begin to describe it. But then again, you wouldn't want to do that, would you? Imagine the mess," I cooed, my voice dropping to a conspiratorial whisper.

His eyes narrowed, a flicker of something akin to fear replacing the defiance. "What are you talking about, woman?"

"Why, everything, of course," I replied, my gaze flitting across his features, taking in the subtle tremor in his hands and the frantic darting of his eyes. "The fear, the regret, the gnawing sense that it's all about to unravel. Don't worry, Mr. Patterson; it's perfectly normal in these situations. The human psyche tends to play these little tricks on us, doesn't it?"

He remained silent, his jaw clenched tight, but I could sense the carefully constructed walls around him starting to crumble.

Leaning in closer, I lowered my voice to a barely audible murmur. "See, Mr. Patterson, here in therapy, we see everything. We delve into the deepest recesses of the mind, unlock those hidden truths you try so desperately to keep buried."

A bead of sweat trickled down his temple, his bravado completely shattered. "Lies! You're bluffing! There's no way you could..." his voice trailed off, replaced by a choked sob.

A cruel smile played on my lips, but I maintained the facade of a concerned therapist. "Now, now, Mr. Patterson, there's no need for that. Let's just talk. Tell me about yourself. What brought you to this point?"

He remained silent, his gaze darting around the cell like a trapped animal searching for an escape route. The seconds ticked by agonizingly slow, the tension in the air thick enough to choke on.

"I'm not telling you a damn thing."

"Oh, Mr. Patterson," I replied, my voice laced with amusement, "you already have." The tremor in his voice, the fear in his eyes – they spoke volumes.

"You see," I continued, "we all wear masks, Mr. Patterson. We present public facades to the world. But beneath that surface, there's a churning sea of emotions, anxieties, and secrets. And in this quiet space, without judgment, those secrets have a way of revealing themselves."

Seven minutes.

He shot me a venomous glare, but the defiance was fading, replaced by a dawning sense of unease. The knowledge that I, a complete stranger, seemed to see right through him was unsettling, to say the least.

"You think you know me?" he spat, a hint of desperation creeping into his voice.

"I see the fear, Mr. Patterson," I countered, my voice gentle yet firm. "The fear of what might happen, the fear of losing everything. It's a heavy burden to carry, isn't it?"

He remained silent, his gaze flickering between me and the observation window. I knew the detectives were watching, no doubt bewildered by my approach. But it wasn't their approval I sought; it was a confession from Patterson.

"Tell me, Mr. Patterson, how are you holding up?"

He scoffed, his tone humorless. "Just peachy, Doc. I'm enjoying the hospitality of this fine establishment."

I fixed Patterson with a penetrating stare, determination coursing through my veins like a surge of electricity. "Why did you kill Steven's grandmother, Henrietta Roseblood-Gundel, and frame Steven?" I demanded, my voice a firm challenge.

Patterson's demeanor remained stoic, a veneer of indifference masking his true emotions. "I have no knowledge of any such events," he retorted smoothly, his tone measured and controlled.

I leaned in closer, my eyes boring into his, refusing to back down. "That's alright," I countered coolly, my voice steady despite the adrenaline coursing through my veins. "Because I know exactly what happened."

A faint flicker of uncertainty danced across Patterson's features, barely perceptible but enough to betray his facade of calm. "And what, pray tell, do you think happened?" he inquired, his skepticism thinly veiled.

I settled back in my chair, a small smirk tugging at the corners of my lips. "It all started with your relationship with Henrietta Roseblood," I began, watching intently for any sign of reaction from Patterson.

A subtle shift in Patterson's demeanor betrayed his discomfort, a fleeting glimpse of unease flickering across his expression. "I fail to see how my personal relationships are relevant to this discussion," he retorted, though the tension in his voice betrayed his unease.

"But they are," I insisted, my voice firm and unwavering. "Because Henrietta discovered your deceit, your manipulation of her cousin, William Williamson."

Patterson's facade cracked, a hint of panic flickering in his eyes. "I assure you, I have no knowledge of any such deception," he protested weakly, though his voice lacked conviction.

Undeterred, I pressed on, my gaze piercing through Patterson's facade. "Henrietta knew the truth," I continued, my voice laden with accusation. "And she wasn't afraid to expose you for the fraud you are."

A shadow of uncertainty crossed Patterson's features, his composure faltering under the weight of my words. "This is preposterous," he insisted, though his voice trembled with doubt.

"But is it?" I challenged, my tone laced with determination. "You framed your own cousin, William, and let him take the fall. And you would have done the same to your new associates, Gundel and Jorges if they hadn't been too smart for you."

Patterson's eyes widened in realization, the truth of my words sinking in like a heavyweight. "You have no proof," he declared defiantly, though the desperation in his voice betrayed his crumbling resolve.

A triumphant smile played at the corners of my lips as I met Patterson's gaze head-on. "Who said anything about proof?" I replied, my voice brimming with confidence. "Sometimes, all it takes is a keen eye and a sharp mind to uncover the truth."

Patterson's facade shattered, a mask of defeat settling over his features. "Who has been feeding you these lies?" he demanded, his voice tinged with desperation.

I leaned back in my chair, my smile unwavering, my gaze unwavering. "Nobody," I replied simply. "I simply know how to connect the dots."

As I went deeper into my theory, Patterson's demeanor shifted from composed to visibly unsettled. Each revelation seemed to chip away at his facade, revealing the guilt and fear lurking beneath.

"Henrietta tried to help Williamson," I pressed on, leaning forward with an intensity that matched the gravity of the situation, "but by then, he was already wanted by several authorities. You planned to eliminate him, but Williamson did something unexpected."

Patterson's eyebrows furrowed in a mix of curiosity and apprehension. "And what, pray tell, did Williamson do?" he interjected, his voice betraying a hint of unease.

"He wrote a new will," I announced, watching Patterson closely for any sign of reaction. "A will that transferred all his earthly possessions to Henrietta Roseblood. If Williamson were to die, Henri stood to inherit everything."

The room seemed to crackle with tension as Patterson's facade faltered, revealing a flicker of panic beneath the surface. "And what does this have to do with me?" he demanded, his voice tinged with skepticism.

"Everything," I countered firmly, refusing to let him off the hook. "Because you couldn't afford to let Williamson die. Not when Henrietta stood to inherit your wealth."

A spark of recognition flashed in Patterson's eyes, his composure slipping as the pieces of the puzzle began to fall into place. "That's preposterous," he protested weakly, though his wavering voice betrayed his growing uncertainty.

"But is it?" I challenged, my tone dripping with conviction. "Think about it. Henrietta had entered into a relationship with Akiva Gundel, and together, they were too smart for you."

Patterson's facade crumbled further, a glimmer of fear surfacing in his expression. "What are you suggesting?" he demanded, his voice laced with apprehension.

"I'm suggesting that you couldn't afford to let Williamson die," I asserted boldly, my gaze piercing through his defenses. "Not when Henrietta and Akiva were onto you. So you kept Williamson alive, biding your time."

Patterson's eyes widened in realization, the weight of my words sinking in with each passing moment. "And what of the will?" he inquired, his voice amused.

I leaned in closer, my voice dropping to a conspiratorial whisper. "That's where Henrietta's quaint little jewelry store comes into play," I revealed, relishing the flicker of panic in Patterson's eyes. "The store that had been in her family for generations. You needed a way to get your hands on that will."

As I watched the turmoil play out across Patterson's face, a sense of vindication washed over me. I had him on the ropes, and I wasn't about to let up now.

"So what does Mr. Patterson do?" I asked theatrically. He hires Jake Hail to cozy up to the grandson right after Mr. Akiva Gundel, his son, and his daughter-in-law die. The boy is vulnerable and hurting, so he's susceptible to influence."

Patterson's jaw tightened, a flicker of unease crossing his features as my words hit their mark. I could see the pieces falling into place in his mind, each revelation driving home the extent of his deception.

"Gradually, the group gets closer," I continued, my voice rising with conviction. "And they soon start breaking into places, with the final goal being to have Steven help them break into his grandmother's store."

The tension in the room was palpable as Patterson's facade crumbled, the weight of his guilt bearing down upon him like a lead weight. I could almost taste the desperation radiating from him as the truth threatened to consume him whole.

"But Jake gets greedy one night," I pressed on, relishing the way Patterson's facade wavered under the weight of my accusations. "And the group is arrested. This allows Steven's grandmother, Henri, to step in and sever the bonds between Steven and Jake. Once again, his plan has been foiled."

At this point, Patterson cracked, his composure slipping as a wave of panic washed over him. "Stop," he pleaded, his voice strained with desperation. "Stop this madness."

But I couldn't stop. Not now, not when I was so close to unraveling the truth. I was like an avenging angel, driven by a singular purpose to expose Patterson's crimes and deliver justice to those he had wronged.

Patterson recoiled, his facade crumbling completely as the weight of his sins bore down upon him. "Please," he begged, his voice barely above a whisper. "Have mercy."

But there would be no mercy, not for a man who had preyed upon the vulnerable and betrayed the trust of those closest to him. I was the instrument of justice, and I would see this through to the bitter end.

Patterson hung his head in defeat, his resolve broken as he finally began to unravel the web of lies he had spun. As the truth came pouring out, I couldn't help but feel a sense of satisfaction, knowing that justice would finally be served.

As I stood before him, the weight of his crimes pressing down upon us both, I couldn't help but feel a surge of righteous fury coursing through my veins. Every word I spoke echoed with the weight of truth, each syllable a damning indictment of his deceit and treachery.

"Some time in your underhanded dealings," I began, my voice rising with indignation, "you made Williamson hire Dr. Thorne, an assassin you found through your underworld connections. Using Williamson as a frontman under the name Taskin, you funded Thorne's work and bided your time. You used Thorne to eliminate rivals and enemies, and no one was the wiser because Thorne was a brilliant man."

Patterson's eyes flickered with a mixture of fear and defiance as I laid bare the extent of his machinations. He squirmed under my gaze, the facade of control slipping with each damning revelation.

"But then," I continued, my voice thundering with accusation, "during one of his checkups, Thorne found out that Williamson was dying. He could no longer wait, so he tried to get the will again from Henri, but the store was from Steven, who had now been put in charge of the business. But Steven would not sell; he was as stubborn as Henrietta Roseblood-Gundel, his grandmother."

I could feel the tension in the room crackling like electricity as I vividly imagined Patterson's elaborate schemes unraveling before his very eyes. He was like a cornered animal, desperate and dangerous, but I would not back down—not now, not when I was so close to uncovering the truth.

"So what do you do?" I thundered, my voice ringing with righteous fury. "You make a plan, a perfect plan. You will use Williamson for one last crime and frame Henri's grandson, Steven, for it."

The words spilled from my lips like molten lava, searing through the air with the force of a hurricane. Patterson's facade crumbled before me, his composure shattered by the weight of his guilt.

"You kept badgering Steven to sell his store," I continued, my voice rising with each passing moment. "And then, when all was ready, you headed to Henri's house. Typically, you would not be present at the scene of the crime, as you always kept yourself away from the crime, but this one was personal. And that was your first mistake."

I could see the realization dawning in Patterson's eyes as I recounted the details of his carefully orchestrated plan. He had thought himself untouchable, invincible, but now the walls were closing in around him, suffocating him with the weight of his own guilt.

"You entered the house," I pressed on, my voice cutting through the silence like a knife. "But everyone was asked to turn their backs, and you did not speak loudly. You asked Henri where she kept Williamson's new will, but she does not tell you. And you left, by the back. After this, Dr. Thorne killed her, and they used the hallucinogen he made to suggest to Steven that he had killed his own grandmother."

The room seemed to pulse with tension as I recounted the final moments of Henri's life, each word a dagger aimed at Patterson's heart. He writhed in his seat, his facade crumbling under the weight of my accusations.

"It was the perfect vengeance," I declared, my voice ringing with triumph. "You killed Henrietta, who scorned you, killed Williamson, and set Steven up after framing him for their deaths, thus destroying everyone who stood in your way."

Patterson's mask slipped, his resolve shattered by the relentless barrage of truth. He pleaded for me to stop, to spare him the agony of his own guilt, but I would not relent. Not until every last shred of his deceit lay bare before me.

"Did I get anything wrong?" I demanded, my voice sharp with accusation. "Tell me, Timothy. Tell me where I went astray."

"Stop," he pleaded, his voice barely above a whisper. "Please, stop."

But I would not be deterred. Not now, not when victory was within my grasp. I pressed on, relentless in my pursuit of justice, each word a hammer blow against the fortress of lies he had built around himself.

"Did I get anything wrong?" I demanded, my voice ringing with accusation. "Tell me, Patterson. Tell me where I went astray."

As I outlined Patterson's missteps and exposed the flaws in his meticulous plan, his facade of defiance began to crumble further.

With each revelation, his desperation became palpable, a tangible force filling the room with its suffocating presence. "And then," I continued, my voice unwavering, "realizing that your initial attempts had failed, you resorted to more drastic measures. You sent those threatening letters to Steven, hoping to coerce him into selling the store. But when Steven proved to be more resilient than you anticipated, you committed yet another grave error. Even though you knew Steven could not be framed this time, and he had gotten me involved." I watched as Patterson's eyes widened in realization, a flicker of panic dancing across his features.

He knew that I had uncovered the truth, "And that's when you killed Mr. Simmons," I declared, each word laced with condemnation.

"An innocent man caught in the crossfire of Patterson's insatiable greed and ruthless ambition. But it was too late for regrets, too late for remorse." As my accusations reached their crescendo, Patterson's resolve finally shattered. His mask of indifference fell away, revealing the terrified man beneath.

"I killed her, alright?!" he screamed, his voice raw with emotion. "Shut up, please shut up."

With a satisfied nod, I turned on my heel and walked out of the interrogation room, leaving behind the shattered remnants of a once-powerful man. Justice had been served, and I had been the instrument of its delivery.

Closure

As we returned to the observation room, the atmosphere was heavy with tension, the weight of the recent revelations pressing down on us like a suffocating blanket. Steven, whom I had asked to come here before I asked Captain Denver for permission to speak to Patterson, now clung to me, his tears soaking my shirt as he expressed his gratitude for what he perceived as my salvation. "Thank you," he whispered hoarsely, his voice trembling with emotion. "Thank you for believing in me, for fighting for me."

Reynolds and Patterson's lawyer entered the room, their expressions a mixture of disbelief and resignation. But before they could utter a word, Patterson broke the silence with a confession. "I did it," he admitted. "I killed her." He had been muttering that since I left the room.

The captain wasted no time in informing me that my patient was off the hook. "You did it, Olivia," he said, his voice filled with admiration. "You cracked the case."

Detective Miller and the captain offered their congratulations, but their earlier skepticism was now replaced with genuine respect. "We owe you an apology," Miller admitted, his expression contrite. "We should have trusted you from the start."

I waved off their apologies with a small smile. "You were just doing your job," I reassured them. "We all make mistakes."

I turned to the captain, curiosity burning in my gaze. "What will happen to Patterson and Thorne now?" I asked, my voice tinged with a mixture of apprehension and curiosity.

The captain's expression darkened, his tone grave. "Considering the gravity of their crimes, the best they can hope for is a life sentence," he replied, his words heavy with finality. "Justice will be served."

Three days later, the investigative journalist released a damning exposé detailing Patterson's extensive criminal activities. William

Williamson's name will finally be cleared, but the vindication came too late, as he passed away just days after the truth came to light.

That night, after reading the article, I sighed. It was a sigh of true relief. It was all over; I could go back to my old, regular, boring life now.

"I did it, Gojo," I said.

She did not even look up to acknowledge my words.

Small Town Secrets

Thank you for reading Silence of Secrets, and if you enjoyed the story of Dr Olivia Jenson, please leave a review of your thoughts! Thanks, Stella

Small Town Secrets

After Sheriff Heston's shocking revelation as a murderer, Watson Bay is in turmoil. Amid the chaos, Parker Rose finds herself entering a new phase of her career. She is now a private investigator. She's determined to leave her past failures. But, her latest case throws her into a web of mystery and danger. Dr. Marshal seeks Parker's help to remove ransomware from his laptop. She finds a message accusing him of a heinous crime. Tensions are rising and relationships are tested. Parker's investigation leads her to surprising allies and risky revelations. As Parker delves deeper, she sees the full extent of the hacker's scheme. It threatens the whole town's infrastructure. Time is running out and lives are at stake. Parker must face the hacker's motives and race to save her community. Amidst the chaos, Parker's relationship with Jake Squire faces challenges. They grapple with trust and loyalty. They uncover shocking secrets as they navigate the stormy waters of the investigation. The secrets will change Watson Bay forever.

Small Town Secrets:

Chapter 1:

Bang.

Parker turned her attention to the front door, which loomed at her in the encroaching darkness. Evening was settling into the salty skies; the early shadows of winter reached their tendrils across Parker's living room. An inkling of regret pounded through her veins. What gave her the bright idea to run a repair shop out of her home? It was one thing to operate as a solo agent when she was a private investigator, but now that she had expanded her business to include computer and phone restoration, customers were showing up on her stoop daily. Small-town logic prevented Parker from seeing anything wrong with that arrangement—she knew everybody, and everybody knew her. Her address was never a secret. But now, all alone with an angry fist pounding at her door, she wondered just how bright that idea was.

Bang-bang-bang.

Maybe it was the memory of Sheriff Heston that made her so afraid. She didn't use to think her neighbors were capable of heinous things. That was until the man who kept her bills paid with constant work as a private investigator and promised to safeguard the community was found guilty of murder. The sheriff's plot to somehow bring media attention and tourists to Watson Bay by killing off beloved locals in prime spaces was hackneyed—not the sort of stuff Parker expected from someone she put her faith into. He'd also endangered her, chasing her through empty alleys in the hopes of making her his next victim. Thank God Jake Squire was there to ward him off. Unfortunately, Parker was embroiled in the belief that Jake was guilty up until that very moment, just as the sheriff had intended. Though it was discovered Jake had been framed, and he and Parker were trying to make their way as friends, things were still occasionally tense.

One of the reasons she branched out into computer repair, to begin with, was so that she could lessen her relationship with the police department. They were still looking for a replacement, and that gave her an opportunity to step back a little and create space between herself and the people she was slowly beginning to distrust. Without regular assignments from the police, though, she had to make ends meet somehow. Lo and behold, Jake stepped in with all his business know-how and helped her broaden the scope of her work.

Self-employment suited her, too. She liked dictating her own schedule, even though sometimes she thought she could have benefitted from more structure. Someone breathing down her neck and telling her what to do. But she chalked that up to misery talking—a strand of self-doubt that convinced her she wasn't capable of leading a normal, busy life on her own. She didn't need her hand held just to get through the working day.

Bang-bang.

"Parker Rose?" came a voice from behind the door. It sounded muffled and masculine but not as threatening as she presumed.

With a sigh, she got up from the couch and warily looked out the peephole.

"I know you're still open," said the man.

She could hardly see him in the dying light. She decided, against her better judgment, to open up. "How can I help you?" she asked with a forced grin. She swung the door wide—another mistake—and the man came barging in.

Before she could demand to know his identity, he whirled around, practically flinging his laptop at her in his flurry. It was Doctor Marshal, a notable practitioner in town who most everyone tried to see when they had a problem. He had a reputation for patience and compassion, but Parker wasn't getting much of that tonight. Instead, he glared at her with red eyes and a scowl fixed on his dry lips. His puckered expression aged him by a solid decade, and even when he caught himself in the throes of his anger, he didn't relax. He just stood there frozen, waiting for Parker to request to know what was wrong. When she didn't, he finally conceded.

"My laptop is broken," he muttered and waved the machine in her face.

"Okay," she replied, feeling herself unravel. At least he was just a customer with a regular problem. He was more mad at himself than he was with her. This was a standard issue. "What seems to be the problem?"

"How should I know that?"

"Um... I just mean, like, when did you start noticing it didn't work properly?"

"Today. Yesterday. I don't know."

Parker saw his arm buckle as he fatigued from holding it up. She motioned for Dr. Marshal to give it to her, but he hesitated. "I need to have a look," she offered. He didn't budge. "You know, to help you."

Dr. Marshal reluctantly handed her the device, and Parker strolled over to the coffee table. In an attempt to diffuse the situation, she pretended as though nothing was wrong: not his attitude, not her own feelings, and certainly not the ransom message that populated as soon as she turned the computer on. Patting a couch cushion for him to sit on, she smiled at Dr. Marshal until he joined her. Sinking into the sofa with a huff, he started at the blazing laptop screen forlornly.

"I almost wish the damned thing didn't turn on," he admitted.

Parker focused on the alert. A large pixelated rectangle announced in a retro font:

You can get your life back for a small fee of $15,000. I wish I were as lucky as you.

A clickable *next* button followed the message. Parker wanted to ask the doctor what it meant, but she figured he wouldn't be honest about it. She decided to be professional, refrain from prying, and just do what was asked of her.

"You have a couple options," she announced. "You can either pay the ransom, which I doubt you wanna do, or we can wipe this baby clean."

"What—" His rage had reignited, and he sat up straight.

"That being said, even if you do decide to wipe your hardware, that might not get rid of the virus. For all we know, the ransomware is installed on internal chips and could very likely repopulate once you reboot."

"So... aren't you supposed to *help* me?"

"I am."

"This doesn't sound like help; this sounds like pure laziness. *Just pay the ransom*. If it was that easy, I would've done it myself!"

"Doctor..." Parker took a deep breath, "I'm not trying to wind you up. I'm just being honest. Of all the viruses you could've caught, ransomware is easily the worst of the worst. Even getting a new computer might not solve it if the hacker finds a way to infect all the devices on your network."

"A hacker? You mean a *person* did this?"

"Well, I mean, yeah. What else?"

"I don't know... AI. *The machine*."

Parker let a laugh slip. "A person is always behind it, Doc. What would AI gain from duping you out of money?"

He shrugged his shoulders but didn't reply. Instead, he crumpled in his seat, bringing his hands to his forehead to rub his wrinkled skin. He looked weary as if he had just come home from performing 10 surgeries in a row. Parker felt bad for the guy, wishing she could do more to help him but not wanting to get his hopes up on a futile venture. While ransomware wasn't novel, it was also above her pay grade.

"Do you remember what link you clicked on?" Parker asked in an attempt to bring him back to the present.

"What are you talking about?" His words were aggressive, but his cadence had softened. He was just a dejected man searching for answers.

"In order to get the virus, you had to have clicked something. An ad, maybe, or visited a website. Generally, these messages don't just show up on your computer one day. Unless this hacker is super advanced, maybe, but then they'd probably be asking for more than fifteen grand."

"And going after someone who actually has that kind of money," Dr. Marshal snapped. "I can't just buy a new laptop, and I certainly can't lose what's already on there. I have pictures... memories... I can't start over."

"I'm sorry, Doc."

"Please tell me there's another way. Aren't *you* a hacker? That—that's why I came to you. I can't be royally fucked like this... Pardon my French."

"I guess I could take a crack at it," Parker finally offered. She wasn't happy to do it, but then again, she was never going to improve her craft if she refused to take on challenges. The doctor was right; she did make it her job to hack into other people's devices, so why would this be any different? But she also didn't want to bear the brunt of his ire should she be unable to fix the problem entirely. "There's a chance I could access the source code of the virus and disable it that way."

"Only a chance?"

"Correct," she nodded, pleased that she had chosen her words carefully.

"You're not guaranteeing me your services, then," he scoffed.

"I don't make promises I can't keep. Like I told you, ransomware is no joke. Pretending like it's a simple process would be a lie. I'll do my best, believe me, but that may not be enough."

"I should take my business elsewhere," the doctor grumbled as he reached for the laptop.

Parker didn't swat him away, but she did say, "To who?"

He let out another defeated groan. There wasn't somewhere else for him to go. She was the only technician in town and certainly the only person he could rely upon to be discreet. Someone in a different county wouldn't owe him privacy—they'd have asked him a lot more questions about just how and where the virus came from. But Parker understood it was a source of shame and that if his reputation was spotless, something like this could mar it. He may not have been nice to her, but she figured he was just having an off day. Who wouldn't be angry in his shoes?

"Just have it ready for me in a week," Dr. Marshal demanded.

"I don't—"

"*Please*, Parker. Please. If you really wanna have a successful business and be worth a shit, you'll do it in a week."

Parker opened her mouth to retort, but the doctor was already gathering himself up off the couch and storming toward the door, still ajar. She followed after him half-heartedly, leaving his laptop open on the coffee table. The ransom note continued to blaze, even without their eyes to witness it. He had already disappeared into the dark; not even the glint of the paint on his car could be seen. She had a strange feeling like she had been accosted by a ghost. Gone before she could register—much less prove—what had happened. She locked the door behind him, thankful to be alone again but troubled by what just occurred.

His moods were torrential, shifting from second to second regardless of how or what Parker said to him. She wanted to believe he was a nice guy who had fallen on a hard time, lashing out at her solely because he wasn't used to being vulnerable and unsure. He was the person everybody went to, who trusted that they were in good hands—his hands. Of course, he didn't want to admit he had done something wrong, or stupid, or both. He didn't want Parker and the community at large to think of him as a failure in any respect. That still didn't excuse the way he spoke to her, ordering her around like she was a dog rather than someone he ought to respect.

Parker shuffled back to the living room, mulling over the conversation and failing to see where she had slipped up and deserved to have her fingers bitten off by Dr. Marshal. She couldn't identify a snide comment or malicious request but decided not to stew over the matter. She would just find herself resentful of the doctor, adding him to her list of Watson Bay members she could no longer look at the same way. Maybe that was part of his issue, too, and why he was so hostile—he didn't want to become the second pariah in just a few short months.

Could this ransomware really denote something so distasteful he had to behave in such a manner? She figured it was something lewd like pornography but expected every older man in town to occasionally partake in it. It wasn't like she was going to retrieve the exact link he followed and blast the video to the whole world.

She pulled the computer onto her lap and reread the warning a few times, wondering what would happen if she hit *next*. Surely, things couldn't get worse. The virus had already been installed, and that was the climax of the attack—anything from here on out would merely involve more taunting... right? She bit her lip as she kept her eyes glued to the screen, the ominous words burning into her retinas.

No, she should try other keys first and see what was still functional. But when she hit *command*, *control*, and *enter*, her fingers felt as though they were pressing down on hardened glue. Why couldn't Parker just do as she was told? Her flesh was gliding along the traction pad, and suddenly, the mouse hovered over the button. That terrible, intriguing button. Curiosity always got the better of Parker. She hit it.

The screen stayed the same, but the message shifted:

$15k is to be sent in Bitcoin to wallet address bc13lm2.

She grimaced at the standard attachment. Nothing left to see here. But the *next* button was still present. She clicked it again. This time, she'd landed on the jackpot.

You will pay for your crimes, Doctor Marshal. The depths of your evil will be made known to the public if you don't act quickly. I would ask you to choose wisely, but that would be asking too much.

She hit *next*.

Be warned, Doctor: I make good on my promises.

Download Small Town Secrets to keep reading now...

Don't miss out!

Visit the website below and you can sign up to receive emails whenever Stella Mace publishes a new book. There's no charge and no obligation.

https://books2read.com/r/B-A-KHASB-GWNPD

BOOKS 2 READ

Connecting independent readers to independent writers.

Milton Keynes UK
Ingram Content Group UK Ltd.
UKHW052042140824
446844UK00017B/739